A Shaft
of Light

JOHN FINCH

CHAPTER ONE

In the long days of that summer before the war, the sun shone on the South Yorkshire mining village of Cuddon as a mixed blessing. It ripened the corn in the fields where it grew to the very edge of the slag heaps, gold against the dull red shale that streaked the grey, dusty slopes. It shone through the windows closed against the same dust which distributed itself evenly across the long rows of terraced houses, and on the roofs of the separated houses of the tradesmen, managers and professional classes. As the shale dried in the heat, the dust increased and the occasional breeze distributed it classlessly across the landscape.

In the mornings, as the sun rose above the eastern slopes of the Cuddon Main Colliery stacks, the half of the working population that was unemployed turned over and went back to sleep. For some it had been the pattern for most of their working lives, for others only since the colliery had closed its gates some two years before. Later, as sleep ebbed from them like the fading effects of a drug, they would rise reluctantly and squat on the steps outside the houses, or congregate on the street corners away from the complaints of the women. They would be shaven or unshaven according to the degree of hope which survived in each, and would chide or accept the rowdiness of the children in the same measure. Occasionally a man would pass down the street whose dress, manner and walk would mark him as employed to any normally perceptive observer. His passing would be acknowledged by a nod, a casual, 'Now then, Norman', according to the way he wore his relative wealth so as to make the gulf between them tolerable. Often his passing would be marked by a silence, brief but totally shared, before the conversation would start again, compulsively, but on a different tack.

On this morning in August 1939, Denis Russell opened his eyes in the bedroom over his father's small hardware shop in the main street of Cuddon. He heard his mother come out on to the landing outside his bedroom door and then go downstairs. Soon afterwards he heard his father follow, and then in the routine pattern that always followed this waking, the bus that brought the night shift from the Parkway Colliery some ten miles to the south pulled up outside and the men poured out of it. They came out silently as always, but the iron clash of their clogs on the stone pavements echoed in the streets long after the bus had gone, as did their silence.

He saw them now in his mind, faces blackened by pit dirt, but white around the sockets of the eyes so that they seemed to stare through and beyond with a strange unseeing innocence. The Dudleys in which they carried their water to work were slung underneath their stained and tattered jackets, making them appear to have a grotesquely shared deformity. He knew their silence to be the silence of physical exhaustion. They would carry it with them into the houses and the women would greet them with silent attention to their needs.

2

It had been so in the house they lived in when his father had been in the pit, before the fall which had amputated his arm. His entry into the home had been the arrival of a presence. The announcement by his mother, 'Your father'll be here in a minute', was both a warning and a request which rarely had to be repeated either to Denis or to his brother Stan who was still living with them then.

This was how it had been five years before, when Denis was nine and Stan was barely eight. In bed now, looking up at the ceiling as if the past was writ there on the distempered plaster, it seemed to Denis like another world. The loss of the arm had been like the passing of an era. He did not know to what extent the tragedy had brought about the change. Stan's illness and subsequent incarceration in a mental home was something separate, though belonging to the same time. On the other hand, the loss of work and the subsequent deprivation was directly attributable to the arm, as was also the change in his father, and in the routine pattern of their lives.

It was the more subtle change in the relationship between his mother and his father which Denis, acutely aware of it as he was, could not pin down. It was as if the presence around which their lives had orbited had departed, leaving a vacuum.

So it had been for the last five years. In terms of survival they had been saved by his father's brother, George, who had loaned the modest capital required to rent the shop and buy the initial stock. His mother's brother, Maurice, had also contributed, or at least Denis had always assumed so. He could remember how at the time of the crisis he would come in from play in the evenings sometimes and find his mother, father and Uncle George whom he liked and Uncle Maurice Horsborough whom he didn't like, sitting in the living-room in the evening gloom. His mother would rise to light the gas as if it was a signal, and the conversation would cease until Denis had gone upstairs to bed. Afterwards he would hear them from his bed, the occasional raised voice of his mother and his uncles. He never heard his father's voice.

Climbing from his bed at last, he dressed in the new long trousers which he had been given for his fourteenth birthday the week before. There had actually been two pairs, so that he did not have the embarrassment of reverting to shorts for everyday use as was usually the case. In some way he knew that his father had been responsible for this, possibly because of the grudging way in which his mother had presented them to him. He knew that sooner or later she would insist on his wearing out his old shorts, but he felt he could live with that temporary embarrassment. Putting his new longs on for the first time, he had his first tentative awareness of the potential of approaching manhood, the outward and visible sign of the inward stirrings that had been going on for some time now inside him. This would have been his last year at school if his birthday had not fallen as it did. In the event he had one more year to go.

He wondered now as he dressed, what the future held in terms of work. He had failed his scholarship examination for Grammar School, though failed was hardly the right word when there were so few places and so many capable of filling them. It was, nevertheless, he knew, regarded as a failure by his mother and by his Uncle Maurice Horsborough. They had imparted in him a sense of shame and lack of achievement in the way in which they expressed their regret. Because he knew he had worked hard he resented it. The choices that were open to him now were few. Most of his contemporaries at the school would go down the pit, but he knew that neither his mother, nor his father for different reasons, would countenance this.

That they talked about his future, and argued at length, he also knew. They were discussions in which he had no part. It was not just that the possibility of asking him what he would like to do did not occur to them, though it did not since the choices were few as to make discussion meaningless: in their minds they saw it as their responsibility to select from what there was on his behalf. It was an attitude of the time, conditioned in his father's case by the circumstances, which, also because of the time, he did not question. He simply awaited their decision.

Once in the last year he had taken from the library a book on careers. He had read it as some, accidentally falling across a work of imaginative fiction, are excited into reading for the rest of their lives. That was to come later for him. What the careers book did for him at that time was to give him an awareness of his place in society that perhaps no other book could have done, not simply because of the doors which it opened and then, for him, closed, but because it gave him an awareness of his own situation in comparison with that of his own blood relatives.

Going down the stairs, the long trousers rubbing still strangely across his knees, he heard the sharp ting of the shop bell and heard his mother go in there from the kitchen. He hoped that the customer would be one of the kind that kept her talking, which she was never loath to do, so that he could have his breakfast and go out without being intercepted.

He passed through the living-room which was her pride and joy, inasmuch as pride and joy played a part in her life. The pride was somewhat diminished by the fact that most of the furniture had at some time been discarded by relatives.

In the poky little kitchen at the end of the short dark passage which hid the pantry, his father sat reading the

5

paper. The table almost filled the room and his father always sat in the corner by the fire, the paper propped at an angle against the wall so that he could read it while eating his breakfast with his one hand.

'Oven,' his father said as he came in.

Denis opened the oven and took out the breakfast left there by his mother. If he ate it quickly he could be out before she returned. He sat down at the table and started to eat.

'Don't gobble,' his father said, his eyes still on the paper.

Denis slowed to something which might be accepted as less than a gobble and looked at the paper. There was a photograph of Mussolini on the front page. There were often photographs of Mussolini, and of Adolf. 'The terrible twins' his father called them.

Somewhere beyond the dark little passage the shop bell tinged again. Denis wondered whether it was the same customer going out or another one coming in. Customers came in more frequently these days, since Parkway Colliery had opened up again. There were more travellers too, and his mother went more frequently to the bank. The stock in the shop had grown from its earlier thin beginnings, especially the tin Dudleys, and the snap tins. Brushes and mops seemed more in evidence, almost as if there was a concerted campaign to clear away the dust of the Depression. 'Things are looking up,' he had heard his Uncle George say once. 'They need coal to fight a war,' his father had replied, simply, looking at Denis as he said it with that deepening in his eyes which he had learned to recognise as affection, mixed with concern.

'What's the programme today?' his father asked him.

'Decontamination centre,' said Denis.

'You mean the baths,' his father said, as if Denis's description of the new function to which the local swimming baths had been put was offensive to him.

Denis himself liked it. It sounded official. It went with the steel helmet and the more sophisticated gas mask with which he had been issued when he joined the ARP, with Ted, as a messenger boy. In the beginning they had been used almost solely as casualties for the older personnel to practice first aid on. Since early summer, however, the swimming baths had been closed to the public and a messenger boy and at least one adult were always in attendance. It had made their summer one to be remembered, for usually he and Ted stayed together throughout the day, regardless of whether they were on duty or not, and were allowed to swim in the pool, which was always kept full. The macabre purpose behind it all, which in their minds was all tied up with Adolf and Mussolini and not to be taken too seriously, had not been impressed on them by the brief course on gases used in a possible war. Even the solemn occasion at the police station when they had entered a cell filled with a relatively harmless gas, to demonstrate the effectiveness of their masks, had not really penetrated. They were far more impressed by the awareness of being confined in a cell frequently occupied by various notorious local drunks.

Finishing his breakfast now, Denis rose to go.

'Ted working yet?' his father asked.

'No,' said Denis.

'His dad in work?'

'Don't know,' said Denis, lying. Doug Hoyle, Ted's father, was definitely not in work, for this was the reason Ted would never come to the matinee at the Hippodrome with him. The previous week, having money left from his birthday, he had suggested paying for Ted, but his friend had simply said, 'I don't like the Hip' and was abrupt with him for an hour or two as if he had been reminded of something unpleasant. It was something to do with Ted's pride, Denis thought. He knew about Ted's pride from incidents at school over the years. Ted's pride was easily hurt. He didn't know why, but he knew that it was so. It was something you just accepted about Ted.

He hesitated a moment, listening at the same time for the sound of the shop bell that might herald his mother's return. She would find an errand for him. If there wasn't one she would invent one. It was something she did on principle. In the event she had done it already, for his father, reminded by his hesitation, said:

'That envelope on there. Your mother wants you to take it to your Uncle Maurice's.'

Denis took it and went, while the going was relatively easy.

Ted lived in Little Moscow. Like most of Cuddon, it was just fifty yards or so off the main Cuddon Road. Once regarded as a hotbed of Communism, it now housed most of the congenitally unemployed. While the rest of Cuddon looked like a village on the way to giving up hope, Little Moscow presented no such uncertainty. Built originally by the owner of Cuddon Colliery, who had also donated the baths, it was now owned by the Council. Into the forty or so houses which faced each other across a square were packed the poorest families, later to be called the Problem Families, of the area. It teemed with children of all ages, for while hope had died, the instinct to perpetuate the misery and squalor which Little Moscow represented had all too obviously survived.

The houses had not been painted for some years, for the Labour controlled council had plans to demolish them and build anew in their place. Even the demoralisation engendered by the, as they saw it, abdication of Ramsay MacDonald, their King, and the

8

subsequent humiliating defeat at the polls had not caused these plans to be shelved. Periodically they were brought out, dusted and discussed. Like the Tablets on Mount Sinai they were a confirmation of the Word. They sustained the Faith against the day of the Second Coming. Meanwhile the houses decayed where they stood. Some had newspapers at the windows. In other areas this indicated an empty house. In Little Moscow it simply meant that the occupants were unable to afford curtains.

The children were for the most part bare-footed. The few that had shoes rarely had socks. Toddlers toddled early in the square, there being distinct advantages to mobility. In the summer they staggered around the rubble strewn area naked below the waist, apparently unwatched but in danger from nothing more than the odd passing bicycle. The staple diet of bread and jam was often evident in the tongue drawn circle stickily red around their mouths as they played, little white Bantus of another culture, in the dust of the earth from which they came.

Ted had been born and had lived his fourteen years in this same square. He had a sister, Jessie, one year younger than himself, and then progressively downwards in nine or ten month intervals, two brothers, and a sister, who had died the previous year. In all the four years or so that Denis had been his mate he could recognise, of the others, only Jessie, for they all played in and out of each others houses and no outsider could be sure to which family each belonged. Among themselves there were rarely any doubts. In such a tight community unwritten laws were broken at great peril. In such strange climates does morality flourish.

Jessie came to the door when Denis knocked. He was glad it was Jessie. Ted's father always seemed to look through and beyond him as if he had answered the door to find no one there, while his mother seemed to resent his coming as if she suspected he might carry some contagious disease. Jessie always seemed, in a way, glad to see him, or at least he always felt that she was.

She called back inside the house for Ted. She never asked him in unless it was raining. Nor did Ted. Yet she stayed at the door, the baby in her arms, waiting for Ted to come, not wishing to leave Denis standing there alone.

'Tucker's Fair's here tonight and tomorrow,' he said.

'Yes,' she said, 'I know.'

Across the Square voices were raised in anger. A woman shrieked and a man's voice bawled back at her. Watching Jessie he saw her flinch as if the sounds were directed at her, as they probably sometimes were in this place that was her home.

Ted came round from the back eventually, pushing his bicycle, and Jessie nodded at him and went back inside.

'You've forgotten your tin hat and gas mask,' Denis said.

'Leave 'em at the baths now,' Ted answered. 'Kids play with 'em if I bring 'em home, and I've nowhere to put 'em.'

Denis remembered the envelope.

'I've to call at my uncle's,' he said.

Ted mounted his bike of many parts and looked down at his front tyre through which the inner tube would soon be showing.

'I'll see you at baths then.'

'They've got two tyres in a shed up there,' said Denis. 'They're worn but they're better than yours. We can see if they're right for size if you come with me.'

There was a moment of silence, then Ted said 'Aye, all right then.'

Even a pride such as his had its limits, it seemed. He stood on the pedal and started to ride across the Square.

Denis followed, dodging the bricks, the broken glass and the occasional baby.

A mile from the crossroads that marked the centre of Cuddon, if indeed Cuddon could be said to have a centre, a tree covered slope topped by a fourteenth-century church broke the skyline. A handful of stone cottages and houses marked the original village of Cuddon, for the bulk of the population lived in the long sprawling rows of terraced houses built by the colliery company. The place had expanded almost overnight with the sinking of the first shaft in the middle of the previous century. The agricultural community, divided from what must have seemed an incoming multitude by only a short length of road, stayed on the hill. They were joined by the tradesmen and professional people who came to the area over the years, and paid good money for land on which to build their houses away from the sprawl in which it was earned. Physically they were little more than a stone's throw from the nearest terrace, as Little Moscow was from its more respectable neighbours, but the gulf was symbolically the same.

Maurice Horsborough was not an incomer. There had been Horsboroughs in Cuddon for as long as he could trace his ancestry back. Almost all of them, up to his father's generation, had been farmers. His grandfather left the soil, as others in Cuddon did, when the colliery company bought their land for housing. Sooner or later most left the area. They were glad to do so when they saw the slag heaps building up and the land despoiled. One or two, perhaps, looked at their money and wondered if it had been worth it.

Not so the Horsboroughs. Perhaps they remembered the Parable of the Talents. Perhaps they just got a taste for more and remembered the old Yorkshire saying, 'Where there's muck there's brass.' Whatever the instinct that made them stay, it eventually paid their wages.

In 1939 Maurice had been running the various family businesses, mostly men's outfitting and numbering over a dozen shops scattered over a fairly wide area. His father had died some ten years before and since then Maurice had added two more shops, both in middle class suburbs of Leeds. He could have moved to a better area, of course, as his father before him could have, though like many Yorkshire businessmen he had developed the habit of pleading poverty to the point where to some extent he believed it.

'It's all in the business,' he was fond of saying. 'Can't call a penny my own. It's all on paper,' he would add, as if implying that the money didn't really exist.

Inevitably a Tory in a Tory tradition, he had never dabbled actively in politics. A hard man where money was concerned, he was insensitive rather than unkind. When in church he repeated in prayer, 'We have not done those things we ought to have done', it did not occur to him that the words were an apt description of himself. He sinned, as many do, by omission.

Over the years he had acquired a wife from a family very similar to his own, two children now in their early twenties, and lived on the hill above Cuddon in the house in which he was born and which his father had left to him.

It was to this house that Denis came now with Ted. He left his bike outside the gates at the end of the drive. He also left Ted, who in any case had no inclination to enter. He had only once even taken a friend into the house of his mother's brother. The day after, his mother had spoken to him on the subject, telling him that he must not again take his friends there. His Aunt Clare, it seemed, was 'peculiar'. Precisely what form this peculiarity took was not explained, his mother simply used the word in full explanation, looking beyond him out of the window into the back yard as she spoke to him. She had chosen a time when his father was out, or Denis might have gone to him for a definition, and when he saw him again it had ceased to be important. The word, after all, did fit his aunt. She rarely visited them. If his uncle called when she happened to be with him she stayed in the car outside more often than not, rather than enter.

Denis approached the house now, wondering how to broach the subject of the tyres. He knew the tyres were hanging in the shed in the garden because he had come here with his mother the previous month when the Horsboroughs were on holiday. She had come every day to feed the cat, for their daily help was also away. Getting bored in the garden where she had told him to play he went to find her to ask if she was ready to go.

He had found the front door open. Normally he would have knocked and waited, but since only his mother was in there he pushed the door open wider and entered. The hall was empty, and the door to the kitchen was open so he could see she was not there either. Thinking that perhaps she had gone upstairs to the bathroom he stood in the hall a moment waiting. He had not really looked at the house before, his visits being brief and usually on some errand. Looking around him now, at the expensive furniture, the spotless decorations, and feeling under his feet the rich soft pile of the carpet, he suddenly became conscious of something he had always taken for granted; how very much different it was from their own. He had a sense of being an intruder, of having no right to be there in their absence, with an accompanying sense of guilt. Wanting now to go, he had called:

'Mum!'

She had answered him from a nearby room and he had crossed the hall and entered. It was the lounge, a large and sumptuously furnished room which he had rarely been in. His mother was sitting on the couch in the centre of the room, her hands clasped round her knees. She looked entirely at home, as if she belonged there quite naturally, and because he felt an intruder he had a sudden sense of alienation from her also.

She had looked up at him, but almost without seeing him, and he had seen the marks of tears still wet on her cheeks.

He remembered this briefly as he walked down the drive to the rear of the house and knocked on the kitchen door. He waited but no one came. He knocked again. Beyond the far hedge at the bottom of the garden, where there was a tennis court, he heard someone laugh, and a faint murmur of voices. He waited a moment longer, then walked down the path to the gap in the hedge which led to the tennis court.

His cousins were there with a man and a woman he did not know. They were lying in the sun, looking up at the almost clear sky, or with their eyes closed. The strange woman had her head resting on the abdomen of the man he didn't know. They had been playing tennis. Rackets lay on the grass where they had dropped them, and the court was littered with balls. As Denis came through the gap in the hedge his cousin Tim sat up and saw him.

'It's young Denis,' he said.

His cousin Doris opened her eyes, looked at him, and then closed them again.

'How's Denis?' said Tim, squinting against the sun.

Denis, shy as he always was with Tim, though he liked him, scrabbled in his pocket for the envelope and produced it.

'Mum sent this for Uncle,' he said, almost at attention like a messenger from the Front.

Tim dragged himself to his feet and took it. 'They're out,' he said. 'I'll see he gets it when they come back. Like some lemonade?'

Denis would have liked some lemonade, but he thought of Ted. 'My mate's waiting,' he said.

'Waiting?' said Tim. 'Waiting where?'

'Out in the lane.'

'What's he want to wait there for? Fetch him in!'

'He won't come,' said Denis.

'Won't come?' said Tim. 'We'll see about that.'

He jogged off through the gap in the hedge. Denis remembered what his mother had said about not taking his friends here and decided the matter had been taken out of his hands.

'Aren't we going to play?' said his cousin Doris, not opening her eyes.

The strange man sat up suddenly, so that the woman's head fell back on the grass.

'Don't mind that,' she said. 'It's only my head.'

The man looked at Denis and smiled.

'Who's this?' he said.

'Denis,' said Doris, not opening her eyes, or mentioning their relationship.

'Hello Denis,' the man said. Then he lay back on the grass and the woman again put her head on his abdomen.

Tim was in his second year at Cambridge, and Denis assumed from their soft southern accents that they were visitors from there. He looked at them curiously since they were not looking back. They looked to his fourteen years very adult, though neither of them would be more than twenty or so. But then the boys he occasionally saw wearing the brightly badged blazers of Caselborn Grammar School always looked much older than himself, and were of course if they were in the sixth form. It was because he lived with the, for him, natural assumption that one left school at fourteen that he was never able to think of them as representing the next stage in his own development, for by then he would be working.

He felt an odd pride in this that in some way compensated for his own inarticulate feelings of failure in not achieving the scholarship, for the fact that so very few did had not entirely diminished such feelings. The two in his own year who had done so, rarely joined with those they had been in the same class with now. In the evenings or on weekends or holidays when the mass of the children played on the stacks, or in winter under the lamps in dark passageways, the successful were sat at cleared kitchen tables, ploughing away at homework.

Jessie was one of these. He wondered how and when she did it in that house that was almost entirely occupied and surrounded by children and in which, as the eldest, she had duties to perform.

He became conscious suddenly that the woman visitor with the southern accent was smiling at him. He flushed, and looked away, embarrassed, and was relieved to see Tim come through the gap in the hedge propelling Ted before him. Ted looked embarrassed too, but not too averse to being brought here, Denis thought with relief.

Tim filled two glasses for them. 'There you are,' he said. 'Help yourselves if you want any more.' Then he sat down on the grass and contemplated his friends.

'Couple of soft southerners, these,' he said with a sideways glance at Denis and Ted.

'Oh drop it, Tim,' said Denis's cousin Doris. 'We went through all that last night.'

'She's a southerner at heart,' said Tim. 'She hates it round here, don't you?'

'I can think of better places to live.'

'Where does Ted live?' Tim asked Denis, as if Denis were some official spokesman for an absent Ted.

'Little Moscow,' said Denis, not looking at Ted. If

Ted had not been there he would have invented some fictitious address. He tried to make it sound as if it was just another place.

Tim's friend sat up and the woman's head again fell on the grass.

'Thanks,' she said.

The man looked at Ted with interest.

'Little Moscow?'

'Former political capital of Cuddon,' Tim explained, grinning, suggesting old, dubious glories.

'How come?'

'Most of the well-known Blackshirts lived there at one time,' said Tim.

'Blackshirts in Little Moscow?'

'That's what they call them round here, at either end of the political scale … Party members, Mosley's lot … They dress them in one shirt – a black one.'

'I find that hard to believe,' said the man.

'Yes, I daresay,' said Tim, 'but you're politically educated and they're not. Anyway, you can't expect to know about Northern working-class politics down in Canterbury.'

'What do you know about Northern working-class politics?' Doris said, briefly opening her eyes at Tim.

'Damn sight more than you do,' he replied, a note of irritation in his voice, because she criticised his local knowledge to his friends on his home ground. Then he ignored her and concentrated on the man.

'They get their political opinions from reading the *Express*,' he said.

'At least the *Express* supported us in Spain,' the man said. 'The usual stupid stuff, of course, but their intentions were honest.'

Doris opened her eyes again. 'I was in London in February. I walked down Whitehall to see Charlie Forrester. There was a parade. A lot of odd-looking characters with sandwich boards. "Why silence about Communist Spanish atrocities?" they said.'

'Fascists,' said Tim.

'Rubbish,' Doris said. 'They were from the International Brigade. It said so on the posters. "We who fought in the International Brigade give you the truth".'

'The disenchanted are like the poor,' Tim said. 'They're always with us.'

'They fought there,' she said. 'They know. You didn't.'

Tim looked at her but didn't immediately reply. His face had the look of one who has been through it all before. 'Pointless to argue with her,' his expression said.

She took advantage of his silence.

'All this fashionable political rubbish you pick up down there,' she said. Then addressing herself to the man, 'Are they all like that at Cambridge?'

'The usual mixture,' he grinned.

Denis waited for Tim to speak. He did not understand the argument, but neither did he like Doris. He didn't want her to have the last word.

It came in a burst of adrenalin, from Tim: 'We're going to have a war because we didn't back the Popular Front in Spain. Europe's going to tear itself apart again because people like you don't care. You're like Chamberlain with his bit of paper, you think it can all be sorted out between gentlemen. And if the other bloke turns out not to be a gentleman, well there's always the good old British Navy, and the good old British Tommy, to sort it all out for you in somebody else's front garden while you just sit in the sun back home, or play Lady Bountiful to the wounded!... You're like the rest of this family, you can't see the bomb because you're sitting on it, and you can't hear it ticking because you're deaf!'

There was a brief silence before Doris jumped to her feet and walked away. She vanished through the gap in the hedge. Denis and Ted sipped their lemonade, as if there was no one else there. Tim looked down at the grass, his face hidden. The girl opened her eyes then closed them again. After squinting thoughtfully up at the sun for a moment, the man said:

'I have all this sort of stuff with my brother. Edmund, you know – the one in the Foreign Office. Always telling me stories about when Labour were in power and how the Lads at the Foreign Office kept Ramsay MacDonald in his place.'

'MacDonald's had it round here,' said Tim. 'A. J. Cook's the only bloke they trust round here.'

'He's dead, isn't he?'

'Is he? They don't talk about him as if he was.'

'What will they do in a war, the sort of blokes you have round here?'

'What sort of blokes? We're not on another planet, you know.'

'They've got a lot of grievances, haven't they?' the man asked. 'I mean, all the damned unemployment after the General Strike.'

'They can smell work now,' said Tim. 'We need coal to fight a war. Besides, they're as patriotic as anybody else when it comes to the crunch – any time now on my reckoning.'

Tim jumped to his feet.

'Come on, you'd better start getting fit! Your King and country are going to need you!'

He turned to Denis and Ted. 'You two want to be off? You can stay and watch if you like. We're not much cop though, I warn you.'

'There's a tyre in the shed,' said Denis, suddenly.

'Is that an observation or a request,' Tim asked, smiling. Then seeing that Denis was embarrassed and didn't totally understand him: 'You want it, is that it?'

'If it fits,' said Denis.

'If it fits, it's yours.'

Tim picked up his racket. 'How's your mother?' he asked, and not waiting for the answer: 'Tell her I'll pop down and see her before I go back.'

The shed was on the other side of the hedge, just through the gap. Denis went inside, brought out the tyre and gave it to Ted. 'You'd better go and try it,' he said.

Ted trotted off with the tyre as Doris came from the house. She watched him vanish round the corner and then came down the path.

'Who gave him the tyre?' she asked.

'Tim said we could have it. He's gone to see if it fits.'

She looked at him. He waited for the complaint, but instead she turned her back on him and walked back to the house. He felt suddenly ashamed, without knowing why. He would have liked to have put the tyre back and gone, but it was Ted who needed it.

Waiting for him to return he heard the man on the court say something to Tim, and Tim said, 'He's my cousin. Dad's sister's boy. They live down in Cuddon, the poor end.'

Denis thought indignantly, 'It's Ted who lives at the poor end!' It was as if Tim had taken away from him what little supremacy he had in relation to Ted.

CHAPTER TWO

You could, to some extent, measure the relative poverty of the various strects in Cuddon by measuring their distance from the foot of the stacks. The least desirable were closest to the dust and the smell, and the Square was closest of all.

The gritty sulphurous taste of dust from the slag heap was in Ted's mouth and throat when he woke that same morning. He lay for a moment, befuddled with the afterbirth of sleep, waiting for the room to form round him. Through half open eyes he could see his clothes piled on an orange box by the side of the bed, and on the floor beside them the clothes of his two younger brothers who shared the bed he slept in. The smell of slag was always discernible in the room, but this time it was worse than it usually was; and then he remembered that he had woken in the night, unbearably hot, and opened the window an inch or two. He got out of bed now and closed it, then got back in, the thickness in his head from a night of polluted sleep still not clearing.

If it had been a schoolday, he would have dragged his

clothes on and made his way down the stairs to the scullery to sluice his head under the tap. As it was, he could afford a few more minutes in the no man's land between consciousness and sleep. His mother and father would sleep into the late morning. His mother was idle and his father had long since given up the attempt to maintain some sort of pattern that related to his earlier working life, as if he had abandoned altogether any future hope of work.

His brothers beside him were drugged as he was. They would wake in their own good time. They had nowhere to go as he had. Until he had joined the Civil Defence it would have been the same for Ted, and it was only the prospect of a day on duty at the baths with Denis that urged his mind towards consciousness. As school drove him through the motions of living in the weekdays, forcing him into the action of maintaining a routine, so the otherwise pointless spells of duty at the baths had kept him active at weekends and in the otherwise interminably boring school holidays. Before that he had woken with the rest of the house.

He would not be the first up though. Already his ear had caught the sounds of movement from downstairs, and the rattle of the pipes in the wall as the tap was turned in the scullery. Jessie was always awake, even before he was. When he went down she would have mustered whatever breakfast she had, and would be sitting at the square scrubbed table in the living-room with her school books spread before her. It was the only time in the day that she could work in the silence which he imagined her work would demand. Respectful, almost reverential in his attitude towards her schoolwork, he would descend the stairs quietly and close himself in the scullery so as not to disturb her.

He dressed and made his way down there now, though still bemused by the heavy night. He closed the door to the stairway behind him, glanced at her briefly, then turned towards the scullery. With his hand on the doorknob her voice stopped him.

'You don't have to creep, you know,' she said.

He turned and looked at her. She was smiling at him. She had never spoken before, always allowing him to pass through in silence.

'I'm all right,' he said, as if to assure her that the effort caused him no pain.

'I've to work with all the racket going on mostly,' she said.

'You don't like it though.'

'I've got used to it.' She picked up the lid of the teapot that was on the table beside her and peeped inside. 'I've only just made this. There's one for you. Get yourself a mug.'

He hesitated, as if reluctant to lose this little ritual he had kept up so long, then did as she said, bringing the mug and holding it out to her.

'You can sit down,' she said.

'You're working.'

She said, 'I've been up for hours. I'm ready for a rest.'

He sat on the other side of the table from her and waited for her to pour the tea. She was clean and fresh and tidy in her face and dress, though her eyes were tired with the concentration of reading, as if she had not yet totally emerged from the book. She shone in the scruffiness of the room and everything in it as if she had stepped from another world, and yet she had been born on the heavy flock mattress on which his mother and father slept in similar squalor, and had been totally bred in the world of the Square. Everything in it that he hated was magnified by contrast with her. It was a contradiction which he could not comprehend and at times seemed to him to have an almost supernatural unreality, as if some force was at work in all this darkness, though such thoughts were alien to him both in his years and, such as it was, his upbringing.

Sitting across the table from her, with the rest of the family asleep, he felt alone with her in the house, as if none of the others existed. He had a tolerant affection for the younger ones, a dislike which verged on something much stronger for his mother, and only for his father a feeling which approached the strength of his feeling for Jessie. He had imagined sometimes what sort of life they would have had if there had been just the three of them. Even in the circumstances in which they lived he knew it would have been more tolerable. Much of the aggravation came from the sluttishness of their mother and the overcrowded conditions in which they lived. That her sluttishness was a reaction to these conditions, perhaps, it was beyond him to analyse, though sometimes he would think back to a time when, vaguely, he could remember that things had been better. But his father had been able to pick up the odd casual job then and, for all the hardness of the times, this had held them back from the abyss into which they now seemed to have fallen.

As he sipped his tea his mind returned, as it often did, to what always inevitably seemed the potentially panacea for all their ills. He broke the silence across the table and said, 'Think Dad'll ever work again?'

Jessie considered the question, looking beyond him as if she used the wall behind to work out the calculations that would produce the answer.

She said, eventually, 'If the war comes they reckon everybody'll be in work.'

He had heard that before. It was something, he remembered, Denis had quoted his father as saying. Since there was no further deprivation he could think of which a war might bring about, the possibility instilled no great fear in his mind. You could lose your life in a war, of course, but that could happen in the pit also and the odds were probably no greater with one than the other. He had no real fear of the pit. He had, if anything, a longing to be done with school and into the world of men which the pit represented.

He said, 'I shall go down the pit then,' knowing that she hated the thought of him doing so because they had talked about it once before. It warmed him that she should be concerned for him, that in all the world probably only she would regret the rough, hard, dangerous life he would have to live, for his father would simply take it for granted.

He said, wanting and yet not wanting her to fear for him, 'I shall like the pit. It'll suit me.'

'Why will it suit you?'

'I shall be a man,' he said, simply, as if there could be no other valid reason.

'You don't think about things,' she said accusingly. 'You don't look to make something better of your life.'

'How?' he asked, not using what he saw as the impossibility of what she wanted for him to confuse her, but rather as if he said to her, 'If you can show me some way I'll take it.'

Then there was shouting upstairs from her younger brothers and she stood as if to go up to them immediately.

'Let Mam see to it,' he said, with sudden anger, not wanting to lose her or the moment.

'She won't,' Jessie replied, with simple fact which he could not deny. Then she was gone upstairs and the contact between them was broken.

Later, as he stood outside the Horsboroughs' waiting for Denis, he went through this conversation with Jessie again in his mind. He knew what she meant when she said he did not look to make something better of his life.

It was true. Once she had tried to get him to read some of the books which she read for school, as if she thought it might create an ambition which he did not seem to have. He made a pretence of doing it simply to please her, and in a sense this was so, but there was also the fact that he was curious. Respecting her own achievements in gaining a scholarship, how could he reject her efforts to help him without belittling her. So he had ploughed on through *Wuthering Heights* and *Jane Eyre*, which were her favourites at that time, finding nothing with which he could identify or which in any way shone a light on the kind of world she saw in them which, it seemed, he did not. He had lied to her, saying that he liked them, but he could sense that she knew he was simply trying to please her in saying so. She had tried him once more with a rather second-rate middle class novel of the time, and he abandoned this after reading the first three chapters. Set in an upper middle class suburb in the South of England it was totally alien to him. This time he had said so.

'Why do you like it?' he had asked her, almost angrily, as if, by liking it, she had in some way demeaned herself. The answers she had given were confused, and hesitant, so that in the end he had made some joke against himself to stop her further embarrassment. It was something that stayed in his mind though, and a long time later, looking back with adult understanding on his childhood and youth, he had come across a copy, remembered it and flicked through the pages; and it was suddenly apparent to him that what this rather poor novel represented to her was something that saddened him always – the working class dream, to be middle class.

Now, standing in the lane outside the drive to the Horsboroughs' house, he himself experienced no such dream. He stood as a man in a strange country who fears that someone might ask him to produce the passport he does not have, and longs to be back where no such passport is necessary. Not able because of this feeling simply to stand and wait, he made a pretence of fiddling with his bike. Neither tyre was good, but the front one was almost finished. It was a mongrel bike, made up of various parts from other bikes gleaned over a long period, and it was his pride and joy. It took him out into the countryside surrounding Cuddon, and was his qualification for being a messenger in the Civil Defence unit. It took him away from the Square. Only his increasingly desperate need for another tyre would have brought him to this part of Cuddon. It was Indian country, but where the Indians were all big chiefs. No fences surrounded it but the very atmosphere of the area said 'Keep Out!'

Concentrated on his bike, for its familiarity in these unfamiliar surroundings as much as anything else, he was not aware that Tim had come down the drive until he spoke to him.

'Come and have some lemonade,' said Tim.

Ted looked up and saw a good-looking youth, some six years older than himself, smiling at him. Tim was wearing a white shirt and tennis shorts. His accent, after two years at university, had no connection with the area if it ever had. His hair was long compared to the local short back and sides. There was an easy confidence, even a slight touch of what at a stretch might be called arrogance, in his manner which, if Ted had been able to analyse it honestly and with a self-awareness which comes, if ever, later in life, he would have recognised as the only obvious trait they had in common.

He said, to this alien figure, 'I'm all right,' then added, from some past influence instilled by his grandmother rather than either of his parents, 'Thanks.'

'I'm sure you're all right,' Tim smiled, 'but come and have some lemonade and then you'll be all righter.'

Ted searched in his mind for some other kind of refusal but could find none. The worn tyre caught his eyes. He was here for the tyre. It dangled like a carrot in front of Tim's smiling eyes, offering him no alternative. He turned his bike round without speaking.

'That's more like it,' Tim said, and Ted followed him down the drive, pushing the battered bike.

He sat on the grass with Denis, sipping lemonade, but only when Denis did, as if he feared there might be some ritual; as at the time in life when, faced for the first time at a meal with a multiplicity of cutlery, the inhibited initiate waits for the order of use to be revealed to him.

Although sat beside him he felt cut off from Denis in a way that was strange to him. For Denis was related to all this; for the moment was one of them. That Denis might be experiencing similar feelings of alienation did not occur to him.

The conversation would probably have passed by him, for his eyes were busy absorbing the scene, if Tim had not asked Denis where Ted lived. He listened then as they spoke about him as if he was not there. It was when Tim said to the other man, in explanation of the political confusion over the local use of the word Blackshirt, that while he was politically educated the people of Cuddon were not, that Ted felt the first stirrings of something that was neither embarrassment nor discomfort.

His father knew about politics. There were books from the Miner's Welfare library in the house at the present time which he knew, from the titles, were about politics. There was one about the Spanish Civil War, for his father had picked it up and had turned to a list of British dead at the end of the book and had pointed a name out to Ted. 'Know who that is?' he had asked, and

Ted had recognised the name as that of a man who had been sacked from the pit at the time his father was, and who had sometimes come to the house. Then his father had said, 'He died for you,' as if he spoke of the dead Christ.

There was also the fact that his father had been sacked from the pit for his political activities in the General Strike. This he had heard not from his father, but mostly in overheard conversations or when one man would say to another, 'This is Doug Hoyle's lad that was crucified by the owners for keeping us out after t'General Strike.' This had happened to him three or four times now. Though he knew neither the facts nor the circumstances he knew, from the way in which it was said, that it was an accolade; something of which he could be proud. Then, too, there were his mother's frequent complaints, stridently voiced, sluttishly trumpeted across the Square for all to hear. 'You and your bloody politics!' she would scream. 'I pay the price for your bloody politics!' And his father would look at her, then leave the room without speaking, followed by a stream of foul-mouthed abuse.

So Ted listened now as the group on the lawn spoke of politics, though he did not understand. What he did understand, though it puzzled him, was that in speaking about the war Tim spoke as his father might have spoken. Vaguely he knew that Tim was at least to some degree on his father's side. Yet he was a boss, or at least he belonged in that camp, and it was the bosses who had put his father out of work.

When the two men jumped to their feet to start playing again, and Tim said that he supposed they would want to go now, Ted remembered, with a sudden awful fear, the tyre. Were they not, after all, to have it? Then he heard Denis say, 'There's a tyre in the shed,' and it quickly became apparent they could have it. He felt a sudden great warmth for his friend, his saviour. He was, after all it seemed, not one of Them.

The final anxiety came when he looked at it in the shed and it came to the question of size, for even the size marking on the side was worn off on his own. He took it and ran almost to the drive where he had left his bike against a tree. It fitted! His relief was such that he almost wept.

CHAPTER THREE

The tyre fitted. They took a short cut from the Horsboroughs' that led across the pit fields, by the long line of slag heaps which were fed by overhead buckets from Cuddon pit, and stopped by the stream into which the slag heaps drained. Denis sat in the sun and watched while Ted wrestled with the wheel, prising the old tyre off and replacing it with the new one. The strong smell of sulphur from the stream, which would have driven strangers away, was something they were used to, as was the clatter and squeak of the buckets on their never ending journey along the overhead cable. As country-born children remember the sounds and scents of the countryside as they lie in adult wakefulness in the dark night of the city, so in later years they remembered these sounds, and the odour of the stream, and their childhood.

'What's it like inside?' said Ted, suddenly, struggling to get the new tyre on without nipping the inner tube.

'What?'

'Horsboroughs'. Where we've been. Their house. What's it like?' Ted asked.

'Posh,' said Denis, as if he was a constant and welcome visitor. He said it with that mixture of pride and embarrassment which always confused his association with his relatives. He remembered the words he had heard from the man on the tennis court that same morning: 'Poor relations.' Some feeling stirred inside him. Not resentment; he was too young, too accepting of life as it was, yet for that. Picking up a stone from the ground beside him he stood and flung it up the stack.

'Posh,' he said.

He ran at the stack with a sudden burst of energy, mounting the shallow lower slopes with ease. He went on with increasing difficulty as the gradient beat him and his feet sank into the shale as it became softer higher up. He reached a point where an old pram lay half buried, probably left there by coal pickers, and sat on the wheel, swivelling backwards and forwards as he looked back down the slope.

He was forbidden to play on the stacks, as were many others, but they all did. The strange lunar landscape had a fascination only equalled by the thrill of defying authority. His presence there having been reported once to his mother by a sharp-eyed customer, she had used the misdemeanour in an attempt to forbid him also to play with Ted. His father had sent him upstairs and then had intervened, for Denis had crept back down to overhear.

His mother, bitterness and resentment in her voice, was dominating the conversation when Denis reached the bottom step and stood outside the closed door to listen, poised for a rapid exit should either of them come out.

'What's he going to grow up like?' she asked.

He did not hear his father answer this, though he listened, for he would have liked to hear his father's opinion on his future prospects, not having one himself.

His mother went on: 'Those Hoyles, they're the worst

of a bad lot. She comes in the shop sometimes, thinking we'll let her have stuff on the slate because Denis plays with Ted Hoyle. You should see her face drop when she sees it's me come to serve her and not you. You'd let her run up debts she'll never pay off, wouldn't you?'

'I worked in the pit with Doug Hoyle,' his father said. 'Side by side in a two-foot seam.'

'He hasn't worked for years.'

'Neither have I.'

'Only because of your arm.'

'There hasn't been work.'

'There is now, for those that want it.'

'Not for everybody. Not yet.'

'They live like animals!'

'They live as they're able!'

'Others that have no more than them live better – live clean!'

'All right,' his father said. 'He married a slut! He knows it. He has to live with it. He's learned his lesson too late, the hard way, like you've learned yours with me. He regrets it like you do, but he has to go on because what else is there?'

His voice choked into silence. When Denis's mother spoke again, her voice was softer, gentler.

'How can you compare?' she asked. 'How can you?'

'Worst of a bad deal, you got,' his father said.

'Have I ever said that?'

'It shows through,' said his father. 'It shows through. You want for Denis what he'd have had if you'd not gone against your father, not what I'm able to give him.'

'Only for him,' she said, 'not for me. You know that. You know it.'

In the silence that followed, Denis had crept back up the stairs.

He looked down now on Cuddon from his modest perch on the stack. In the fourteen years since he had been born he had left it not more than half a dozen times, all but one of them for a boarding house on the East coast owned by a distant relative. The other time had been to Keswick where he had camped for a week with the school. He could remember still the tree covered slopes around Derwentwater, and the craggy heights of Helvellyn, so different to the stacks on which he now stood; unsoiled by the afterbirth of the Industrial Revolution.

His mind had not yet begun to question the reasons for the differences in the quality of the lives of the people he knew, but he was aware of those differences. Most immediately he was aware of them in Ted and himself. The fact that Ted lived in Little Moscow for example, between which and the meanest adjacent street there was a great gulf fixed. They were all working class, but some were more working class than others. He knew already that his mother and father had different conceptions as to why this was. His mother blamed the people, and his father blamed life.

There were other contrasts, like those between his own life and that of his cousins. He felt it most with his cousin Doris. She seemed in some way to resent him, as if the fact that he was her cousin somehow diminished her. Tim was different. The contrast here was almost solely to do with the differences in their ages. When Tim called him 'young 'un' there was warmth in his voice. Moreover Tim came to visit them, not in the way his father did out of an evident sense of duty, but giving the impression that he wanted to. Moreover, Denis knew that between Tim and his father there was a mutual respect. Tim was, for instance, the only person he knew with whom Jim Russell discussed politics. That they disagreed was apparent, but that they enjoyed the thrust of the argument was equally apparent. Denis could never remember the content of any of their arguments, but something Tim had once said to his father had stuck in his mind:

'You're a working man! How can you believe what you do?'

His father had simply smiled.

They were late when he reached the Baths. Old Maddy Thomas was in the ticket office which was now an administration centre for the First Aiders. She was writing in a book. Whenever they saw her she was writing in the book. It was called the Incident Book, but there were never any incidents apart from the odd Sunday exercise.

Maddy was almost eighty, but fantastically spry. Her hair, pure white, was drawn back in a bun and she wore elastic sideboots which had not been made for years. She had come to Cuddon from Wales as a child when her father had come to help to sink a new shaft, and they had never returned, for the mine from which he came had been destroyed in a major disaster. She had never married, but had found her vocation in an involvement in almost every charitable enterprise in the area.

She looked up at them now over her wire-rimmed spectacles as they passed through the turnstiles. The thrill of not having to pay still not having quite died, they usually passed through the turnstiles.

'You're late,' she said.

Denis wondered if she would write it in the book. Whereas most of the Air Raid Precautions volunteers were never quite sure whether they took it seriously, Maddy Thomas seemed to have no such doubts. Though she was greatly respected in Cuddon, the fact that she had been placed in charge of the Decontamination Centre, a name by which the Baths never quite became known, was generally regarded as a joke. It was part of the game of preparing for a war which few totally believed would happen, a social pastime which brought status to some and companionship to others. It was an opportunity to get together, and the fact that Authority had placed Maddy in charge indicated that Authority too did not believe it would happen.

Since Hitler had invaded Czechoslovakia in March of that year the climate had subtly changed. Hardly anyone now said with conviction that there would not be a war, and those who had always said there would be continued to say it. The air raid practices became more frequent, and more air raid shelters were built. Families with cellars began to convert them by strengthening the supports of the joists as the booklets which were issued instructed them to do. Some even tried to make them gas proof as the booklets also instructed. Air locks were made at the entrances with blankets, which had to be soaked with water when the gas rattles were sounded. Denis had never heard a gas rattle, for Cuddon had been accidentally bypassed when they were issued. He imagined that a gas attack might sound something like the annual Boxing Day football match when Cuddon played at home and rattles were much in evidence.

It had never truly entered his mind that the practices which were held and in which he usually played the role of casualty might actually become a reality: that bombs would fall and that people would suffer the injuries for which he was crudely treated by half-trained volunteers. That there had been a war some twenty-odd years ago in which gas had been used he knew, for they had a distant relative living in Cuddon who had been gassed at the Front and was still coughing his way towards the grave in a front room from which he had rarely since had the strength to move.

After all, Maddy Thomas was still in charge. It was all a game, he thought. Authority must surely know better than the people.

***

They swam for the rest of the morning, just the two of them in the large empty pool, jumping into the slipper baths whenever they started to turn blue with cold. Occasionally Maddy would come and peep at them through the rubber curtains over which the notice 'Mortuary' had been mounted, and aware of an audience they would erupt in an exuberant display of aquatic gymnastics. Ted would race up the ladder and holding his nose would jump into the deep end and swim under water to the side where Maddy was and cling to the rail, hiding below the edge of the pool in an attempt to deceive her into believing that he had drowned. He never succeeded. She would simply vanish as quietly as she had come. He would complain to Denis:

'You should scream,' he would say.

But Denis could never bring himself to join in the deception.

The only other visitors they ever had were Harry Colthard, the baths superintendent, and his daughter Jean. Colthard had been in the pits and, like Denis's father, had been injured in a fall. It had in some way damaged his back and he walked with an odd corkscrew motion, dragging one side up and putting his good side forward and dragging the rest of him after it. He did it now with consummate ease, almost as if it was the natural way of walking. It fascinated them to watch him, and they would fall silent as he progressed along the edge of the pool, ignoring them. When he had gone Ted would climb out and traverse the edge of the pool, imitating Colthard's motion, and Denis, feeling obliged to, would follow. Once that summer when Colthard passed through, Ted had been in the slipper baths, and Denis had done the walk on his own, pulling his right side after him in what had become a passable imitation.

At the end of the traverse he had suddenly become

aware that Colthard was still there, in the shadow of the exit door, watching him. They had come almost face to face. Denis had frozen into stillness, fear and embarrassment conflicting inside him. Colthard had looked at him for a moment without speaking and then had simply gone out.

The next time Ted had done the imitation, Denis had said: 'We shouldn't do that.'

Ted had looked at him blankly. 'Why?' he had asked.

'We shouldn't,' Denis had said, simply, not telling him about the incident with Colthard.

Ted, looking at him, half opened his mouth as if to probe further, and then had simply dived in the pool. But he did not again imitate Colthard.

They raced now across the width of the pool. Ted always won on the width, but when they raced the length Denis was more often the winner. They raced several times until Ted got bored with winning, and then came shivering out and squatted in the slipper baths where it was warm, watching the surface of the pool become still again, their sinuses stinging with the effect of the chlorine.

'Maddy Thomas is dying,' said Ted, suddenly, lowering his usual speaking voice which tended to boom with the odd acoustics of the building. He repeated it again, lower, almost in a whisper, as if he might have been too loud before and by doing this might cancel it out.

'Dying?' Denis looked at him incredulously. He said, 'She can't be. She's in there.'

'She's six months to live,' said Ted, dramatically, almost forgetting to lower his voice.

'Who says?'

'It's gone round. It's known. Everybody knows it.'

'I didn't know,' Denis said.

'Everybody knows it,' said Ted. 'You ask your mam.'

They sat with their hands clasped round their knees, still shivering slightly, watching the dying ripples in the pool.

'Does she know?' Denis asked eventually.

'Me dad says she does,' Ted said. 'She comes to our house. She knows me dad well. She brings us clothes that get given her.'

An association with Maddy Thomas was not something he would normally bother to mention. It was as if she had acquired a new status.

They were swimming again when Jean Colthard came in. Denis was not aware of her until she dived into the pool beside him. She had been in the pool when they were there once or twice before, and in the last week or so had occasionally turned up to watch them. It was Ted who had made the first overtures that started her talking. He would plunge into the pool beside her, grin at her then swim away. She would go on her back, paddling the water, looking after him with a wary smile. Then she would follow him and they would swim side by side for a time without speaking. It was like a language between them, and Denis was reminded of something he had become aware of in the last year or so when they passed girls coming home from school, that where girls were concerned Ted had the edge on him, for he himself was immensely shy.

As she came out of the water now beside him she smiled and for a moment he thought she was about to speak. To his relief however she turned away and swam towards Ted. She said something to him which Denis did not hear, and Ted laughed and started to splash her, lying on his back and flailing at the water with his legs. Suddenly she swam straight at him and they both went under in a thrash of limbs and Denis could see the bright red of their Corporation costumes below the surface oddly distorted by the refraction and the light.

They came up gasping, their faces flushed and bright, and then suddenly it was she who was swimming away from Ted, and Ted who followed. She proved herself the faster swimmer now, something she had not revealed before, as if it was a card up her sleeve. She swam the length of the baths, Ted following at a lengthening distance. Reaching the bar at the end she waited and then, as he came up, dived underneath him and swam away from him again.

The next time she did this Ted was ready. As she passed underneath him he went down. Denis saw them struggling beneath the water, then part. Ted shot to the surface with a gasp of triumph and made for the side. She followed, gasping for breath as she came above the level of the water, pulling at the strap of her costume with one hand while she tried to keep afloat with the other. As she thrust upwards with her feet to keep above water Denis had a sudden glimpse of the curve of her breast before she pulled the costume back over it, and he realised what Ted had done.

Ted was at the rail now as she turned and looked at him, undecided how to react. He looked back at her, not with his usual grin, waiting for the outcome. She swam towards him using a slow breast stroke as if not to alarm him, but as she came closer he used the rail to pull himself out of the water on to the concrete edge of the pool. She looked up at him as he stood out of reach, a half smile now on his face, then she plunged for the ladder to climb from the pool. He waited till she emerged and stood at the top of the ladder shaking her hair. The grin was now strong on his face again, as if he now knew the answer and simply waited for her. Her own face was expressionless. Then suddenly she ran at him and Ted became the pursued. They raced round the pool as Denis watched, gasping with a mixture of breathlessness and emotion that echoed in the emptiness of the building like startled little cries of pain.

Suddenly they were gone through the curtain that divided the pool from the small plunge where the younger children learned to swim. He heard them for a time, and then silence.

Denis was dressed and was drying his hair at the mirror near the exit door when Jean reappeared. She leaned against the wall watching him, though he pretended not to notice.

Eventually she said, 'Going home?' as if it was not already obvious.

'Dinner,' he said.

'Coming back?'

'I'm on duty all day,' he said, as if suddenly remembering his supposedly real purpose there; giving it an importance.

He heard a splash and looking beyond her saw that Ted was back in the pool.

'Will you be long?' she asked, as if there was no one else there. It was an ability in women that he was to recognise later in life, and be reminded of this first recognition.

When he got home Tim was there, drinking tea with his mother and father who had already eaten.

'You're late,' his mother said to him, but the complaint lacked the usual sharpness, because Tim was sitting there.

She changed whenever Tim came. It was not that her relationship with Denis lacked warmth, but that her resentment at a way of life which was less than her childhood and upbringing had promised rubbed off on him. She wanted for him what life had held out to her from an early age and then had taken away, and she could not give it. His friendship with Ted was part of this resentment. It was not so much snobbery, though it was that too, as a refusal to totally accept what had happened, and to shield him from the effect of what she regarded as the disaster in her life.

Eating his dinner in the kitchen, he only half listened to the voices in the next room. Sometimes the shop bell would go and his father would answer it, for she never liked to be dragged away when Tim was there.

Denis ate voraciously. With no one there he could not be chastened for gobbling, and the hours in the pool had sharpened his appetite. As the satisfaction of his hunger warmed his empty stomach he thought of Ted, who would not go home until late in the day, for if he did there would be nothing for him. The events of the morning passed through his mind. Maddy Thomas was dying. Or perhaps it was just another of those stories which went round the village and were eventually proved to have no basis in fact. His mother would know. Perhaps he would ask her, not telling her that Ted had told him for she would simply say that Ted should mind his own business. He only half believed it himself, and the half that did believe was simply curious. He had always seen Maddy as perhaps most others saw her; a slightly eccentric old woman, who had been old when they were young, hurrying along the mean streets of Cuddon on the charitable errands which were her life. Other people died but you never really believed, expecting them at any time to pass you in the street, until eventually they were forgotten.

More sharply he remembered the incident with Ted and Jean Colthard, the almost ritualistic communication of their silence as they swam, side by side, and their expressions as the incident reached its climax. He remembered too their silence after they had disappeared into the small plunge.

Jean had left school the year before, being older than Ted and himself. He remembered seeing her over the years as the children of the village walked backwards and forwards to school, usually with the same group of girls, always a year older than himself and therefore always apart. She lived in a house which was part of the baths and went with the job, and not being attached to any other added to her status. This was already considerable, not just because she was almost startlingly blonde in a basically dark community, but because she had become the epitome of what a generation of adolescents vaguely knew as sex. There was a boldness about her which was masculine and yet, at the same time, provocatively feminine. Stories about her were circulated around. She had been seen in the pit fields at night while still at school, in the company of Sid Crossley, a miner and former centre forward of Cuddon school team. The fact that Sid was only sixteen did not abate the scandal. He had been two years in the pits. He was therefore a man.

Reflecting on all this, Denis was at the same time amazed at and envious of Ted's boldness, even though he had become accustomed to his friend's relaxed and easy approach to girls. When she had started to swim with them in the pool at the beginning he had slightly resented the fact that where there had been just two of them there were now three. The last few times, when she had come to watch them, he had felt a vague interest in the comparison between Jean dressed and Jean in her swimming costume, a thin, cotton, Corporation issue that clung tightly to her figure. He speculated on the silence which had followed their disappearance. Would Ted tell him what had happened? He had boasted once before of an incident with a girl in the pit fields, but Denis had not believed. Boasting of this kind was normal practice.

There were girls who would have been either horrified or delighted if they could have heard the descriptions given to their fictitious ability to arouse and satisfy adolescent desire, who walked through the life of the community with their inhibitions intact totally unaware of their role in the fantasy lives of the boys who passed them by with furtive, slightly embarrassed glances. In later years, when the fantasies became a reality, there were those who looked back on the years of delight in speculation with a sense of regret for their passing.

Denis sat for a time, unusually, behind his empty plate and considered the possibility that the images conjured up by his imagination were fact; that what was fantasy for him had been reality for Ted. He longed to know the truth. He saw again the curve of the girl's breast as she struggled to raise the strap of her costume, and remembered how she had stood near him after the silence of the plunge to ask him if it would be long before he returned.

Why had she asked him this? His mind grappled with the possibilities, straining to remember the exact intonation of her voice, her expression, and the deeper expression somewhere behind her eyes which, when his own had met them briefly, remained steadily on him so that he had had to look away.

Lost in the effort of all this he became suddenly aware that his mother had entered the kitchen and was looking at him.

'Penny for your thoughts,' she said.

He stood to avoid looking at her and took his empty plate to the sink.

'Going out again?' she asked him.

'I'm on duty,' he said, suddenly panic stricken in case she had some errand which would delay his return.

'Your towel's still wet,' she said, and then, to his relief, 'I'll get you another one.'

He followed her into the living-room, where Tim was still sitting with his father, and waited while she went up the stairs.

'If I do my thesis on this place,' Tim was saying to his father, 'I shall need to go down the pit.'

'No problem there,' his father said.

'There's a man called Longley who led the strike here in 1925.'

'Ted Longley? He works for the Council. Sweeps the road.'

'He didn't go down the pits again then?' Tim asked.

'The owners wouldn't have him,' Denis's father said. 'They look on him as a troublemaker.'

'And you?'

'They were bad times. We're only just coming out of them. Longley fought back in the only way he knew how. It was a war. The women and children were suffering too. If the owners cared they showed no sign of it. They kept him out of work because he fought against their indifference.'

'You agreed with him then?'

'In that situation I did.'

'But not with his politics?'

'Politics change,' his father said warily, knowing Tim and sensing a trap. 'In any case,' he said, 'I don't like victimisation. Look what we did to the Germans after the war; look at them now, after vengeance!'

'Is that all it is?'

'It's part of it,' Denis's father said. 'It's human nature … What they don't teach you in college.'

Tim grinned, accepting the point.

'I'd like to see Longley,' he said.

'I can show you his door. He lives in Little Moscow. He'd have nothing to say to you if he saw you with me. Denis could show you. His mate, young Ted, lives next door. Doug Hoyle might put a word in for you.

Longley's more time for him. They've neither of 'em worked in the pit since the strike. You can risk it if you want, though you'll probably get door slammed in your face. Don't tell your dad that I put you up to it – or your aunt come to that.'

'Where will you be?' Tim asked Denis.

'At the baths,' Denis said, fearing another obstacle to his return.

'I might come round later,' said Tim.

'Talk about summat else eh?' said Denis's father, winking at him as they heard his mother coming down the stairs.

Maddy Thomas was asleep when he peeped through the ticket office window on his way into the baths. She was sat in a chair by the window, her head bent forward on her chest, her hat still balanced precariously on it. Although it was summer she wore a long cardigan which, whenever she stood up, came almost to her knees. He stood for a moment watching her in the privacy of her sleep. He had not asked his mother to confirm that Maddy was dying, for even if it was true he did not imagine she would tell him. It was quite possibly true, he thought, for there were many things he knew to be true the facts of which his mother had evaded, or which he had not troubled to ask. Things from which he was protected either by evasion or by silence, as other children were, and which they ultimately passed among themselves in a process of self-education.

Then as he looked her head jerked briefly on her chest, the eyes opened, her hands moved in her lap and the knitting needles were clicking as if they had never stopped. It was like a resurrection, for the thought had occurred to him that perhaps what he watched was death. He passed through the turnstile and ran … ran … ran into the baths.

Ted was in the slipper baths but there was no sign of Jean. He looked cold and was quiet, his hands clasped around his knees. There was an expression on his face which Denis recognised but could never have described except in later years. He had seen Ted in such mood before and knew that there was nothing to be done except to wait for it to pass.

'Going in?' Denis asked.

'No,' Ted said briefly. 'I'm getting dressed in a minute.'

Denis wanted to ask him where Jean Colthard was but decided not to. Instead he said:

'Tim wants to see your dad.'

'Tim?'

'Him that gave us the tyre this morning.'

A brief flash of interest momentarily broke the withdrawn expression on Ted's face.

'What's he want to see him for?'

'He's doing a thesis.'

'What's that?'

'Something they do at college,' Denis said, not having knowledge to explain beyond this. 'He's calling later. I said you'd take him round. You will, won't you?'

'If he wants,' Ted said, his interest apparently gone. He stood up, gasping slightly as cramp gripped his legs. He said, 'I'm off up to Cuddy Fair.'

'Doesn't open till tonight,' Denis said.

'I'm just off to look.'

'We're on duty.'

'You'll be here if the Germans come.'

Ted grinned, and Denis saw that his mood had gone.

Left alone he swam for an hour or so but, alone, was soon bored, so dried himself and got dressed. He hoped that Ted would return before Tim came. That Tim should find some value in talking to Ted's father he saw as being in some way a bridge across the divide which his mother was always trying to create between Ted and himself. She respected Tim, looked up to him even as young as he was, and was grateful to the point of excess for his visits. Perhaps Tim might even persuade her to let Ted come to the house, to stay with them even, for they had a spare bed.

Lost in daydreams of a life in which people were more reasonable, unprejudiced and responsive to his hopes he did not see Jean until she stood before him. She wore a light summer dress and sandals and carried a costume and towel over her arm. The sun was high above the roof lights now and it caught her hair as it fell loosely towards her shoulders, untidily natural as she had simply let it dry after the morning swim. Everything about her was natural, fresh, uncared for except by the benevolence of nature.

She said, 'Where's Ted?' But not as if it was important.

'Cuddie Fair – to look,' Denis answered, his tongue getting in the way of the words so that they sounded to him as if he was speaking with his mouth full. He became aware of a tightness in his chest. His vision too was slightly distorted as if his eyes were having difficulty in relating the reality before him to the image he had carried around in his head for the last few hours.

'Swimming?' she asked him, her eyes holding on to him as they had done that morning so that again he had to look away.

He nodded and she smiled and vanished into the nearest cubicle, not fastening the door and he averted his eyes as he hurried past in a turmoil to change in another cubicle at the far end.

When he came out she was already in the pool. He dived in at the side furthest away from her and swam a couple of breadths, then dived to the bottom of the pool and retrieved one of the lead weighted wooden floats they used for such exercises. When he came up she was at the rail beside him. She took the float from him, dropped it again and then went after it. He saw the red costume and the dark shape of the float, distorted by the movement of the water, and then she was back beside him with the weight. She gave it to him, smiling. He smiled back and was briefly aware that he was feeling more relaxed, his shyness beginning to slip away. He threw the weight far out into the deepest part of the pool and then went after it, forcing himself down, searching the bottom of the pool for the dark shape. He had spotted it when he felt a movement beside him and was aware that she had followed him down. As he reached for the weight she reached for it too, holding on to his arm, her body hard against him. He made a pretence of holding on and then let go and thrust himself from the bottom back towards the light. He had been down for longer than was usual for him, and he floated for a moment on his back, replenishing the air in his lungs, until he suddenly realised he was alone.

He turned over and looked down into the pool but could see nothing. He glanced quickly around the surface again to confirm that she was still not there. Panic seized him briefly, and then he dived until he touched the bottom. He started to move around but again could see nothing, and soon the need for air forced him back to the surface. As his head came out of the water he caught a quick glimpse of her costume as she dived and, realising that she was playing some game with him, swam quietly to the rail and waited.

She came up close to him this time, the weight in her hand, smiling.

'Were you going to let me drown?' she asked.

'You shouldn't have done that,' he said, remembering his moment of panic. 'You shouldn't have done it.'

She swam to the rail and took hold of it, still gasping slightly as she took in air, pushing her hair, still gold but darkened now by the water, away from her face.

'I swim a lot with Dad working here,' she said. 'I do that to everybody. I can stay down longer than most people.' And then when he didn't reply, she said, honestly and without smiling, 'I'm sorry.'

It made him shy again that she should take him seriously, though he wanted desperately not to be so. He reached out suddenly, scooping the water with his hand, and splashed her. Then, astonished at himself and at the same time suddenly beginning to feel relaxed again, he swam quietly away, this time taking the length of the pool in a slow easy breast stroke. On the return she joined him, swimming alongside, quietly keeping pace with him as he had seen her do with Ted. They swam several lengths. Even at the pace it was more than he usually managed, but then this confidence was new to him also, and he had the feeling even when it came to an end that he could have gone on for ever.

Later, sitting in the shallow warmth of the slipper baths, she said, 'Your hands are nice,' embarrassing him but imprinting the thought in his mind. Throughout his life, from time to time, he would look at his hands, seeing nothing very special but always believing that it was so, as she had said it.

One other thing she said that stayed with him. It came out of remarks she made relating to the fact that both their fathers had been seriously injured in the pit. She had said, 'Old Horsborough cut your mother out of his will because she married a collier.'

It astonished him that she should know this. It should equally have astonished him that he knew it himself, for it had never been said to him. It had become part of his consciousness simply through things overheard, through simple observation and the fitting together in his mind of these various processes, so that when she said it he knew it to be true. The fact that he thought of 'Old Horsborough' as Tim's grandfather rather than his own, though he had in truth been so, was part of the confusion and the reality. That other people should know this was new to him. Perhaps they also knew things which he did not. He remembered that it was Ted who had told him that Maddy Thomas was dying. Did Maddy know, he wondered, herself?

He said now, to the girl, lowering his voice: 'Maddy Thomas is dying.' He waited for her reaction.

'I know,' she said. 'I heard my mam tell my dad.'

So it was true, or most likely true. Even peeping at Maddy in the ticket office as she sat in a stillness that had made him suddenly afraid, he had only half believed it. Gripped by the now almost firm reality, lost in his thoughts, he did not notice that the strap of Jean's costume had somehow slipped from her shoulder, exposing a fair part of one of her breasts, or if he did he paid no attention. The excitement of the morning had gone, and the incidents of the afternoon had not recreated it in him; rather they had conditioned him to something else. He did not at that moment know what it was, though he was soon to know.

She stood up suddenly, lifting the strap to her shoulder as if she was hardly aware that it was not already there.

'I'm going to get dressed,' she said, and was gone.

He heard the splash of her feet on the concrete of the pool surround, and the door of her cubicle closed.

He sat for a moment, looking at the pool as he had looked that morning when Ted and the girl had swum side by side. He was aware, though dimly and he could not have reasoned why, that nothing would ever be quite the same again.

As he came out of the slipper baths to dress, Denis heard Jean call to him. She was standing behind the closed door of the cubicle, her head above the open space at the top, her bare feet on the wooden duckboard which showed below the level of the door.

'I've dropped my watch behind the seat,' she said, asking his help.

He was never sure afterwards whether he had pushed the door open himself, or whether she had opened it for him. As it opened and he entered she was behind it for a moment until it closed behind him.

Her costume was pulled down and she was naked to the waist. It hit him like the shock of the water when he first dived in in the mornings and he gasped almost as he gasped for air on surfacing in the pool. His eyes sought hers as if to assure her that there was nowhere else they were looking, for it did not occur to him that the situation was other than accidental. What he saw there convinced him otherwise on later reflection, but not in the shattering enormity of the moment.

The silence could have lasted forever if his eyes, desperate for something to focus on, had not caught sight of the watch on the floor where she had said it was and where, of course, she had put it. He bent with desperate speed to pick it up and held it out to her. His actual exit he could never remember, except that it was wordless, quick, and followed by an immediate sense of release. Back in his cubicle, automatically drying himself, he shook violently, his mind and his body a conflict of new and terrifying emotions and, increasingly as the shock subsided, a vague and barely definable sense of regret. He had been given the opportunity to learn what Ted seemed already to know completely, and he had made a terrible mess of it. What was it he lacked that Ted seemed instinctively to have? Could he ever acquire it?

CHAPTER FOUR

When Ted ran through the curtains of the small plunge with Jean Colthard chasing him, he knew what the ultimate climax to the chase might be. He knew too that whatever happened would be decided by himself. He had known in the pool that he was the hunted, rather than the hunter, and had used this instinctive knowledge provocatively to stir the excitement of the chase. The fact that Denis was watching had urged him on. To some extent, had Denis but known it, Ted had enjoyed demonstrating his competence with the other sex as much, if not more, as the anticipation of the ultimate climax.

Driven to the far corner of the plunge, though he could have escaped by jumping in, he turned to face her. She stopped, breathless with the chase and with laughter, but there was a watchfulness in her eyes which awaited his next move though she, too, was aware that the moment had come. They remained a few feet apart, watching each other, as their breathing quietened and the echoes died away. He knew that she waited for him, that the chase was over and that she would acquiesce in whatever approach he made. Or would she?

His instinct told him that she would, but he knew from the talk that went on between boys of his own age that she had the reputation of being a 'teaser'. What basis, if any, there was for this he did not know. Boys of his age group were prone to sexual boasting, to the invention of experience, and she was an attractive girl; a prize to be boasted of in the sexual stakes. He looked at her now across the gap between them. It would have been so easy for him to reach out and test her willingness. She stood, her breathing almost normal now, waiting for him. And although the chase was over it was as if the wish to provoke her further remained in him, and, he stayed as he was, half smiling, watching her. Then he turned away and walked to the edge of the pool and squatted there, looking down as if he watched for something in the water.

After a moment he looked up. She was still there, but was no longer smiling. He looked at her seriously as if to say, 'That game's over now; this is another game,' then he looked back down at the water and waited.

She came eventually and stood close beside him as he had more or less thought that she might. After a moment she squatted, her leg touching his, and looked down into the water as if he had invited her to look at something he saw there. He stayed silent so that eventually, as he had also anticipated, she broke the silence and spoke.

'I like your friend,' she said.

It was an unexpected move, savouring of his own provocative mood. He felt a sudden anger towards her, and a lessening of interest, not because she had used a profession of interest in Denis to change the tone of the game but because she chose to play by his rules rather than her own.

'He doesn't like girls,' said Ted, vaguely aware that

what he really meant was that Denis was shy.

'He likes me,' she said.

'He'll not do anything about it even if he does.'

'Like you, you mean?'

The sharp suggestion that he had taken the situation no further with her because he was shy irritated him.

'Maybe I don't like you.'

'You do.'

'Only same as anybody would if you chuck yourself at 'em.'

'Think I chucked myself at you, do you?'

'Of course you did.'

He was under her skin now. A new kind of game could be starting, but he would not let it. He had had enough. He stood up. He said, 'I'm off now,' and looked down at her, grinning, as if to say that even if he was attracted to her he was free and would take her or leave her in his own time. He was himself again, master of his own fate where girls were concerned, belonging to no one. Yet as he looked down and saw in her face the curious mixture of emotion that was anger leavened by disappointment he had a feeling of regret that it was ending like this. He hesitated briefly as if to give her time to ask him to stay, but she did not move or even look up at him.

Denis was in the water when he went back into the large pool, and did not see him. He took his clothes from the cubicle and went into the room which had the notice 'Mortuary' on the door. Then he dried himself, dressed, and left the building.

Ted would have liked to have gone home. He desperately wanted to talk to someone, though not at all sure precisely what he wanted to talk about. There was only Jessie he could have talked to, but now his mother would be banging around the house, making a pretence of working, flailing his father with her tongue, and screaming at the kids so that the noise she made far outweighed their own shrill decibel output. There were many loud voices in the Square, but none was louder than hers. She had the reputation of being a bad payer in the shops, too, which if they didn't give credit or were heavy-handed in demanding payment suffered in reputation. No doubt fear of her loud voice was the only reason she could still get credit at all.

She took in washing now, much of it from the tradespeople in the shops who no doubt saw it as a way of giving in order to receive. Almost every day in the house was a washday, the living-room festooned with other people's clothes and sheets, the steam rising up the stairs to the bedrooms so that the whole house was permeated with the damp and the smell.

Ted hated it. He knew his father and Jessie did too, though they had no alternative but to live with it to survive. The house had long ceased to be a home to him. It was simply somewhere where he ate and slept. He was glad almost for the hours that school had kept him out of it, and for the rest of the time, in the evenings and at weekends he got out on his bike as much as he could. Three evenings in the week there was relative peace in the house. For this they were indebted to the Hippodrome which changed its programmes three times weekly, and from which a proportion of the money from the washing went. His mother would sit in the ninepenny stalls, her discontent feeding on the affluence portrayed in what were largely American films.

Now, in the warm sun of the afternoon, Ted pedalled viciously away from Cuddon towards one of his favourite haunts in the countryside. As he went past the park and down the hill away from the last of the houses, the slag heaps vanished behind him and the smell of

sulphur faded too. He turned off the main road down a
road which ran through the farming country, where the
flatness of the landscape was broken by copses of trees
on strange mounds which seemed almost to have been
put there for the purpose. He pedalled furiously now,
persuading himself that the new tyre had given added
speed to his mount, until the hedgerows ended and the
countryside opened out into what seemed an endless
stretch of unfenced common land with heather, trees and
clustered rocks and in the far, far distance the beginning
of the hills. Side tracks which led to farms, or the ruins
of what had once been farms, led off from the road at
intervals and eventually he turned down one of these
towards his objective.

He came to it after a rougher and much slower ride
some half a mile after leaving the road. A small, ruined
farmhouse built some two hundred years ago, it stood at
the end of the track in a yard approached through a gate
which had long ceased to function. He passed through it
now, into the overgrown cobbled yard and climbed from
his bike, leaving it where he always left it, by the low
stone wall which surrounded the small garden in front of
the house.

Ted had found the house two years before when out
on his bike exploring. Since then he had visited it several
times each week, whenever he could no longer bear the
atmosphere of the house in the Square. Although the
roof was sound, the windows in all but one of the rooms
were broken. The plaster ceilings of the lower rooms
were cracked and there were large gaps where some of
the plaster had fallen. When he first came to it the
ground floor had been littered with rubble, the remains
of broken furniture and discarded remnants of carpeting
covered in mould. It had been winter and he had left his
home for the usual reasons, heightened by some family
row. Not wishing to return until the last possible moment

he had lit a fire in what had been the living-room and stayed on long after dark, huddled in front of the bright blaze and barely conscious of the cold wind blowing through the broken windows. There was a fireplace in the bedroom with the unbroken windows and the next time he had stayed he had lit the fire here, closing the door. The heat of the fire warmed the small room quite rapidly and he had fallen asleep on the bare boards, only waking when the fire went out and the room became cold again.

From then on he had made the room his own, making a bed from straw and some of the pieces of carpet which he washed in a trough in the yard and dried in the sun of the summer that followed his discovery. He made shelves using bricks and odd planks of wood from the barns, and eventually on the shelves there appeared the bits and pieces of bicycles which he scavenged from anywhere and everywhere and stored against the possibility of a breakdown. A cup without a handle, a kettle and a pan were other things he acquired over the months, together with a scantily bristled brush and an old shovel.

His constant fear as his attachment to and need of the place grew was that someone would discover him here and order him away, but in all the time he had been coming he had, miraculously, seen no one. More recently, though, he had made a lock for the door of the upstairs room. It worked by the simple expedient of sliding a plank through the plaster wall of the adjacent room into a metal bracket from one of the stable doors, so that anyone trying the door would simply think it blocked by rubble on the other side.

His latest acquisition was a blackout curtain made from material left by the men who had blacked out the baths. It meant that he could have his fire at night without fear of being seen.

Only Jessie knew where he was on his long stays away from home, but she had never been. He had made her swear to tell no one, but once in the winter of the previous year when he had left the house with his mother's screaming ringing in his ears his father had, so Jessie told him, turned on their mother. 'Damn you, woman,' he had said, 'for driving him out on the streets in this perishing weather!' Then later Jessie had said to her father, 'Don't worry about him, Dad, he's got a place to go.' His father had simply asked, 'Is it all right?' and she had said that it was and, knowing her, he had asked no more.

Ted entered the house now like a man entering into his own. His fears of being driven away had been pushed into the background so that he now felt safe and in possession. He was proud of it, too. Sometimes in his mind he would recreate the house as it might be if it was really his own and he had the wherewithal to do the necessary work. Because he was proud of it he was tempted, sometimes, to tell Denis and even perhaps to bring him to see it, but although he trusted his friend as perhaps he trusted no one else other than Jessie and his father, he resisted the temptation. Too much was at stake. He had been tempted, too, to work on the garden, discovering in himself a delight in growing things and the feel of the seasons in the thrust of the daffodils through the neglect of what had once been cared for flower borders. The slag heaps represented neglect, too, but nothing grew on the stacks. Man had made the stacks.

Looking down at the garden from the window of the room he now entered, and beyond to the wide sweep of common, farm land and the distant hills, he was aware that over the past two years something had grown in his mind, too; a puzzled awareness of the difference between the two worlds he now lived in; of the sterile desolation of Cuddon itself, and the living miracle of what survived around it. Sometimes, when he was recreating the house as he would have had it he would see Jessie in a room, or from the window would look on his father in the garden. Once even his mother passed across the window of his mind and entered the kitchen. She was slim and smiling and the lines of discontent had been wiped from her face, and somewhere along the line that divides the reality of what is from the so near reality of what might have been he began consciously to link his two worlds to the greater world outside and to what was happening within it; and to the past.

He lay on the bed by the fire that warmed him in winter and closed his eyes. He was tired from his long swim in the pool and from the fury of his ride away from Cuddon, but most of all from a confusion in his mind arising from his reaction to Jean Colthard and the incident in the pool. Although he had gone through the motions of being himself, manipulating the event even to the point of allowing himself to be hunted, he was aware that hunter and hunted had fused in him and that, in some way he could not fully understand, he had emerged the victim rather than the victor. He saw now, with a sudden clarity of image that surprised him, her still figure as she looked down at the water after he said he was going. With equal clarity he remembered the expression on her face; the mixture of anger and disappointment; the conflict that in a way was reflected in himself. He had a sense of pain that was new to him outside his family, and an awareness that the compassion which in the past he had felt only for his father in his silent acceptance of the awfulness of their life in the Square, and for Jessie, had, however briefly, been extended to someone else. He did not, of course, recognise it as such. Compassion was not one of the words in his vocabulary, for all that he experienced it and had need of it. It was just another pain.

He fell asleep no less confused than when he had started to think about it, or rather he thought that he had slept. In fact he only lost consciousness for a brief few minutes, tired of grappling with feelings he did not understand and lulled by the singing of the birds in the garden outside and the warmth of the day. He had no watch, however, and it could be that hours had passed. It was a perpetual problem with him, not knowing the time. Moreover, he felt guilty now at deserting Denis. It was not the same to simply walk off, presenting his back, and to be seen to go, as he sometimes did.

He closed the door and fastened it and went down the stairs into the garden. He felt, as he always did when he had to leave, resentment at having to go. The track rose sharply beyond the gate to a rise which hid the house from the road. He pushed his bike to the top of the rise, looked back once, then mounted the bike and started to ride back to Cuddon.

CHAPTER FIVE

When Denis had finished dressing, he rolled his towel and costume up and sat quietly on the bench in the cubicle, listening. Would she come and see him before she went? He could not imagine so, for already the feeling he had had earlier was growing strongly within him, that she had intended him to see her as he had, and that in the way he had behaved he had somehow failed her. What should he have done?

Guilt was grained in him by the morality of the times in which he lived, but the conflict which raged inside him now obliterated any feelings of guilt. Obsessed by the possibility of the apple, he was oblivious of the serpent.

The confidence he had felt swimming beside the girl in the pool, the feeling that at last he was about to enter that world in which Ted moved with such assurance, had deserted him. Something else too had gone. It had gone and yet it was there, somewhere in the shadows which clouded his mind, as if reluctant to leave him. He was aware of it as a presence without a substance he could cling to; as something he could forever again reach out to but never touch. It was not guilt that reared its ugly head over the events of the day; but innocence.

An age seemed to pass as he sat on the bench. He had heard no movement from the cubicle farther up the line. The thought came into his mind that perhaps she still waited for him, that perhaps there was still time; though time for what he could still not have defined. He crouched down on the duckboard and, bending his head below the level of the dividing wall, peered along the line of cubicles. They were all empty. She had gone and he had simply not heard her. A bitter sense of disappointment and loss overwhelmed him. He stayed grotesquely bent for a time, hoping that perhaps for some reason or other she had stood on the bench and was out of sight, but he knew that in this he was fooling himself. He was still in this position when he became aware of other feet outside the door of his own cubicle, and looking up saw Tim peering down at him over the cubicle door.

'Lost something?' Tim asked.

He almost bolted upright, ignoring a sudden sharp cramp in his leg, his face red with both the effort of bending and with embarrassment. He heard himself mumble something to the effect that he thought he might have but did not now think that he had.

'Where's your mate, young 'un?'

Denis remembered that Tim had come so that Ted could take him to see Doug Hoyle.

'He's gone to look at Cuddie Fair. Just to look at it – he'll be back soon.'

Tim looked at him, not smiling now, with an expression that was in fact concern.

'You all right?' he asked.

Denis wondered for a moment if some drastic change

in his appearance had taken place, for he had once heard his father talk of a workmate whose hair had turned white overnight.

'Bit of cramp,' he said, and grimaced as if to emphasise that the pain was purely physical.

'Swim all day?' asked Tim.

'Most of it.'

'Lucky devil!'

'We're on duty,' Denis said, defensively.

'Bobby's job!' Tim said, grinning, unimpressed. 'I'd better go and ask Maddy Thomas if I can borrow you both. You don't mind hanging around a bit?'

'She's dying,' Denis said, suddenly remembering the other event of the day. 'Maddy Thomas is dying.'

'Yes,' said Tim, not smiling any more. 'Yes, I know.'

He looked at Denis again as if trying to read something he could see only faintly written on his face.

'I'll be talking to Maddy when your mate comes back,' he said.

Half an hour later when Ted returned, Denis was still sitting on the bench in the cubicle, but with the door open now, his eyes hypnotically held by the sparkle of the pool as the late afternoon sun cut through the glass roof into the water.

'Your cousin's talking to Maddy Thomas,' Ted said.

'I know.'

'What's he want to see me dad for?'

'I told you.'

'Maybe me dad won't see him.'

Denis could find no answer to this. The possibility had not occurred to him. Ted rammed the point home.

'He might not want to.'

Denis shrugged. Ted's mood was back again. Denis had known it the minute he returned, seeing it in the slightly hunched shoulders, the eyes directed downwards, the feeling that any minute Ted would turn and walk away, without explanation or farewell, just a silent presentation of his back. It was Ted. It was something that happened to him. Denis wondered why it had happened now. Was it something to do with Jean Colthard as he had suspected earlier on? If so, what? He had forgotten the incident in the plunge that morning, but now it came back again, and because of what had happened since, it came with a startling revelation. He was jealous of Ted.

He wanted to reject it but he couldn't. It had entered his mind directly as a new and immediate experience, and immediately it spread. The need to know what had happened between them in the silence that had followed their disappearance was overwhelming, but he knew he could not ask directly, and immediately he began to phrase the devious approach in his mind whereby Ted might be prompted into telling him, an image erupted in his mind. She was standing as she had stood in the cubicle, naked to the waist, her eyes deep, lost, waiting; but standing where he had stood was Ted.

Beyond that moment was a darkness he could not comprehend, into which he could not reach, not merely because of the boundaries of his ignorance, but because defensively, reaching his limits, he turned away and was physically sick.

They walked to the Square, leaving Tim's somewhat battered Austin Seven in the yard at the baths. It was Ted who had suggested they leave it there. 'You might get a brick through the window if you bring it down our way,' he said, making no apology, but simply stating a fact.

Outside the shabby exterior of Ted's house they stopped. 'It's here,' he said, but did not invite them to enter.

He looked beyond them, as if addressing someone

immediately behind, and said 'I'll tell him,' then left them and went inside, closing the door behind him.

Tim smiled slightly, as if something in Ted's behaviour amused him. Denis, forgetting his jealousy, said 'He's got one of his moods on today.'

'Got one of his moods on, has he?' Tim said. 'Why?'

'Wants to go to the fair and he can't.'

'Why not?'

'Got nothing to spend.'

'Have you?'

'I've a bit.'

'Can't you share it?'

'He won't,' said Denis. 'He won't have it from me.' He wasn't too sure that he wanted to give it now, anyway, but it was true still.

'I see,' Tim said, as if he had arrived at some firm understanding of Ted, and no other comment was needed. He looked round the Square, at the houses with newspaper at the windows and at those where some attempt had been made to present some kind of appearance, if only by sand-stoning the steps.

'A long time since I was down here,' he said. He gave no intimation of his feelings, but he was no longer smiling and there was a strange tightness about his face which Denis did not remember having seen before, giving him an older look. It reminded Denis of the difference in their ages, which he was never usually aware of in any strong sense. It reminded him too of the other difference, the one he was often aware of, and he looked at Tim's clothes now to reassure himself that Tim did not look too out of place, as he himself did when his mother insisted he should wear his better clothes. Tim was wearing an old shirt and slacks, however, not specially but because he usually did. Even so, it was obvious that he did not belong here, though Denis could not have explained why he recognised this fact.

The door opened now and Ted came out, his father behind him. He nodded at Denis and looked at Tim.

'He shouldn't have left you out here,' he said. 'Come in.'

He stood to one side to allow Tim to enter, then said to Ted, 'You and your mate play out for a bit, eh?' Then he went inside and the door closed behind them.

Denis and Ted climbed the slag heaps at the back of the Square. A hundred or so feet up, the slag levelled out, forming a grey plateau almost the size of a football pitch. They played here often for the slag had become hard and firmly bedded with use. Planks and bricks had been carted up over the years and were used to form benches on which you could sit and look at the view, such as it was, for it consisted mainly of the Square, the rooftops of the houses beyond, and Cuddon Colliery effectively breaking the skyline. The slope up which they climbed ended at its lower reach at the very backyard gates of the houses that backed on to it. In some cases the heavy rain had carried the slag on into the yards, so that it was no longer possible to close the gates. There was speculation as to how many years it would take for it to reach the back doors of the houses themselves.

They had brought with them a shaft and a short, sharp pointed piece of stick with which to play 'Peggie'. The stick was laid on the ground, the pointed end hit with the shaft, and the distance it travelled was the extent of the achievement. When they were younger they would play the game for hours, but in the last year or so had soon found themselves becoming bored. At the end of half an hour or so, Ted threw the shaft down the slope to where he could pick it up later, muttering something to the effect that he had had enough.

They sat on one of the plank seats and looked down at

the Square. The sun was already entangled in the pit headstock as it travelled down towards the horizon. They watched it silently, their faces tinted by its orange rays.

Denis said suddenly, as if he could contain it no longer: 'Jean Colthard came back.' He picked up a stone and tossed it casually down the slope. Ted picked up another and outdistanced him.

'What did she want?' he asked.

'We swam,' said Denis.

He left it at that and waited, but Ted said nothing more. Instead he picked up more stones and tossed them, without real effort, down the slope.

Denis could bear the silence no longer. Some impossible tension inside him forced the words out:

'I like her,' he said.

As if he had clapped his hands and startled a flock of starlings, voices were raised in the Square below. A man bawled and a woman screamed back at him. A child started to cry. Denis was dimly aware that Ted had turned his head and looked at him briefly and was now looking away. He was also aware of the import of what he had said, for they were the simple words that were used that said everything. There were other words, bawdy words, that were used to shock, to imply some knowledge that you did not have, to join in a conversation on a competitive, knowing level. The words he had used were generally acknowledged to convey something different; unspecified, but not carnal. Later generations sought to express both the sacred and the profane in popular music, but popular music was almost totally directed at adults in the world of Denis and Ted. All they had was the words; the ache in the heart that no words could express; the desperate incommunicable reality of adolescence.

'She's just a teaser,' said Ted.

Denis knew only vaguely and instinctively what he

meant, but he knew enough to be agonised by it.

'She's not,' he said, 'she's not,' and then, almost pleading, as if at the same time he was saying unknowingly something he later read and recognised – 'Tread softly, because you tread on my dreams'; he said: 'I like her.' It was again the equally inarticulate repetition of a later age, and Ted made no answer. Instead he got up from the seat, picked up more stones, and threw them, this time up the higher slopes of the stack. He threw them tirelessly, but with an increasing ferocity, as if at an alien target.

Denis watched him for a time, but there were no more words. The vocabulary was exhausted. Alone in his misery he got up from the bench and started to plough down the slope towards the Square below. Towards the lower reach he was aware of Ted behind him, and they reached the flat together. He leaned against the backyard wall of one of the houses as Ted, exhausted, gasped out his chosen words of comfort:

'She's just a teaser,' he said.

When they went back to the house, Tim and Doug Hoyle were deep in conversation. Ted closed the door behind them and they sat down quietly on a horsehair sofa from parts of which the stuffing was escaping, not daring to interrupt.

Denis had, of course, seen Doug Hoyle before, for he came to the door sometimes when Denis called for Ted. Only once had he been in the house before, a time when it had been raining and Ted was there alone. He looked at it now as he looked at it then, in comparison with his own. It had not been papered for many years and much of the paper had peeled off, but the paper and the walls were soiled so as to present an almost uniform colour, making the patches less noticeable. Apart from the sofa there were three upright chairs in the room, a battered sideboard, a square table covered with American cloth, and little else. The gas light had no shade on it, and half the mantle was broken away.

He observed Ted's father closely now for the first time. He wore a shirt which had originally been white with thin black stripes woven into the coarse cloth. He did not wear a collar and tie, though he had once appeared at the door wearing a black tie and white collar. The shirt was tight on his body, but the wide bottomed trousers were gathered in at the waist by a broad leather belt, as if he had shrunk inside them and gathered them around him as he shrank. His hair was dark and close cut to his head, as if roughly trimmed by a razor, except on the crown where it was heavy and licked down by water. His cheeks were sunken, making the bones of his face stand out, giving him an ascetic look. It matched his eyes which, when they were still, had a distant, despairing look; lifeless. They were bright now as he talked to Tim; alive with interest. Even Denis, accustomed to the tight, lifeless faces of the Cuddon unemployed, and used to a figure which simply came to the door in response to his knock, was aware of the difference. For much of the time Hoyle listened as Tim spoke. Although it was Tim who had come to ask the questions, it seemed that the conversation had now turned round, and that it was Hoyle who was asking the questions. He leaned forward now, as Tim fell silent and said:

'They can't fight a war without coal. You think we should let 'em take us into war after what they've done to us?'

'It'll be a war against Fascism,' said Tim. 'Can Labour turn their backs on that?'

'Labour!' said Hoyle. He spat in the empty grate. 'We asked for bread and they gave us Ramsay MacDonald!'

Tim looked down at the floor as if seeking the truth

behind an enigma that was to pass into history.

'Only Cook spoke out for us of them that had the gift,' Hoyle said. 'I heard him once…' He paused, then said again, as if it was all that need be said: 'I heard him.'

The sun had dropped out of sight behind Cuddon pit headstock when Denis walked back to the baths with Tim. The pit wheel, motionless now against the orange sky, hung like a crown of thorns over the rooftops and the quiet streets.

'It's lighting up time,' Denis said.

'You've a lamp on the bike, haven't you?' Tim asked.

'It's done.'

'Fat lot of use you'll be if Miss Maddy wants a message taken!'

'There'd be a blackout then,' said Denis. 'War'd have started. They only play in daytime now.'

'Play?'

'That's what me dad calls it.'

They passed the Miners' Welfare and the County Library branch which had been completed the year before.

'Off to the Fair on your own?' asked Tim, as they neared the baths.

'Mum won't let me now,' Denis said. 'She'll say it's too late.'

'Want me to ask her?'

Jean Colthard would be there, Denis thought. The possibility that he might see her was gold and dross.

'Yes please,' he said.

'What about Ted?'

'I told you. He'll not let me share with him.'

'His father's been a big help to me,' said Tim. 'I couldn't offer him anything, but he might let me give your mate a shilling or two. I could run you home and

71

then run you back there. What about it?'

'Yes please,' said Denis, pushing his fears aside.

Jessie came with them to the Fair at her father's request. Denis could see that Ted was pleased that she was with them. His relationship with Jessie was not like the relationships of many of the other boys who had sisters, and who either tolerated them or pretended they didn't exist.

Uncle Maurice Horsborough had been at the house when Denis and Tim arrived there. He was standing in the poised way he always seemed to do, as if to indicate that his stay was purely temporary and that at any moment he would be taking off. Denis could see, both from his uncle's expression and from the attitude of his mother and father, that, for some reason, his uncle was not pleased. His mother, not raising any objection to Tim's suggestion that he should be allowed to go to the Fair, had sent Denis upstairs to change. Although other thoughts were filling his mind he had, once or twice, tried to listen to what was being said downstairs, for occasionally the voices were raised and angry. When he had come down his uncle had gone, and later in the car Tim had been quiet and withdrawn, lacking his usual sparkle and good humour. When he had dropped them at the Fair he had for a moment smiled; 'Enjoy yourselves,' he said, and then drove off, but not before he had thrust two halfcrowns into Denis's hand.

Cuddon Fair came once every year. There were other Fairs at some of the surrounding towns, most of them bigger than Cuddon's, but this was the one that they looked forward to most for everyone knew practically everyone else. It was held on a piece of waste ground that formed the approach to Cuddon Football Club, and the lights and the noise brought Cuddon awake as no other event of the year did. Faces bobbed into the light from the outer ring of darkness, already smiling with the expectancy of an event in a long uneventful year, for in such a tight, closed little community, where not everyone had even a wireless, the events of the outside world seemed far away.

All the usual stalls were there, and at the coconut shy a queue of white-muffled, cloth-capped young miners, keen and half-jokingly aggressive in their wish to compete, had already formed. There was one large roundabout, and several smaller ones; the dodgems and the 'Wall of Death'. Beyond the fortune tellers' stalls was a small marquee which was the boxing booth.

They wandered around at first, taking it all in, exchanging rowdy greetings with others they knew. When the money started to burn a hole in Denis's pocket he bought some brandy snap and distributed the balance between the three of them. The music of the steam organ filled the night air so that they had to raise their voices almost to a shout to make themselves heard. It stood at the centre of the largest roundabout which was called The Farmyard and the animals went not just round it but up and down as they went at what seemed enormous speed. They waited for it to stop, then scrambled on as the last lot staggered off, choosing the animal which had seemed to move up and down the fastest, or the slowest, according to their fear of what the ride might do to their equilibrium.

Then they were off, slowly at first to temper their apprehension, and then increasingly faster so that they seemed to rise above the rest of the fairground and look down on it. It seemed strange to Denis, unbelievable almost, that people were passing by and paying little if any attention to this extraordinary phenomenon of which he was a part. Then, as they reached their fastest speed, he saw Jean Colthard in the crowded area by the coconut shy. She was there, and then as he orbited, was gone.

She was there again, laughing, and was gone. He stood in the stirrups of the horse he was riding, straining to see her the next time round, wanting her to see him. She was there still and this time he saw that she was not alone, but with someone he did not know, and the next time round he saw that it was a youth some three or four years older than himself, and then they were gone.

He wanted the machine to stop now, but it seemed to go on for ever, his eyes continually searching out the same spot, seeing her in a series of broken moments, like a film pieced together after every other foot had been cut. When it finally started to slow down she was gone, lost in the crowd, and although he searched for her face for the rest of the evening he did not see her again.

When they were down to their last sixpence Ted wanted to go in the boxing booth, but was worried that Jessie could not come with them. They were arguing the point, she trying to persuade him, when one of her schoolfriends joined them. Happy to leave her in company, Ted pulled Denis towards the booth. As they queued to pay they examined the two professionals who stood on the platform outside, on either side of the notice which announced that anyone who could last five rounds with either of them would win ten shillings. The men stood poker faced, their arms folded, aloof from the crowd, knowing that every man who went past the pay box wanted them to lose; that they were friendless in a hostile environment, in an inbred community which was hostile not just to them but to any outside force which would challenge it.

Inside the booth, the early comers were impatient for it to fill so that the fighting could begin. Individuals among them were being persuaded to have a go, or in some cases dissuaded from doing so, for each defeat reflected on everyone there. Denis and Ted wriggled their way to the front, helped by an occasional push and a shout of 'Make way for t'young 'uns.' They would never have been allowed to do so had they been taller, and Ted, accustomed to watching Cuddon from the barbed wire enclosure known as 'The Pen' when they played rugby at home, had instructed Denis to keep his knees slightly bent so as not to look like a possible obstruction.

The promoter entered the ring and looked around to see how the place was filling. He was subjected to immediate barracking: to shouts of 'Get on with it! ... We're not bloody sardines, you know! ...' which he totally ignored, chatting to one of the seconds in the corner. Eventually he looked at his watch, as if it was this that controlled the start rather than the size of the audience, and made a signal to the door. A cheer went up and the men in the audience, tightly packed to the point of suffocation, swayed with excitement. One of the professionals appeared in the ring, how he got there being something of a miracle, and arms were raised as men indicated their wish to take him on. The promoter eventually pointed to a young, well-built miner, slightly taller than the rest, as if to indicate from the start that his men were prepared to take on the best.

The bell rang for the first round and the two men met the referee in the centre of the ring, the young miner looking slightly incongruous in comparison with his opponent, for he wore long, wide-bottomed trousers, the waist of which had been folded over to hold them up in the absence of a belt. Within less than half a minute, in which the men had scarcely done more than size each other up, the trousers dropped around his ankles to the accompaniment of a great cheer. From somewhere in the crowd a belt was produced and the man, looking slightly sheepish, put it on and the fight was started again. The rest of the round was tame and lacking in aggression, the professional being content to play with his opponent and give him a chance to warm up.

The second and third rounds were lively, for the challenger boxed well and landed some well-timed punches, encouraged by shouts from the audience who warmed to him, scenting a possible victory. In the fourth round he came out on the bell bouncing with confidence and with a series of short arm jabs to the professional's face succeeded in raising the atmosphere in the booth to fever pitch. Towards the end of the round the professional actually walked into a right hook which landed him on the canvas for a count of five, but shortly afterwards the bell rang for the end of the round, and the men returned to their corners.

The young miner was bombarded with advice, while in his corner the professional sat still, his arms on the ropes, his expression emotionless while his second worked on him silently.

The challenger came out confidently on the bell, moving jauntily on his feet, scenting victory rather than survival. He was immediately in trouble, a series of hard rocking blows to body and head confusing him, for he had not expected them. Within a minute he was on the canvas for a count of eight, and when he got to his feet it was with difficulty. Within thirty seconds he was down. He did not get up again.

For most of the time Denis's eyes were on the professional. For some reason he could not have articulated, he was on his side; wanted him to win. When the victory came he actually cheered, a dig in the ribs from Ted silencing him for the cheer was not echoed around him. He noticed, however, that when the professional left the ring to be replaced by his colleague, he received friendly pats on the head from some of the miners in the crowd.

The man who replaced him was cast in the same

mould, though physically different. The man whom the promoter selected as the new challenger, however, was not at all like the man who preceded him. Smaller in height, some years older, he revealed when his shirt was stripped off a body so thin as to be almost emaciated, though with the muscular remains of hard physical work at some time in his past. The crowd were silent now, not simply because of their disappointment with the previous fight, Denis sensed, but with a still anticipation for the one which was now to take place which was totally different from their mood before the previous fight started.

Aware that Ted was saying something to him in a low voice, Denis bent towards him to listen. 'It's me uncle,' Ted said. 'He's out of work. They've had a baby.'

Denis looked at the man in the ring. His face had the same ascetic look that he had seen in Ted's father earlier that day; the same sunken cheeks and prominence of bone structure. He wondered how such a man could be chosen to fight the professional in the opposite corner who, although a lightweight and markedly slighter than his colleague, was obviously fit.

Almost total silence reigned in the booth after the bell for the first round. Ted's uncle came out fighting as if he had decided that, whichever way it went, it would be best to have it over and done with. He landed several punches within the first minute, but even Denis could see that they had little or no effect on his opponent. He retreated under this wild attack, dodging or riding most of the blows so that the audience became impatient and murmurs of a 'Fair feight' were heard. As if responding to this the professional came back with a loosely aimed punch which, almost accidentally, it seemed, connected. It opened a cut above Ted's uncle's eye from which the blood now started to trickle. There was a murmur from the crowd, and the other man started to dodge and weave again as if he did not wish to offend them.

Even at the start of the second round Ted's uncle was obviously tiring. He collected several other punches, seeming to run into them almost. Once he tripped and fell for a count of two. When he got up again it was as if the ten shilling note had been wafted under his nose like smelling salts. Sensing his fading strength would not carry him through the remaining rounds to win it, he attacked in a desperate frenzy, like a cornered animal. The crowd came to life, seeing it no longer as a fight which one or the other might win, but for what it was: a battle for survival, to simply stay on his feet and punch long enough for the other man to put himself in the way of one of the punches that might, by a stretch of the imagination, allow him to pretend that he had been knocked out. The crowd shared his desperation; became part of it almost. They cheered, groaned, and urged him on, and he responded, blindly now but with some reserve drawn from within himself. He collected another blow, running into it as before, and the cut opened wider and the blood poured over his face. He swung out of his agony and the blow miraculously connected and the professional went down for the count.

Denis turned to Ted and saw that his eyes were filled with tears.

'They let him win,' he said.

Spent up, they walked back across the pit fields to the lower end of Cuddon where they lived, the noise of the fairground receding in the distance as they followed the track that skirted the slag heaps.

Ted was back inside himself again, shoulders hunched, hands deep in his pockets as he walked, occasionally aiming a savage kick at the night air as if he had spotted some invisible antagonist. It was his third 'mood' that day, Denis thought, suddenly amused by it.

It was, he decided, what his mother used to call 'One of those days'. It had been one of those days for him, too. Somewhere inside him there was still a small ache, a sense of loss and of failure, but also a feeling that somehow his life had moved forward.

Ted started to increase his pace and vanished into the darkness, leaving Jessie and Denis to follow. Jessie made no attempt to keep up with him, and Denis matched his pace to hers.

'It was your cousin that gave us the money, wasn't it?' she asked suddenly, out of the darkness.

'It was Tim,' he said.

'He's a Horsborough, isn't he?' she asked, as she might have used the name Rockefeller.

'In a way,' Denis said.

She laughed. He said, defensively, 'I mean he's different.'

'He's nice,' she said. 'I like him. He's quiet, like you.'

The statement confused him. He equated quietness with shyness, which was what made him different from Ted. That anyone might find it likeable was a new thought.

It stayed with him as the street lights came into view. Where the track led on to the end of the streets, Jessie stopped. There was no sign of Ted.

'I can cut down the ginnel,' she said.

She waited as if for a dismissal, shadows flickering across her pale face as the gas light wavered uncertainly in the night breeze. He wondered what it would be like to touch her. Amazed at himself he reached out and put his hand on her cheek.

It was cold, though the night was warm. He smiled as if to say, 'I'm only touching you to see if you're cold.' She looked back at him, not smiling, her eyes waiting. 'She likes me,' he thought, 'because I'm quiet.' He said, 'Goodnight, then,' taking his hand away.

'Goodnight,' she said, and went off up the ginnel. He watched until she turned the corner at the end and was gone.

It had been one of those days.

CHAPTER SIX

When Ted swung off into the darkness of the pit fields
he was barely conscious of leaving Jessie and Denis. He
strode into the night as if it might offer the same
oblivion as if he entered the sea and allowed the waves
to engulf him. The darkness outside him merged with the
darkness within, so that the confusion of thoughts which
had raged in his mind since they left the fairground
echoed in the night around him, refusing him the
oblivion he sought. He did not know why the fight in the
fairground boxing booth had moved him to tears. In a
sense he was ashamed that it had done so, for boxing
was one of the manly sports he had been taught to
respect both at school and in the more overt violence of
life in the Square. On Saturday nights when the public
houses emptied it was the exception rather than the rule
for peace to prevail. Where no aggravation existed, men
would create it, as if following some ritual which
demanded a climax of violence in return for the
consumption of sleep; a kind of exorcism.

He had, of course, like Denis, seen Jean Colthard.

Unlike Denis, however, he knew the youth she was with. His name was Jack Dakin and he lived in the council estate that bordered the edge of the park. A somewhat fleshy youth with darkly brilliantined hair he worked as a delivery boy for one of the local butchers and was reputed for the length of time he stayed in the houses of some of the women to whom he made deliveries. Early that summer his bike had been taken and left all night outside the house of a widow who was strongly involved with the local Methodist Church. Not knowing his reputation she remained blissfully unaware of the reason for the averted grins which she sometimes encountered on passing faces.

That Jean should choose to be at the fair with someone like Dakin sickened Ted. He reacted to it with almost the same kind of horror he would have felt if it had been Jessie who had accompanied Dakin. It angered him, too, but his anger was directed at Jean rather than Dakin who, for all his years, he regarded himself as totally superior to, for Dakin was a delivery boy and he himself would soon be in the pit.

He longed now to be at work, to be in the pit, to be a man. He had spoken of it already to his uncle who was a member of Gospel Hall. Most of the deputies and undermanagers at the pit were members of Gospel Hall and had survived the closure of Cuddy Main, transferring to Cuddy Hall Colliery at the expense of others who were not Gospel Hallers. To get work in the pit some connection with Gospel Hall was more or less essential.

He had, however, said nothing of this to his father, though he suspected that his uncle had told his father of his request. That his father should not then discuss it with him did not surprise Ted. There was a deep bitterness within Doug Hoyle towards the pit which was more than the usual colliers' heartfelt desire that their sons should escape their own fate. It was rooted, too, in the resentment he felt at the victimisation he had experienced following his militant stand in the General Strike. Very rarely it erupted in the form of a tirade of abuse directed at the present union leadership. They had let such as himself pay the price and had not closed ranks to prevent it, he claimed. When he spoke of it Ted felt himself the weight of the pain inside the man, heavier because of the rarity with which he exposed it.

What he did not take to himself was the fear that such might be his own ultimate fate. That the owners were men to be feared he did not doubt, but they were beyond his ken. His mind could no more conceive of them in human terms than it could the devil. The men of the pits, for him, were those whose blackened, weary faces looked down at the pavement as they made their way home after shift. The same men who, fresh from sleep and jaunty with the prospect of a few idle hours, walked scrubbed and clean as choirboys with their eyes fixed lightwards as if they sang some anthem to the sun. They were, too, the few legendary faceworkers; the kings who walked like kings, but were gentle. His uncle was one of them. It was his great hope, his one connection in life, somewhat like Denis's relationship to the Horsboroughs, but proud. Ted was related to a king. The gates of the cage which would carry him darkly into the deep soul of his manhood must surely be opened to him. That it might not so happen he never let himself think.

He had strayed from the track now. The night was almost moonless but the sky was clear. Over to his right the first street lamps flickered like lower stars at the point where Cuddon met the edge of the stacks, close to the entrance to the Square. He was tired now, more from the mental confusion that had accompanied him from the fair than from the effort of walking, but he could not yet go home. Always he waited for the two he shared the bed with to go to sleep before he joined them, and to wait meant sitting in the living-room with nothing to do while his mother dozed or fumed and his father read in silence. He bore left in the direction where he knew another track had earlier branched from the one he had lost. It led towards the baths which, at this hour, was the only place he knew to which he could go. The night duty people would be there. With luck he might get a mug of tea or even, as had happened once, be asked to join in a game of cards.

He found the track and started along it, the lights in the distance before him glowing more brightly. The hard mud surface was rutted and difficult to walk on and the boots which he wore were sizes too big so that his feet seemed to catch at every rut. Slow as he was he became aware that he was catching up the shape of someone who walked before him. He saw that it was a woman, for trousers were rarely worn as yet by the other sex. Then, at the same time as he became aware that she was limping, they entered the dim reach of the first of the street lamps and he saw that it was Jean. She had stopped, as if she recognised and waited for him, and he stopped too though something inside him urged him to ignore her.

He saw her hair flip backwards as she jerked her head in a gesture he recognised, and he knew her eyes would be bold and challenging as if they spoke and said, 'I'm not going to start it, it's up to you.'

'What's up?' he asked, roughly, reluctantly.

'Oh, it's you,' she said as if he might just be anybody.

'What's up?' he repeated, to let her know that he had only stopped because she was limping.

'I've ricked my ankle,' she said.

'Serves you right,' he thought, though he said nothing. He was suspicious too. She could not have known he would take this path, but she might have recognised him first in the darkness. He was not in a mood to play the hunted.

'Walked on without you, did he?'

'Who?'

'Dakin.'

'Jack Dakin? What's Jack Dakin to do with it?'

'You were with him at the fair.'

'Was I?'

'I saw you.'

'So what?'

She had him boxed in the corner. He looked for some move which would get him out so that she wouldn't think he cared that he had seen her with Jack Dakin. He said, 'He's a nice chap, Jack.'

'You know him?'

'I've spoke with him. I know a mate of his. He doesn't believe what they say about him either.'

'About who?'

'What people round here say about Jack.'

'What do they say?'

'I can't tell you.'

'Why not?'

'You're a girl.'

'Maybe I don't need telling. Maybe I know.'

'It's all talk, what they say about Jack.'

'You think so?'

'Don't you?' Ted asked, strategically.

Now he had her boxed. He grinned in the darkness. There was a moment of silence before she answered him.

'I don't think it's talk,' she said. 'Anyway, why don't you say what you mean? You mean he's supposed to be fast with women, don't you?'

Oh, but she was bold! She was bold as brass! It was, he suddenly realised, one of the things he most liked about her, her boldness. She had an open, fearless quality that could take his breath away and make him afraid of the excitement she generated within him as she had done at the baths.

'You ought to know if you're going out with him,' Ted said, coming straight back at her. 'Now answer that,' he thought. 'Bloody well answer that!'

This time she paused more briefly, then said, 'Yes, I suppose I ought to if I am.'

The excitement became irritation now. He was bored with the game. He wanted to put all the questions straight and get straight answers, but if he did she would think he cared. And he did care. The back of his mouth was dry with an emotion which he supposed was jealousy. He had brought it with him across the pit fields. Some of it had dissipated, but now she brought it all alive again. His hands were clenched deep in his pockets now. The mood was returning.

He was on the point of walking on when, as if she could read his mind she said, 'I'm not going out with Jack Dakin. He's not my type. He came after me at the fair, that's all. I told him to buzz off.'

So again she disarmed him of even the weapon of his mood that would have made it possible for him to turn his back on her and simply walk away. She had taken a step backwards and now it was up to him to follow, but somehow he could not expose his wish to do so, as if he feared some kind of trap.

'Shouldn't we be getting on?' he said.

'You'd better go on without me,' she answered. 'It'll take you ages if you wait for me.' She hobbled a few steps as if to make the point, then waited. There was no answer to that one except that by walking beside her, as he now did. Matching her pace, he acknowledged to some extent his defeat.

A minute or more passed in silence before she spoke

again. 'Where's Denis and Jessie?' she asked.

'They were dawdling. I left 'em.'

'I like Denis.'

He thought for a moment that she was playing with him again, but it had sounded genuine enough. She had used the word 'like' in a general way and not as he and other boys used it as a substitute for 'love', or so it sounded to him.

'He's all right,' said Ted, condescendingly acknowledging that his friend might possibly be likeable.

'He's not like you.'

He was curious as to what she meant by this but refusing to betray his interest he simply grunted.

'He's shy. He's interesting,' she said. 'He's got brains, too,' she added, as if Ted was some sort of imbecile, though he knew it was not what she meant.

'He didn't get a scholarship like our Jessie did,' said Ted. He made no claim to academic prowess, but he liked being related to it as he liked being related to a king.

'He'll not go down the pit.'

'He will if he's lucky,' said Ted. 'There's nowt else for him round here.'

'He'll not,' said Jean, as if she gazed into a crystal ball and saw the future. 'He'll not go down the pit.'

'I shall go down the pit.'

'Because you'll have to, you mean?'

'Because I want to.'

'More fool you, then!'

She spoke it bitterly, with a trace of the deep resentment which sometimes surfaced in his father. He accepted it in his father, sensing the deeper reasons for his bitterness that were personal to him. He could not accept it in her.

'You know nothing about it.'

'I know enough. I know what it did to my dad.'

He had forgotten that she was a collier's lass and that the mine had crippled her father. He said nothing more and she did not pursue it. A moment later she stopped and said, 'Can I lean on your arm?'

She took his silence for assent and put her arm on his, clasping her fingers around his wrist so that her arm would not slip from him. They moved on, more slowly now and awkwardly. He was very conscious of the movement of her body against him and of the weight of her arm. He was conscious too of a physical stirring within him. It was deeper and more urgent than the feeling he had experienced in the baths.

They were almost up to the first of the houses when she said, 'Cat got your tongue?'

He stopped, not knowing whether it was the proximity of the houses or the tone of her voice or perhaps both of these which told him to stop. For all his boasting and his brashness with Denis he had never before touched any girl. Even in the street games they played which were in some ways designed to give them the opportunity to pair and to hide in the darkness of the alleys he had not touched any girl, though on occasions he might have felt the desire to do so.

He reached out his hand now, and as it touched her waist she came towards him and against him and his other arm went round her. Her dress was thin and through it he could feel the strong warmth of her body, and then her arms encircled him too so that she was completely against him, and yet, as if denying it all, she suddenly said, 'I shall never marry a collier … Never … Never …'

But he shut her mouth with his own and she did not resist him.

It was not very late when he eventually got home, but it

was later than usual. His mother had gone to bed, but his father was still in the living-room. He had been coal picking that day and the remains of a fire still glowed in the grate. A fire was his great enjoyment in life and even in summer, on all but the hottest of days, the fruits of a day scratting on the slopes of the slag heaps would liven the room, heating the water in the iron box at the side of the grate for they only had one cold tap in the house.

He was not reading as he normally did, until the book was put down reluctantly a moment before he mounted the stairs. He was sat in his usual chair, leaning slightly forward as if to catch the last of the fire's glow. For a moment he did not seem to hear Ted enter, then he looked up, his eyes seeming to re-focus from a great distance, and Ted waited to be chastised.

'Where've you been?' asked Doug Hoyle, but without admonition in his voice. 'Your sister got home an hour or more back.'

'Took a walk to the baths,' said Ted, half truthfully.

'Got one of your moods on, she said.'

His father's eyes were half smiling now, as if it amused him that Ted should be prone to moods as he was himself. Ted grinned at him, sheepishly.

'Maybe,' he said. 'Maybe I had.'

'What about this time?'

'Nowt much,' said Ted. 'Summat or nowt.'

'You can tell me, you know,' his father said, as if unwilling to accept Ted's dismissal. 'We can talk can't we?'

'It was just for a change, that's all.'

'Nowt for you to do back here, you mean?'

'Aye, that's it. Nowt to do.'

'You could read like I do.' Hoyle picked up one of his books as if to offer it.

'Our Jess lends me books. I can't take to 'em.'

'What sort of books?'

'Story books mostly, about rich folk and such, and olden times.'

'Don't you like reading about rich folk, then?'

'No.'

'Your sister does.'

'Happen she'll marry one. Women can do that, can't they?'

'Marry out on it, you mean?'

'Men can't.'

'Some do,' his father said. 'Gigolo blokes and such.'

'What's them?'

'Men that lives off t'earnings o' women.'

'Men?'

'Aye,' his father said. 'Men that trades their bodies to women for brass.'

Ted flushed. Not with embarrassment for his sex, or because he could not remember his father speaking to him in any way about sex before, but because he was reminded of Jean's strong, wanting body against his own. Yes, he thought, there could be women who could want so much they would be willing to pay. It was new knowledge to him that women could experience desire in the same way that he knew it to be for himself. He had never really believed the stories he had heard about Jean. He would not believe them now. Only that she wanted himself.

'There's other books than story books, you know,' his father said now, bringing his mind back to the moment. 'Library's full of all sort o' books. Books about life as it is … history, science, lives folks have lived, politics … there's no end to books. Get down to t'library – you can pass your time usefully reading books.'

'I should be bringing money in,' said Ted, 'not reading books.'

'It applies to me more than thee does that,' his father said. 'It's me that should be bringing money in, not thee.

Thou't a lad, just left school. In a better world you'd be learning yet, not worritting yourself about bringing money in.'

'I'm fourteen. I'm a man.'

Hoyle looked at him, struggling not to deny him his manhood but with a deep sadness behind his eyes. 'I were a man at twelve. So it were thought in them days. That were t'age I went down pit. They make men of us afore us time. What sort o' men do they call theirselves I wonder.' And the old bitterness was there in his voice again.

'I want to be a man,' said Ted.

'You think I blame you for that? It's not thee I take issue against. It's a man's world, by God! There's damn little in it for women. What's your sister to do in life, for all her brains and her study. She'll be needing to bring money in an' all when she's done at school, not going to college as she should.'

'You'll let her go though, should she pass?' Ted queried anxiously.

'I'll have your mother to fight.'

'I shall bring money in.'

'It'd take a rich man's fortune to get us out o' t'hole we're in.'

'I shall get to the face. I shall be a king,' Ted said, his eyes smarting with unshed tears of desperation.

His father looked at him then back at the fire, as if what he saw in Ted's face caused a pain in him.

'You're a good lad,' he said. 'It does you credit to feel as you do. Do you think I feel no shame that I can offer nowt better to none of you?'

He looked up again, and Ted saw almost with terror that his eyes were filled with tears.

The other two younger ones were sleeping soundly when Ted climbed into bed, but he himself could not sleep. It was hot in the room, but remembering the sulphurous poison that filled it when he opened the window he left it shut. From time to time he felt the instinct to turn and twist and bury his head in the pillow, but because of disturbing the others he dare not move. It was an agony of frustration to be awake, not to be able to sleep. His mind was full of images of Jean that generated a heat in him that he did not fully understand. Sex had always been half a joke, not totally real but for the most part fantasy blended with lewdery and the need to brag of manly accomplishment. He was afraid of this feeling in him, for it dominated him and would leave him helpless before her. Yet he knew he could not let this happen. He would have her, but he would not bow down. But in a sense it was what he wanted, what part of him wanted; to bow down, to give himself, to make of himself an offering.

His mind tossed and turned while his body lay in forced stillness, longing to move, to be carried with the tide of feeling that engulfed him in a fever of wanting. Eventually he could stand it no longer. He slid out of bed, pulled on his trousers and shirt and tiptoed down the stairs in the darkness.

The fire was out now and the room was in darkness, but he knew that there was a candle on the dresser kept for the occasions when the gas mantle would be broken and they would have to wait until they could afford another. He found the matches and lit it and the dim light flicked around the room, licking at the glass of the solitary framed picture of his grandfather who had been killed in the last war, and catching brightly on the surface of the few china ornaments and the lacquered text that read 'Thou God seest me'.

'I shall never marry a collier,' she had said. His father, too, hated the thought of him going to the pit. He had never before queried his future. To have a job at the pit was his ultimate ambition, the only doubt the possibility of his getting such a job. Without it there was nothing, no fixed point in his life to which he could move. What did they want him to be? Did they want him to be an errand boy like Jack Dakin? Even had the chance been available to him he would not from choice have taken it. When he thought of the pit it was not of the darkness below him he thought. He saw it, in a sense, in reverse. He stood in the darkness and looked towards the light, to the moment when the cage lifted and carried him up; to the moment of coming home.

CHAPTER SEVEN

On the 2nd September 1939, Arthur Greenwood, acting Labour Party leader, rose in the House of Commons to reply to a temporising speech by Chamberlain. German troops had moved into Poland the previous day, Warsaw was being bombed. An endless stream of mothers, children and cripples evacuated from London and other major British cities left the mainline railway stations that day and headed for the rural counties as the official evacuation began. The world's first television service closed down, and the twenty thousand screens in existence went blank for the duration. But Chamberlain's speech carried no hint of a coming declaration of war.

As Greenwood rose to reply, a veteran Tory imperialist shouted, 'Speak for England, Arthur.' To Tory cheers, the Labour spokesman did his best. 'I wonder how long we are prepared to vacillate,' he said, 'at a time when Britain and all Britain stands for, and human civilisation, are in peril.'

***

The following day was Sunday. Early that morning Maddy Thomas, roused from her sleep in the middle of the night by a harassed Council official, descended on Cuddon Station with a retinue of Civil Defence workers and members of the Women's Institute. Denis and Ted, bleary eyed but excited, were among the Civil Defence contingent.

A train loaded with evacuees from London was expected to arrive at Cuddon at 8 a.m. After its occupants had been fed it would then proceed to an undisclosed destination. A siding had been prepared to distribute the food and to deal, it was said, with any casualties. Precisely what casualties could be expected since no shot had yet been fired in anger on British soil had not been stated, but a rumour that the train had been machine gunned from the air by German planes at a precisely named spot in the Midlands became firmly established throughout Cuddon by 9 a.m.

Considering the short notice and the unexpected nature of the emergency, Maddy Thomas had coped well. An expert delegator of authority, she had set up headquarters in the station master's office and had formed a committee before the dawn chorus began in the few trees that remained in the scrubland that separated Cuddon station from Cuddon pit. She would have been better equipped, it was true, to deal with a gas attack on the civilian population, but that not being forthcoming, this, she told them all, was a heaven sent opportunity to demonstrate their usefulness and efficiency to those who had greeted their earlier exercises with a mixture of scorn and hilarity.

As the organisation swung into action of a practical nature, Denis and Ted were kept busy taking messages from Maddy's headquarters to various other points in Cuddon. Food was commandeered from shops in

Cuddon and outlying areas on promissory notes signed by the Council official who assumed, for he had had no firm instructions, that the procedure would be approved. Shops whose stocks had already been depleted by hoarding housewives, and who were reluctant to part with what remained, were visited personally by Maddy, travelling in an ancient field ambulance with a large red cross on the side, and castigated for their lack of patriotism. Few stood out against this, for already the Nation was dividing into the patriots and those few who were designated by the majority, for various obscure reasons, as unpatriotic.

Denis was at the station when the train arrived. It was packed with exhausted looking women, and children of various ages up to the early teens. A handful of despairing looking men who were in charge of the occupants descended from it and entered the station master's office, after giving instructions that no one was to leave the carriages. They might have saved their breath, for despite the fact that the doors had been locked from outside by the guard, several of the older boys were out exploring within seconds of the office door closing.

One of them cornered Denis. He was a boy of about the same age and, despite the strong London accent, he reminded Denis of Ted. It was not so much the clothes, which were shabby as Ted's always were, as the impression he gave of being older than his years.

'Going to feed us here are they?' he asked.

Denis assured him that they were.

'Stinks in there,' the boy said. 'Kids have been wetting theirselves all night. Our Arthur wet himself. He keeps crying for me mum. Me dad wouldn't let her come with us.'

He pointed to a dirty, tear streaked, nine-year-old face watching them rigidly through the window of the nearest carriage. The eyes, like his brother's, were older than the face, but had the weariness of immense age, as if in the past twenty-four hours they had experienced all life and wanted no more of it. In the way in which he watched his brother there was a kind of terror, as if he feared that the train might move on, leaving all that remained to him in life that was familiar standing on the platform.

Later, as the train started to lurch out of the station on its desperate journey North, leaving an appalling mass of litter where it had stood, Denis found himself watching for the face. As the carriage heaved past him his eyes searched each compartment, flashing from face to face, imprinting the image on them so that, in the end, as the last carriage rolled from the station, they had become one tear-stained, terror-stricken image which was his memory of the incident.

Ted joined him as it disappeared up the track. He looked around at the litter.

'Mucky buggers,' he said.

Denis had a sudden sense of divergence from his usual mood of agreement with Ted. It flushed into his consciousness as a kind of anger that was new to him, in that it overcame his usual willingness to agree simply to avoid disagreement.

'It's not their fault,' he said.

'Whose is it then?' Ted challenged, his eyes sharp as if he was aware of this departure from the norm in their relationship. He repeated again, 'Whose fault is it then?' in a tone which defied disagreement.

Denis searched for words but could find none. It crossed his mind to mention that he had equated the boy who had spoken to him with Ted, knowing he was on dangerous ground. As he sought for a way to express this he became aware that Ted had lost interest in the conversation. His eyes were on the ground among the litter. He moved a few paces and then stood still, put his hands in his pockets and looked around with a casual, relaxed expression. Evidently reassured that he was not observed he bent suddenly, picked something up from the ground, put it in his pocket, and as casually returned to where Denis was.

'Half a crown,' he said. 'Down there. Just picked it up. Half a crown!'

'You'd better give it to the station master,' said Denis.

'Why?'

'Or Miss Maddy.'

'Why? She'll only ask who's lost it, and when they all say they have she'll give it to me for being honest.'

He took it out of his pocket, looked at it, then put it back again. He was a complete realist in those days, was Ted.

Later in the morning they were dismissed by Maddy, who looked at them through her tired old eyes and said, 'Home to bed. You've done your bit. A few more willing lads like you and we'd win the war.'

Her words implied that, willing lads not being available, it was lost before declared. They protested feebly that they were willing to carry on with helping to clean up the debris, but she insisted, and in any case the excitement had gone.

He thought about it as he made his way home. No one had told him they were officially at war, but Maddy had spoken as if they were. If anyone knew, Maddy would, for she spoke on the telephone to people in places as far away as Manchester, and one day at the Baths someone had telephoned her from London. There were the people on the train, too. What were they fleeing from, if not from an enemy? Was it just another exercise, perhaps?

The tear-stained face of the brother of the boy he had spoken to came back to him. Was the terror in the face of the boy who missed his mother, and was afraid in an alien land, simply the result of a demonstration of, as one of the ARP booklets put it, 'What the population might expect in the event of hostilities.' If it was, why had they not been told, for it was obviously life he feared, not death at the hands of an enemy.

Denis wondered about death, for he equated war with death most of all. The annual service at the Cenotaph, the wreaths to the fallen, the long procession that passed down Cuddon Main Street on its way to the annual ritual. The long line of women dressed in black; mothers, sisters or widows of the men whose names were carved on the phallic stone. Old Mrs. Hough who had 'water' and whose flesh hung over the tops of her tight shoes so that, looking down, she could never see them. She had fainted once, and the Major who was reading Binyon's poem had ignored her and carried on. 'They shall not grow old as we that are left grow old,' he said, triumphantly, as if Mrs. Hough had proved the point.

Would his own name be there one day, perhaps? He saw his mother, part of that long procession, dressed in black. 'Their name liveth for Hevermore,' the Major proclaimed, ignoring the logical extension of the thought that damned his own to oblivion. The 'H' he prefixed eternity with was an addition of his own, adding emphasis as his later deletions of it did the opposite. Denis, who had joined the choir at the Anglican Church two years before to please his mother, was familiar with the Major's mode of speech, for the Major was a lay reader at the same church. Some of his modulations, when reading the Lesson, produced a rigid suppression of smiles among the congregation, and the sound of strangled laughter from the choir. It was odd in a Major, his mother had commented once, but then his grandfather on his father's side had been a working man. His father had smiled, enigmatically.

***

He entered the house at the rear, down the alleyway at the back of the grocer's where the rats came out at night to scavenge the dustbins. The little yard at the back of the house was dark and sunless, even on this sunny Sunday morning. He had missed church he remembered now, but then it was an emergency and for once he did not have to manufacture an excuse.

The house seemed unusually empty as he entered it, but the radio was on in the small room in which they lived between the kitchen and the shop. He called, 'Mum', but softly, for she had a rooted objection to raised voices on Sunday. There was no reply, and he went to the door which led to the shop and opened it and went inside. The blinds were down, but a beam of sunlight came through a tear in one of them and illuminated the inside. It was spotlessly clean and tidy as it always was on Sundays, for on a Saturday night after closing his father would spend a couple of hours or more in what had become a weekly ritual. He would tidy, dust and polish, using his one arm vigorously, perspiring with the extra effort that this involved. No one was allowed to help him.

He came down the stairs now as Denis came out of the shop. He went to the radio and switched it off.

'Mission completed?' he asked.

'They were women and kids from London,' Denis said. 'They were mucky,' he added, a traitor to his earlier enlightenment.

'Hungry?'

'They gave us something to eat,' said Denis. He asked, 'Where's Mum?'

'She's upstairs lying down,' his father said. He looked at Denis quietly, and added, 'Chamberlain was on the radio ... We're at war with Germany, it seems, but you expected it I daresay?'

Denis nodded. His father said, 'Your mother's a bit upset. I daresay a lot of women are. Women with sons. I've told her it won't affect you. Have to last longer than the last one before you'd be involved. Anyway,' he said, 'it'll all be over by Christmas.'

Denis went upstairs to his room. As he passed the door of his parents' bedroom his mother called his name. He went inside. She was lying on the bed, looking up at the bedroom ceiling. There was a dent in the feather mattress where his father would have sat, comforting her. As Denis entered she turned her head and looked at him. It was the second tear-stained face he had seen that day that had troubled him. She was his mother, and he would have been disturbed to see her so at any time. It was something that happened with people who were close to you. The face at the railway carriage window had been something else. Nothing could have been more remote from him, he thought, than that small alien face. It did not occur to him then, with one foot in childhood still, that what he had seen was a mirror image of himself. That what he had experienced was the beginnings of a process of learning to empathise; to enter the minds of others and to feel their pain so that it became your own.

His mother held out her hand and he sat on the edge of the bed where his father had sat and took it. She looked at him searchingly without speaking so that he felt embarrassed and longed for her to look away. He was tired, too, and as the thought entered his head he yawned, suddenly and without restraint in the face of her tears.

She laughed. He looked at her for a moment in astonishment, not immediately understanding that she was laughing at him.

'You're tired,' she said, almost happily, seeing the child again where she had been looking for the man.

He admitted he was tired, not understanding the transformation in her, or his own part in it, but glad that it had taken place.

'Well,' she said, 'I can't stay here all day.'

He left her and went to his own room, closed the door and lay on the bed. He would be back at school next week. Ted would soon be at work at the pit, his self-contained quality even more pronounced. Denis suspected that most of the money Ted would earn would go into his home, but even so he would have money in his pocket for the first time.

Most of the boys he was friendly with at school would be working too, because of the accident of his birthday that put him a year behind the majority. His life was beginning to change, but the biggest change of all was a year away and he was impatient for it to happen. When he went back to school, he knew he would feel left behind. Even Ted, perhaps, would abandon him, seeking his friends in the new world of work and the other world that went with it; the world of making your own way, making your own choices, not having to be in on time every night; the world that he sensed his mother wanted him to stay in forever.

Two weeks later, he deceived her seriously for the first time. There had been small deceptions before, of course, mostly for convenience, or to avoid reproach. This, in his mind at least, was something quite different.

Ted, who was working nights, had waited for him outside school on the Wednesday before that weekend. Seeing him there Denis was embarrassed, for he wore short trousers to school on occasions, not having thoroughly worn them out, and Ted was now wearing long ones all the time. Denis had approached his mother more than once on the subject, but she had been adamant that he should wait until he left school. It seemed to be part of a policy she had adopted to prevent him growing up, or at least to slow the process.

'I'm going out with Jean Colthard,' Ted suddenly said as they walked back down the road.

It jolted Denis. Since the incident at the Baths he had had dreams about Jean Colthard. They were not the sort of dreams he could have told Ted about, even had they involved another girl. Nor could he remember them in detail, but only in general terms. He knew that in them he was much older, very much his cousin Tim's age in fact. He was also much more sophisticated, and remarkably like Tim in this, too. Also he had a car, which was precisely like Tim's except that, for some reason, it was a different colour. The situations in which he, Jean and the car were involved, were rather like snatches from the American B films which he and Ted had seen at the Hippodrome on the rare occasions when they were allowed to go in the evenings, usually to see the main picture which had to be one which could be loosely considered as being educational.

'Well then?' said Ted, and perhaps attributing Denis's silence to the conversation they had had earlier that summer he added, 'You don't still like her, do you?'

'Me? I don't like her. Why do you think I like her?'

'You said so once.'

'Oh, that,' said Denis, as casually as he could. Then a trifle vindictively, 'I didn't think you liked her. You said she was a teaser.' He was tempted to add that he had been teased, but sensed he would be on dangerous ground.

'I like her,' said Ted, and from the way that he said it Denis knew that he was well and truly hooked. In spite of his own conflicting emotions, he was impressed. There were other situations he could imagine Ted in with girls, but for him to actually 'like' one was something quite new. Now as they walked he glanced sideways at his friend and thought that he saw in his expression some of the inner unhappiness that he knew from experience was a part of 'liking'.

'You sure you don't like her?' said Ted, as if unable to believe that anyone might not.

'I like somebody else now,' Denis said, instinctively. As he said it he found himself almost wishing it was true. The wish, perhaps, may have made the statement convincing, for Ted seemed to accept it. A hundred yards or more may have passed in silence before he took the plunge and said, 'She teased me, too.'

Ted almost stopped in his tracks, but somehow or other he managed to keep moving. The silence this time was shorter.

'When did she tease you?' he asked.

Denis wished now that he had kept silent, but it was too late. In an odd sort of way, he was glad that he had said it. He was beginning to feel top dog. Dreams he might have, but it was Ted who was stuck with reality.

He said, 'She teased me at the Baths, that day we went to Cuddon Fair.'

'You're fibbing.'

'I'm not!' He felt he was gaining prestige. They passed the Junction Hotel where the colliers fought on Saturday nights and the women waited in the darkness outside to take the casualties home from motives of love or revenge.

'How did she tease you?' asked Ted.

Denis piled agony on agony. He said, 'She asked me into her cubicle to find her watch and she didn't have her cossie on.'

'That's not teasing,' Ted said, with the voice of one who wants to believe.

'She was teasing,' Denis said, as if he spoke from a lifetime's experience of being teased. Moreover, to be one up on Ted was a new experience. He forgot about his short trousers.

'I don't care anyway,' said Ted, morosely, stating a fact of life. 'I still like her.'

They walked in silence for a while. Ted still did duty at the Baths, but Denis had been moved to the ARP centre attached to the police station. The long summer when they saw each other daily had come to an end and, coupled with the fact of Ted's work, they had begun to lose the closeness in their relationship. The new situation had brought them together again.

'We've got some blackout masks for bike lamps in the shop,' said Denis. 'You can have one if you want.'

'Thanks,' said Ted, which again was something new. Gratitude had always been something which implied a debt.

As they turned the corner into the main street, the wind blew the dust of the slag heaps into their faces. It had settled on the rooftops in the long dry summer, and the occasional rainfall had only washed it into the gutters. Soon the winter would come and blow it all away. They stopped by the ginnel which would take Ted down to the square.

'I'm going in Dakins,' said Ted. 'Wait for me a sec.'

He vanished inside the small sweetshop, which also sold tobacco and took bookings for the two cinemas in Caselborn four miles away. Mrs. Dakin was a widow now. Old Dakin, who used to sit outside on the step in summer, had died the day after war broke out. His last words, she had said, were, 'I hope you get through it all right,' then he had sat up, looked at his watch which was always hung on the end of the bed, said, 'It's half-past four,' and died. He had had a deep scar in both cheeks where a German bayonet had gone right through in the First World War.

From where he stood, Denis could see his parents' little shop. He hoped that his mother did not come out, for he knew that she was even more averse to his relationship with Ted since Ted had gone to work and become a man. Less than a week ago she had said, 'Have you made a new friend yet?' as if she assumed that his friendship with Ted had come to an end. But he knew that it was her way of asking him if it had, and he had answered neither one way nor the other. At the top of the street he could see the double-fronted men's outfitters which was one of his Uncle Horsborough's shops. He wondered if Tim had gone back to University yet, for they had not seen him lately.

Ted came out of the shop with a paper packet holding five Woodbines in his hand. Denis wondered at his audacity until he remembered that Ted was now a man and could more openly display his vices if he wished.

'Want one for later?' Ted asked him.

'No thanks,' Denis said, with an anxious glance up the street. At this short distance from home it was guilt as much as the risk of discovery which made him refuse, for they had smoked occasionally throughout the summer, mostly cinnamon cigarettes from the chemists in Caselborn. Ted lit one and puffed. He did it not as you did it in front of other boys, with a self-conscious display of manliness, but as if it was one of the natural functions.

He said, suddenly, 'Want to come to the pictures at Caselborn?'

'What's on?' Denis asked.

'Three Stooges,' said Ted. He usually quoted the supporting programme. He added, 'I've booked three seats, but there's four together if you'll come.'

'Four?'

'I'm taking Jean. She's told her mother she's going with our Jessie so she's to come as well. They don't let her go on her own. They go to Chapel.'

Denis wondered what prayers might be said in Chapel

if her parents knew what had happened at the Baths. Ted's offer tempted him. She was going with Ted, of course, and behind Ted's offer he could sense self interest at work, but it was tempting all the same. In spite of the situation he desperately wanted to see her. 'I'm like him,' he thought, 'I don't care. I still like her.'

'Jessie asked me if you'd come,' Ted was saying. He looked embarrassed. She was his sister. It was hard to think of her in a similar situation to Jean and himself, especially with Denis involved. But he had obviously promised her he would ask and he had done so. 'She's taking her matric next year,' he added, inconsequentially but with pride, as if he were announcing some special attraction.

'I'll have to ask,' Denis said, becoming conscious again of his short trousers. He couldn't go in those for a start.

He didn't tell his mother he was going with Ted, he told her that he was going with a friend from school whose brother went to the grammar school and who was going with them. She would like that, he knew. She had always hoped that he might develop friendships in the class from which she herself came. 'Why can't you make friends with "nice" boys,' she would say, as if the 'nice' ones were always precisely located in the social scale. Recently she had spoken to Tim about him. Denis knew this because Tim had talked to him as he had been asked to do, and had not hidden from him the fact that he had been asked. 'Your mother thinks you ought to have wider interests,' he had said, and then putting things on the line as he always did, he had added, 'I think in a way she's right.' They would talk about it, he said, before the end of the holiday, but the holidays were already over. He wondered again why Tim had not been to see them. It was not like Tim to forget.

***

They were supposed to go on the six-thirty bus but when Denis boarded it at his own stop only Jean Colthard was on it. She was sitting at the back for which he was thankful, for old Mrs. Wilks, who was a regular visitor to the shop, was seated at the front. He made his way to where Jean was sitting and sat down beside her. He had not seen her since the incident at the baths and had difficulty in looking straight at her. She seemed to have no such problem, however, smiling at him as if her rendezvous was with him and with no one else.

'Don't ask me,' she said, answering his unspoken question, 'they weren't at the stop.'

'What shall we do?'

It wasn't quite as it was in his dreams. In his dreams there was no uncertainty. In his dreams he looked her straight in the eye and told her what they would do, and she simply complied.

'They'll probably be on the next one,' she said.

'What if they aren't?'

'We'll have to go without them, won't we?'

He knew, though he could not look, that she was smiling as if it was what she really wanted. He sat stiffly beside her, aware of her closeness, loving and hating her at the same time. 'She's just a teaser,' he thought, and he let the thought go on and on in his mind. It made no difference at all.

When the bus stopped in Caselborn he remembered old Mrs. Wilks, but she was no longer on it. She must have got off at one of the other stops without him noticing. He wondered if she had seen him. It would be half an hour before the next bus arrived.

'We'll miss the Three Stooges,' he said.

'Good!' she said. 'I don't like the Three Stooges.'

'Ted does.'

'Doesn't mean I have to.'

There was a park not far from the cinema and they decided to go there to pass the time. Caselborn was built on a hill and from almost anywhere in the small town you could see the flat surrounding countryside away into the distance. Most of it was fertile agricultural land, but it was impossible to look in any direction without seeing, in the far distance, a pithead, or the dark outline of slag heaps. From where they sat on the grass now you could see the distant cluster of houses, pit and slag that was Cuddon, but you could not have imagined it from here as it was. Caselborn was clean, tidy and cared for as Cuddon was dirty, poverty stricken and forgotten. He thought of this always when he came here, of this difference, and wondered why. For much of his life he classified places in this way, from this early memory; this being a Caselborn, and that a Cuddon.

Jean said now, as if she could read his thoughts, 'You won't stay in Cuddon, will you?'

'I don't know,' he said. 'Why shouldn't I?'

'It's a mucky hole.'

'What about you?'

'Fat chance I have of getting out of it!'

'As much chance as me,' he said.

'Men can find work away,' she said. 'We marry into it, women. Who else do we meet but Cuddon men?'

'Caselborn men,' he said.

'They don't want to know you if you live in Cuddon. Cuddon women are different.'

'How?' he asked.

'I don't know,' she said, 'but they are. Do you like Cuddon women?' she asked, suddenly smiling, looking into his eyes. He loved this directness in her. It softened the shyness that had stiffened him all the way here on the bus. He found himself smiling back, and something in his smile seemed to worry her so that she looked away.

'I like you,' he said, appalled and delighted with himself at the same time.

'You shouldn't like anybody that much,' Jean said.

'How much?'

She thought about it, then eventually she said, 'Too much.'

'How do you know I like you too much. I just said I like you.'

'You should laugh about things,' she said. 'Everything. You shouldn't take anything too seriously. If you care for anything too much, even a dog, you get hurt in the end.'

Her face clouded over as she said it, as if contradicting her words. She looked utterly unlike herself, vulnerable, gentle, caring, tragic almost too, quite different from the way he always imagined her. A thought came into his mind, something that always came back to him when she did, whenever she floated into his consciousness looking as she did at that moment: 'Women are older than men,' he thought.

When the next bus came in, Ted and Jessie were on it. Jessie looked at him quickly, then away. 'She's shy,' he thought, 'like I am with Jean.' Ted glanced at him with what Denis thought was suspicion when he saw him waiting there with Jean. 'He thinks I've been having a quick tease,' Denis thought, grinning. Then he knew that Ted had seen the grin and that it had irritated him, for his shoulders hunched up and the dourness came over his face. He had one of his moods on again.

He could never remember the title, or the actors even, but he always afterwards remembered the film. When he saw it again years later, he was appalled that it should have made such an impression on his mind. It was the story he really remembered. Banal, not in any way original, it must somehow have fitted his mood at the time. Perhaps he identified with one of the men, or maybe the woman reminded him of Jean. Or perhaps it had nothing to do with either, but was just a part of the evening that saw the twilight of his childhood and the beginning of his youth.

They sat on the back row, traditionally, the boys on the outer seats and the girls in the middle. Denis was right when he had said they would miss half the Three Stooges. That wouldn't please Ted, he thought, but then nothing was likely to please Ted in one of his moods. Denis sensed that he was inhibited too by the fact that his sister was there. They spoke very little in the interval, mostly the two girls chatting about the film, Ted sitting hunched in his seat. Denis joined in easily where he could. He noticed how much more interestingly dressed Jean was than Jessie, and was intuitively aware that Jessie was conscious of this. Once Jean turned away from glancing at Ted, caught Denis's eye, grinned at him and winked. 'Oh you teaser!' he thought. It delighted him, the intimacy between them.

They came out more or less as they had gone in; Ted morose, Jessie shy, Jean amused and Denis caught somewhere between pain and exultation. He was with her, but she wasn't his. It had been enough up to now, but as they came out of the cinema and broke into pairs, Jean and Ted walking ahead, he realised that nothing had changed except that they had established some sort of relationship. He found himself walking quickly, almost running at times, to keep up with the two ahead as Ted, head down, worked his mood off in movement.

'Are we late for the bus?' asked Jessie, a bit breathless, hurrying along beside him.

There was something in her voice, an edge of sarcasm perhaps, that made him glance at her.

'I'm trying to keep up with them,' he said, not really able to see her in the blackout. They were getting used to it now, the blackout. It had helped in a way that it had happened while the days were still reasonably long. Even so there had been accidents as people stumbled through the unaccustomed darkness. Harry Byte, who was in Denis's class at school and was also in the choir with him, had been knocked down by a car with excessively dimmed headlights and crippled for life. Casualties on the roads in the country as a whole had more than doubled.

They missed the last bus that passed the end of Cuddon Main Street and had to catch the one that took them to Cuddon Top. It meant walking back across the pit fields, but was better than walking the whole four miles. In the bus the lights had been blacked out all but for tiny areas which emitted a dim blue light that made normally healthy looking people look pale and ill. It was not this so much as the sight of Ted and Jean sitting together on the seat in front of him that depressed Denis. She sat by the window and he watched her face reflected in the dark glass. Jessie spoke to him twice, but nervously and inconsequentially and as if she simply felt the need to break the silence.

When they got off the bus at Cuddon Top, Ted set off into the darkness at his previous pace as if he cared not at all whether they followed or not.

'Oh well,' said Jean, 'here we go again!'

'Let him go on his own,' Denis said, with unusual disloyalty, and was aware that even in the darkness Jessie had glanced at him sharply as he said it.

'I'd better go,' she said, after a moment's hesitation. 'Like doing the cross country at school again!'

She set off after him at a trot. Cloud had cleared from the night sky since they had left Caselborn and a thin moon dimly lit the landscape. He watched her shadow go with an ache and a longing to follow her, but set off more slowly with Jessie, remembering her previous rebuke. It had rained heavily the previous day and pools of water obstructed the path so that they had to slow down to avoid them in any case. Most of the time they had to go single file, and Denis led the way, waiting for her whenever the track broadened out and then walking on again in silence, his eyes forever searching for the figures ahead, his mind not at all with her. Increasingly he forgot to stop and his pace quickened.

He had almost completely forgotten Jessie when he heard her cry out behind him, and he stopped and turned. She was back along the track, just a vague shadow in the darkness, but he could not see what it was that had made her cry out. Reluctantly he made his way back. She was sitting on an old overhead bucket that had toppled down the slag heap at some time in the past and landed on its side. She was unfastening one of her shoes.

'What's wrong?' he asked her.

'I walked into that,' she said, pointing to a large pool of water across the track. 'My shoes are soaked through.'

They would never catch up now, he thought, frustrated and impatient with her.

'You can't dry them here,' he said.

'I'm emptying the water out.' Her voice sounded cold and unlike her.

'You'll be able to dry them if you get home.'

'Have you tried walking with shoes full of water?' she asked, and started to cry. He could tell she was crying by the sound of her voice, for her face was in darkness. There was just a quiet, weary frustration of tears in her voice. 'I went in there trying to keep up with you,' she said, trying to be sharp, as if anger might quell her tears.

He said, 'I'm sorry,' meaning it, feeling suddenly ashamed. The heat of the chase had gone out of him. He was resigned. He sat on the bucket beside her.

'Trying to keep up with Jean Colthard,' she said,

bravely, for he could sense that she forced herself to say it, as if to bring things to a head.

'I'm not.'

'Yes you are. You've been doing it all night.'

'I haven't.'

'You're wasting your time, anyway. It's our Ted she's after this week. Next week it'll be somebody else.'

His sympathy for her, suddenly created, began as quickly to evaporate. He said, 'She's not like that.'

'You know her well, do you?'

He wanted to say, 'I've seen her without her clothes on,' as if it was a kind of marriage between them, but of course he didn't. Instead he said, 'She's not like you think she is.'

'Men are stupid,' she said, as if they were two grown-up people. They were silent for a moment while she took off her other shoe and emptied it.

'I've got to wear these to school tomorrow,' she said. 'I've only one pair. We're not well off like you are.'

It pained him that she should attack him with his relative wealth. Ted never did. The consciousness of it was always between them, but it was only through his own awareness that he felt it, not through Ted. On the point of becoming angry with her again, he felt it subside, being replaced by a genuine sympathy. He remembered the Square; the squalor of the house in which she lived. Her father's face came before him, shadowed with poverty and frustration and, though it was only years later that Denis recognised this, the agony of not being able to provide.

'What do you like about her?' Jessie asked, bringing his mind back to Jean.

'I don't know,' he said, making his admission.

'She's pretty, of course.'

Immersed in his first adolescent expedition into love, he did not realise that this was an invitation for him to salve her own pain by telling her that she was just as pretty. She could not know that in fact, when she said it, this was what he thought. He glanced sideways at her, but she was only a shadow. It entered his mind that he must have noticed before as a simple fact. 'She is pretty,' he thought.

With the thought came another thought. She had asked Ted to bring him that night. She 'liked' him. Perhaps she felt about him as he felt about Jean Colthard, though he could not imagine that anyone could match his own pain of love, the heaviness somewhere between the stomach and the heart, that held him down. How simple it would have been if he had felt for her what he felt for the other. What unimaginable joy!

'Why don't I?' he asked himself, as so many have.

All night he had held in his consciousness, aware and yet unaware of his dawning sexuality, the memory of Jean Colthard's breasts as he had seen them the day at the Baths, and as he saw them all that evening through the clothes she wore that covered them.

'We'd better get on,' he said now as Jessie finished fastening her shoe. Some kind of panic rose within him. He had remembered how he had touched Jessie's face before he left her on the night they had gone to the Fair. How easy, these strange new longings told him, it would be now to reach out and touch her breast. Into what exciting, strange new land of as yet unexperienced sensations would it lead him? Would it take away that other pain; the heaviness within him? Was that what he wanted, that it should go and be replaced by something more pleasurable, more immediately satisfying?

'We'd better get on,' he said, as if the floods were rising to engulf them.

CHAPTER EIGHT

Ted did not see Jessie the following day, but when a day later he rose from his bed in the early afternoon, which was the pattern when he worked nights, he was surprised to find her at home and washing in the scullery. He stood in the doorway, his eyes still heavy with sleep, and blinked at her. 'What are you doing here?' he asked. 'Shouldn't you be at school?'

She looked up from the dollyboard, her hand still clutching the grey sheet which she had been rubbing over the corrugations in a vain attempt to return the sheet to its natural colour. All the sheets were like this since Ted had started at the pit, for only at weekends did he manage to get his body completely free of the black dust of the mine.

'Mam's not well,' she said.

'What's up with her?' Ted asked, only half interested, and mostly because it affected Jessie.

'I don't know. Dad's gone down to the surgery to get the doctor to call.'

'You shouldn't have stopped at home, you'll miss

your schoolwork.'

'There's work to be done here. Who else is to do it?'

'Me and Dad can manage.'

'That's what he said. It's my place to stop` here anyway.'

'Your place is at school.'

'I'll be able to go tomorrow,' she said, as if to placate him and avoid an argument. 'Aunt Dolly's taking the kids for their meals.'

Aunt Dolly was his father's sister. She was a spinster; stout, amiable and with an enormous capacity for mothering which had saved them from more than one disaster.

Ted grunted, dourly accepting the situation. It never occurred to him to go upstairs to see his mother.

Jessie twisted the sheet to wring the worst of the water from it, then carried it out to the yard where the mangle was and inserted it between the wooden rollers. Ted followed and started to turn the handle on the large iron wheel which turned the rollers, and Jessie fed the sheet through them, and then again, and the water trickled greyly on the flags beneath.

She allowed him to take the sheet from her and followed him out of the yard to where the clothes line hung at the foot of the stacks, handing him the pegs as he hung the sheet on the line.

'You've had a visitor,' she said.

He concentrated on the sheet as if he had not heard her, making a labour of it. She smiled as if something about him amused her, but he did not see this.

'It was Jean. She said she didn't catch you up the other night.'

'Come after me, did she?'

He had wondered. It had been his intention that she should, and that he would allow her eventually to catch up with him, but somehow they had lost each other in the darkness he supposed. He had tried not to feel concerned at the thought that perhaps, after all, she had not followed him. He did not want to admit, even to himself, that it was of any great importance to him.

'I'll get your breakfast,' said Jessie.

He followed her back into the house and sat on a stool in the scullery while she busied herself with preparing his food. Once before when their mother had been ill she had stayed away from school to see to them all and the house. She seemed to enjoy it, as if it was some kind of therapy from the mental weariness of weeks and months spent ploughing through books.

'What did you and Denis get up to?'

She looked away from him and concentrated on the work of her hands.

'We just walked home,' she said, and then, as if she could not let it go, 'He's keen on Jean Colthard, like you are.'

'Who says I am?'

'You go out with her.'

'Once out to t'pictures?'

'You see her other nights, I know you do.'

'Why shouldn't I then, if I want? Don't you like her.'

'She's all right,' said Jessie.

'You don't like her do you?' he asked.

'She's got a name.'

So even she knew, lost in her world of books. He looked at her, bent mock busy over preparing his meal.

He said, 'It's all talk that.' Then because he knew she did not believe it was just gossip, he said, 'I don't care anyway. I like her as she is.'

'I do in a way,' said Jessie, as if anxious that Jean should not become an issue between them. 'I'd like to be like her in a way.'

'What way?'

She thought about this, then said, 'She's full of life.

She's straight. She knows what she wants.'

'What does she want?'

'She wants you.'

'She'd never marry a collier. She's told me.'

'She'd marry you.'

'How do you know?' He flipped the question at her casually, but waited for the answer as if sentence was about to be pronounced on him.

'I just know,' she said, with a total conviction which he accepted. A kind of exultation rose in him. So whatever game she might play he had her. Or perhaps it was simply that the game was now played out and he had won. He had no sense of danger in this attitude. It was how things should be. In his fears that things might have been different he had sensed a softness in him that was unmanly and unworthy of a man who worked among men. It was not how things should be in a man's world. He was in charge of himself again as one who aspired to kingship should be, and already he could see the shape of his life. He would win through to the face, and he would come home to the woman he had chosen.

'What about you then?' he asked, suddenly, for there was nothing left to say about himself.

'What about me?'

'Isn't there anybody you like?'

Her back was turned to him. He could not see her face. She said, 'I don't think so.' But he knew from the way she said it that there was.

'Who is he?' he asked, finding himself more than mildly curious.

'Nobody you know.'

'Somebody that goes to the grammar school?'

'Who'd look at me from grammar school?' She turned, and he saw that her face was flushed.

'Why shouldn't they?' he asked, not grasping the point she was making.

'We live in the Square,' she said.

'You can't help it. What's it to do with you that we live in the Square?'

'It's how things are,' she said.

'Nay,' he said, and it was at the tip of his tongue to continue and to tell her that she was not as others in the Square – the loud women, the perpetually haggard men, the crawling off-spring of poverty. Yet he had said to her, 'You can't help it,' and now, at the point where he would have denied them, he suddenly asked himself, 'Could they?'

There was a banging on the floor above. Jessie said, 'Mum wants me,' and left the room to go upstairs, promptly as if she was drawn there by love rather than the nagging compulsion of guilt because love did not exist in her as it should. He knew this was so, though he did not know how he knew. As much as any woman in the Square his mother epitomised her environment. He knew that Jessie shrank from her and was ashamed, and yet again he did not know why he knew this. Was it because in the books she had lent him and tried to persuade him to read she had experienced, albeit vicariously, another kind of life which made her own seem, by contrast, an abyss? Yet she would accept the inferiority which he himself denied though he disliked the squalor of the Square as much as she did.

In his relationship with Denis he had often been aware of the physical difference in their two lives. Denis slept in a bed alone and did not have to share it with two others. They had a bath and a toilet inside the house and the house, although not architecturally much better than the one Ted himself lived in, was clean and cared for. They lived as the better off miners lived, some of whom even owned their own houses, bought in the days when colliers' earnings were higher than most in their class. Denis ate, he had often hungrily suspected, better and more regularly than he himself did. Yet Ted felt no inferiority. On the contrary, more often than not he had a condescending attitude towards his friend, and more than ever now that he had won Jean whom Denis 'liked'.

Doug Hoyle came into the room now, back from the doctors. He blinked as he entered, although he came from the light into the darker light, as if the darkness hurt his eyes. He dropped his cloth cap on the table, then dropped himself in his usual chair and sat silent, looking at the empty grate as if unaware of Ted. Feeling a sudden compulsion to draw his father's attention, Ted took a packet of Woodbines from his pocket and held the packet out.

'Take one,' he said, as if issuing an order.

'Nay,' said his father, waving the packet away, though Ted knew he loved to smoke, though he could not afford to.

'Take one,' said Ted, a new force in his voice.

Hoyle looked at him and their eyes met as they rarely did when there was any emotion between them. Then he put out his finger and thumb to take a cigarette.

'Take the packet,' said Ted, the new force growing stronger.

Hoyle paused and looked at him again, his hand still outstretched. Something akin to a smile touched the corners of his mouth and glowed briefly in his eyes. He said, taking the packet, 'Thou't a man at last then, eh?'

An hour later the doctor came and went up the stairs. He was a dour but likeable Scot who called all the women by their Christian names and the men by their surnames. His questions were always brief and to the point, and at times he hardly seemed to speak at all, but would look around the room as if it was more interesting than the patient, or as if somewhere the diagnosis was written on the walls. To all but the few on his panel who had tasted his rare but legendary wrath he was 'a good doctor'.

Jessie busied herself in the kitchen while the doctor was upstairs. Hoyle, deep in a book he had picked up from the library on his way back from the surgery, had simply looked up and nodded when the doctor entered, and then gone back to his book. Ted went and sat on the doorstep in the manner of miners, his back hunched against the wall at the side of the door as he had seen his father do. It was something he had done as a child, sitting on the other side of the door imitating his father, dragging at an imaginary cigarette.

He had been at the pit for two weeks now. Coming home at the end of his first day's work, the shock of it still reverberating inside him, he had seen his father sitting here on the step as he crossed the Square towards him, and had thought, 'He knows what I feel, but he'll say nothing.' And that was how it had been.

He looked across the Square now, remembering the silence in the cage as it carried him down on that first day into the blackest night he had ever known, the dim, flickering oil lamps seeming only to emphasise the darkness, catching occasionally at two tiny red stars which he eventually realised were the eyes of rats or mice. He remembered the creaking of the roof timbers as the strata settled on packs and roof supports, and the feeling of the weight of the earth above him. Left alone, two miles from the pit bottom, he filled four tubs on that first shift, that being the task that was given him. It was dust, not coal, and the dust added a fog to the darkness. He had wondered what he would do if the oil in his lamp ran out, for the shift seemed endless and a lifetime passed before he heard the tap of the deputies stick and knew that his first day's work was almost done.

Two miles back to the pit bottom, then, and the blackened faces of those who had travelled down with him in the cage. Their faces were tired, but they were no longer silent. Their voices chattered like larks as the cage rose to the light and released them.

Off the bus he had walked proudly through the streets to the Square, proud to display the blackness that announced he was a worker and a man and with something of a swagger in his walk.

They were waiting for him at the house. When he opened the door they were there, all of them, silently waiting for the only breadwinner in the family. The smell of bacon and eggs drifted from the scullery and instinctively he knew it was for him, and his mother, who had looked at him without emotion, said, 'You're back then,' and vanished into the scullery. His two young brothers were all round him then, looking at him as if for the first time, endless with questions. And then he had looked over their heads and caught his father's eye and they had looked away from each other. Jessie had simply sat there in silence, looking at him also, an odd smile on her face as if she did not entirely believe that he had been there and had now returned.

He remembered it all, squatting there on the doorstep waiting for the doctor to come downstairs. He lived it again, as he did sometimes still on shift when work and time dragged hard at him. No homecoming would ever be the same again.

Only Jean had shown no interest at all, for even his mother had listened as he had answered the boys' interminable questions. He had seen Jean the following night, since for some reason she was not allowed to go out on Monday nights. He had met her on the road that led out of Cuddon to where the farms were, and she had greeted him as if nothing unusual had happened since they last met. He had waited for her to ask him about his first day, and had almost started to tell her anyway but that some obstinacy created by her lack of interest, or such he took it to be, had silenced him. 'All right, then,' he had thought, 'if you're to say nowt then neither will I!' His irritation towards her as both maintained a silence on the subject over the following two weeks had culminated in the mood which had driven him to walk away from her on the night they went to the pictures with Denis and Jessie. That it was really lack of interest he only half-believed. In some way, he sensed, it had to do with her hatred of the pit.

She had been that morning while he slept, Jessie had said. Let her come then, for he would not go to her, lounging at some distance from her home as she had told him to do, so that she would see him and come to him without her parents knowing. Such skulking offended his new found dignity in any case. And yet he desperately wanted to see her; wanted her understanding even if she could not bring herself to approve of his work.

Now through the open door behind him he heard the doctor's voice. He had come downstairs and was speaking to Doug Hoyle in the living-room, an event unusual in itself. Ted stood so as not to obstruct the doorway, and a moment later the doctor came to the door with his father.

'I'm just across the Square with the doctor here,' his father said, and Ted nodded then watched them go. They walked slowly, stopping occasionally as if their conversation had reached some kind of punctuation mark.

Ted went back into the house. Jessie was in the living-room. She had laid her schoolbooks out on the table as if she had intended to work, but was sitting in the chair by the fireplace where his father usually sat, looking at the empty firegrate as his father sometimes did when he was deep in thought.

She looked up when she heard him enter.

'What is it?' he asked, reading some trouble in her face.

'It's the doctor.'

'What about him?'

'I didn't like to seem to listen. I couldn't hear it all, but I think it's serious.'

'Mum?'

She nodded, looking at him.

'What did he say then?'

'He kept talking about a growth.'

The word meant something to Ted, though not a lot. He knew that it was a word with serious implications, but there were people he knew that had had growths removed.

'Nellie Machin had a growth removed,' he said, mentioning someone they both knew to be alive.

'I thought about Nellie Machin,' Jessie said, as if she had sought round for comfort, and yet he knew that she did not greatly care for their mother, for it was another of the things they were conscious of sharing. Yet a cloud had come over the day, and inside him something had stirred that he did not even now recognise, as if he had remembered a face but could put no name or place to it.

He abandoned his pride that night after tea, and after slicking his hair back in the cracked scullery mirror, and telling Jessie he was going out, he went out of the house and walked in the direction of the baths. Then almost halfway there resentment had built up again inside him while he walked, so that he turned and walked back again. But tomorrow was Sunday and this was his one free night of the week, and if he did not see her now another week would pass unless she came to the house the following day. Yet she knew this was his free night and she had not returned after calling earlier when he was asleep.

He saw her in his mind.

'It's your turn now,' she said.

'Playing your bloody games again!' he swore at her image.

'Takes two to play games,' she replied.

'It's all a game to you!'

'No it isn't!'

'Yes, it is!'

'You don't care for me,' her image said. 'You want me to come to you all the time.'

It was true. She had come to him too, that morning, though he had been asleep in bed after work. He got his bike out of the yard at the back of the house and rode to the baths. He stood with it in view of her house and fiddled with the brake.

'You and your games,' he kept saying to himself, castigating himself for his weakness.

'I came to see you this morning,' she said. 'I'd forgotten you'd be asleep.'

They dismounted halfway up a steepish hill on the road out of Cuddon. She had seen him from the house and had brought her own bicycle out, following him at a distance until the houses were behind them.

All his earlier doubts and uncertainties, and his resentments too, had disappeared. As they had gone so had his confidence returned. With his gesture he had asked her to come to him and she had come. He could ask no more of her. There was a warmth and awareness between them now which seemed to heighten all his senses, so that he was more aware of her as a person, and not just a girl, than he had ever been. He liked the way she dressed too, and it was as if he noticed this for the first time. She wore colour as if she flaunted it like a wickedness.

He had chosen the direction out of Cuddon instinctively, though without any conscious destination, but already a thought was growing in his mind.

As if she could read him almost, she said, 'Where are we going?'

'I know somewhere we could go.'

'Well then?'

'Nobody knows it but me.'

'Want to keep it secret, do you?' she said, smiling.

'Aye,' he said, seriously, looking at her.

'You trust me, don't you?' she asked, serious herself now.

It reminded him of the moment in the baths when the game had stopped and she had sat on the edge of the pool, vulnerable and prepared to lose.

They had reached the top of the hill now and the farmland spread out before them with the familiar hills in the distance. Again he had the feeling he had had only with Jessie and his father, perhaps, of wanting to give of himself for their happiness and of not feeling unmanly or 'soft' because of this.

He said, suddenly, 'Come after me,' and mounted his bike and rode off, not looking back, confident now that she would follow. When he reached the track to the ruined farmhouse, and turned down it, he had one brief moment of doubt and glanced back, but she had turned too and was following him. He did not stop again until he reached the yard where he dismounted and leaned his bike against the low stone wall and waited for her to come.

She stopped in the yard, but stood astride the bike still and looked at the house.

'Whose is it?' she asked.

He said, half-jokingly but with a serious pride of possession, 'It's mine.'

As if she understood the feeling behind his claim, she did not laugh, but asked again, 'Whose is it really?'

'I don't know,' he said truthfully. 'I just found it.'

It was a still August day, still with the heat of summer

but with a tiredness in the long green grass and the green dressed branches of the trees as if they longed for the coolness of autumn. You did not notice such things in the Square. In the Square the temperature and the light overhead simply changed.

She leaned her bike against the wall beside his own then came to stand beside him.

'How long since you found it?'

'Two years. I've done things inside,' he said, as if apologising for the shabby exterior.

'It's lovely,' she said, and he knew from the way she said it that what had got hold of him when he first saw it was echoed in her. Because he had expected her to make fun of him, and think him odd, it was a further bonding in the relationship between them.

'Aren't you going to show me round?' she asked, smiling.

So he led the way down the path and they entered the house.

'I've not done anything in here,' he said quickly as they entered the kitchen of the house. 'It's a room upstairs that I've done.'

She stayed still though as he moved towards the stairs and looked at the room as if she was furnishing it in her mind. A long shaft of sunlight had entered the room with them through the open door. It caught at her hair and at the soft outline of her body, and the gentler reflection illuminated the quiet, serious expression on her face. Although he was anxious to show her the room on which he had worked he waited for her, following her gaze, and something of what she was thinking entered his own thoughts so that he began to see the room in some measure as she saw it, furnished and cared for and occupied with life. Then she sighed and put up her hand to her hair as if she felt the warmth of the sun there and wished to hold it, and her arm shadowed her face, and as it fell again her expression was that of a sleeper who has dreamed and is now awake again.

When they opened the door to the room upstairs and went inside he was embarrassed by his claim to have 'done things', for imagination had shown him in the room downstairs far more expansive possibilities.

'I've not done much really,' he said, excusing himself, not looking at her.

The sun streamed in, for the old blackout curtain was drawn back out of sight. It was tidy though, for he always left it so. The remains of a pile of wood he had gathered the last time he had lit a fire were stacked on the hearth.

He glanced at her quickly now, ashamed, but she was smiling, not in a denigrating way but with warm amusement.

'It's a man's room,' she said, as if it was what she had expected anyway.

'Aye, well it would be, wouldn't it,' he said, with a touch of the old banter, 'me being a man.'

'A man,' she said. 'You?'

'Think I'm a lad still, do you?'

'All men are lads. They never grow up.'

He wanted to tell her about the pit, but she hated the pit. To talk about it would put a barrier between them and he would have lied in his teeth sooner than risk the loss of this warmth between them.

'I've grown up,' he said. 'I'm grown up enough for you.'

'Oh, are you then? And how grown up would that be then?'

'More than Jack Dakin.'

'Still jealous of Jack Dakin?'

'I'm not jealous.'

'No need to ask me about him then, is there?'

She stood away from him, her back to the light so he

could hardly see her face, only the shaft of the sun shaping her pale hair like a frame around it. Was she smiling at him still? The light dazzled him. He felt exposed and vulnerable, and now a new weakness troubled him as he grappled with it for the first time; a sense of awkwardness in his handling of the situation, an ignorance of what to do next. He had always been able to cope with the game, with the boy girl banter of it, but the reality was not as he had expected it to be. He felt frozen in his awkwardness. Almost he wished that she would move and take the initiative. He had a sudden fear that she might reject him, and yet he knew she would not.

He said, for it was beyond the power of his legs to carry him: 'Come here.'

'What for?'

It was the game, and yet it was not the game. It did not occur to him that the moment might be as difficult for her too.

He said, 'Come and see.'

'An order, is it?'

'Come and see.'

'I don't take orders, nor ever will.'

'I want you to.'

'Want me to what?'

'Want you to come.'

'Try saying please, then.'

'Please,' he said, his mouth dry.

'Please come,' she said, insisting.

'Please come.'

She came then. She stood almost touching him. It had been easy in the pit fields in the darkness, and it had been spontaneous anyway, not in his mind for that last half hour that now seemed an age. He put out his hand and touched her hair where the sun caught it. Then the other hand reached out to her breast. His mouth reached hers, but gently, not in the rough curiosity of the first time he had kissed her but in a new way that was another first time, never to be forgotten. Then they were on the bed of straw and old carpet on which he had lain while her image taunted him after the game in the baths. Then he had felt himself the loser, the victim, and had suffered the pain without knowing what it was. He knew it now.

'Why do you say "like"?' she asked him.

They were still on the bed, but the light in the room was dim and soft. She had asked him to pull the curtain, and he had done so, and now the sun crept in around the edges where it could.

'Are you awake?' she asked, after a moment, raising herself on an elbow, looking down at his face which was turned away from her.

He turned in answer, but still did not speak. He simply looked back at her.

'What is it?' she said, gently, as if she had found him weeping, a child.

'Nowt,' he said, after a moment of looking at her.

'Nothing?'

'Nowt. It's nowt,' he said, reaching out with his hand to touch her face, sensing her need for reassurance, her fear that in some way she had failed him. Then again to reassure her, he asked, 'What did you want? I was thinking. What was it you asked me?'

'Why do you say "like"?' she asked him again. 'You kept saying you "liked" me.'

'Did I?'

'You wouldn't hardly have done it if you didn't like me, would you?' she asked, half-smiling.

'No,' he said.

'Why do you think to say it then?'

'I don't know.'

'Maybe you meant something else.'

'Maybe.'

'Say it then.'

'I don't know what you mean.'

'Yes, you do.'

'What do I mean, then?'

'I want you to say it.'

'If you know what I mean, I've said it.'

She lay back again on the bed. He heard her voice say, 'I want you to say it,' as if she knew it was asking too much for him to say it while she looked at him.

He lay on his back beside her looking up at the old, cracked ceiling that other eyes than his must have explored in their time.

He said, 'I love you,' though barely believing that the voice was his own. He found it, oddly, easy to say.

For a moment she was silent, and then she said, 'I love you.'

Then again for a moment there was silence, until she asked, 'Why do you say "like" instead of "love"?'

'You know why,' he said, wondering why she asked when she knew the common language and why it was so.

'Because love's supposed to be soft?'

'That's what they say.'

'You think it is?'

'Not now.'

'Say it again.'

He looked at the ceiling. He could see the line of the laths that supported the plaster through the grey white lime covered skin.

'I love you.'

This time he turned and looked at her. She looked back at him and then away. 'Nobody can have felt like this before,' she said, ageless in her youth. 'Nobody.'

The word echoed in his mind. He thought of the people he knew. Denis 'liked' her; 'loved' her; or thought he did. Then there was Jessie. Faces he knew entered his mind at random, paired in marriage, or others he knew who were 'courting'. He could relate none of them to what he now knew was love, for it was so intensely new that he had no doubts. He could only assume that it happened to some, but not to others, and that it had happened to him. It did not occur to him at that moment that those in whom he did not see it had, perhaps, once had it, only to lose it. That he himself might wake one day to find it gone. That it was not a reality, but an illusion.

CHAPTER NINE

A week later Tim appeared at the house. For a couple of
days before he came, Denis had noticed an oddness in
his mother's attitude towards him. She was more than
usually silent when he was in the house, and when she
spoke to him she spoke sharply as if he had done
something to irritate her. Coming in quietly one night he
had heard his mother and father arguing in the living-
room. The sound of the door closing behind him had put
an end to the argument, but not before he had gained the
impression that it was in some way connected with
himself. Then, too, he would lift his head when eating or
reading a book and find her watching him with a curious
expression on her face. It occurred to him once that
perhaps Old Mrs. Wilks had been in the shop and
revealed that she had seen him on the bus to Caselborn,
but then his mother knew he had been to Caselborn that
night and the fact that he had sat next to Jean Colthard
could have had no real significance since the bus was
almost full.

Tim appeared unexpectedly on the Sunday afternoon.

His mother was more than usually pleased to see him, as if he had lifted some burden from her by his coming. Denis and his father were listening to the radio. She took Tim in the kitchen as if to have him to herself. From time to time Denis noticed his father listening, as if he would have liked to hear what they were talking about, but the radio made it impossible. Once Denis went in to help himself to bread and dripping.

Tim was saying, 'I'll have to let them know at home. Mother's expecting me for tea.'

His mother said, 'Denis can go and tell them.'

'That's all right,' said Tim, 'I can phone from down the road.'

'It'll get him out of the house. He can go on his bike. He needs the exercise. He's done nothing but mope in his room these last few days.'

This last bit was true. Most of his time when he was not at school was spent lying on his bed, immersed in a daydream about himself and Jean Colthard which had soon developed into a serial, which he would pick up from where he had left off the previous session. He would have protested now that he was listening to the radio, but knew from the past day or two that his mother would tolerate no such excuse and he had no wish to be embarrassed in front of Tim.

Denis said, meekly, 'I wanted some bread and dripping.'

'You can have your tea when you get back,' his mother said, adding to Tim, 'He's eating us out of house and home these days.'

'He's a growing lad,' said Tim, smiling.

On his way to his Uncle Maurice's with the message, Denis took a detour past the Baths and the adjacent houses where Jean lived, hoping for a glimpse of her. He circled it twice, not daring to go beyond this, but saw no sign of her though he almost fell off his bike peering through the windows as he freewheeled past them. He had seen neither her nor Ted since the night in Caselborn, and had no idea of the state of their relationship. It was a warm, dry autumn day and he imagined they would be out walking down Smokers' Lane where the courting couples went, as did the illicit smokers. He had experienced the guilt of smoking down there himself but not, he thought with regret, the even more illicit experience of courting. He would detour down Smokers' Lane on his way back, he thought, though what precisely he hoped to achieve if he saw them did not occur to him. At the back of his mind, too painful to dwell on, was the thought that Ted might be being treated to a tease. The thought had amused Denis once, but no longer. His imagination had already carried him beyond the point where teasing stops and what Ted would call 'The real stuff' begins.

His aunt opened the door to him. She was a stoutish, tweedy woman with greying hair and a hearty, confident manner. Denis didn't dislike her as his mother did, and she seemed to bear no grudge against him for the hostility she must have sensed in his mother.

'Tim's at our house and he says he won't be home for tea,' Denis said as soon as she opened the door. Having delivered his message he waited to be dismissed, but instead she invited him in. Unable on the spur of the moment to find an excuse, for by now he was impatient to visit Smokers' Lane, he had no alternative but to enter.

He followed her into the lounge where he had once found his mother sitting, the stain of tears still on her cheeks. His Uncle Maurice lay on the sofa, asleep, a Sunday paper over his face.

'Oh well,' she said, as if she had previously moved

about the house without noticing him, 'It's time he woke up.'

She prodded the paper.

'Maurice,' she said, 'we have a visitor.'

Maurice Horsborough appeared from behind the paper and looked at Denis through the spectacles he was wearing, then took them off as if better to see.

'Young Denis, is it?' he said. 'What are you doing here, my lad?'

'He's come with a message from Tim. Tim won't be home to tea.'

Maurice exchanged a glance with his wife, then looked again at Denis.

'Not home to tea,' he said, 'I see.' He looked suddenly tired, as if he would have preferred to retreat back into sleep, but instead he put on his spectacles again and stood up.

'Like to take your mother a cabbage from the garden?' he asked, and since it was hardly a question to which he expected a negative answer, he added without waiting, 'Come with me and we'll see what we can find,' as if cabbages were things which got lost and had to be found.

Denis followed him into the garden. They walked down the pathway to the tennis court, though Denis knew that the vegetable garden was the other way. The leaves had mostly fallen from the trees and had stayed where they had fallen, or where the wind had blown them. The garden had a neglected look, quite different from the day in summer when Denis had come here with Ted, but more than seasonal. There were signs of activity at the far end of the court, where a hole had been dug into a slope, and curved sheets of corrugated iron were propped against a tree.

'Air raid shelter,' his uncle said, as if anticipating the question. He looked at the lawn, morosely, as if it irritated him.

'I suppose we'll have to dig that up, like we did in the last lot,' he said. 'Dig it up and plant things,' as if it would be a ritual rather than a necessity.

He stood looking at it for a moment, as if planning it in his mind. Then he said, unexpectedly, 'Your mother used to play on there when she was a girl, before we dug it up for the war.' And again there was the suggestion of a ritual offering.

'Young Johnny Molesworth was after her at that time,' he went on. 'He was at Cambridge like Tim. He was killed at Ypres the year I went to France.'

He looked at the lawn as if seeing ghosts flitting through the thin autumn sunlight, Denis forgotten beside him. 'A lot of things would have been different if it hadn't been for the war,' he said, and was silent again as if he speculated on that other world that never happened. Remembering him again, he put his hand on Denis's shoulder.

'We'll find that cabbage,' he said, mundanely.

Riding back towards Smokers' Lane, having eventually made his escape, it occurred to Denis that his reception at his uncle's had been unusual. It had been unusual in that he had rarely in the past been encouraged to stay, and had even more rarely been spoken to as if he was an individual. After the cabbage was, with no great difficulty, found, he had been pressed to stay and eat something, and had only escaped by inventing a fictitious stomach complaint.

Freewheeling down the road, the cabbage slung from his handlebars in a carrier bag, he remembered something he had read in his father's newspaper to the effect that people were actually beginning to talk to each other on trains. 'It's the war,' he thought. 'It's just the war.'

Smokers' Lane was a disappointment. There was no sign of Jean and Ted. There were courting couples in profusion, handholding couples who immediately relinquished their grip when he approached; couples with arms round waists who brazenly kept their grip and simply stood to one side and ignored him, for he was only a boy. If he had but known it, in the dark undergrowth of the plantations on either side of the lane, there were undoubtedly other couples for whom handholding and the thrill of putting an arm round a waist had become somewhat tame. In that still protective but increasingly less effective, leafless environment, which was all they had, couples anticipated the coming 'Goodbyes' of war; the men snatching at what was being given as it had never been given before out of love, but could now be given in moral abundance, surely, to those who would soon be called upon to give their all! In any case, contrary to the impression held by succeeding generations, it had never been a question of knowing how to do it, so much as of having a place to do it in!

Tim was sitting with his mother and father in the living-room when he got back. The radio was on but turned low. He could tell that the conversation had been about himself because of the moment of silence which followed his arrival, before his mother stood up and turned up the radio slightly as if they were really listening to it. Someone was singing the currently favourite popular song, 'There'll always be an England,' the banality of the words of which seemed to have little effect on its enduring quality, for it lasted throughout the war. Before it ended Tim suddenly stood up, said 'Do you mind?' and without waiting for their answer, switched it off.

'If we start to believe that,' he said, as if to explain his action, 'we'll sit on our backsides and wait for God to win the war for us.'

'I'm sure He's on our side, Tim,' said Denis's mother.
'If He wants to take sides He hasn't much option,' said
Tim. 'Not when He looks at the others. It doesn't mean
that we've all that much to be proud of.'

He had worded it gently so as not to offend her,
knowing how much a part religion played in her life, but
he could not keep the strength of his feeling out of his
voice. A brief shadow of sadness passed across her face,
as if she sensed a gulf between them which would never
be bridged, but loved him for all that.

'You were going for a walk weren't you?' she asked.

He looked at her as if from a long way off. 'A walk?'
he said, as if it was the first time it had been mentioned.
Then, coming back from wherever it was he had been,
he jumped to his feet briskly and said, 'Of course I am!
Of course!' and looked at Denis. 'Come on young 'un,'
he said.

'You're to go with Tim,' his mother said, as if it had
been prearranged.

'He doesn't have to, but I'm sure he will,' Tim
rebuked her. 'You'll keep me company, won't you,
young 'un?'

Denis nodded his agreement, sensing some
prearrangement, but willing to go along with it. He liked
to be with Tim anyway, but was also curious. So much
seemed to have happened to him lately. Perhaps this was
something else. He had the feeling, which he had had on
and off for some time now, of being carried along on a
tide of change over which he had little or no control.

They took a short cut by the side of Cuddon rugby
ground which led to the park. It took them past the side
of the dark Victorian vicarage which adjoined the
Anglican church.

'You're in the choir, aren't you?' Tim asked him.
Denis agreed that he was.

'Like it?'

'It's all right.'

'What does all right mean?'

'We have some fun.'

'What sort of fun?'

The answer to this was longer in coming. Eventually Denis said, 'We laik about a bit,' using the old word of Norse origin which his father used to describe days off from the pit as play days. 'We work five and laik two,' he would say.

As if the word had reminded him, Tim asked, 'How's your friend who lives in the Square?'

'Ted? He's all right,' said Denis, reminded not of Ted, but of Jean.

'Father got work yet?'

'Not up to last time I saw him he hadn't.'

'When was that?'

'Last Friday week. We went to pictures in Caselborn.'

'Good?'

'It was all right,' said Denis, taking it all as small talk, half of his mind still on Ted and Jean. He was beginning to have a definite feeling about Ted which was new to him. It was jealousy.

'Who was the girl you were with in the park?' Tim asked. Coincidentally they were turning into Cuddon Park as he said it. It put all the other thoughts out of Denis's mind. It was like being caught with the burning cigarette and no redeeming excuse. 'Why are your fingers brown?' his mother had once asked him after a smoking session with Ted, and quick with inspiration he had said, 'I was holding Jack Hollis's cig for him.' The sick fear that was guilt stirred sourly in the pit of his stomach.

He said, because there was nothing else to say, 'It was Jean Colthard. Her father works at the baths.' Then he waited.

The park was almost empty. The young had gone home to tea, and their parents would not stroll there until evening was firmly established so that they could walk back in the intimacy of dusk.

'Is she your girl friend?' Tim asked.

'She's Ted's,' Denis said, with the hard bitter edge of truth which silenced Tim for a moment.

'Well,' he said eventually, 'I daresay you've gathered that your mother asked me to talk to you. One of her customers saw you in Caselborn, and the girl has a bad name it seems.'

Denis wondered if the bad name was 'teaser'. Instinctively he spoke in her defence.

'She's all right. There's nothing wrong with her.'

'I'm sure there isn't. I take all that with a pinch of salt. I know the kind of fictions invented in a small community. I said I'd have a word with you anyway about …' He paused, as if in some difficulty over the right expression, then said, 'Well, about girls and so on.'

Denis was silent and Tim took his silence as reflecting embarrassment, which to some extent it did. 'I daresay you know most of it anyway,' said Tim, reassuringly. 'Your father said he'd had a word with you.'

Denis remembered. Some three months before his father had taken him to a farm run by a tenant farmer who had been at school with him. He had launched into an unusually frank explanation of the processes of animal procreation. There had been some brief initial embarrassment, but then it had become simply interesting. Not a word had come from his father which might in any way have suggested any possible link with human behaviour, or any devious reason for the visit. When it was over his father had simply said, 'Well there you are, that's what it's all about!' Beads of perspiration had stood out on his forehead, but then it was a warm day. He had looked into the far distance, and repeated,

'That's what it's all about!' like a man who had been into battle and had, to his total surprise, survived. That Denis may not have grasped that the intention was to link the human situation with the cows and the sheep had not occurred to him.

'I suppose we can take that side of it as read?' said Tim.

Denis nodded thankfully.

'I wanted to talk to you anyway,' said Tim. 'Not just because your mother asked me to. I thought there'd be time enough when you were older perhaps, but now this damn war's on us we're all in a hurry to bare our souls.'

He was silent for a moment as if not knowing quite how to begin. Then he said, 'I've packed up at college. I'm joining the army. I'll have to sooner or later, so I reckon I might as well dive in. Your uncle's furious, thinks I'm chucking away my education not waiting till I've taken my degree. He's like a lot of other people, he thinks it's all going to be over by Christmas.'

'That's what Dad said. I don't think he believes it,' Denis added, 'I think he was saying it so I wouldn't be worried.'

'Are you?' Tim asked, glancing at him.

'Haven't thought about it.' It wasn't entirely true, but it was partly true. He thought about it rarely, in those terms. They would win, of course, he knew that. The possibility of defeat had not occurred to him. When he thought at all about the possible effect of the war on his own life it was in terms of excitement and glory rather than in terms of death or mutilation. The manuals on the treatment of gas victims had worried him somewhat, but his mind had not really accepted these things as potential realities.

'It wasn't the war I wanted to talk to you about anyway,' said Tim. 'If it goes on long enough for you to be called up you'll have to sort it out for yourself like the rest of us. Girls too,' he added, with a quick grin. 'All part of life's rich tapestry. What I really wanted to talk about was you, me, the family ... I don't suppose anyone's ever talked to you about that?'

'No,' Denis replied, truthfully.

'Your mother may do sooner or later, or maybe not. I don't know how she feels about it, not really. Up to a point, maybe, but it's not easy to really understand someone else's pain. Your father wouldn't speak unless she did. It affects him too, of course, but not in the same way.' He paused, then added, 'You don't know what I'm talking about, do you?'

Disconnected fragments of snatches of conversation between his mother and father overheard in the past flashed through Denis's mind. With them came the more recent image of his mother, sitting alone in the room at his uncle's house with her unexplained tears. From somewhere in his subconscious, as if in some dark little room in his head someone else had been working it out, he said, uncertainly, 'Grandfather?'

Tim glanced at him. 'How did you work that out?' he said.

'I don't know,' Denis said, which was also true.

'You're right, anyway. When your mother married your father, your grandfather cut her out of his will. He didn't want her to marry a collier. A lot of colliers feel the same way, but for different reasons. Your grandfather was a swine. I'm sorry about the word but I can't think of another. Your mother wouldn't want me to say that either, but it's true and I want you to know it ... Any questions?'

Denis shook his head.

'If it hadn't been for that,' Tim said, 'you'd have had the same opportunities I've had in life, for what they've been worth to me. I'm telling you all this because I've got a conscience about it. Not that that's any help to you.'

He glanced at Denis again as he said it, as if he expected some reaction, but Denis was silent, content to listen.

'What's your ambition in life?' Tim asked him, suddenly.

Denis thought for a moment, then said, as it came to him, 'I don't want to go down the pit.'

'Nothing you desperately want to do?'

Denis thought hard. It was as if someone had granted him a wish and he could not think of one. Eventually he said, 'I wanted to be a doctor once. I told Doris, but she said we were too poor.'

'She said what?'

'She said we were too poor,' said Denis, in a simple, matter of fact way.

'The cow!' said Tim, and Denis, glancing at him, slightly shocked, saw that his face was tight with anger.

He said, not in defence of Doris, but as a simple statement of fact; 'It's true!'

'That's not the point, is it?' Tim said, as if he expected Denis to understand what the point was. He started to walk faster so that Denis had some difficulty in keeping up with him. They had arrived at the far side of the park now. Tim stopped and looked back across the distance they had covered.

'If I get angry sometimes,' he said, 'it's because I think differently to the rest of the family. Your mother too. Even your father, though God knows why. It's something called politics, but I'm not going to bother you with that either, except to say that if ever you want to know why I think as I do you've only to come and ask me. You understand?'

'Yes,' said Denis.

'I'm going to speak to Dad. He should have done more. He'd probably say that he couldn't go against his father's wishes. That's just claptrap as far as I'm concerned. He's not a bad man. He's what he was brought up to be. I'm not apologising for him, I'm just apologising for his generation. You might have to apologise for mine one day.'

'I'm better off than Ted,' said Denis. 'He's down the pit.'

In bed that night he thought about the day. He always opened the curtains before he got into bed, so that the light from the street lamp outside would illuminate the room. Now, with the blackout, only the moon in the darkness. There was a searchlight on the common five miles away which occasionally probed the night sky as if searching for an enemy who inexplicably failed to appear. Bill Godber, the warden for the street, would sometimes find delight in the form of a chink of light from someone's carelessly blacked out window and would be aggressive in exercising his authority. He was a big pudding of a man who had been a sergeant in the army in the last war, but had been unemployed for the last seven years. Reinstated to a rank in society which gave him power, he secretly hoped that the war would never end.

As they had walked back home from the park, Tim had asked him again about his future and Denis had told him about the careers book and the few ideas he had had, most of which he had long discounted. He had asked him which other books he had read. It was a poor list. At school they were reading 'Wind in the Willows'. Denis loved it, but they were not allowed to take the books home.

'I'll lend you my copy,' Tim had said, 'in fact I'll rake out whatever I've got that I think might interest you. Read all you can. Anything you get excited about, follow it up. Use the library. Whatever they haven't got they can usually get. Books are a weapon in another war

– one that goes on for ever. That's why Hitler burned them.'

Back home, Denis's mother had made a fuss of Tim, grateful for the interest he was taking. His father too, Denis sensed, was pleased. They cared for him and were frustrated by their own inability to help him. His mother particularly, Denis sensed, wanted something for him she could never truly articulate. It was something, he knew, that women were prone to, this desire for ambition in their men. He wondered to what extent the fact that Ted was working, and not at school as he himself was, influenced Jean. He felt that he had some sort of attraction for her because of her general attitude and the confidence she bred in him, but she had gone with Ted, not to mention others he knew little of, when he felt sure that his own feelings were totally on display, that she must know he was hers for the taking. It must be school he thought. That and his age.

He wished desperately that there was something in the future that he could offer, but there was only himself. 'What's your ambition in life?' Tim had said, and he had been unable to think of anything except the negative answer, 'I don't want to go down the pit.' Would he go down the pit for Jean Colthard, if that was the qualification required? His mind fled from the thought.

Then again, the future seemed far away. It was like the war. People were called up, appeared briefly in uniform and then disappeared, but to where? Occasionally they came home on leave and walked down the street in uniform with some newly acquired gait, steel-shod boots clicking sharply on the pavement, people who were already apart, belonging in another place and now here simply as visitors.

He would go away, Denis thought, when he was old enough. 'You won't stay in Cuddon,' Jean had said, adding, 'It's a mucky hole.' He knew that himself, though with his limited experience of the world outside he had little to set it against. There were the films they saw occasionally, most of them American and as far from anything he could relate to as the moon. Once he had seen *David Copperfield*. He remembered it vividly, particularly the death of Ham Peggotty which had moved him, as nothing had ever done before, to tears. He also remembered Peggotty's boat, but then it reminded him of their own small room and kitchen which enclosed his life with the same warmth. It was familiar, something he knew and could identify with.

Where would he go? No picture formed in his mind for there was little to base it on. The darkness of the room was like a sea which his eyes could not penetrate, and beyond it outside the vaster darkness of the land in which he was born and which now was at war. He lay with his eyes open in the darkness, straining as if by some enormous effort he might be able to see. Sometimes he slept and then would be awake again, and eventually he could sleep no more and lay with his face to the window, eyes open, waiting for the light.

CHAPTER TEN

The first Christmas of the war was not very different from the last Christmas of peace the year before, so far as Cuddon was concerned. The blackout went on of course, and more uniforms were seen on the streets as men came home on leave, but most of the young males in Cuddon were exempt from military service by reason of working in the pit. Those who were not exempt but did not want to go were absorbed in the drive to recruit men for the mines as the arms drive built up and coal was needed to fuel the factories.

In the Square the change in the weather was more marked than any changes due to the war, with one exception. Men who had been out of work for years were now employed and money started to flow into homes which for years had known little but poverty and deprivation. Unemployment became the exception rather than the rule.

Doug Hoyle was one of the exceptions. His political role in the strike some fifteen years before still, it seemed, stood against him. Even the combination of the changing situation and his own brother's connection through Gospel Hall was not enough, it seemed, to overcome the prejudice against him. His bitterness towards the Union and their neglect of him in the past did not help, for he had developed a pride in his isolation that made it impossible for him to make the first approach. Even his handful of friends on the far Left were unable to persuade him to go and ask for work. They made the attempt, probably because even now they were ashamed of their inability to help a man who, more than most, had suffered for the obduracy of his beliefs.

'What do you want of us, lad?' one of them asked impatiently, meeting him on the street when Ted was out with him one day.

'If you need to ask you'd not understand if I told you,' his father had replied, and the man had shaken his head as if it was beyond him, with the implication that Hoyle was being unreasonable.

Even Ted began to feel that his father had pushed the point too far, though he would never have told him so. His heart ached as his father's isolation increased. For a time, after Ted first started work, they had taken to walking out together in the evenings when Ted was not seeing Jean, but as winter came on his father would rarely leave the house.

As if he sensed Ted's concern, Hoyle suddenly said one evening, 'It's as well I'm not in work. Who'd see to things in the house with your mother as she is?'

'Aye, well it'd mean our Jessie stopping off school and missing her education,' Ted said, wanting to assure his father that he had a valid function in life.

'It might come to that anyway, if your mother goes,' said Hoyle, giving the first indication that he knew his wife was dying, for it was no longer a question of if she would die, but when.

In the early stages of her illness she had spent some

time downstairs, sitting silently for the most part opposite to her husband, watching him read. She read nothing herself, though she would listen interminably to the radio which Ted had bought them.

For some weeks now she had remained upstairs in bed, her condition gradually deteriorating. They had taken the radio upstairs for her, and sometimes Hoyle would put down the book he was reading and say, 'I'll happen go and listen to the wireless a bit,' and go up to the bedroom. It was always for the radio. He never once said that he was going to see his wife.

Yet Ted knew that this was often the reason he stayed up there, listening to programmes in which he could not possibly have had any interest. It was as if he had to have another reason to go. As if the real reason might suggest that he was 'soft'.

A slash of colour in his otherwise grey, meandering routine was the visits Jean made. Regarding their relationship as permanent and settled since their first visit to the ruined farmhouse (there had, of course, since been others) he had brought her home to the house one evening shortly afterwards. To his father he had simply said, 'This is Jean,' and had gone upstairs to the room where he slept, to change. When he came down again they were deep in conversation, and his father had suddenly laughed at something she said, a rare sound in the house. Whenever she came after that he would brighten at her entrance. She would quip at him and he would quip back, sharpening his wits on her, enjoying the pretence she made of disagreeing with him on almost everything simply to draw him out. Then they would both turn on Ted, joining voices to make fun of some of his more obvious failings. It was always him against the two of them; a game.

When she had gone Hoyle would go back to his book again, but from time to time would look up and smile, as if going over their conversation again in his head. Jessie too took pleasure in the brightness this brought to her father's life, and her own relationship with Jean became warmer because of it so that soon a real friendship developed. It was as if they had added someone entirely fresh to their family, and the newness lightened the added depression brought to the house by the constant reminder of the dying woman upstairs. Then, too, the children had stayed on at Ted's aunt's since their mother first became ill and it began to look as if it might be a permanent arrangement. To Ted it meant that for almost the first time he could remember he slept alone.

Sometimes when he came in the house Jean would already be there. He would hear the laughter from the scullery, and Jessie would join in, and his father would look up as he entered and smile as if to say, 'Just listen to those two.'

On the day before Christmas Eve, when he came off shift the house was empty downstairs. He looked in the oven, but almost unbelievably there was nothing there. He had never known his father not have food ready for him when he came off shift. In the scullery there was no sign of any having been prepared for either himself or Jessie who would soon be home from school. He went back into the living-room to see if his father had left some message to explain his absence, but could not find one.

With his foot on the first step of the stairs it came to him suddenly, the thought of why this unusual state of affairs should be. He stopped and looked up the narrow, dark stairway. He listened, but heard nothing. He thought, 'She's dead,' and listened again while the thought echoed through his mind. Then he started to climb the stairs.

At the door to the bedroom he hesitated. Since he was a child he had hardly entered it. It was not just the thought of her death that made him hesitate now, but something which had existed for a long time in his mind, a kind of taboo which he could not have begun to explain. Then he went inside.

The curtains were closed, but then they were closed for most of the time now for she had complained that the light hurt her eyes. There was light in the room, though, for the fabric was thin and faded with constant washing over the years and in places was coming apart.

As his eyes became used to the dimness he could see her outline on the bed. Since she had taken to it he had seen her only once, when his father had said, 'Your mother wants to see you.' He had gone up the stairs and put his head round the door only, thankfully, to find her asleep. Then he had conveniently forgotten and his father had not reminded him, as if he understood that there was no one there that Ted wished to see. It had troubled Ted, though, this reluctance to see her even when she had asked that he should. At times it almost brought him to make the attempt, but never quite. It was for most of the time as if she had already gone.

He would not know death if he saw it, for he had seen no dead person before. Why he moved to the bedside now he did not know. He simply found himself there looking down at her. He had no memory of her other than as a heavily built woman with a loud voice, slatternly habits and, grotesquely, beautiful bright gold hair. It lay on the pillow now, spread around her casually as if she had simply dropped it there, but the body under the thin layer of blankets was not that of the woman he had known. So emaciated was she by the illness that it was almost as if she was no longer there. The face too was hollowed down to the bone so that he barely recognised it. There was only the hair. The eyes opened and looked at him. She was alive. His instinct to flee was stronger than if he had found her dead.

She said, 'You've come back then,' and the voice was thin and brittle like that of a child.

'There was nobody in,' he said, finding his own voice.

'He was called to a union meeting.'

'Dad?'

'They sent for him.'

Her voice had no expression, as if she knew that what she said was important but that it no longer mattered to her.

'Will he be working?'

'We shall see,' she said, as if even at the point of death she trod still the path of uncertainty. She turned her head away for a moment, then looked back at him. 'You've got a girl he tells me?'

He was embarrassed. Her eyes troubled him so that he could not bring himself to look directly at her.

'Aye,' he said, simply acknowledging the fact.

'Colthard's lass from the baths?'

'Aye.'

'Lively young lass … full of life …' The word reverberated around the room. She said it again. 'Life,' she said … Her eyes travelled the room as if she looked for a familiar face in a crowd.

'I was like that when I was a lass.'

He remembered the time at the farmhouse when in his mind he had seen her pass through the garden, young, slim and smiling, someone he knew and yet had never known. He looked down at her and the two figures blended, never to be separated, another pain that would never go away.

Seeing him looking at her she put up her hand as if she would hide the face he saw, but then dropped it as if she realised the hopelessness of it all.

'I was like that when I had you,' she said, 'but the Square soured me.'

Her eyes closed. He waited for a moment, but she did

not open them. He no longer had the urge to flee. For some reason he wanted her to go on talking. Perhaps if he waited she would. He walked to the window and looked through the gap where the curtains did not quite meet.

The Square was below in all its barrenness. Now that it was winter the smaller children who were not at school stayed in the small, steamy kitchens to play. He liked it better in the winter. In the winter you simply passed through it to the house, and the life in the other houses was contained in them so that it was quieter and more private. He liked it best of all when the snow fell and covered the slag heaps and the debris in the Square so that it was almost like any other place.

It had soured her, she had said, yet it was the only home he had known. He could not dream of another different life as he suspected Jessie did when she read her books. He could not live, he would have said had he known the word, vicariously. He could only live with facts.

His mother as he had known her was a fact, as was his indifference to her in recent years. It was a fact, too, that she was dying. Who was this other woman then of whom increasingly a picture was forming in his mind? 'I was like that when I was a lass,' she had said, speaking of Jean.

Would it be for them as it had been for his mother and father, this erosion of life? He turned to the bed as if she might give him the answer, this new wise woman whom he had spoken to as if for the first time. But her eyes were closed and he could see that she slept. It had all come too late.

He was in the scullery when his father came home, preparing a meal for himself as best he could, for he was hopeless in the house.

'I was hoping to be back by the time you came off shift,' said Hoyle. 'I'd to go out.'

'Mam told me,' said Ted.

'You've seen her?'

'I went up and talked to her for a bit.'

Hoyle looked at him, as if he would ask him something more, then simply said, 'I'm glad you've seen her.'

There was a straightness about the way he stood as if he had been crouched for a long time and was drawing himself up to stretch the unused muscles out.

'Harry Barnes came for me,' he said, almost casually, as if it was an everyday thing for him to leave the house for some definite purpose.

'Oh aye?' Ted said, pretending no more than usual interest.

'They've taken me on as checkweighman.'

Ted turned and looked at his father. The eyes shone clear and bright out of the thin, lined face.

'That's what you wanted. What you've always said.'

'Aye, a job given by the men, not the management.'

'It's been in their power to give it for years.'

'Management would have said nay to it. They've the right.'

'Why not now?'

'They can't afford to fall out with the union now, we've a war on.'

'All these years,' said Ted.

'Aye, well they've done it now,' said his father, seeing only the bright moment, as if the years of depression no longer counted.

'All these years,' said Ted.

Ted's mother died on New Year's Day and was buried four days later. He had gone up the stairs to see her every day since the first time, but she rarely spoke again

156

for she was now heavily sedated with morphine. Doug Hoyle spent most of his time in the room, though he slept now in the same room as Ted.

Jean was at the house the night she died. They had arranged to go to the pictures, but when he said he would rather not go she did not press him. Because of the atmosphere in the house she was more subdued, helping Jessie with jobs in the house or sitting with them listening to the radio while Jessie did her homework. She could never understand how this was possible.

'How can you do it with this racket going on?' she would ask.

Jessie would simply smile, for except in the early mornings she had rarely had better conditions. The evening her mother died she was out, having, she said, arranged to see a friend. He wondered if it was the secret boy friend, and who it might be, and what their relationship would be. He could not equate the physical excitement of his own relationship with Jean in terms of Jessie. It was not in her character as he knew it, or thought he knew it, except in terms of marriage which was a long way off. Not that he thought less of Jean for the way in which she had given herself. It was just that they were different people.

So they were alone in the room, but she would not sit with him for long. She was restless, frequently getting up to examine something in the room.

'Why can't you settle?' he asked her, a touch of irritation in his voice, for after the first few weeks they had ceased to handle each other with the delicacy of new lovers.

'You're watching me all the time.'

'Who is?'

'You are,' she said. 'You've been like it for days, now.'

'You're kidding yourself.'

'Why do you watch me?' she asked, instinctively aware that he knew it to be true.

'You're nice to watch,' he grinned, and she was obliged to accept this though she knew there was some other, deeper reason.

'I'm not going to fly away, you know,' she said.

He could not tell her that whenever he looked at her he remembered what his mother had said when he talked to her about Jean. 'I was like that when I was a lass,' she had said. It had become an obsession with him, now, watching Jean and seeing the woman upstairs.

'The Square soured me,' his mother had added.

Would it sour Jean, too?

CHAPTER ELEVEN

Still hoping that Britain and France would sue for peace after his rapid conquest of Poland, Hitler held back from further attacks on other fronts while the other two countries used this respite to build up their forces. Later known as the 'phoney war', it lasted until the spring of 1940. The only activity was at sea. An aircraft-carrier, the *Courageous,* was sunk in September, and the battleship *Royal Oak* was sunk in Scapa Flow the following month. Shortly before Christmas, morale in the Navy was boosted by the scuttling of the *Graf Spee* in Montevideo.

Morale in Cuddon was higher than it had been for years. The beginning of the end of the long lean period of the depression had started with rearmament, and already an era of possibly full employment was in sight. In the first months of the war there seemed to be no real shortage of anything, and the growing earning population spent its new found wealth largely in hoarding things which instinctively, and with the experience of a previous war, they knew might eventually be in short supply.

In the cellar below the shop, Denis's mother hoarded tins of food and all the sugar she could get her hands on. 'You're like a bloody squirrel,' his father complained once when she entered the house, flushed with triumph, bearing another twenty odd pounds of sugar. He muttered something about it being unpatriotic.

'If you want to carry on with that dirty habit,' she had said, meaning his cigarettes, 'you'd better start hoarding yourself. It all comes in ships,' she added, with the instinct of an island race.

Months later, accidentally pulling out a drawer so that it fell off its runners, Denis had found the space beneath packed with cartons of Goldflake. He had taunted his father with the discovery.

'I thought you said it was unpatriotic, Dad,' he had said.

'They're all at it,' his father had said, somewhat shamefaced. 'Not that that's any excuse. We give in to the Devil and call it human nature.'

'Shame!' grinned Denis.

'I am ashamed,' his father said. 'But don't tell your mother. I should never hear the end of it.'

Tim had joined the army. Towards the end of March 1940 he came home on leave in his private's uniform, calling in at the shop on his way from the station to his home. Denis came home from school to find him asleep on a chair in the living-room. As he came into the house from the shop he had shouted, 'I'm back, Mum,' in his usual way, and she had darted in from the kitchen at the back with her hand to her mouth, bidding him be silent.

She was too late, for the shout had awoken Tim. He opened his eyes and looked at Denis; 'Hello, young 'un,' he said.

He was thinner, Denis thought, than when they had last seen him. His hair was trimmed short back and sides, whereas before it had covered the tops of his ears and had occasionally hung down over his eyes in a rather poetic way. The uniform fitted him loosely as if he was caught between sizes, and the roughness of the cloth contrasted sharply with the smoothed out, tircd face. There was a canvas pack with webbing straps from which a tin helmet hung on the couch, and a kitbag which was bulky and looked impossible to carry.

'I'm sorry he woke you,' Denis's mother said.

'I'm not,' said Tim, 'it's time I got on home.'

'They're expecting you?'

'Tomorrow. I got here faster than I thought.'

'I could use the telephone at the bottom of the road. Your father would bring the car down.'

'He's still running it?' Tim asked.

'He was down in it yesterday.'

'We're living in a fool's paradise, aren't we?' Tim said. Denis's mother did not reply, but from her expression he could see that she knew what Tim meant.

'I can carry his kitbag,' Denis said, optimistically.

They both smiled, but Tim said, 'That'll be a help. Better just try it for size first.'

Denis lifted one end, put his back to it and tried to raise it on to his shoulder. He got it there, almost, but the weight made him sit down suddenly and they both laughed.

'There's a knack to it you see,' said Tim, covering Denis's embarrassment. 'If you can carry the pack it'll help.'

The pack was heavy, but easier. He trotted along beside Tim up the dark road, wishing it was light and that his friends could see him. Already there was an aura about a uniform, and a resentment of this from those who were civilians and wanted to stay civilians. Later, when they opened the new munitions works at Raison, some twelve miles away, the resentment developed into bitter hostility on both sides. The men in uniform resented the high wages paid to the workers in comparison to the pittance of their service pay, but even more they resented the stories of skiving and the fact that it was a reserved occupation. Few of them resented the fact that mining was also a reserved occupation, for they were aware of the danger, and danger they understood. Though not yet bloodied in battle they were more aware of the possibility than the average civilian whose life had barely altered for the worse. Moreover, at this stage in the war many were volunteers, like Tim, who had joined up idealistically to fight Fascism rather than wait to be conscripted.

'Any ideas about what you want to do yet?' Tim asked him suddenly as they walked.

Denis was silent for a moment. Since he had last talked to Tim he had formed a very definite idea of what he wanted to do. He had not spoken about it to anyone, because he knew instinctively that for a number of reasons it was impossible. If he could mention it to anyone at all it would be to Tim, but even so it was a moment or two before he said, 'I want to go to sea.'

Tim was as slow in replying as he himself had been in the telling. Eventually he said, simply, 'Why?'

Again Denis found difficulty in answering, and when the answer came it was inconclusive. 'I don't know,' he said, shrugging his shoulders against the weight of the pack and at the same time wondering if it was strictly true. Did he not know or did he not want to say? At the back of his mind there was a reason, but it was a reason he instinctively knew that Tim would not approve of. He tried to bring himself to express it, searching for words, for it was easier to say some things in the darkness, even to Tim.

'Just something you feel, is it?' Tim asked, making Denis's struggle towards what he sensed was an important truth no longer necessary; letting him off the hook.

'There's an advertisement in *Boy's Own Paper* for Sparks,' Denis said. 'You do six months at a college and then you go to sea.'

'What's the problem?'

There was more than one. Two seemed insurmountable.

'Mum,' said Denis, rightly expressing the worst.

'Yes, I can see that,' said Tim.

They plodded again into silence, Denis aware of Tim's mind at work beside him, grateful that the whole idea had not been immediately shot to pieces as he instinctively knew it would have been had he mentioned it at home.

'She must know if the war goes on, as I think it will, you'll have to go into something or other,' said Tim, eventually. 'What did she say when you told her?'

'I haven't told her.'

'Your father?'

'I haven't told anybody but you,' Denis said, conferring his trust, and Tim, as if he recognised this, again blessed it with a moment of silence, before he asked, 'Any other problems?'

'You've got to pay,' Denis said, realising as he said it that it was almost as insurmountable an obstacle as the first.

'Nothing else?' Tim asked him.

Again Denis struggled to bring himself to express his reasons for the desperate longing he had for this thing. They had learned a poem at school once, learned it to the point of boredom as they learned so many things. It was 'Sea Fever' by John Masefield, and he could have recited it accurately and even discussed it with some understanding. But the feeling he had was not the feeling behind the poem; the interest he had was more material than that.

'Your mother's bound to worry,' Tim said, eventually. 'It's not much of a war to date, but the ships are going down already. The sea's our lifeline and if it's cut we've had it, and the Jerries are going to bash at it as hard as they can.'

'I know,' said Denis, feeling already the danger and the glory. He would have discounted the danger, but without the danger there was no glory. He had no fear because his mind would only really comprehend it when faced with the cause. You did not learn fear from books.

'The money,' Tim said; 'well, that's easier.'

Denis was surprised at this. Money had always been the most insurmountable aspect of any problem. He could think of very little, being young and without it, that could not be solved by the availability of the right amount of money.

'You want me to help?' Tim asked eventually. 'I mean, you want it badly enough to face the consequences? I can't protect you from your mother's feelings. I can only try and smooth the path and see if something can't be done about the money.'

'I want to go,' said Denis.

'But you don't know why?'

Again Denis struggled with the words and the desire to be honest that might compel him to speak them and lead to some kind of understanding that he felt a vague need to achieve.

'It's just a feeling,' he said, ultimately, opting out on the moment.

It was years before the reasons were eventually clarified and, but only retrospectively, he understood.

Maurice Horsborough and his wife were having tea in the kitchen when Denis and Tim entered the house. Horsborough greeted his son almost shyly, standing back to allow Tim's mother to embrace him, then holding out his hand to be shaken. It was an oddity to Denis, this shaking of hands between father and son. His own father would have reached out his hand and roughly rubbed his hair, or taken his shoulders and looked into his eyes with warm affection. Was it something that happened as you grew older, he wondered, this distancing? He found himself fleetingly hoping it would not happen between his father and himself.

Tim, his mother's arm still round his shoulder, said, 'This lad's carried my pack all the way up from their house and he's not had his tea yet.'

Denis's aunt looked at him, smiling. Her eyes were slightly moist and there was a softness and unsteadiness about her expression that did not fit his image of her.

'We can soon see to that,' she said. 'Sit down, both of you. Let me take this.'

She tried to lift the kitbag from where Tim had leaned it against the wall, but it refused to be lifted from the floor.

'Oh my God,' she said, 'how do you manage it?'

'Easy when you know how,' said Tim.

'We used to carry that lot and a fourteen pound rifle as well,' said Maurice Horsborough, as if to reassure her that the lot of the private soldier had improved. He tried the kitbag himself, then put it down. 'I wouldn't like to do it now,' he said.

They sat at the table while Margaret Horsborough vanished into the recess of the pantry.

'We've lost Mrs. Williams,' Horsborough said. 'Her husband's got work on munitions. They've moved. Nobody seems to want to take the job on. In any case,' he added, in the phrase that came to be used as an explanation of any departure from a previous norm, 'there's a war on, isn't there?'

'Where's Doris?' Tim asked.

'She's running the Caselborn shop for me. Young Charlton's been called up, and Barton's ill. Discovered some sort of muscular complaint. Probably getting ready to try and dodge the call up when his age group's called.'

'You think they'll ever get that far?' Tim asked.

'Twenty-seven's the top age now,' his father replied. 'I reckon they'll be calling the forty-year-olds before the year's out! The price of clothing's doubled already. Sixty shilling or more for a suit at the Thirty Shilling Tailors now. They'll bring in rationing soon. They say Churchill's against it, but it's got to come.'

'You're not one of these people who think it'll all be over by Christmas then?' asked Tim.

'I said that before last Christmas. Not any more. We're just waiting for it to start, aren't we?'

Tim fiddled with the cutlery on the table. His eyes went to the pantry from which his mother had still not emerged. He lowered his voice; 'I might be moved on soon,' he said.

His father looked at him, then at the pantry door.

'What am I thinking of,' he said. 'You must be dying for a drink. Come in the other room.'

Tim stood up. 'You stay and talk to Mum, young 'un,' he said to Denis. He followed his father out, saying, 'You've still got a drop or two left, then?'

The door had barely closed when his aunt came out of the pantry.

'They've gone for a drink,' Denis volunteered.

'Left you to be conscripted? Can you peel potatoes?'

Denis nodded.

'You'd be a bit of a dim wit if you couldn't, wouldn't you?' she said, smiling.

Helping her while the two men were away he found some of the shyness he had always felt with these relatives, even at times with Tim, gradually disappear.

She chatted to him constantly, though her eyes were always going to the door, asking him about his mother and father as if they were people she had not seen for years, as indeed they were in any real sense.

'We must get together more,' she said, once. 'We've all got to stick together through this, haven't we?' And again Denis was aware, as he had been on his previous visit, of a warming in a relationship that had always seemed to him to lack anything but the accident of birth.

Then Doris came home and immediately everything was as it had always been. He carried on peeling the potatoes, glad to have something to do. It was better to be ignored while you worked than while sitting, waiting to be noticed. There was something in her manner, which he could not at that time have described, which diminished him. In a vague sort of way he was conscious that she herself felt diminished by the relationship. It was a feeling compounded of various incidents in the past when, being with friends of her own class, she had ignored him; or the fact that in all the years he could remember she had never visited them at home as Tim did. There was an arrogance in her manner which he was mostly conscious of because of its absence in Tim. Why she should feel this way and Tim should not was an enigma to him, and in spite of Tim he was conscious of being hurt and belittled by it. Lately there was another feeling which only later he recognised as resentment. In an odd sort of way it was tied up with other influences in his life; with his relationship with Ted and his mother's attitude towards this; even with his reasons for wanting to go to sea, so far as he understood them, for it was all complex and beyond him at this point in his life. He had once complained to his father that Doris had passed him on the street in Caselborn and had affected not to recognise him. His father had simply said, 'Take no notice. Take no heed.' Then had added, 'There's nowt so queer as folk,' as if this was the full and satisfactory explanation.

'Tim's come home,' his aunt said when Denis entered the room.

'I know,' said Doris. 'I went in the lounge. They're having a man to man.'

'Not argument?' her mother queried, anxiously.

'Not the usual raised voices and spiky silences if that's what you mean.'

'I think they're beginning to understand one another.'

'You're an optimist, aren't you?'

'They're trying, anyway.'

'There's a war on. We're all pretending we're one big, happy, united family. What rubbish! I mean, look at this family. What have we in common with ...' She stopped abruptly and Denis, looking up, saw in the mirror that hung over the fireplace that his aunt was shaking her head and pointing ... Because of the reversal in the mirror it was a moment before he realised that she was pointing at him.

After tea Tim said, 'I'll walk back down with Denis.'

'Good heavens, he's not a baby,' said Doris.

'You don't mind, do you?' Tim asked his mother, ignoring Doris. 'I've a whole week's leave.'

'No, of course not,' his mother said.

'I've some books to get from upstairs,' Tim said to Denis. 'I'll not be a couple of minutes.'

He left the room and with his going Denis felt lost among strangers, and sat there waiting to be spoken to or not as the case might be. Doris stood up from the table and started to clear it, sharply and more noisily than was necessary as if by doing so she wished to make a point.

'I cleared some of his books into the spare room,' said Denis's aunt. 'I'd better make sure he can find them.'

She went out and Doris, the table cleared and the pots

piled on the draining board, vented her feelings, whatever they were, in the process of washing up. Denis, who had removed himself from the scene in the usual way by looking down at the piece of table immediately in front of him, lookcd up and saw that his uncle was watching him. There was a not unkindly look in his eye and his expression was friendly and interested.

'Tim tells me you want to go to sea,' he said.

Denis, as if to affirm that he knew the impossibility of his ambition, and largely for Doris's benefit, said, 'It was just an idea. I could join the navy when my call up comes.'

His uncle smiled. 'A good three years before that happens. They can raise the top age but they won't lower the minimum.'

'You'll be going down the pit, won't you?' said Doris, throwing it from the sink as part of her vendetta.

'Mum and Dad won't want me to,' Denis said.

'There's a lot of things we don't want in life. We just have to face up to facts, don't we?' she replied, as if she was a veteran in the art of facing facts.

'This course,' his uncle said, as if Doris had not spoken, 'where is it?'

'It's over in Lancashire,' said Denis, with the same sort of finality as if it had been on the other side of the Atlantic Ocean.

'You'd have to live in then,' his uncle said. 'How long does it last, this course?'

'Six months.'

'What's your mother going to think about it?'

'She wouldn't want me to.'

'Your father?'

'Dad wouldn't mind,' Denis said.

'But you've not asked him?'

'You've got to pay,' said Denis. 'We couldn't afford it.'

'Of course they couldn't!' Doris chipped in from the sink.

Maurice Horsborough looked at his daughter's back, his face expressionless, except that for a moment there was something akin to disagreement in his failure to react. Then Tim called Denis from upstairs and Denis rose to go to him.

'Not just a passing fancy this business about wanting to go to sea?' his uncle asked.

'No,' said Denis, hoping that he wasn't again to be asked his motives, which always confused him, and Horsborough's eye was sharp and enquiring as he asked.

'Better go and see what Tim wants then,' his uncle said, and Denis left the kitchen and mounted the stairs. Near the top he dropped his cap over the banister and had to go down again to retrieve it. As he picked it up he heard Doris's voice through the half open kitchen door.

'Of course they can't afford it,' she was repeating. 'Why didn't you pooh-pooh the whole thing?'

'If it hadn't been for your grandfather they'd have been able to afford it,' Horsborough said, 'just as we've been able to afford things for you.'

'His mother was a fool to marry the man,' said Doris. 'You can tell she's regretted it.'

'You don't know that. If she hadn't married him she'd have had half your grandfather's estate. I'd have said she must have cared quite a lot to sacrifice that.'

'Infatuation,' said Doris. 'It passes. Then you pay the price.' Denis wondered what infatuation was, then heard her say, 'In any case, if you've such a conscience about it why haven't you done something?'

He listened for his uncle's reply, but at the same moment heard his aunt descending the stairs and started towards them as if he had only just left the kitchen.

'Tim's room's the first on the right,' she said as she reached the bottom of the stairs where Denis was waiting. She looked at him, and again there was the unsteadiness in her normally placid expression which he had seen when she looked at Tim. She put out her hand and touched his hair.

'You're far too young to go to sea,' she said, 'far too young!' And he realised that Tim must have told her too.

He had never been in Tim's room before, and only up the stairs after having asked permission to use the toilet. It was a large room, as big, Denis thought, as the whole of the upstairs at their own house. Framed photographs from school and university hung on the walls and, incongruously, an official looking sign which read 'Ladies Only'. It was furnished as a bed sitting-room, and almost the whole of one wall was a large built-in bookcase with the shelves completely filled. Tim was stood in front of it as Denis entered, selecting books from the shelves. Denis waited, looking round at the room. It impressed him and was the kind of room he would have expected Tim to have, and in future years, whenever he was preparing a room for himself, he was conscious of the fact that to some extent he was trying to recreate his first impressions of the room in which he now stood.

Tim turned with a handful of books and held them out to him. 'Ever read Joseph Conrad?'

'No,' said Denis, taking them, unsure whether the name Joseph Conrad was the author or the title of a book.

'They'll tell you as much about the sea as pretty well anything,' Tim said. He picked up another pile. 'These are for your friend's father, the one who lives in the Square. I promised them a long time ago, but with one damn thing and another … They still live there, do they?'

'Yes,' said Denis, surprised at the question. If you

lived in the Square you lived there for ever. There was nowhere else to go.

'If you want to borrow them after he's finished them you can. They're politics. You might not be interested, but you'll find that out for yourself. I thought I'd walk back down with you and take them on. He must think I've forgotten. If I don't take them now I probably will forget. I might be away for quite some time.'

He looked round the room as if he had just become aware of it.

'Always used to take this place for granted,' he said. 'The army's cured me of that, among other things.' He didn't say what the other things were.

CHAPTER TWELVE

The library was the most modern public building in Cuddon. Big enough to serve a large community, it had been built following a comment by the Prince of Wales on a tour of the depressed areas in the late Twenties. The Prince, it was said, had asked to see the library and had expressed his disgust with the county authority on being told that no library existed. 'Bloody disgusting' was the expression attributed to him when the story was recounted locally. True or not, it fitted the character of a man whom many working class people had come to have a high regard for, and the library came into being the following year. Largely patronised by children who queued at the librarian's desk to ask for 'a love book for me mam and a thriller for me dad', it had a less used but reasonably adequate non-fiction section and a small reference library.

Ted paid his first visit to the library in the winter of 1940. The shift his father was working made it difficult for him to change his books and Ted had offered to do it for him. He was surprised to find that most of the books his father read were specially ordered from lists which he supplied to the librarian, a service with which Ted was impressed. On the evening Ted visited the library none of the books Hoyle had ordered had yet come. Rather than return empty handed he accepted the cards the librarian gave him and went inside.

The choice staggered him as he wandered from shelf to shelf. It seemed to him, to whom reading was an alien occupation related to school or to the boredom created in him by the books Jessie had tried to get him to read, that all the books in the world must be gathered here. He did not know where to start. Occasionally a title would catch his eye and he would take down the book and open it, but with no means of knowing whether it would meet his father's needs. As closing time approached and the library emptied he had found nothing he could confidently have taken away and was relieved when the librarian approached him.

'You brought Mister Hoyle's books in, didn't you?' she asked.

'Aye,' he said, 'but I'm dashed if I know what to take him back.'

'There's a book on William Lovett I've been saving for him,' she said, 'and a Worker's Educational Association pamphlet on Education. That's my own, but I thought he might like to read it.'

He accepted them with relief and she stamped the book and took back one of the cards.

'You're not a member yourself,' she said. 'I'm surprised your father's enthusiasm hasn't rubbed off on you.'

'I work at the pit,' said Ted, as if this excluded him from the world of books, but then he remembered that his father, also, worked at the pit and felt ashamed of the way in which he had excused himself. So he said, 'I'd like to join, though,' and accepted the application card she gave him and made his way home.

Jessie was out, visiting the children at their aunt's where they had taken up permanent and happy residence in the comparative luxury of that spinster's home. He made up the fire and switched on the radio to listen to the news. With little to report in a war which had been declared but was not it seemed actively happening, the news was largely composed of trivialities. Sporting events continued as usual and the lives of the great were reported in detail.

Bored and indifferent he eventually switched it off. He wondered if Jean would come that evening. She had lately shown a disinclination to visit the ruined farmhouse, complaining that it was too cold, which in truth it was despite the fires, for the wind howled through the gaps in the floorboards and around the door, cooling even his own more or less permanent passion. He longed now for the time to come when they would be of an age to marry. A man in all other respects, he lacked only the final consummation of the double bed under a roof which, although rented, he could regard as his own.

That she sensed his frustration he did not doubt, for he made no secret of it.

'You don't care any more,' he had said to her one cold night when she had simply wanted to stay in the house with Jessie and himself. They had quarrelled, and on more than one occasion since. He did not realise that her frustration was as real, if not as intense, as his own. She had also shown a reluctance for the kind of urgent but ultimately frustrating petting in alleyways on their way home from the pictures, places to which they were driven because there was nowhere else to go.

One evening, coming home on the last bus from Caselborn which meant that they had to walk across the pit fields, they had a long stumbling argument in the darkness as they walked. It had been the usual glossy

American film about cosy middle class American life, where everyone seemed to own a car and a house of more than ample proportions.

'Why can't we live like that?' she said.

'Who wants to?'

'I do.'

'You'd better go there then,' he replied, feeling on safe ground, for he scarcely believed that America existed except as a background for the film makers. He added, 'It's not real. Nobody lives like that.'

'Some people here do, anyway,' she said. 'People like the Horsboroughs.'

'Those buggers!'

'Don't swear. What do you know about them anyway?'

'I've been there. I went there with Denis one day.'

She was silent for a moment. He could tell she was impressed. He fictionalised to impress her further.

'We played tennis. We played tennis and drank lemonade and talked about politics.'

'What do you know about politics?'

'I read about politics,' he lied.

'You'd be better reading about something that'd get us out of this mucky hole.'

He had been through the argument about Cuddon too often to want to repeat it now. She hated Cuddon.

He said, 'Politics can take you away.'

'How?'

'Like it did for Jack Dawson.'

Dawson was the local member of parliament, a man who had risen through the ranks of the union to represent the constituency. There was a drawback to Dawson, however, in terms of the argument. He lived in the same terrace house he had always lived in and his lifestyle seemed hardly to have changed. Even Ted found this difficult to understand. He expected Jean to pick on it, but she didn't, and then he understood why.

'He's got a flat in London,' she said.

It was something he hadn't known. He realised it was something that impressed her, the flat in London. She was in some ways, he thought, like Jessie. She dreamed of another world. The fact that she lived outside the Square in a house attached to the baths which had a bathroom and a toilet inside the house was not enough. To meet her dream it would not be enough for him simply to leave the Square for one of the better streets in Cuddon. Her sights were set beyond Cuddon, while his own ambitions were firmly rooted here; in his desire to ultimately work at the face; to be a king, within the confines of the world he knew.

She said, after a time, 'Will you go in for politics?'

'I expect I will,' he said, to please her, though nothing at that time was further from his mind.

Things had been better between them for some weeks after that. Then one night in the house she had picked up one of his father's books and had browsed through it, and then had turned to him and said: 'I don't know how you can understand all this.'

His father had looked up from the book he himself had been reading.

'Him? Understand that? He's never read a book on politics in his life.'

So they were back to where they had been, except that now she queried everything he said and their relationship was less than it had been. Yet he wanted her more than ever and was ashamed that he had lied to her. Yet had it been a lie? More and more at the pit he had realised that politics were woven inextricably into the working life of the miners. In the disputes as to the amount of dust in the tubs as distinct from good saleable coal; demands for greater safety, and for pithead baths so that men could return from work clean and not to houses where all too often their only facility was a hand-filled tin bath on the hearthrug so that, often too weary to rid themselves of their ingrained dirt they would carry it with them between the bed sheets.

He thought of all these things in the silence that followed when he switched off the radio. His father had studied politics for most of his adult life, yet where had it got him. Condemned to a wilderness of no work after the General Strike, bitter at the inability or indifference of the union for which he had fought to prevent his victimisation, did he still believe in the fair and effective power of organised labour? He read about politics, but without involvement. When the union sent for him because they no longer needed to strike to have him reinstated in work he had gone cap in hand, giving them his immediate forgiveness for the failure to even care about his lost years, seeking even to excuse them the failure.

At work he had heard men talk of the class struggle, using political words and phrases which he did not understand as neither, he felt, did the majority of his mates. For most of them politics was simply the battle for higher wages with better conditions dragging some distance behind. That it might affect their lives outside work as some of the more politically minded would argue, the great mass of the men seemed neither to care nor to wish to understand. What was actually meant by the class struggle, Ted himself did not really comprehend. Though knowing very clearly that he belonged to the working class, and that somewhere above him in that other world which people like Jean and Jessie presumably aspired to were those like the Horsboroughs, he could not relate the strata between. Where, for example, did Denis fit in the scheme of things? That he was better off than the Hoyles, or anyone else in the Square for that matter, was obvious. The gap was nothing like so wide, though, as the gap which he sensed existed between Denis and his family and the Horsboroughs to whom they were related. There were men in the pits who, he felt, were far more affluent than the family of his friend. Yet Jean had been right, he sensed, when she said that Denis would not go down the pit as he himself had done. Why he sensed this he did not know, nor did it occur to him that it might have nothing to do with class. Perhaps, he thought, it was simply something that rubbed off on you if you happened to be related to people like the Horsboroughs, some mystical influence conveyed by the accident of birth. It would account for the fact that Denis's mother, he knew, disapproved of their friendship so that it had existed outside the influence of their respective homes. Yet now already, as if by some predestination, they were growing apart.

He reached out and picked up the book the librarian had given him to give to his father, and opened it at the title page.

He read: 'The Life and Struggles of William Lovett, in his Pursuit of Bread, Knowledge and Freedom'.

The name meant nothing to him, though he had heard the names of political writers like Marx and Trotsky mentioned at work and had seen their names on books his father had been reading.

He opened a page at random and started to read:

'The House of Commons is not so much ignorant of social evils as indifferent to them. While our social evils and anomalies have repeatedly been brought before you, you – whose duty it was to provide a remedy – have looked carelessly on, or have been intent only on your own interests and pleasures. Your own Commissioners have reported to you that thousands of infant children are doomed to slavery and ignorance in the mines and factories while their wretched parents are wanting labour and needing bread.'

The word 'infants' stuck in his mind. Surely that was not true. You were not allowed in the pit before the age of fourteen, though in his father's day it had been twelve. He returned to the title page and saw that it had been printed in 1876. Yet dimly he could relate it to his own situation. His father had wanted labour and needed bread while others had been intent on their own interests and pleasures.

He remembered his mother, her hair loose on the pillow, and of the other picture of her that had come into his mind when she had said of herself in relation to Jean, 'I was like that when I was a lass.' Tears smarted in his eyes for the woman he had never known, though he fought against them for tears were 'soft'. In the deep, dark corners of his mind a golden head bent over him and he suckled at a warm, generous breast.

He turned back to the first page of the book and started to read again.

CHAPTER THIRTEEN

On Cuddon Main Street where a side street cut off to the
Square, Tim stopped and said, 'If you want to cut off
home now I can manage those other books.'

'I'd like to come and see Ted,' Denis said.

'No homework?'

'We don't do homework.'

'No, no of course you don't,' Tim said, 'I forgot.'

They turned down the street and walked towards the
Square. Dark as the other streets in Cuddon were with
the blackout, the streets around the Square were even
darker. In earlier years, playing hide and seek with Ted,
they had been a haven of darkness, but now they
emphasised the general gloom that was the war, even the
lights from the windows being obscured by the wooden
frames with tarred paper covering which people used as
blackouts and which were cheaper than the heavy double
curtains used by others. In the Square itself the blackout
was said to be rarely complete, with almost every
household an offender at some time or other. It seemed
at times not so much an uncaring attitude as a gesture

which said, 'Well drop your bombs then! What have we got to lose?'

Light peeped faintly through the cracks in the door when they reached Ted's house. Tim tapped on the door somewhat gently as if their visit was clandestine. Denis had not seen Ted for some weeks now, and rarely before that since his relationship with Jean Colthard had started. He knew that it was still going on, for occasionally he would see them together. She always waved to him, but Ted would simply nod and grin and carry on. Once, alone, he had stopped to talk, but in a stilted, embarrassed way as if he felt responsible for a progressively dying relationship and as if this implied some guilt. Denis, left to his own devices by a natural adolescent process, and having no other deep friendship, had increasingly spent more time at home. He had asked about Jessie, for he thought of her sometimes in the speculative way he had observed her on that last evening together. Especially when he felt lonely, or felt the stirrings of approaching manhood, he thought of her. It had been a possibility into which he could have fallen so easily, and with so little effort. He never asked about Jean. He thought about her often, but with a muted acceptance now of something that would never be.

No one came to the door, so Tim knocked again sharply. Almost immediately they heard movement inside and after a moment or two the door was opened and Doug Hoyle, making a feeble attempt to pull some sort of light trap to behind him, peered at them in the gloom.

'It's Tim Horsborough,' Tim said. 'I promised you some books a long time ago.'

There was a moment of silence as if Hoyle had not comprehended, then he said, 'Aye, I remember. Come in, lad ...'

They pushed their way through the canvas light trap

into the room.

'Awkward bloody thing,' said Hoyle, struggling to close the door behind them.

The room was as Denis remembered it, but somehow tidier and cleaner and the sour smell of poverty which had permeated it before was less conspicuous.

'The kids are at my sister's,' said Hoyle, as if to explain the silence. He took the books that Tim held out to him and looked around for his spectacles. Putting them on he squinted at the titles. 'I shall have to go to Woolworths again,' he said, 'these damned glasses aren't what they seemed when I tried 'em on at the counter.' Then, as if to explain the sudden affluence that made it possible for him to purchase a sixpenny over-the-counter pair of spectacles he said, almost shyly as a modest man would explain some unexpected honour: 'I'm in work again.'

'At the pit?' Tim asked.

'Aye, at the pit. Onsetter at the bottom of the shaft.' He paused, then said, 'Came too late to benefit her, though,' and seeing Tim did not understand, he added, 'My missus. We buried her yesterday.'

As he said it, his eyes filled with tears. It surprised Denis, this visible sign of affection. He knew his father's dislike of the woman, his feeling that she had made a bed of shame and misery for a man he liked and had once worked with, but he knew from things he had heard over the years that it was also a view that was generally shared. Ted's silence on the subject of his mother, and Denis's brief contacts with her at the door, had confirmed this. He did not know then that it is sometimes possible to weep for one's enemy, to see the destroyer as a victim as well as the destroyed.

Hoyle took the books from Tim and inspected them, and then noticing that they were still standing he said apologetically, 'Sit yourself down … sit down!'

They sat and waited while he looked at the books, handling them carefully, rubbing his hands on the back of his trousers before he inspected each one. He looked at the titles first and then at the opening pages, reading a few lines to himself so that for a moment Tim thought, ludicrously, that perhaps he was going to read them and return them while they waited.

Eventually he put them down on the table and sat by the fire and looked at them. 'It'll take me some time to get through yon,' he said.

'There's all the time in the world,' said Tim.

'I'll not be able to take in best part of yon Marx,' Hoyle said, almost apologetically. 'I borrowed him from the library once and I couldn't make top nor tail of him, but I'll have another go. I've to take him at other folk's valuation as it is. You should make your own valuation, not depend on other folk, but then I'm not an educated man. It maddens me at times that I can't understand.'

'I'm not a religious man,' said Tim, 'but I know that the Church puts religious experience before theology. Maybe it should be the same with politics.'

'I know what you mean,' Hoyle answered. 'My dad was a religious man, but he broke with Chapel.' He looked at Denis as if to include him in a conversation that was obviously beyond his grasp. 'God knows where young Ted is,' he said, 'but happen he'll be back before you go. You'll know he's courting. She usually comes round for him about this time.'

'You'll enjoy the Jack London,' Tim said. 'Gissing's a bit of an acquired taste, but he's local to some extent. You might find him interesting.'

The subject of the books exhausted, they were silent for a moment. Then Tim said, 'I wanted to bring you the thesis I wrote that brings in the stuff you helped me with when I was here last, but I couldn't put my hands on it. I'll search it out before I go back off leave and give it to the young 'un here to bring to you.'

'Ted'll enjoy these,' Hoyle said. 'He's taken to going to the library and getting himself some reading since he went down the pit. It's mainly politics he reads. Talking about starting classes at the Worker's Educational next autumn. There's a lot of the younger end that come in the pit these days that go to 'em.' He looked at Tim's uniform, and added, 'You'll be finding it a bit of a change from college where you are.'

'It takes a bit of getting used to.'

'Where have they got you?'

'I'm not supposed to say,' Tim replied, apologetically.

Hoyle grinned. 'I could be a spy I suppose. Living in Little Moscow I'd be for Uncle Joe, I reckon. Do they damn well know what they're up to, the Russians?'

'This treaty with Germany you mean? I don't know what to make of it … I'm a bit shattered by it all as a matter of fact.'

'We'll know what it all means in the end, I suppose, after it's all over. Only happen we'll all be dead then and it'll not matter.'

Then there was a knock at the door, but before Hoyle could rise to answer it, it opened, the blackout screen parted and Jean Colthard came in.

She wore a bright red mac and a yellow scarf tied over her head as if to defy the blackout. Her entrance brought a new feeling to the room. She sparkled against the shabby background, and Hoyle himself seemed to straighten and quicken with her entrance.

She glanced only briefly at Denis and Tim, then spoke to Hoyle.

'Where is he?'

'How would I damn well know where he gets to. He tells me nowt.'

'You should have brought him up right.'

'Don't you cheek me! You're as bad as him!' said

Hoyle. He grinned, delightedly, enjoying the banter between them.

'Anyway, I only came to tell him I couldn't come.'

'Well that's double Dutch if I ever heard it.'

'I've to go to my aunt's the other side of Cuddon. Tell him I came and since he wasn't here I went.'

'Tell him a lie, shall I?'

'I'd not have waited for him, choose what,' she said. 'I can be independent too, you know.'

'If he doesn't know it now he never will.'

'Not knowing, is it?' she said. 'It's caring!'

'He cares nowt for nobody, him,' Hoyle said, betraying his affection.

'I'll be off then!'

'Watch yourself in this blackout. There was a young lass from top end molested at Christmas.'

'Chance'd be a fine thing,' she said.

Tim, who had watched her since she entered the room, spoke: 'I'm going that way.'

'Which way?' She looked at him, as if for the first time.

'The other side of Cuddon.'

'There you are then,' said Hoyle.

'Spoiling my fun,' she said. 'Who's going to molest me if the army's with me?'

'This is Tim Horsborough. He's related to young Denis here. Cousin is it?' he asked, stumbling with the introductions. 'You know young Denis.'

'I've seen him somewhere before,' she said, smiling, teasing. 'Now where was it?'

'Stop teasing the lad,' said Hoyle, unaware of how emotive the word was for Denis, who could feel the colour now rising in his cheeks. Confused and speechless, her entry had brought everything back to him.

She looked at Tim now. 'We'll have to get off if

you're coming because I'm late.'

Tim stood and said, 'Ready if you are.'

'You'll want to stop and see Ted,' Hoyle said now to Denis as he was about to rise and go with them, and unable to say that he didn't, Denis remained where he was.

Ted came in a quarter of an hour later carrying some books. Surprise at seeing Denis flickered briefly in his eyes. He nodded and said, 'Now then,' which was the common form of greeting between the men in Cuddon.

'Jean was here for you,' his father said. 'Did you know she was coming?'

'I've been to the library. It takes time picking books. Couldn't she wait for me?'

'Had to go to her aunt's t'other end, she said.'

'Coming back is she?'

'Not tonight I reckon.'

'She'll please herself anyway,' said Ted, as if uncaring, adopting the surface attitude to women of most of the Cuddon men, a mixture of perplexity and indifference.

'Now you're back,' his father said, rising, 'I'll get off down to t'pub. Kids are next door. Our Jessie'll fetch em. She's upstairs doing her homework.'

'Aye then,' said Ted.

'You'll be all right then,' said his father, hesitant.

'Why shouldn't I be?'

'I'll be off then.' Hoyle paused again at the curtain as if to repeat the remark, then pushed his way out, again cursing the awkwardness of the contraption, and the door closed behind him.

'He was asking permission,' Ted said, grinning.

'Permission?'

'Permission to go to the pub. He's not been able to afford it for years. Feels he needs somebody to tell him as he can.' His smile faded, and he said, 'I grudge him nowt. Nowt.'

He picked one of the books that Tim had brought from the table. 'Where's these from?'

'Tim promised them your dad that time we came before. I came with him and stopped on to see you.'

'Thought he was in the army.'

'He's on leave.'

'Officer, is he?'

'Not yet,' said Denis.

Glancing through one of the books Ted said, 'Politics is it? What's he know about politics?'

'He's studied 'em.'

'Is that why he came to see us, because he's studying politics?'

'He came to bring the books.'

'I read books on politics. A few of us do at the pit. We're going to get on the Council. We're going to change things.'

'Labour's in already in Cuddon,' said Denis. 'They're all Labour. If they put a pig up with a red ribbon round its neck they'd vote for it round here my dad says.'

'What do you vote?'

'I don't know about politics.'

'Everything's politics,' Ted said. 'Everything.'

There was a silence then. The conversation had produced a kind of hostility between them although Denis had taken no stand except to quote his father on the popular vote. He sensed another ending in his life. Not the end of a relationship, perhaps, but an end to the kind of relationship it had been.

Perhaps Ted sensed it too, for his tone became more friendly. 'What's it like at school these days?' he said.

He had chosen a sore subject, though unintentionally. It reminded Denis that Ted was technically a man of sorts. He worked with men and brought in a wage. It had changed him already. Denis had noticed it tonight more than before. There was an assurance about him which had always been there and which Denis had always envied, but which was now reinforced. It was physical, too. Denis could sense the muscle beneath the shirt. Ted was a man and he had asked him what it was like at school, as his father might have asked. It put years between them.

There was Jean Colthard, too. Seeing her earlier and now seeing Ted it seemed to him that there was a gap between himself and each of them that could never be bridged, as if they belonged to another world almost. He felt again the old sense of inferiority which for a time he had almost shaken off.

'You never come to ARP duty these days,' he said.

'I've enough on with work. It's only a lark anyway.'

There was a silence between them before Denis stood and said, 'I'd better get home.'

'Aye,' said Ted.

He fiddled with the blackout curtain at the door and cursed it as his father had done, then held the door open oblivious to the light that streamed out into the Square.

'To hell with 'em,' he said, not specifying whether he meant the government or the enemy.

Denis went out on to the step.

'I'll see you,' he said.

Ted said, as if to part on a caring note, 'You'll leave school this summer. What will you do?'

Out of the blue Denis grasped his ambition and made a reality of it and of the reason for it which sprang from his need for the kind of assurance that he was aware of in Ted; his need for manhood.

'I'm going to sea,' he said.

Without waiting for Ted's reaction and the dangerous details which would involve him in lies, he walked off across the Square, only vaguely aware that the light still streamed out into the night from behind him as Ted watched him go.

CHAPTER FOURTEEN

Jessie came down the stairs as Ted came in from seeing Denis off. Her eyes were still lost in the small print she had been reading and she blinked in the bright flare of the gaslight.

'Where's Dad?' she asked.

'Gone to the pub.'

'Thought I heard somebody here.'

'It was Denis and that cousin of his. Him that came once before. One of the Horsboroughs.'

'He's gone?'

'Denis? Aye, he went just now. He's off to sea.'

'To sea?'

She seemed startled.

'I doubt we'll see much more of him in Cuddon,' said Ted, as if he was writing off the past.

'It'll keep him out of the pit, anyway.'

'What's wrong with the pit? You're like Jean, too quick to talk about summat you know nowt about.' He tried to keep the edge out of his voice, for he hated arguing with Jessie, but Jean had been voicing her dislike of the pit too often recently. 'It's all right all these blokes going into uniform. It's coal that'll win the war. You've heard Dad say so.'

'It'll not get us out of the Square though, will it?' she said.

'You'll get out of the Square.'

'Will I?'

'You'll pass your exams. You'll go to college.'

'And the kids?'

'They'll stay where they are at me aunt's.'

'Suppose they do,' she said, 'what about you two? You and Dad?'

'I shall wed Jean when we're an age, you know I will.'

'She'll have you, will she?'

'What makes you think she won't?'

'You do nothing but fall out these days.'

'Only because she goes on about the pit.'

'And Dad?'

'Dad'll be right,' said Ted. 'There's lots of blokes like Dad that fend for theirselves. You worry too much.'

He grinned at her, making light of it, but it was true. She had hardly known childhood, the burdens that had been thrust on her as their mother had faded with despair. He hated that she should become like the older women of Cuddon, old before her time. He feared it as he feared it for Jean.

He said, 'You'll marry out of this, you see. You're better than the others round here.'

'I'm from the Square. Who'd marry somebody from the Square?'

Grained in her as it was by circumstances beyond her control, it angered him that she should so belittle herself. It angered him too that he should be obliged to belittle others to try to lift her self-esteem.

'The Square won't be here when the war's over.'

'Going to pull it down, are you?' she asked, smiling for the first time.

'Aye,' he said, 'that's what we're going to do!'

His anger was young and blind and he had no firm idea of the targets at which he wanted to aim it. There seemed to be so many of them. He was at the stage where much of what he read confused him with apparent contradictions, like the sound of many voices in his ear, each giving contrary advice. To pull down the Square was an ambition to which he could direct himself, an act of positive destruction.

He said, 'I shall go on the Council when I'm of an age.'

'I can see you on the Council,' she said.

'I mean it. Don't make fun.'

'I'm not,' she said, seriously now. 'I meant it too.'

He looked at her searchingly, to see if she was humouring him as Jean would have done. What he saw reassured him.

'I wish I'd done more at school,' he said, opening himself up to her now. 'Not to stop out of the pit. I belong in the pit. But so I could have better understanding of what I read.'

'You should talk to Dad more.'

'He's gone soft. He reads books but does nothing. It's taken all the bite out of him being out o' work all them years. Union did nowt for him, blast 'em, yet he'll not hear a word against 'em since they had him made checkweighman.'

'They did that at least.'

'Only because there was nobody else could be trusted for the job. Shonny Daws told me. They respected him because he suffered to stop out on strike when the rest of 'em trailed back to work with their tails between their legs. They can see he was right now, though none of 'em would be man enough to say so.'

'Better late than never. I think you're wrong about him anyway. He knows the right and wrongs of it. He chooses to keep his counsel, that's all. It's all there in his head.'

'Why will he not be straight with me then?'

'Union's his staff of life. What did you do at school when kids from Bessie Street used to call us for that we lived in the Square?'

'I used to feight 'em,' grinned Ted.

'If you fight the union he'll fight you if he thinks you want to stand outside of it. He's given his life to it for all it let him down.'

'It did that all right.'

He turned the radio on, but it was an orchestra playing a classical piece so he switched it off again.

'Don't you like music?' Jessie asked.

'For dancing I do.'

'I mean real music.'

'That I just switched off you mean? You like it?'

'Why do you think I go to concerts at school? It's not compulsory you know.'

'You can have it on if you want,' he said generously, switching it back on again. He listened for a moment with apparent respect, then said, 'It's a mystery to me what you see in that rubbish.'

She said, 'It's a mystery to me why you like reading politics when you won't read real books.'

'Sort of rubbish you used to give me to read?' he said, amiably. 'There's nothing more real than politics.'

'Life's not all politics,' she said. 'Is that what we live for – politics?'

'You call it life, what we live?'

'And when you've got it all straightened out,' she asked him, 'and we're living in Jerusalem, what will you do with your time?'

'What's Jerusalem got to do with it?'

'You call yourself a socialist,' she bantered at him, 'and you don't know that.'

'What do you know about it?'

'I'm doing it for English,' she said. 'Poetry by William Blake.'

She took a book from the sideboard and searched out a page then held it out to him.

'Read that.'

'Poetry,' he said. 'It's soft, is poetry.'

'Read it!' she commanded, thrusting it at him. 'If it's only to humour me.'

He took it and started to read. She busied herself around the room, tidying away the things the two men just left where they put them. When he came to the end he looked up.

'I like the last bit,' he said.

She took it from him and read it aloud:

'I shall not cease from mental fight,

Nor shall my sword sleep in my hand,

Till we have built Jerusalem

In England's green and pleasant land.'

'I like that,' said Ted. 'It's fighting talk is that.'

An hour or so later he followed his father round to the pub. Things had picked up at the pub. There was money around and the miners were swilling the coal dust from their throats as they hadn't done for years.

His father was at the bar, alone. Ted wondered if he often stood there alone, and suspected that he did. He would be happy enough, Ted thought, taking in the life around him, for he would have little enough inclination to join in idle pub chatter himself. Years of hiding away in the house because he could not afford to go out had given Doug Hoyle an acceptance of the monastic side of life. He had the look of a solitary man. Not arrogantly aloof; simply a man content to look and listen. 'He knows the rights and wrongs of it,' Jessie had said. 'He chooses to keep his counsel, that's all. It's all there in his head.'

Ted went and stood beside him. 'I'll have a pint,' he said.

'You shouldn't be in here be rights,' said Hoyle, digging in his pocket nevertheless.

'I know,' grinned Ted. 'I should be up at King Billy. Beer's better.'

'You know what I mean.'

'Nay, Dad,' said Ted, 'if I'm old enough for pit I'm old enough for pub.'

'Not much I can say in answer to that, is there?'

'That's what I said it for.'

An argument broke out at a table nearby over the precise limits of the call-up age.

'What did the Horsborough bloke want?' Ted asked.

'He brought me some books he promised me a long time back. I helped him out when he was doing something on pit villages for his studies.'

'Aye, I remember that,' said Ted. 'What sort of books?'

'Spanish Civil War. A book of Tawney's I haven't read.'

'What's a bloke like him know about politics?'

'Why shouldn't he?'

'One of that lot?'

Hoyle looked at him and smiled. 'All the more credit to him,' he said. 'It stands to reason we'd look to politics to better us lot in life. We'd have damned little chance without. He stands to lose, not gain, if socialism comes to power.'

'He's one of them.'

'Them and us? I don't see it as being as simple as that, lad.'

Ted grinned to take the edge off it as he said, 'You've

gone soft, Dad.'

'You reckon I've gone soft, do you?' Hoyle smiled, gently.

'Not just you. Union, Labour Party … Look at Attlee, we'd as well have Mickey Mouse in charge!'

'Happen he's like me, Clem Attlee, not so soft as he looks. They named a Brigade after him in the Spanish Civil War.'

'They talked about Spanish Civil War that day I went to Horsboroughs and got that tyre for me bike. Young Horsborough and some of his university mates. They're all wind that university lot.'

'Aye, well they've allus been given to spouting a lot, but there's some of our lads there on union scholarships, you know. It's to be hoped they're not all wind.'

'Denis is a bit like that.'

'Your mate?'

'I don't see much of him these days,' said Ted.

'He's always seemed a decent lad to me.'

'He's all right. He's a bit soft that's all.'

'Takes all sorts to make a world, you know.'

He didn't have a bad word for anybody these days thought Ted. All it took to take the fire out of him was to give him work. Yet he respected the martyrdom which, in a sense, he had shared. The political arguments could have turned bitter and sour with anyone but his father.

'You steer clear of politics usually when you're talking to me,' his father said, as if he could read Ted's mind.

'Do I?'

'Politics tore families apart in the Spanish Civil War,' said Hoyle, returning to one of his favourite subjects. 'Not just Left and Right. They fought each other on the Left as well. Brother against brother, father against son.'

'It'll not be like that for us,' said Ted. 'I shall not let it.'

'By biding silent? Can we not talk politics without getting at each other's throats then?'

'I'll not feight you,' said Ted.

'Happen I shall have to feight you, then.'

'Nay, Dad … let it not come to that,' said Ted.

He sought to change the subject. He said, 'Why did Jean not wait for me?'

'She'd somewhere to go.'

'She looks down on me because I work at pit.'

'She says nothing I've heard.'

'She does, though.'

'She's a good lass. Is it wrong for her to want something better for you?'

'Better for me, or better for herself.'

'You don't do credit to yourself when you say things like that.'

'Where was she going? Did she say?'

'I don't remember whether it was her grandmother's or her aunt's. Young Horsborough said he'd walk her there anyway.'

He waited for her close to the house next to the baths in which she lived. He felt safe standing across the road because the curtains were closed, but he resented the feeling; that it was necessary because her parents did not know of their relationship. Perhaps she had already come home and was in there. He had no way of knowing except to knock at the door and ask for her.

'That'd put the cat among the pigeons,' he thought, tempted.

It was cold, waiting. It added to the mounting frustration inside him. So Tim Horsborough had accompanied her wherever she had gone, had he? She would like that, thought Ted. She would like being walked through the streets of Cuddon by one of the upper crust, the masters. He beat his feet in cold and fury on the pavement, the picture of Jean and Tim injecting political iron in his soul. The Colthards wouldn't have objected to her bringing Tim Horsborough back to the house; their eyes would stick out like chapel hat pegs. He could imagine his own cold reception, tarred as he was by the brush of the Square. Some better understanding of Jessie's fears began to dawn on him as he stood there. Yet Colthard had been a miner before being crippled in the pit and given the job at the baths, and had lived only a street away from where he himself lived. Again his mind battled with the difficulty of comprehending the strata in society, the divisions within his own class. What hope was there of unity while they existed? How would they ever overcome them? The difference between the inside toilet and the cold walk at night to the earth closet across the yard. Into his mind came the germ of the awareness that he would have realised motivated his friend if he had talked to Denis about these things. He became conscious of the way out that meant that you packed your bags and went. It was not open to men to marry out of their stratum as some women did, but he had two legs, he could walk. His imagination created a portrait of himself as he might return; he brushed the dust of the Square from immaculate clothes; reached in his pocket and pulled out a wallet bulging with notes. He did it while standing in the door of the Colthards' house, opposite. They watched him. Their eyes stood out like chapel hat pegs. Then he turned and walked away.

He stood at the crossroads then, had he known it. What he dreamed of was not impossible. He was aware of a latent ability within him which could make it come true. Yet almost at once he rejected it, though why he rejected it he did not know. His hands thrust deeper into his pockets and his shoulders hunched, Ted was in one of his moods.

She came like a lamb to the slaughter, smiling when she saw him waiting there, as if she was glad he had come. 'Oh, you can smile,' he thought. 'You can bloody smile!'

'You shouldn't have come out tonight,' she said. 'I was going to come round again tomorrow.'

The civil defence workers came out of the baths. The night shift would be on. He would have liked to have been in there with her, naked in the pool, chasing her in the moonlight, playing games. So real it was at that moment that he almost reached out and touched where his hands would have played.

'You don't have to bother yourself,' he said, looking away from her into the night.

Her smile faded.

'In a mood are we?'

'I've to wait out here with me cap in me hand, haven't I?'

'I can't see a cap.'

'You know what I mean.'

'I can't help it.'

'Why don't you tell 'em you're going out with somebody from the Square?'

'It's nothing to do with the Square. It's them, as they are. It's their religion.'

'Some bloody religion!'

'They can't help it. It's how they were brought up.'

'A bit above everybody else, you mean?'

'They'd be the same about anybody.'

'Tim Horsborough? Be t'same about him would they?'

'So that's what's wrong? He walked me to me aunt's, that's all.' He looked at her. She looked away.

'Enjoyed it though, didn't you?'

Jealousy raged in him, explosive as fire damp in the pit.

'Made a change from moods,' she said, suddenly abandoning conciliation.

He turned his back on her and walked away.

CHAPTER FIFTEEN

The day after Tim came home on leave, Maddy Thomas died. She died in the ticket office at the baths, sitting in the same chair and in more or less the same position as on the day when Denis had peeped through the window and had, for a moment, thought she was dead. It was in fact Denis who found her, but this time he had walked into the room, thinking that she was dozing as usual. He had spoken her name but she had not replied, and then he had coughed and shuffled his feet but she had remained quite still, her head slightly turned away from him. Later he could not remember quite when he had realised she was dead, or how, for the first time in his life, he had recognised death. He had not shouted or run out, but had stayed for what seemed a very long time, simply looking at her, sharing her physical stillness but with a storm rising in his mind. He had not known it then, but later in life he came to realise that it was his first experience of genuine grief; a genuine sense of personal loss.

Jack Thomas, the leader of the demolition squad, had

come into the room behind him then and had immediately recognised the situation. He had touched her gently, to confirm it, but as if he would comfort her in some pain.

'Poor old love,' he had said, but to her, gently comforting, as if she was alive and could hear him. He was normally a roughish, hard-spoken man who had often expressed irritation at Maddy's precision when it came to observing the rules. Watching him now, transmuted briefly by the situation, Denis found that his eyes had blurred with tears. Throughout his life he would experience the same reaction whenever he discovered humanity in unexpected quarters, as if he had uncovered some universal vulnerability, some confirmation of the fact that we are all lost.

Thomas, looking at Denis, had seen the shock in his face.

'You go on home, lad,' he had said, 'I'll see to this,' and Denis, after one last look at his first experience of death, had gone.

When he got home Tim was there, sitting in the room behind the shop with Denis's mother and father. He had entered through the shop and as he came into the room his mother was already rising to answer the bell, for normally he would shout, 'It's me,' when entering that way.

'You might have shouted,' she said, but as if there was some other irritation behind the words, for she sounded genuinely angry.

'Maddy Thomas is dead,' said Denis.

He had caught them in the middle of a conversation, and their minds were slow to adjust.

In the silence he said, 'I found her,' for already, in the short journey from the baths, the shock had mostly dissipated and had been replaced by an awareness of being at the centre of an occasion.

'Where did you find her?' his father asked.

'Sitting in her chair at the baths,' said Denis. 'I knew she was dead,' he added, as if claiming credit for an accurate diagnosis.

'Who have you told?' his father asked.

'Jack Thomas came in. He said he'll see to it. He sent me home.'

The words tumbled from him and came to an end. The whole story in a nutshell. Nothing more to be told, for the rest was not communicable. He waited for the reaction.

'You're pale,' his mother said, her voice now free of irritation, concerned for him. 'Are you all right?'

'I'd like a drink,' said Denis, already feeling a sense of anticlimax.

'There's a pot in the kitchen just made. Go and help yourself, there's a good lad.'

She reached out her hand and touched him on the brow as she did sometimes when he complained of a headache, as if by touching him she would feel his pain. He was reminded of Jack Thomas touching Maddy and again, suddenly, he felt the tears flood up again and turned his head so that she should not see them.

'Go and help yourself,' she repeated, and he went out, glad to be able to hide himself from them. He had always hidden his little griefs, creeping into the house and up the stairs, clutching them to himself as if they were a precious possession. For many years, in a sense which he would not then have comprehended, he remained ignorant of the fact that this was what they would become.

The kitchen was the darkest room in the house for it faced the high wall of the yard which was only feet away. It was the room into which his mother never invited anyone, or allowed any visitors to help with the washing up in case they saw it, although, to his father's amusement, she would complain if they did not offer. It was the shabbiest room in the house as well as the darkest. Everything in it was old and worn with use and the square, scrubbed table filled at least half of it. It was the room which Denis loved most.

Having poured himself some tea he sat now, his elbows on the table, his fingers warmly wrapped round the enamel mug with its chipped blue rim. In the range the fire flickered briefly then subsided to a glow. His mind followed the example, having churned over the event and spent itself in the process. In the exhausted calm of the aftermath he existed in the glow of the fire, the hot taste of tea, and the rough familiarity of his elbows on the scrubbed table top.

He was still sitting there, his mug emptied now, when his father entered from the other room.

'Tim's going,' he said. 'You'd better go and thank him before he's off.'

'Thank him?'

'You want to go to sea, don't you? You want to go on that course?'

'Yes,' said Denis.

'He's persuaded his dad to pay for it, and your mother to live with it, so you'd better go and thank him, hadn't you?'

Which of the events of the day – the death of Maddy Thomas or the changed pattern of his life – were to make it stand out most as 'one of those days' only time would show. He had thanked Tim, conventionally as was expected of him, but unable to convey his true feelings. Then, after Tim had gone, he had mounted the stairs to his room, closing the door behind him. He had lain on the bed, looking at the ceiling, the most familiar pattern in his life, and had tried to take it all in. He was not to know that in the course of Tim's leave there was one more event to come, to which, perhaps, he would be less able to adapt than the others.

The following day his father wrote to the wireless school to secure a place. It was March and he had only four more months before he left school. Walking there that morning he had the feeling that it was already behind him, that he was moving into an adult world. He knew that there would be no sadness, no regret in his departure. He had not enjoyed his schooldays, and since Ted had left he had felt there was nothing there for him at all, he had not replaced that solitary friendship with any other. The English master, who was the only one who ever marked him out for praise or attention, had departed to join the army on the outbreak of war, and his successor seemed to have little interest in either the work or the class. He would set them something to read and would then sit staring out of the window, as if in the far distance he could see the postman coming with his call-up papers.

It was cold in the classroom despite the heat from the forty odd bodies sitting at the desks. At break they congregated around the radiators in the corridors which could warm only by contact, so that only the biggest and strongest had any relief from the cold. When the bell rang they shuffled back into the classrooms where dreams were made, for there was little else to do but dream. Most of them probably dreamed of the small, steamy kitchens at home where at least it was warm. Some, like Denis, would have their private dreams, their minds leaving their chilled bodies to experience some fantasy existence far removed from the tedious reality of their present.

He dreamed of being at sea, or at least as he envisaged it would be. It was a recreation from many strange sources: from boys' magazines, books, films he had seen at the local cinema. It bore as little relationship to the reality as dreams of that kind ever do. Most of all he dreamed of coming on leave in his uniform, for this was the real motivation, the true reason for his ambition which he had held back from telling Tim. Now that the reality was already within his grasp he felt already the fulfilment of a need. His need to be different, to be apart.

Where it had come from, this need, he did not know. When he had felt it stirring within him it had sometimes been associated with Ted, with his envy of Ted's confidence and an apartness he could sense in him even though they were friends. But it was more than that. In the confusion of images that accompanied his dream of coming on leave, the figures of his Uncle Maurice Horsborough, his aunt, Doris and even Tim, were usually present. To them more lately had been added Jean Colthard, dominating them all, so that although they remained in the background his scenes were all played out with her. They were romantic rather than erotic, and again they were in the manner of the films he had seen; fictional recreations in which the main characters bore some highly romanticised resemblance to Jean and himself. Later in life he remembered that classroom with its dreaming figures seated quietly at the desks. He remembered the master, forever gazing out of the window, waiting for the war to release him. It seemed to him, looking back, that there must have been one overwhelmingly common feeling which they all had but rarely communicated to each other – the wish to escape.

Now that his friendship with Ted had all but been severed by the process of growing up, his life at home was increasingly tedious too. Where once he had come into the house from school with a happy sense of release he now entered quietly. More often than not he would go straight up the stairs, after a brief greeting, and would lie on the bed and look at the ceiling, continuing the day's dream as if it was a particularly exciting novel that urged him on to the end.

Today, unusually, his tea was waiting when he got home. He sat at the table in the small dark kitchen with his father, and his mother brought it to them from the oven.

'One of your favourites today,' she said, putting a large piece of cod in front of him.

His father looked across at him, smiled, and said, 'See how she spoils you!'

As she brought her own the shop bell rang as it often seemed to do at meal times and she put it back in the oven, closed the door and went to answer it.

'All the day to come in,' his father said, 'and they always come when you eat!'

The shop bell rang again, but she did not return which meant another customer. His father had tried to get her to close at meal times once, but she had refused, fearing to lose the trade. 'We can always take it in turns,' she said, but it was always she who answered the bell, rising quickly before his father, as if he was still the breadwinner, still the man come home from the pit to whom attention must be paid before all.

Denis watched his father now as he ate with his one hand and remembered the time when they had watched, and yet not dared to watch, as he had struggled to use his fork as a knife as well. He remembered the day when for the first time his mother had cut his father's meat up herself before serving and had presented it to him. He had looked at it and then at her, and she had smiled at him as if to say, 'Will you fight me then for this little thing I do for you?' It was as if something passed between them, but nothing was said.

'Do they dream too?' Denis wondered suddenly,

looking at his father. He rarely thought of them in relation to each other, almost always as they related individually to himself. It occurred to him, perhaps for the first time, that they had a life of their own in which he had no part and which he knew nothing of. 'What would they dream about?' he wondered, not able to imagine that they could ever have experienced the kind of fantasies that he created himself. The thought reminded him of that day's dream and he started to pick it up where he had left off, losing himself.

The shop bell rang again, jolting him back to reality, and glancing across the table he saw that his father was watching him. He flushed as if caught in some unseemly act and bent to his plate again.

'You're quiet these days,' his father said. 'Missing Ted, are you?'

'I see him now and then,' said Denis.

'Not much though?'

'No,' said Denis, 'not much.'

'I'd a mate a bit younger than me when I went down the pit. He stopped at school a year and I went down in the cage with the lads. I see him now and then. We're mates still in a way, but not the same. You'll be away yourself before long.'

'Yes.'

'You'll see things I'll never see. You'll grow up. You're halfway there already in your mind I'll bet.'

He looked up and his father smiled. 'How could he know that,' Denis thought.

'Coming home in your uniform. The lasses after you. Your mother jealous to death.'

Denis felt as if his most private thoughts had been plucked from his head and laid on the table. It did not occur to him that his father had simply described a natural ambition, universally shared. He felt his face tighten and warm with embarrassment. He almost expected his father to say, in the next breath, his eyes hard on him, 'I know what you've been up to with that teaser Jean Colthard.'

Instead he said, 'Don't talk about it much with your mother; going to sea I mean. She's hard put to accept it.' He paused, and then went on, his voice different in a subtle way to the voice in which he usually spoke to Denis. It was more the kind of voice with which he spoke to other men.

'It was nothing I said that persuaded her. She trusts young Tim, you see. And then her brother, your Uncle Maurice, paying for you, it makes her feel a part of them again.' He spoke without rancour about something which must have caused him a certain humiliation in the past, for he was a big enough man to take it and lay it beside his experience of life, discounting petty pride for the greater pride of knowing he had learned to live with reality without losing his self respect.

'Her father, your grandfather, was a hard man,' he went on. 'Hard by anybody's standards even for times like them. She broke all the rules when she married me, but she broke his heart and he never forgave her. She lives like she does, in comparison to what they've got, because she'd not throw me off for what he could give her that I never could.'

He turned his direct gaze away from Denis for a moment as he said, 'There's not many women like her. She's just your mother to you, I daresay. You'll see her differently one day.'

Then he looked at him again, with his straight, honest eyes and flushed slightly as if what he had said had been something of an effort for him, an embarrassment.

'There,' he added, 'it's been said. It had to be told you one day. It's part of your life. You'll have wondered about it a bit I daresay without us saying anything?'

Denis nodded. It was all he could do. There were

things he would have liked to ask but he shared his father's silent embarrassment. He needed time to digest this new, more open kind of communication between them over things which had always been locked away. Something else which had remained unspoken emerged now, as if one more door had to be partly opened before everything was locked back away; one more cupboard explored, looked at.

'I'd like you to go and see Stan, your brother, before you go off to sea when you've done your course,' his father said. A great sadness came into his eyes as he said it, as if he spoke of someone dearly loved, now dead. 'He'll as like as not know you, or so it'll seem. That's what they say at that place where they look after him. They know best I suppose, but I'm never too sure. He shows no sign to me or your mother when we go. We could be strangers. I don't know though. I caught him looking at me once …'

He stopped as if unable to continue, not for lack of words, but simply because the memory was too much for him. Then after a moment he simply said, 'I'd like you to go, anyway,' and the subject was closed between them, to Denis's relief. It was a door he himself could not open, and had no wish to. He had been asked once some years before if he would like to go and see Stan, but had refused in a strong way as if he feared there might be some compulsion to do so, and he had not been asked again. Vaguely at the back of his mind there was a memory of a time when the other bed in his room had been occupied, and of the figure who occupied it, but it was blurred and not recognisably human. In time he had come to think that there had never been four of them in the family, as if the existence of Stan belonged to a dream, though not the kind of dream he indulged in nowadays.

Later when his mother came from the shop he went

upstairs, lay on the bed and looked at the ceiling, and waited for the other dreams to come. Nothing much happened. Vague images flitted across his mind, but without the pseudo reality he was accustomed to. It was as if the machine had stopped working because the arc had grown dim; the celluloid was spinning, but the image had lost the light. Reality was too much with him.

It was dark almost before he became conscious that it was getting dark. Below him in the shop he heard his father bolt the door. His mother called something and his father answered and then the house became silent again. Because there was no longer any reason to lie there he got up and lit the gas. What few possessions he had were in the room. A few books, old toys, his clothes in the wardrobe. Soon he would leave even these behind him.

He combed his hair, looking at himself in the mirror as he did so. This was what other people saw, this embryo youth who looked back at him. He looked himself in the eyes, and then looked away as if he saw something there that disturbed him. He felt his chin where the down was dark in the mirror but non-existent to the touch. He would start to shave he decided. There was no real need except in his mind, as if he needed some physical confirmation of the changes that had taken place and were about to take place. When he ultimately went to sea, he thought, he might well grow a beard. The down on his chin derided him and he turned off the gas and went downstairs.

The radio was on in the living-room and they were listening to it, his father with eyes half closed and his mother knitting. It was a dark, navy blue wool and he thought it would probably be something for himself. Everybody was knitting for the services these days. She had knitted a scarf for the son of the vicar at the church she went to, and also one for Tim. Now she had someone of her own to knit for.

She smiled at him as he came in the room. Earlier in the evening before he went upstairs he had felt her eyes following him. It had irritated him at first, but then he remembered what his father had said and put it from his mind.

He said, 'I'm going out.'

'Oh?' she asked. 'Where?'

He simply wanted to walk, but he knew that would not satisfy her, so he said, 'I'm going to the baths. They might want me, to talk to me I mean. I've not been back since I found Maddy Thomas.'

'Watch the road in the blackout,' she said, as she always did, and again he felt the slight irritation of being talked to as if he was a child.

He went down the side passage that ran beside the shop and out into the night. The Cresford bus was stopped across the road where it always waited until the advertised departure time. Vaguely through the darkness he could see the faces of passengers, blue in the dimmed masked lighting, like travellers from some other world. He stood for a moment, undecided which way to go, then turned left on the road which would most quickly take him away from the houses, walking briskly into the dark as if he had a purpose other than simply to go.

The moon came from behind the mass of a moving cloud and suddenly the night was less dark. He was glad, for he rarely walked at night and in the blackness it had begun to seem pointless to be out. Now, as the moon shadows of the houses and then the trees grew on the silver ribbon of the road he became aware, too, of the silence, and of the contrasting sound of his footsteps on the rough asphalt. He came eventually to where the slag heaps had spilled almost to the pavement edge. They rose up and away from him far into the night, so that looking up it was like seeing the dark edge of a wave about to plunge into the trough and engulf him. Looking down again his eyes were caught by tiny sparklets of light where the bright moon reflected on polished fragments of coal scattered among the shale.

As he walked he became more and more aware of his aloneness, for the distant houses would have carried lights in peacetime, and since leaving the last houses of Cuddon he had seen no one. The air, too, seemed part of the silence. It was fresh and free from dust, for rain in the last few days had damped down the slag and even the night breeze failed to raise it.

He saw himself, a tiny speck, on the map of Britain that hung on the classroom wall at school. The ragged edges of the drawn coastline expanded as his mind tried to grapple with his minuteness. He could not conceive of himself as a grain of sand, his mind rejecting the anonymity of such a conception. He needed the relativity of familiar things to retain any sort of concept that could be meaningful to him. For a moment as his mind hovered on the edge of infinity he experienced a sense of panic, of standing on the edge of an abyss. Would he ever understand it, his place in what his mother was fond of calling 'the scheme of things'? Did he have such a place? How would he find it and to what purpose? Already he was committed to leave the place which he now called home, and as the realisation entered his thoughts he had a fleeting moment of uncertainty, of near panic, as if again he stood at the edge of an abyss. Then, restoring him, saving him, came the image of himself as he appeared in his dreams – the returned traveller; the man who had been and seen and had come home again; the man apart. It was Ted who would stay here, within the confines of this familiar world, growing only to the extent that the slag poisoned soil would let him.

Denis stopped and looked back down the road in the

direction of Cuddon from where he had come. It did not occur to him that perhaps he would go and never return. The returning was part of the going, part of the pattern he shaped for himself.

The shadows on the road diminished as the moon passed behind a cloud, and the night closed in around him. Looking up he saw that the cloud was small and that the light of the moon had already turned the far edge silver. He waited for it to reappear, standing still on the road, the silence around him.

It was broken then by the sound of other footsteps. They came from the direction in which he had been walking. He turned and looked but could see no one, although the footsteps were now very near. A quiet laugh came through the darkness. There was something familiar about it, and when it came again he knew why. He walked to the side of the road, quietly, and stood in the shadow of a tree, its trunk hiding him from the oncoming walkers. They were almost on him now, but he did not dare to look. So terrified was he at being discovered now that he had chosen to hide that he almost stopped breathing. His thoughts became frozen in the moment, as if to continue thinking even might flood the night air with sound.

They stopped, but he could hear no words that might explain why although they must by now have been only a few feet from him. Then the laugh came again, and it was completely familiar now so that he did not need the light of the moon as it came at that moment from behind the cloud and lit the night again. It was repeated and the blood pounded in his head as his lungs cried for air, and then the footsteps started again and they came into sight, walking past him as he turned his head sideways without moving his body.

He saw, what he had known when he recognized her voice in her laughter, that it was Jean, and he looked beyond her expecting to see Ted walking beside her.

But the figure he saw was not Ted. If it had been almost anyone else it would have come as no great surprise and the shock wave would not have hit him. It was, in fact, his cousin Tim.

CHAPTER SIXTEEN

Ted stayed in the house reading most nights now when he was not at work. Jessie had asked him about Jean and he had simply told her that it was over between them. She had not asked him why. He knew that his father would have asked her, but Hoyle said nothing to him. Ted knew that he was disappointed though at the outcome, that he would miss her lively presence in the house. He wondered once or twice if his father had seen his mother in Jean.

'I was like that once,' his mother had said, 'full of life.'

So far as he could, he put her from his mind, pushed her away whenever she obtruded, or if something reminded him of her he would turn his back on it. It was as if there was a pain inside him which somehow he had learned to control by an exercise of the will, but which from time to time insisted that he should know it was still there. He had not really thought that she would stay away. The day after he turned his back and walked away he had waited for her to appear, as if she would know it was just part of the game. When in the week that followed she did not come he could hardly believe it. Yet he would not go to her, though the thought did occur to him, and the temptation to do so was at first almost unbearable. He would remember his anger at the Colthards' rejection of him, as if keeping it alive would help him not to weaken.

The experience made him wonder about Jessie. That there was someone she cared for she had already told him. He wondered who it was and how she felt, for he knew that she was not seeing anyone. She was too open to have been able to hide the fact even if she had wanted to. That her feelings, her pain, might be as strong as his own, the arrogant illusion that we are all unique in love prevented him from believing. Nevertheless he felt even closer to her for, though different in degree, he felt, it was something they shared. He wondered if she ever saw Jean, and if they spoke of the matter, but he could not have brought himself to ask her, as if to do so would have been a confession of weakness.

From time to time he would visit his brothers, too, whom he had almost forgotten in the weeks before his mother died. His aunt had taken them over completely now, almost as if they were her own, and they seemed to have no desire whatsoever to return to the Square. He felt close to them, and yet apart from them. They liked him to visit them, though. They would press him for stories of the pit, which he knew they would recount at school, re-creating the mythology which makes miners a separate breed, so that they too might ultimately seek their manhood in the pit.

Ted was a pony lad now, in charge of 'gallowas' as they were called. Though everyone knew they were already on their way to extinction as machinery gradually took over their task, he had developed a strong affection for them, a feeling deeper than that of a farmer who breeds to kill. As his love of the light grew with his knowledge of the dark he suffered their blindness as it was his own, and would comfort them with a gentleness beyond that of women, as if he sensed a grief in them which they could not express but which was no less human in its capacity than his own.

He grew closer to his father, too. They would sit on opposite sides of the fireplace, reading the same books but only lately daring to communicate their reactions to what they read, fearing an explosion of disagreement. Over the weeks they had tentatively reached out to one another, glancing away from a subject if it seemed the gulf between them was wide.

'Tha reads nowt that makes sense,' his father would say, gently teasing.

'I read same as you.'

'Tha skips bits that matter. Tha couldn't read that fast if'n tha didn't.'

'I skips bits that don't matter.'

'How does tha know whether they matter or not if tha skips 'em?'

'Sharp as a razor, aren't you?'

'I'm as sharp as thee any day o' t'week,'

'There's rubbish in everything,' said Ted.

'What do you make of this?' asked his father, holding up a book Ted had just finished and which he had previously read.

'What do you make of it?' Ted had countered, ready to counter a dispute.

Then they would grin at each other, knowing that each was unwilling to risk the loss of the warmth between them.

In bed at night he would sometimes think about his father alone in the room across the stairs, the greater part of his life, which had been shared with Ted's mother, now over. One day he would probably be alone himself in that way. Yet he was alone already and because he was now sexually aware of his need, and the emptiness of a need unfulfilled, he would be conscious of the empty space beside him and a conception of his father's loneliness would grow in him which he knew would never be communicated between them. Somewhere outside in the night, the giant doors of the coke ovens would be opened for the period which the blackout allowed and would illuminate the night sky, and the ceiling of his room, for he never now closed the curtains at night, preferring to undress in the darkness. Like a silent cosmic explosion the orange flare would burst into the room so that he could no longer see the stars through the window, as if night was suddenly turned into day.

The days grew longer as spring turned to summer. He rarely went inside the ruined farmhouse now. He would go there sometimes, however, and sit on the wall, looking at it, as if daring himself to go inside and endure the unhappiness of remembering. He could not help but remember, however, the day on which he first brought her there; his pride in the place; the way she looked round the kitchen and, with her imagination, created a home.

How was it possible to own such a place and love in it? With the thought he was back to the crossroads, the night he stood outside the baths and was conscious of the other way; the way which took you from familiar things into the cold world outside Cuddon. The incongruity of thinking of the world outside his barren life in the Square as cold never occurred to him, nor the fact that at the root of things he clung savagely to the familiarity of the things he knew. Nor did it seem incongruous to him that, when he thought about it, he thought contemptuously of Denis for leaving, as if he was running away from something rather than braving the world outside which Ted himself feared. Let him go, he would think. Let them all go. As if the act of staying was a test of endurance; the real trial of man.

He rarely saw Denis these days. Sometimes, briefly, when Denis was on leave they would meet accidentally and pause for a short conversation, broken by embarrassed silences and an awareness of a growing gulf between them. In all of these meetings Ted was aware of accentuating his slightly arrogant stance as a basically superior being, of wanting to be seen to be still on top.

In the past it had been a natural reality brought about by some hesitancy in Denis by which he had seemed to look up to Ted. Now Ted found himself consciously wanting to hold on to the role, as if it had been important to him, which in those days it had not. If anything it had amused him and made him feel protective towards his friend. It was part of the change between them, though he sensed that in a way Denis still looked up to him, and Ted did not understand why he should feel it necessary to make the effort; why he should seem to patronise. He was, in fact, a little ashamed of himself.

After one of these meetings he went home and said to Jessie, 'I saw Denis today.'

'Oh yes,' she said casually, as if it was of no possible interest.

'Looks good in his uniform,' he said, assuaging his shame without abandoning his role in front of Denis.

Jean came one evening when he was sitting on the wall of the farmhouse garden looking at the distant hills. He had his back to the track and he heard the rattle of the bicycle as it came over the cobbles beyond the gate. He heard her dismount and lean her bike against the wall, and knowing well who it was he did not turn.

It had been a warm September day. He had been there for most of the afternoon and it was still a couple of hours before he need go home to collect his snap tin and water bottle from Jessie before heading for the pit. He waited and became aware that she was standing beside him. He blinked at the bright sky as he did when he came out from the cage on to the bank at the end of a shift.

She said, 'I thought you'd given up coming here,' and when he said nothing she added, 'I've been before.'

'Oh, aye,' he said, as if he was being polite rather than interested.

'I've been lots of times. Thought you'd given up.'

'Oh aye?'

'Thought it was mine now.'

He looked at her then.

'Belongs to nobody,' he said. 'Nobody.'

'You found it. Finding's keepings.'

'Who says?'

'I do.'

'Fact is,' he said, 'it does belong to somebody and one day they'll claim it and that'll be t'end of it.'

'Still looking on black side o' life?'

'I face facts,' he said. 'I don't live in dreamland like some folks do. I know what me lot is. It'll not be changed be dreams. Feighting's what'll change it, not dreams.'

'You men!'

'What's wrong wi' us?'

'All you ever think about – feighting. Most of you anyway.'

'All but softies.'

'Like Denis?'

'He's a bit on soft side is Denis.'

'There's a soft side to life as well.'

'Dreamland,' he said. 'Bloody dreamland.'

'Your language hasn't improved.'

'You should hear t'language in t'cage as we come up after shift,' he said. 'You rate me with a lay reader at chapel be comparison.'

'I've heard all about that. Talk about women. Boasting about what they've been doing to their women. They don't know what women are about don't pitmen.' Then she added, quickly as if she had forgotten for a second that he was included, 'Most of 'em don't, anyway.'

'I know what women are about.'

'Do you?'

'Bloody dreams,' he said again, 'that's what women are about.'

'Because they want something better in life?'

He remembered his mother. The dying face framed by the golden hair. Her voice, thin like a girl's. 'I was soured by the Square.'

'I wouldn't deny 'em that.'

'What would you deny 'em then?'

'Taking their knickers off to get it,' he said, assaulting her with deliberate crudity.

'You're crude,' she said.

'Aye, I'm crude. Crude and uncouth, that's what I am. I'm a pitman. I can look on black side o' life without flinching from it.'

He looked at her again but she was looking away from him. There was a sadness in her face that he had never seen in her before, as if he had brought her bad news. A pain rose up in him for the comfort he felt he could not give her without deceit, without denying the honest pessimism that he clung to with such tenacity as if it was a lifeline for him. He loved her still. The word entered his mind easily, pushing out that other deceiving word which they used to deny their gentler natures, 'liked'.

'I love you.' The word ached inside him. 'Oh I love you.'

He said, 'You think I seek to spoil life for you, don't you?'

'No. No, I don't think that.'

'What then?'

'You speak as you find.'

'Do you not find it so then?'

'I look for something better.'

He thought, 'If I could give it you, I would,' as he had sometimes thought in a child's way looking at his father, starved for work.

He said, 'Happen there's better.'

'Where?' she said, looking at him now as someone might look if they had just been told of definite proof of a better life after death.

He looked at the distant hills as if they might hold the answer, for he had spoken instinctively against a deep sorrow he sensed in her; had spoken to give comfort.

He said, 'Soon,' but without conviction, reinforcing it inadequately by adding, 'It'll come soon,' as if he had been told so by others wiser than himself. He searched desperately for the words. 'After the war things'll get better,' he said. 'That's what it's about, isn't it?'

'About fighting Hitler, isn't it?' she said. 'That's as I see it.'

'It's about more than that,' he said, with growing confidence. 'Fighting Hitler's part of it, but it's more than that.'

She looked at him now as if she almost believed, as if he was confirming something she had already been told.

'Somebody else said that.'

'They were right.'

'Tim Horsborough said it.'

The name jolted him. Took him back to the night when he had turned from her and gone away; the long months of misery that had separated him from her. He choked back jealousy or any sign he might give her of the awful fire it created in him.

'He was right,' he said, though he could not help

adding, 'though he knows nowt about it.'

'He's fighting in it.'

'We fight all us lives down the pit,' said Ted. 'All us bloody lives. Not just again such as Hitler.'

There was a silence, as if they had exhausted their capacity to discuss these things, and within that capacity they had said all they had to say, but she had at least not turned on his last remark about the pit as she would have done once.

'Done any more things inside?' she asked eventually.

'I've not been in.'

'Not been in?'

'Not since last time you went in with me.'

It was as near at that moment as he could get to telling her what their separation had meant to him. Yet when they had lain together in the room he had been more articulate, in the half-light that crept around the edges of the roughly curtained window. He looked up now, seeing it curtained as they had left it.

'Has anybody else been in?' she asked him.

'There's been no sign of anybody round here that I could see.'

'I saw a man with a gun one day.'

'When?' he asked, anxiously.

'One day when I was up here.'

'He went in?'

'No,' she said. 'Not while I was here. He was in the trees over there. He shot something. He went away after a bit.'

She looked at the house then started to walk towards it up the path through his garden. She opened the door and went inside. He looked back at the hills. A deep warm happiness was stirring inside him. The blood rushed singing through him. She had come back. She had followed him. It was not a game.

He waited until he could bear it no longer then

followed her inside. She was not in the kitchen, but he stood there a moment trying to see it through her eyes. It saddened him that they should be able to see themselves living here yet knew it could never happen. To believe that it could meant following her into the dreamland he had accused her of inhabiting and abandoning the facts of their life.

He heard her footsteps on the floor upstairs and followed her up there. As he went he thought, 'Sod tomorrow!' The present was brighter than he had known it. The present was real. In his mind, without knowing it, he echoed another Englishman. 'Facts,' he thought, 'are better than dreams.'

CHAPTER SEVENTEEN

The following winter, in the February of 1941, Denis
came home for the last time before going to sea. He had
completed the course and, much to his surprise, obtained
his certificate. He had not expected to, partly because the
principles of electricity and magnetism were new to him
and he had virtually to start from scratch, and partly
because of the social life in the evenings which had cut
down the work he should have done out of class. Very
few failed, in fact, and he did not realise until much later
that due to the shortage of radio operators the standard
required for a pass had been lowered. Casualties were
high and, to keep a full watch, every ship required three
operators.

He had come home on odd weekends throughout the
course. It had not been as he had imagined it would be.
The phoney war was over. In April of the previous year
the Germans had invaded Denmark and Norway.
Denmark had not resisted and Norway, fighting bravely
against impossible odds, had been conquered by early
June. On the 10th of May the German tanks swept into

the Low Countries on a drive which was virtually completed with the evacuation from Dunkirk at the end of that month. On the 22nd of June the French surrendered and Britain stood alone.

In Cuddon the feeling that the war would be a short one had long been replaced by a more realistic view. Although the area was not considered a prime target for bombers, people no longer laughed at the Civil Defence workers. Maddy Thomas was posthumously vindicated, and her hero, Churchill, formed a coalition government. The people of Cuddon were at the beginning of a journey through a long dark tunnel, and for the most part they were aware of it. The losses at sea mounted and rationing began to bite. Familiar faces disappeared from the streets as the call-up was extended to older men and, increasingly, women moved into the factories in the nearby towns to replace them, wearing turbans and, so it seemed, symbolically replaced their skirts with trousers.

Tim had been at Dunkirk and, shortly afterwards, had come on leave. It was before Denis had started his course, but he had seen Tim only once, briefly, while waiting in a bus queue in Caselborn. Denis had heard the familiar, 'Hello, young 'un,' and looking up the queue had seen Tim smiling at him, looking not very much different from the last time he had seen him, but with a deepness behind his eyes and his face, if anything, even thinner. They had exchanged a few words across the people who stood between them, not wanting to risk the hostility which was nowadays directed at queue jumpers. Then the bus had come and Tim had managed to squeeze on it, but Denis was obliged to wait behind for the next one. He had wondered as he waited, how, if at all, his attitude to Tim had changed since the night when he had seen him with Jean, and was surprised to come to the conclusion that it had not. His reaction had been the same as it had been with Ted. It had simply renewed his feeling of inadequacy that had been temporarily obscured by the dreams.

He daydreamed no longer, or rarely. Since he had left home he had moved in a world where he hovered on the edge of manhood. At the old country house on the edge of the North Yorkshire moors, where they trained, there were many like himself, waiting to be initiated, enduring the preliminaries. They slept in metal bunks, six or eight in each of the large bedrooms. Lights out was always the signal for the talking to begin, quite different to the general chatter of the day, as if they held it all back, waiting the anonymity of the dark.

In the room which Denis slept in there was a boy from York who reminded him of Ted. He was always the first to speak, and after the lights flickered out there would be a silence, as if they waited for him; as if he had established some kind of authority. Most of the talk was of girls they knew at home, embellished no doubt but with a frankness they refrained from in daylight. Sexual adventures were recounted, interrupted by the odd wit who would conjure giggles out of the darkness so that the stories were never solemnly obscene. Denis found himself wondering more than once how the girls whose secrets were revealed would have reacted if they could have overheard.

Then, too, almost all of them sounded like Jean; provocatively sexual; taking the initiative. They're all teasers, he thought, disbelievingly. It was as if the images, filtered through the young male minds, became desires rather than realities.

It was this realisation that brought to his mind another. Jean was a reality. She needed no embellishment. She was in life as the fictions that spilled into the darkness of the room. Once or twice he was tempted to reveal her, his own part embellished of course, to join in this masculine world at a practical level. Something always stopped the words in his mouth, denying his sexuality expression. He would simply lie there, erect in the darkness, giggling with the others but never contributing.

Sometimes at night they would go into the nearby market town to a dance, meeting usually at the same public house where the ones who were not of legal age could mingle with those who were, as if the uniform conferred legality on them. At the dances he met other girls, and sometimes he danced, but found himself too physically awkward to enjoy it, shyness again denying his sexuality expression. He was not alone, of course. There was always a small group at the end of the dance hall who rarely danced, but simply stood there, perpetual observers, potential voyeurs. So when he left, his course complete, there was no one to say goodbye to except the friends of his own sex he had made. He had remained true to his early dreams. A couple of years later, on a dark night in the North Atlantic, seated on watch and reading a book of poetry he came across a line which reminded him of that time. Perhaps even, he thought, for it was still true then, of the whole time of his life:

'I have been faithful to thee, Cynara, in my fashion.'

Awaiting the call to join his first ship in this winter of 1941, Denis soon became bored. Once or twice in the first week of his return he thought of going round to see Ted, but found for some reason he was unable to understand himself he did not do so. He was restless now and impatient to go. Even his uniform disturbed him, for at the back of his mind he knew it implied an experience he did not have. Eventually he took it off and started to wear the clothes he had worn before he started the course. His mother was disappointed. She was proud of him in his uniform, though at the same time afraid of what it represented.

'Why don't you wear it?' she had said, one day when she had persuaded him to go into Caselborn with her. And because the answer was too complex he had simply said that he felt like a change.

He was nervous, too, and sometimes irritable, even with her and his father, and this too he did not fully understand and was ashamed of it.

He had been at home three weeks when the telegram arrived, telling him to report to the offices of the shipping company to whom he had applied on the following Monday, and telling him also to come prepared to join a ship. His father had come in with it from the shop and he had opened it and read it to them, smiling, feeling already the cloud of uncertainty lifting from him. Looking at them he could see that they did not share his excitement; that it was a moment they had not looked forward to. Then his mother had said, 'I must finish your scarf,' and had left the room to go upstairs. His father had taken the telegram from him and read it, as if he expected there to be more than Denis had actually read. 'Plenty of time to get packed. No rush,' he had said, and had followed his wife upstairs.

It was a Saturday, a sharp, bright winter day with a clear, blue sky, and a sprinkling of snow from the night before still holding on the slopes of the stacks so that they looked like small, oddly formed hills in another climate. His mood quite changed now, he put on his uniform, and when his mother said, 'You must go and see Uncle Maurice and say goodbye and thank him,' he raised no objection and said he would go right away.

He took a short cut from the Cuddon road on a footpath that crossed the fields. The afternoon sun was warm on his face in spite of the cold, but the rutted soil under his feet was frozen hard and there was ice on a pond in a corner of a field near the school where they

231

had gone sliding when he was a boy. He wondered as he walked where he would go, feeling already the heat of Africa in the sun, and seeing the cold of the North Atlantic in the ice on the pond. For security reasons they never told you where you were going or for how long you would be away, but on the course it had been said that you usually knew within a day or two of joining a ship. Walking across the fields, with the long terraced rows of miners' houses behind him, and beyond them the stacks and the headstock of Cuddon pit, surrounded by the only environment he had ever known, it came to him again, the brief moment of panic that he had felt on the road the night he saw Tim and Jean. It came and was gone.

His Uncle Maurice lay on the couch in the drawing-room, looking pale and ill and with several days' growth of hair on his chin. Not the hard, blue growth that his father had, Denis noticed, but pale and flecked with grey and downy almost like a boy's.

'Flu,' his aunt said. 'It would have been better now if he'd gone to bed when he was told.'

She went out and left them together. Denis sat on the edge of a chair without being asked, something he would not have done a year ago. He sat, not completely at ease, but infinitely more relaxed than he usually was in this house. His uncle looked at him weakly, but with some sort of satisfaction in his expression, as if he had bought a good line in suits and, although too ill to care today, knew it would give him pleasure tomorrow.

'Good stuff that uniform,' his uncle said. 'Doe skin.'

'Yes,' said Denis, and then, presenting a speech he had rehearsed which had never extended beyond two lines, he emerged with a précis and said, 'Thank you.'

'You mean for the course, or the suit?' his uncle asked, half smiling.

'Both,' said Denis, appropriately as his mother would

have wished him to do, but not ungratefully.

'No regrets?' his uncle asked, the eyes becoming more concentrated as if the answer was important to him despite his condition.

'No,' said Denis, meaning it; ignoring or forgetting his second moment of panic.

'Your mother would have done it for you if she'd been able, if it was what you wanted,' Horsborough said. He paused, looked away and said, inconsequentially, 'You can't go against the wishes of the dead.'

Denis was silent. His uncle looked at him. 'You know what I mean?' he asked. 'Did Tim explain it to you?'

'Yes,' said Denis, half truthfully.

'Tim's in Scotland on some sort of course. You know he's on some sort of special operations job? Still won't take a commission. Not aggressive about it, though. He's not the same since he came back from France, but you won't have seen him since then, will you?'

Denis told him that they had met briefly in the bus queue.

'Not the same,' his uncle repeated. He refrained from elaborating on the difference in Tim but said, as if it had reminded him of something else, 'Do you follow your father's line in politics? Or don't you bother at all?'

Denis was not too sure what his father's line was, so he simply replied, 'I don't bother.'

'Not that it matters in wartime,' said Horsborough. 'Coalition government under Churchill, with a few plum jobs for the top Labour men. Work for everybody. Money to be earned but damn all to spend it on. Everything rationed. What's the point in striking for more if your average working man can't spend it? He's no time for banks, for saving. They live for today the colliers. I reckon I'd do the same in their job. If they save they can't save enough to buy their way out of it.'

He lapsed into silence after that, almost as if he had

forgotten Denis was there. Then his aunt came in with a tray and poured them tea.

'Nothing divides people like politics,' his uncle said, suddenly. 'Politics and money, but then they're one and the same aren't they?'

'You're not talking politics to the boy, surely?' his aunt said.

'He doesn't bother about politics.'

'Then why bore him?'

'I wasn't, was I?' He looked at Denis, half apologising, and when Denis shook his head, embarrassed, Horsborough closed his eyes as if withdrawing from the competition in favour of his wife.

She admired Denis's uniform and asked him about the course and where he hoped he would go when he went to sea. He found himself talking to her with little more restraint than he would have talked to his mother, so that the only real diffidence he felt was that of one generation to another. And then suddenly she said, 'Do you know a girl called Jean Colthard?'

He tried to give the impression that he was thinking hard on the subject while his mind coped with the confusion into which she had thrown him. Eventually he said, not daring to maintain the silence any longer, 'There are some Colthards at the Baths. He's the caretaker.'

'That's the one I mean,' his aunt said. 'Do you know her at all?'

He almost denied Jean entirely, with a force that would have made his aunt suspicious, but instead he said, 'I've seen her in Cuddon.'

She seemed to accept his answer, but gave no reason for the question. A minute or two later he stood up to go. His uncle was asleep now, gently snoring, and he followed her out of the room quietly. Standing in the doorway as he stepped outside, putting his cap on, she said, 'I'll tell Tim you came. He'll be pleased. He's often talked about you.'

She stood at the door until he reached the end of the drive, then waved to him as he closed the gate. He was glad to be out in the sunshine again. He walked away slowly, confused still by the question about Jean. Did it mean that Jean had left Ted and transferred her affections to Tim and that Tim had told his mother? Or had someone else seen them together that night? If so, did Ted know too? He would have gone to see Ted before he left home, of course, but now there was another reason for going.

He started to pack after tea in the large blue case which had been specially bought for him to take on the course. He had made little progress when his mother came in.

'You're making a mess of that.'

He acknowledged it, sheepishly grinning at her.

'You'd rather I did it, wouldn't you?'

He agreed that he would, knowing anyway that it would please her. His feelings towards her had changed subtly over the last year or so. Although at times he felt the old irritation, the temptation to hide things from her to avoid the fuss, he was increasingly aware of a growing affection inside him. That it had been latent in the womb, had flourished and been suppressed and was now coming alive again, did not occur to him. He was simply glad of the new warmth between them, and the new respect for her which to some extent his father had been responsible for awakening. He was aware, too, how much of her affection was directed towards himself, how she watched him when he did not seem to be looking. Then too she was at pains these days to avoid the minor irritations, asking where he was going and why, as if she feared any conflict between them that might damage this new relationship. Implicit also in her manner towards him now was a tacit acceptance that he was no longer a child, except to her.

He played on this now, using it to avoid what something inside him deeply feared. He said: 'There won't be time for me to go and see Stan at the Home.'

It was only partly true. It would take up half of the following day which was Sunday, but it was little more than an hour on the bus to the mental home where Stan was incarcerated.

She looked at him, not speaking for a moment. He had promised and she was disappointed but perhaps she saw the appeal in his eyes and understood what he himself could not, but could only express in a turning away. He said, putting off something to which he would never happily agree, simply to push her acceptance: 'I'll go when I come back on leave, honestly!' And then, so like the child she felt she had lost in him that she smiled, he said: 'I'll bring him something back. I'll bring him a present.'

He knew when she smiled that another hurdle had been avoided. That he was reprieved.

Later in the day, when the shop had been closed and they were sitting in the living-room, he played once more on his new found credit.

'I'd like to go and see Ted now,' he said.

His father looked up from the evening paper, not at Denis but at his mother, as if her reaction was more important than his own. But he spoke for her.

'You'll not be late, will you?' he said. 'We've only got you for another day, you know.'

'Just to see him before I go off,' said Denis. 'He'll think I'm a right one if I don't.'

'That's true enough,' said his father. 'Never lose sight of your mates.'

* * *

An hour or so later he went, wearing his heavy greatcoat with the brass buttons to keep out the cold that his father said, missing out the detail of the anatomy, was enough to freeze a brass monkey. They had not yet crossed the line where banter between man and boy becomes banter between man and man. Perhaps they never would, or have occasion to, for he had never heard his father use any expression that, even in those days, could not have been used in 'mixed company', as it was said.

Now that the phoney war was over it seemed that even in the Square they took the blackout seriously. Crossing the normally bog-like earth of the centre, now hard and traversable because of the frost, he stumbled over objects several times in the deep blackness of the night. He had almost to feel his way from the end house, counting the doorsteps, before he reached Ted's. He adjusted his uniform self-consciously, glancing about him as if anyone could indeed have seen him in the gloom, before he knocked, and found himself half wishing he had not put it on. There was a silence which meant he had not knocked hard enough, for he could hear voices inside. He knocked again, harder, and the voices ceased and after a moment or two the door was opened, more cautiously than on his previous visits, the blackout curtain carefully drawn behind it not to spill out the light. A voice from someone he could not see said, 'Who is it?'

He recognised it as Jessie's. He said, 'It's me – Denis.'

There was a silence as if, he thought, she was unsure who he might be and for a moment he thought, ridiculously, of adding his surname. Then she said, 'Come in,' and he followed her inside.

Even the light of the single gas mantle was sharp on his eyes after his journey through the darkness. Jessie closed the door behind him and brushed past him into the room. Ted and Jean were there. She had her outside coat on as if she had either just come in or was about to go out. Ted was combing his hair at a mirror over the fireplace. He looked at Denis in the mirror and turned round.

'It's the navy,' he said.

'Hi, sailor!' said Jean.

He would have thought they were teasing him except that Ted's expression had in it something that betrayed the fact that he was impressed. Jean too was looking at him half smiling but half appraising, almost as if she was meeting him for the first time.

'Sailor without a ship,' said Ted. 'When are you going to finish that course? You spend half your life on course, you blokes.'

'I've finished,' Denis said. 'I've got a ship. I join her on Monday in Liverpool.'

It was his moment. Until he said it then he had not fully realised it himself. He was a sailor. He was joining his ship on Monday. He was going to war.

He took his hat off and unbuttoned the front of his greatcoat and sat down without being asked. He felt enormously at ease and relaxed. For the first time in his relationship with Ted he felt equal.

'All right for some, eh?' said Ted. 'See the world and get paid for it!'

'Take no notice of him,' said Jessie, 'he's jealous.'

Ted said, with his usual directness, 'Of course I'm jealous. Who wouldn't be?'

He looked at Denis as he said it, the faintly bantering smile gone now. In its place was the old assured look which said, as it had always said, 'You might have more than me, but I'm the better man.' Then he turned back to the mirror, as if there was no more to be said.

There was silence for a moment as if the others too had sensed that some kind of war had taken place, and some kind of victory had been declared. Jessie was seated at the table now. There were some books in front of her as if she had been interrupted in the middle of homework. Denis fiddled with his hat. His moment had fallen flat. At the back of his mind was the thought that he should have said something, that it was possible to retrieve it, that there was an answer to Ted. But he could not find it. They were still in the old relationship, although there was a difference perhaps, for he felt the movement of irritation within him that was almost anger; a resentment of a belittling process which he had previously accepted as the norm.

It was Jean who restored the moment for him. Looking at him with an expression which could have been saying, 'Do you remember that day at the baths?' she said, 'We're going to a pub in Caselborn. Why don't you come with us?'

Denis saw Ted glance at her, then back at the mirror. He could see that Ted was not looking at his own reflection, but at himself, waiting his answer.

Denis said, for he had no real option, 'I can't. I said I'd be back early, being off on Monday.' He added, a bit dramatically, 'I might be away for years,' and was aware that Jessie had looked up from her books and was watching him.

'Years?' said Jean.

'The duration, you know,' Denis said, as if it was some kind of infinity.

Ted turned from the mirror. He picked up his coat from a nearby chair and put it on, then looked at Jean. 'Coming then?' he said, roughly, as if there had been some argument and the issue was in doubt.

She looked at him without answering, but followed him as he moved to the door. She was wearing the coat she had worn on the night he came here with Tim and was, as she had been then, a flame of colour in this drab room. Pausing at the door while Ted held back the curtain, she said to Denis, 'Will we see you again?'

He said, with an aching regret that he could not go with them, 'I expect I'll get leave.'

The curtain fell back, the door closed and they were gone. His mind followed them out into the night. They crossed the Square, stumbling as he had done, but with Ted always ahead, not waiting for Jean to catch up with him, arrogant with the assumption that when he chose to stop she would be there. Was that how it was? Denis was used to miners and their attitude to almost any woman who was not their mother; their assumption of male superiority contradicting their reverence for the womb from which they came; their capacity for violence and their capacity for an almost feminine gentleness with those of their own sex and kind who were in trouble. Such gentleness he would have given to her, but she would be denied it with Ted; or would she? How would they be in the darkness when they loved, as he imagined men and women loved, for he had nothing to draw on but his imagination? Was it the kind of life she wanted?

Who was she? The simple question entered his mind and exploded inside him. His adolescent worship was based on an ignorance of women that was almost total, such a mystery they were to him. And yet Ted had solved that mystery, or had he? Did he know about Tim?

Her waywardness baffled him; how she could be so with the two of them. There was himself, too, for whenever he had met her he had sensed that in a way she moved towards him, as if she would explore him because she must, as a climbing plant reaches for its hold on the wall. There had been others, too, for she had been talked about. Oddly, he had had no feelings of jealousy at any time, about any of them. Not even Ted, and certainly not Tim. Envy he had felt and did feel now, but there was no malice in it. Only a sadness for something he yearned for but could not have. It was not what she had offered him that day in the baths that he wanted, though the memory sometimes stirred inside him disturbingly, for he was sometimes sexually aware of other girls. He remembered that Jessie was one of them, and as he did so he remembered the room he was in and that she was there, seated at the table.

She was looking at him. She said, 'You were a long way off.'

He flushed and said, 'I'd better be going.'

'You've only just come.'

Halfway to his feet he sat down again. She looked at him across the table, half-smiling. Her hair was plain and straight and very much a schoolgirl's still. Her clothes were the kind that doubled up for school. She had a pleasant, not unattractive face, but her eyes were what marked her out from others. They reflected her moods. They betrayed her, too. Looking at her now he could see behind the smile a weight of anxiety in her eyes that he should not go yet, and yet they anticipated that he would and that she would be resigned to it as she had had to be resigned to so many things. He wanted suddenly to please her; to see pleasure in her eyes.

'When do you leave school?' he asked.

'This year,' she said. 'I'm going to college if I pass. Ted and Dad are working now. Aunt Dolly's looking after the other two. I wasn't going to go but Ted made me say I would.'

'He's right.'

'No fun for him coming home from the pit to get his own meals. Nor Dad.'

Denis looked away. It had suddenly occurred to him that there were probably things she knew that he did not. He asked, as casually as he was able, 'Will they marry?'

'I don't know,' she answered. 'Why? Have you heard anything?'

He wondered if there was something he should have heard. Instead of simply saying he hadn't he said, cunningly, 'What sort of things?'

'I don't know. They've fallen out a lot lately. I wondered if there was a reason, that's all.'

He wondered again if Ted knew about Tim. Perhaps Tim was the reason.

'They're too young to get married, anyway,' said Jessie. 'Knocking around's one thing; marriage is something else, isn't it?'

She spoke as an adult would have spoken, with the weariness of long experience, and again it was reflected in her eyes so that looking at her he felt, almost as he did with Ted, to be lacking in something.

Then the gas went out. In the darkness she said, 'Oh Lord, the meter's run out!'

His eyes accustomed themselves to the glow of the fire which was also on its last legs. In the semi-darkness she rose from the table.

He said, 'Is there anything I can do?'

'It's all right,' she said. 'I can manage. You stop there.'

She moved across the room like a shadow towards the scullery, passing like a ghost through the door. Now that the light had gone his sense of smell reacted more strongly to what he was always aware of in this house that Ted lived in – the smell of poverty. It was something that even in the small back kitchen at home he was never aware of. And yet they too were poor. Not as this house was poor though. 'They live like pigs,' it was said of people who lived in the Square, a universal condemnation by those who themselves lived on the edge of poverty but had not yet lost what they called their respectability. Did they know how close they were, how in spite of every effort they could make it could overwhelm them? Perhaps it was knowing that shrilled their voices in condemnation; knowing and fearing.

He could hear Jessie moving about in the scullery as if she was lost. Something crashed to the floor and she moaned. He got to his feet and made his way round the furniture to the door and felt his way through it.

It was pitch black in the scullery. He said, 'Are you all right?' not able to see her.

Her voice came from quite close to him in the darkness. 'I think so,' she said. 'The stool broke. I knocked my elbow. The meter's up on the wall, you can't reach it without the stool. If you could lift me up a bit I could reach it.'

He put his hand out and found himself touching her. She said, 'I'll turn round, then if you lift me up ...'

He felt her turn and his hands found her waist. 'Say when you're ready,' he said.

'I'm ready.'

He lifted her up, surprised how heavy she was for she always looked almost weightless. He heard the first coin drop, and then two more. She said, 'You can put me down now,' and he let her slide down through his arms. Then as she touched the floor and her weight passed from him he was aware that his hands were cupped around both her breasts. His face was touching her hair. It had a clean, almost scented smell that made him forget the smell of the room. It brushed softly against his cheek with a sensation that made him move his head so that he would feel it again. His hands were still on her breasts and she had not moved to escape him. He could hear her breathing softly in the darkness, as if she waited, relaxed. He moved both his hands, caressing her gently, with an instinct which traversed his inexperience, and as he did so her breathing changed, but almost imperceptibly, so that it was a moment before he was aware of it.

She turned then, swiftly, as if she had keyed herself to

escape his hands. He stood for a moment in the dark, lost, and then she was close to him again but facing him, and he put out his hands again and touched her and she came softly towards him. His mouth reached for hers and found it, but only gently touching as it is with the young at the first time.

Then suddenly she gasped and said, 'The gas!' and left him and was gone into the other room.

When he followed her in she was reaching up to where the chain hung down over the table to pull it off and there was a slight smell of gas in the air. Turning, she waited for him, not coming to him this time. He went to her and put his hands on her waist. She was still a shadow in the darkness. He put his face against her hair again as if he wanted to repeat the whole thing in the same order. It was as good as it had been the first time. It was good enough to stay with him forever, though other things might be lost. And then again he touched her breasts, and her mouth, and again and again … and over and over … touching … touching … as they sank on the rug in front of the fire … he saying, 'I'm sorry … sorry …' whenever he blundered or hurt her, and she saying, continually, 'It's all right … It doesn't matter … It doesn't matter …' as they stumbled together through the darkness …

The remnants of fog hung around the slab-stoned platform of Cuddon Station just before six o'clock on Monday morning. Denis had said goodbye to his mother at the house. Standing on the platform with his father he preferred not to think of it now. Not that there had been tears. He could have understood tears.

His father had insisted on carrying Denis's case with his one good arm, and after one feeble protest Denis had not objected, sensing that it was something his father wanted to do. They had walked through the dark empty streets in the dank, cold air, mostly in silence.

On the platform his father had run through most of the things he had obviously been trying to remember to say, and had then run out of words. He stood there now, looking intently at a poster on the opposite platform, as if straining to remember something he was convinced he had forgotten. Denis was numbed. He had barely slept, only really sinking into sleep an hour or so before they called him. He had dreamed and half dreamed in a confusion of images shaped from the events of the night before, in which Jessie and Jean were intermingled and reality and fantasy seemed one. He remembered now the moment he had left the house. She had buttoned his greatcoat possessively, but trying not to seem possessive, as if she thought it might offend him. Once she had said, but looking away and almost casually, as if it had to be said but he was not expected to take notice of it, 'I love you.' He had not replied, but had touched her gently with affection as if saying to her what she herself had said on their journey … 'It's all right … It doesn't matter … It doesn't matter' … for some pain he had caused her.

The train came out of the darkness at the end of the platform almost without him knowing it. In a confusion of opening doors, lifting of cases, a fearful hiss of steam and then the doors slamming he was into the compartment and pulling down the window as the train moved out. It stuck halfway and he could not move it. His father's face was working as if he had remembered what he had to say, but too late. Denis tried to smile, his face stiff with the shock of the sudden parting, and then they were past the end of the platform and into the dark morning where everything that was familiar to him was hidden.

Years later his father said, 'I stood on that bloody platform and watched you go. I'd got used to seeing

young lads go down the pit in the cage for the first time
… Fourteen year old, and you looked no older … But
you were going to the other side of the world happen,
with a war on, and we should never know one day to
another whether we'd see you again … I wanted to open
the carriage door and drag you out and tell 'em to stuff
their bloody war!'

CHAPTER EIGHTEEN

The convoy left Liverpool on a grey morning in March. The ships had left the various docks they were in and had anchored in mid-river the day before. The ship to which Denis had been told to report was a freighter of some 7,000 tons gross. It had been ploughing the seas for more than twenty years, mostly carrying the same type of cargo to the same ports. Its grey painted hull was grained with the dust from the coaling wharfs, for the boilers were coal fired. As the dust from the slag heaps at Cuddon crept into the houses and occupied them to the point where the occupants gave up the battle, so it did here, though here the battle was fought by man driving man.

It had been a strange day for Denis that first day in Liverpool. From a sleepy start in the warm familiarity of the kitchen at home, the gradual awakening of a sense of excitement, and then the tearing suddenness of his departure from Cuddon station, he was plunged into another world. Two soldiers had got into the carriage he was in at Wakefield. They had only met while waiting for the train, but already, as happened so often in wartime, they were plunged into each others lives, comparing experiences with an instant communication they could never achieve on leave with the civilians at home. Already the gulf that would never be crossed was forming between those who had been and those who had not.

They had brought him into the conversation on equal terms as one of themselves, offering him a cigarette. He had taken it, instinctively. It was the first he had ever smoked, openly, and as he held it between his fingers and gently puffed as to the manner born, the pain of the image of his father's face as the train had pulled out began to fade from him.

At Liverpool he lost them in the sudden activity that followed the train pulling in. He had known them for a little less than two hours but their going again left him with the small death that accompanies an end too close to a beginning. As he came out into the entrance of Exchange Station, uncertain which way to go, his heavy suitcase was neatly taken from him by a small twisted man who must have been in his early sixties and who had some deformity of the spine which made him appear to be permanently leaning backwards. He received the address from Denis impassively and set off without further comment as if it was of no consequence whether Denis followed or not. In the event they covered, ridiculously, rather less than a hundred yards before they arrived at the premises in question and he accepted, with muted delight, the precious half-crown which Denis's inexperience thrust upon him. Relieved to be free of the embarrassment of allowing a cripple to carry his suitcase, Denis picked it up and staggered inside.

From then, in a confusion of questioning, instruction, filling of official forms and directions which made no allowance for inexperience, he was carried on a tide which deposited him on the dockside where the ship was berthed.

His heart sank as he looked at it. Grey, rust streaked and apparently deserted, it gave the impression that whichever side it belonged to must be the losing side. Despite the twenty-five pounder gun on the stern and the Oerlikon anti-aircraft guns mounted in gun boxes on either side of the bridge, it had the look of total defeat.

As the convoy steamed line-ahead up the Mersey, it threaded its way through a channel of defeat. Sunken ships were everywhere. Some had only their masts showing. One large hull, which must have been resting on a sandbank, had split in two and showed a cross section of cabins and what had been the engine room.

Free of the marked channel, the ships formed into some kind of order and steamed northwards into the Irish Sea, for although their course would ultimately be set for the South Atlantic this was the route which was safest from air attack. Long before they left the estuary Denis had the first awful experience of sea sickness which was to stay with him, on and off, throughout his time at sea, blighting even the potentially happier moments. It stayed with him, this first time, for the whole of the three weeks voyage, until he ultimately vomited blood.

Throughout it he did his four-hour watch. Sea sickness was considered an unfortunate normality rather than an illness for which one could be excused duty. A certain amount of sympathy came his way, but it was not overdone. Each day, just before noon, he would sit upright in his bunk where, lying down, he achieved some slight measure of relief. He would brace himself against the first grim heave and, by an effort of will, survive it. Sometimes the Nigerians who were stewards on the ship would be in there, emptying the slops from the washbasin cabinets, or filling the water tanks above them that fed the basins. They would watch him, nodding and smiling encouragement, sincere in their concern, as if they said, 'We too know how it is'. Once he almost fell and Sam, the eldest, took hold of him and held him. For a moment, until he looked up into the kindly black face with its top of curly, greying hair, he had felt that his father held him.

He felt ashamed that they should have to empty the slops which included, often, the contents of his stomach. It was not because they were black that he felt ashamed; the white man exhibiting his weakness before a lesser breed; but because he knew that others would have it so, and it shamed him to be a recipient of their kindness when he was labelled, whether he liked it or not, with the arrogance of his breed. On deck sometimes, trying to obey the injunction of the chief sparks that it was better to be upright in the open air than on his back in the foetid cabin, he would seek out their company if they were about. They often were, standing at the rail of the ship looking towards the bow, for on this turn of the trip they were going home. He wondered if, on the journey out, they looked towards the stern as he did now. For he endured a double sickness now, his heart aching for the familiarity of the world he had left. It was another weakness he was ashamed of, though he need not have been. Later in the war, on a troopship sailing between Lagos and Karachi, he learned the universality of grief. Talking to the ship's doctor about the large number of Nigerian soldiers who were dying on the trip, he asked him if it was some kind of plague. 'A plague of the heart,' the doctor told him. 'They just curl up and die from homesickness, nothing else.'

Apart from the sickness, he found the watches boring at first. His own watch, usually known as the Death Watch, lasted from twelve until four o'clock, so that he was in the wireless cabin throughout the afternoon and the early hours of the morning. Turned to the distress wavelength for most of the time, with strict instructions to call his superior who slept in the cabin next door should anything untoward occur, he often caught himself on the edge of sleep.

Later, as the sickness to some extent abated, he started to read. Tim had left a dozen or so books for him at home to select from. They were an odd collection, almost all of them written by people whose names were strange to him, so because he had no means of choosing he brought the lot. The night he decided to take one on watch with him he thumbed through them, again finding it difficult to make a choice. Eventually he chose a book by a popular philosopher, one C. E. M. Joad whose name he knew from the radio as a member of the Brains Trust series. Its title, *A Guide to Modern Wickedness*, together with a glance at some of the chapter headings, helped to make his mind up, promising titillation if nothing else. He had little hope that any of them would entertain him, for it was obvious that Tim had chosen them with the object of furthering his education.

He had not yet learned to read a book, other than a work of popular fiction, from beginning to end. Those non-fiction works he had read, usually travel books, were taken in small doses in no particular order. This was no exception. Alone in the wireless room, with static crackling through the headphones, he found a chapter heading somewhere near to the end and started to read. Had he started the book at some other point it might have had no effect on him whatsoever. As it was it had two effects, one long term and the other more or less immediate. He started to think about sex, which was the subject of the chapter though not really the object of the book.

Long before the end of the chapter he put it down. He

was back at home, the evening before he had come away, not in the way he thought of it sometimes, as a warm, safe haven very far away, but actually there on the rag rug in front of the fire with Jessie. He discovered, not for the first time, but at a point in his life where he desperately needed it, the unlimited capacity of the imagination.

She came to him at first erotically. He explored her physically in a way which extended beyond the one actual experience they had had which had been dominated by guilt, fear of rejection, and the blind curiosity of first time love. He did it all again, but did it better. Most of all he did it with confidence and with a growing desire for the time to come when he would do it again, and again, and again.

Even his sickness was almost forgotten in the days that followed as he pursued his new found delight. He came on watch, not with the reluctance with which a man arises from his bed to prepare to go to a job which totally bores him, but with the anticipation almost of a lecher responding to an invitation from a woman with qualities beyond his wildest dreams.

His daydreams at home, which had concentrated on Jean and had been permeated by a romantic unreality, were as nothing compared to the sensual delight he drew from the imaginative repeat of his one real experience. Like music heard too often, which has to be lost for a time before its impact can be experienced in full again, it might be thought that such dreams would have led to satiation. That it did not was due not to the opiate effect it had on his sickness, and the way in which it delightfully filled previously boring hours, but to the way in which his imagination worked so many variations on the basic theme.

He could not have remembered, so varied from watch to watch were his dreams, at what particular point in his headlong flight tenderness obtruded, but it did. Looking down on her in the glow of the fire, her head turned slightly away and always with the same expression, as if at the moment it had happened it had fixed itself forever in his mind, he began to love. It was not that the sensuality in any way diminished, but that it became increasingly imbued with something else, and for a time the two co-existed.

The morning he came on deck and saw land for the first time for three weeks was another time that he could recall throughout his later years, and always he saw it with the same visual impact. The morning was warm and still and there was no hint of the coming heat of the day. They were anchored in the harbour at Lagos in West Africa, some half dozen ships of the convoy having broken away in the night while the rest sailed on to Durban. White buildings, the blue of the water against the sand curve of the shore, and the enormous variety of colour in the vegetation fixed like a snapshot in his mind. His sickness had gone now that the ship was at anchor and was almost, but not quite, forgotten.

Bum boats were already crowding the sides of the ship, loaded with pineapples, massive clusters of bananas and curios made from brass and wood. As he looked down on them the second sparks, his immediate senior, joined him at the rail. A Scotsman from Edinburgh, barely a year older than himself but already a veteran of three voyages, including one sinking, he had been tolerant and friendly with Denis throughout what must have been a trying outward voyage, since he had been obliged to share the cabin with him throughout his sickness. Denis knew little about him except that his name was Andrew Nevin, for there was a quietness about him that reminded him of Tim, so that he had been shy and withdrawn with him in the way that he used to be with Tim, and the conversation had been somewhat limited.

'Better now?' he asked, smiling, knowing the relief.

Denis nodded and smiled back somewhat sheepishly. Too ill at the time to feel embarrassed, he was reminded now of the indignity of the experience. It made him think of Ted. Ted would not have been sick, or if he had been would have found some way of hiding it, in the way that if he ever felt fear in the pit he would have hidden it. Or would the malady have conquered even Ted? There was a distinct possibility, and as he thought of it it became a probability, that it would have. It was another mark on the plus side of the never ending game his memory played with his childhood feelings of inferiority, uncertainty, and an awareness of the shifting sands. Deeply rooted in the eternal battle between Neanderthal and Cro-Magnus, as he later came to think of it, the image of Ted prostrate with sea-sickness added brightness to a morning that shone already.

The sheepishness went from his mind and he said to Andrew, 'When do we go ashore?'

'We'll ask the Chief at breakfast, shall we?' said Andrew.

They went ashore the following day, a crowd of them in a launch owned by the shipping company. There was a holiday atmosphere in the launch, born of three weeks at sea. The Mate and a couple of the engineer officers were in the boat with Andrew and himself and a dozen or so members of the crew. Most of them he knew in some degree or another. The Chippy was there, a man well into his sixties with a long white beard. If you died on the voyage he would sew you in canvas, putting the last stitch through your nose, and would be paid a pound for the job. He sat in the stern now, smiling at the world in general, and wearing a clean white shirt. He caught Denis's eye, watching him, and smiled and shouted across the boat, 'Back in the world now, are we lad?' Everyone laughed and looked at Denis, as if in some way they shared his renewal and were glad for him. He felt a sudden great warmth towards them, a kinship that excluded the officers and Andrew; for they were like the men he knew at home; like his father with the blue scars of his past trade on his face. He wished desperately that his father could see him now, the long voyage behind him, on his way ashore; a man amongst men, come of age.

'Ashore' was not the culmination of the long dream of a voyage that the tone in which it was said at sea promised it to be. Though not the collection of mud huts that the name West Africa conjured into the mind at that time, Lagos was light years, looking forward from then, from the city it ultimately became. There was a temporary air about it, as if the inhabitants had not finally decided whether to stay. It was reflected in the buildings with their corrugated iron roofs and in the dusty unmade roads. Here and there more permanently optimistic buildings had arisen, but the overall impression was of a society marking time.

Only the Africans were permanent, so that you felt that if the buildings were removed they would still be there, cycling leisurely down the dusty roads with umbrellas raised against the sun, or walking silently and swiftly as if on some vital errand along pathways which seemed to lead nowhere.

The strange mixtures of clothing worn by the men seemed to represent the cast-offs of generations of victims of the White Man's Grave, as it was known; their wardrobes emptied by the widows of their grandchildren so that, incongruously, crowned with a bowler which went out of fashion a hundred years ago, some long, lithe striding black figure would vanish across the landscape wearing striped long johns, and barefooted.

Denis was unaffected by the sight of so many black faces in the swarming streets where the white man was the rarity. He was, after all, used to black faces, even if the black did wash off. The dire threats used against naughty children in Britain, that 'a black man would get them', held little terror in Cuddon where the black man could only be Dad. He had, however, been shocked that morning by the routine visit to the ship of a doctor from the shore. The doctor had been invited into the mess for breakfast, where they sat in order of rank. What shocked and embarrassed Denis was not that the doctor was black, but that he had been seated below himself, whose rank was the lowest of all. In Cuddon the doctor was akin to God.

The group from the launch split up on the dockside, and Denis, with half a dozen or so others who included Andrew, set out to walk towards the main buildings. Outside the dock gates they were almost smothered by an avalanche of small black bodies, children who could not have been more than five or six years of age. They were babbling, in English, monotonously but individually, the same phrase. At first, because they spoke as individuals and not as a chorus or as the chanting of a crowd at a football match, it sounded like many different things. Soon, however, as small black hands clutched at his shirt in their anxiety not to lose him, he realised that they were saying, quite simply with the precision of parrots, 'You want my sister? My sister white.' Some of the men in the group, who seemed familiar with the scene, simply pushed them off good humouredly and strode on. The others followed and the little black touts, knowing probably already that it was the wrong time, but ever hopeful, turned back to the gates to await the next launch.

The day was hot now, with a kind and intensity of heat that Denis had never before experienced. Briefly, as they walked through the streets and in and out of the shops, the heat and the strangeness of his surroundings fused in a moment of home sickness and he was back in the kitchen at home with his father seated opposite reading the paper.

As they stopped here and there in the shops the group gradually diminished until there was only Andrew, himself, and, oddly, the Chippy. Soon they were finding themselves in places where they had already been. Chippy, watching their expressions, smiled.

'That's it, lads,' he said eventually. 'That's ashore, more or less. You want the Yankee run next time. New York, Macey's …'

Their expressions registered their disappointment. Chippy said, 'Anyway, you don't want me trailing with you. You go off on your own if you want. It'll happen be interesting to you. I've seen it all before, haven't I?'

'That's all right, Chippy,' said Andrew. 'We might as well stick together. I feel a bit like glue in this bloody heat.'

'Fancy a swim?' asked Chippy.

'There's barracuda in the harbour,' Denis said. 'Fourth engineer told me.'

'He'll swim with the rest choose what he told you. But I don't mean the harbour as a matter of fact, I know where there's a swimming pool.'

'It'll be crowded,' said Andrew. 'We'll never get near.'

'Crowded? There'll be nobody there as likely as not. Want me to lead the way?'

He grinned at them mischievously and, although Denis thought he was pulling their legs they followed him down the road.

A hole had been dug in the ground some twenty feet by ten. A tarpaulin, probably a hatch cover from a ship, was staked around the edges and prevented the water from soaking away. It was makeshift, but it worked. They spent an hour or more in and out of the tepid, murky water, eventually learning to ignore the fact that as they jumped in the lizards jumped out.

Chippy sat on the grass nearby with his friends who had built the pool. They were missionaries, representing some breakaway Methodist group that Denis had never heard of, and lived in a corrugated iron bungalow on the same patch of ground. The man was thin, balding and wore spectacles. For most of the time he smiled gently at no one or anyone, but said little. His accent was what Denis's mother would have called 'educated' and reminded Denis of Tim. The woman was quite different. She was plump, amiable and garrulous and talked all the time to Chippy in a never ending London working class voice, until Denis wondered that Chippy could bear it unless he was quietly asleep. Their daughter was thin like the father and had the same high forehead and, like her father, rarely spoke. She was not very attractive, Denis thought, and his newly awakened sensuality, which might have been expected to respond to almost any woman after three weeks at sea, totally ignored her.

Later they ate in one of the small rooms of the bungalow. There seemed to be only two, and where they slept was a mystery he never solved. The freshness and sharpness of the fruit of which the meal was mainly composed was another new experience, but the most lasting came later, after the meal was over and the conversation, mainly about the war and the life back home, faltered. The man got up from the table and said to the woman, 'I think I'll play now,' and simply vanished into the other room like a child excusing himself but not waiting for formal permission.

They sat in silence for there seemed nothing to be said. Denis thought that Chippy was smiling behind his beard, but his eyes were directed downwards at the table so that he could not really tell. No one moved, as if the stillness of the woman and the girl was a signal for general stillness. The windows were open and the stillness echoed out into the dark of the African night, and came back again as if it would fold itself over them, layer on layer, for as long as they remained.

It came, not just through the door, or through the window echoing back through the night, but through the corrugated iron walls as if there was nothing that could hold or contain it.

In the room next door the man was playing a piano.

CHAPTER NINETEEN

They left an hour or so later. Chippy kept saying they must go because the launch would be coming for them. The man was back in the room now, sitting silently, looking down at the table as if he was listening to himself playing in the other room. The girl was silent too and scarcely moved, except that from time to time she glanced at the man's bowed head. The woman talked almost ceaselessly. In the brief pauses while she took breath Denis, Chippy and Andrew would start to rise but would barely clear two inches from the seat before she started again, so they would sit and wait for the next brief pause, only to rise and fall again.

Eventually they reached the door, and then as if they had not much moved their feet but had been slid by some invisible force, they were outside in the night air. They had thought that she would follow them, but she stayed just inside the door as they started to back away inch by inch into the darkness. The last thing Denis heard before they turned and almost ran down the track was the woman saying to the girl, behind her, 'It's good of him to bring them, to keep them away from the temptations,' and Chippy coughed as if to drown her words, but of course he was too late.

They were a fair way down the track before Andrew, who had obviously heard too, stopped and addressed himself to Chippy.

'Kept us away from the temptations, did you?'

'The what?' asked Chippy, pretending deafness through age.

'The temptations!'

'What temptations?'

'You heard what she said.'

'I didn't hear anything.'

'You old twister,' said Andrew, but amiably.

'Happen she means all these white sisters you were offered down at the dock.'

'White sister my foot!' said Andrew, then, hopefully, 'Are there any white sisters?'

'Not white,' said Chippy. 'Pale shade of khaki's about the nearest you could get.'

'Where are they then?'

'Want to have a look, do you?'

'A look?'

'A look – for the experience, like.'

'You call a look "the experience"!'

'I don't mind you having a look.'

'A quick flash?'

'A look's all you're getting,' said Chippy, adding, magnanimously, 'I was going to give you a look anyway. Why do you think I kept saying the launch'd be waiting for us. It's not for a couple of hours yet. I'm showing you round. You're young. You should see what you can while you're here. I believe in it. But only a look-see, mind!'

'You believe all that stuff then?' asked Andrew.

'What stuff?'

'The religious stuff, back there. All that rubbish we had rammed down our throats.'

'It wasn't him, it was her. He's the Reverend, not her.'

'He should keep her in her place, then.'

'They're good people,' said Chippy, a note of anger creeping into his voice.

'I didn't say they weren't.'

'He can play the piano, any road up.'

'Classical stuff,' said Andrew contemptuously. 'Who wants to listen to that?'

Denis did, but he said nothing. His mother liked what she called the 'light' classics, so opposed, he presumed, to the 'heavy' classics. He did not know to which category the sound they had just heard belonged, or what it was, or who had written it. He only knew that he wanted to hear it again, as he had heard it then, sitting in the corrugated iron bungalow with three weeks at sea behind him, the African night outside, and the face of the girl as she had listened. He had watched her, in brief glances at first in case she noticed that he was watching her, but she was oblivious to everything except the music. As he watched her he had realised that there was something about her that reminded him of Jessie. It was nothing to do with physical attraction, for Jessie was much more attractive, in fact there was no similarity either in colouring or features. It was only when the music stopped and the girl looked up that he realised that the similarity was in the eyes. She had looked directly at him and her eyes had said, 'We have nothing, but we have that, and that is everything,' but with a challenge in her expression, as if she expected him to understand what she said and to deny it.

He wondered about them now as he followed the sound of Chippy and Andrew arguing. The strange mixture that they were, particularly the man and the woman. It was not that you looked at them and thought, 'How did they come to marry?' Most of the marriages he knew were like this, even that of his own parents. The younger ones not so much so, perhaps, but even with them you could sometimes see it begin to happen. Ted and Jean were different, perhaps. If they married it would be, in a way, 'right', whereas in a different situation he sensed, in spite of the strength of the youthful attraction she had had for him, marriage between Jean and himself would be 'wrong'. He felt this instinctively, but did not know why. The strong sense of shock he had had the night he saw Jean with Tim had something to do with the same instinctive feeling. It fitted neither Tim as he knew him, nor Jean as he knew her, except for her reputation as a 'teaser'. He was not to know then that what he lacked was an understanding of the relationship between men and women in terms of sex in all its complexity. The tattered remnants of romanticism, doomed as this was, had gathered themselves together with the outbreak of war for a final orgy. Women gave themselves ritualistically on the altar of parting as if the excuse was necessary for a release of their own sexuality. How could sex be immoral when it was obviously patriotic? It did not occur to him that this could have been the case with Jessie, though in fact it would have happened anyway; but for all he knew at that time it could have been so. It did not occur to him either that one could respectably have one relationship without the other. To him at that time sex and romance were inextricably mingled in an inevitable process which ended in marriage.

That end he had not even contemplated in his dreams of Jessie except in a hazy, romantic way, where they stood at the altar and said, 'I will'. Beyond that point he did not go. His mother, he knew, would have what his father called a 'dicky fit' if she became aware that he was involved in a serious relationship with a girl, particularly with a girl from 'The Square', and Ted's sister at that. It was something he would have to cope with in the future, where marriage lay – in the far, far distant future.

He had written to Jessie on the voyage and had posted it when they came ashore that day. In fact, he had written several letters, most of which he had torn up on re-reading. In the end the letter he posted to her was factual, a fairly brief and formal account of his life since he had left home. There was nothing in it that gave even a hint of his real feelings, except that at the end he had written, 'I miss you', and then, almost as an afterthought, had added … 'very much'. The letters he had torn up were more true to his feelings, were love letters in fact, but the truth had strangely embarrassed him. If she had written to him in such terms he would have been delighted. Did she feel so about him, he wondered? He had no way of knowing. After the suddenness of their intimacy they had both been shy and excessively formal, except that at the moment of parting she had suddenly pulled his head towards her, kissed him on the cheek, and said, 'I'm glad.' It was all he really knew about her reaction for of course there had been no letters. What would she write if she wrote to him? When would he hear from her? When?

He quickened his pace to catch up with the others. Andrew was ahead of Chippy now, striding on as if he knew the way. Coming level with Chippy, Denis said, 'Will there be any letters this trip, Chippy?' as if he thought there might be a different answer from Chippy to the one he had had when he had asked someone else on the ship.

'Might be some at Freetown,' Chippy said, 'after we come from the Congo. We shall pick a convoy up at Freetown.'

'How do you know we're going to the Congo?' It was the first time Denis had heard this mentioned.

'I don't,' said Chippy, 'except that that's where we went the trip before, and the trip before that, and the one before that and all come to think of it.'

'I thought it was secret,' said Denis, remembering what the chief sparks had told him about security. The chief sparks took the war very seriously.

'It is,' said Chippy, 'except to you and me,' and chuckled in the darkness.

'Does Andrew know the way?' Denis asked.

'Not unless he's a mind reader. He's on his dignity. We've had a fall out. He says he doesn't want any sermons from me.'

'About what?'

'About looking out for himself where women are concerned. He's going to get himself a nice big dose one of these days.'

'A dose of what?' asked Denis.

'Clap,' said Chippy, brief and to the point.

'What's clap?'

There was a silence and for a moment Denis thought Chippy had not heard him. Then he asked, out of the darkness, 'Where did you say you were brought up?'

'Cuddon in Yorkshire.'

'I know Cuddon,' said Chippy. 'I was brought up in Rothwell. There'll not be much clap in Cuddon, they don't travel far afield enough. Stick to their own firesides.' He paused, then said, 'I'm talking about VD. You've heard of VD haven't you?'

Denis had heard of VD. Vaguely he had heard of it. He knew that it was a disease that men caught from women, though that it might operate the other way round did not occur to him. It was a joke in a way, or was treated as such in the conversations he had overheard where it cropped up.

'I've heard of it,' he said, slightly embarrassed.

'Heard people joke about it have you?'

'Yes,' said Denis.

'It's no joke. It's a scourge in this business. It finished Beethoven off.'

Because of the way Chippy said it, Denis assumed for a moment that Beethoven must have been a former shipmate of his. Then Chippy added, 'Went deaf, before he died. Imagine being able to make music like that and then not be able to hear it. That we've just heard I mean.'

'That was Beethoven?'

'Who did you think it was – Charlie Kunz? Sonata Pathetique, that was – last movement. Played it the first time I came here, the Reverend did. Was trained as a pianist, you know. Gave it all up to come out here.'

He quickened his step, his interest switching again to Andrew ahead in the darkness but only just discernible now.

'Where the hell does he think he's going. He doesn't know the way.'

Then Andrew slowed down as if he heard him, but only enough to make sure he stayed ahead.

'You'll have guessed where we're going, I reckon?' Chippy asked, in a casual sort of way.

Denis played with the word that had been in his mind since they had had the conversation about the slight shade of khaki girls shortly after leaving the bungalow. He said, trying to sound as casual as Chippy, 'Brothel?'

He could sense that the old man glanced at him in the darkness, and wished he could see his expression.

'Nay, lad,' said Chippy, 'you don't think I'd take you to a brothel? Hotel, they call it. Bit of night life. All there is in this God forsaken hole. There might be a bit of touting on the side, but not a brothel! I'm taking you for your education, that's all. Taking you to see these khaki coloured women we talked about. To see, not to touch mind. Understand?'

'Yes,' said Denis, not understanding at all.

He and Chippy caught thc launch but Andrew stayed. Chippy had simply asked Andrew if he was coming as the time for the launch drew near, had received a negative and had accepted it without further argument. He had not asked Denis, except to say, 'Ready for off then?' in a way which totally assumed that Denis would follow him.

The hotel had been crowded with air force, army and navy, and merchant seamen like themselves, together with a handful of debauched looking civilians, victims not so much of tropical disease, but of the more common and equally incurable disease of boredom.

The women were there, a constant inflow and outflow, their colour aptly described by Chippy's 'slight shade of khaki'. Many were beautiful, too. There was no other word, Denis thought, to describe them. He wondered how they came to be there, aliens to both whites and blacks, and would have liked to have asked the old man except that he feared to seem more than casually interested. Desire stirred in him but only briefly for he was a boy in a hardbitten world of men who treated the women with a casual arrogance which was common among the men in Cuddon. He had envied it in Ted, but did he now? He did not think so, so alien was it to the feelings he had for Jessie. And yet there had been moments in that time he had with Jessie, and in his after dreams, when he had been with her as he imagined such men would be with women. Lust had made him heedless of her pain, though she could not completely suppress it, so that he knew her pain as well as her pleasure. He had felt the surge of it driving him uncontrollably like an enormous wave of darkness that curled over him and broke, obliterating the other more complex emotions.

All this was in his mind as he walked back to the dock with Chippy. Why had Chippy assumed he would come as Andrew had not come? If other men were like that, why not he also? For the seed was there, he knew. Was it simply his age? Would he, one day, be arrogant in desire, seeking nothing but to be obliterated by the wave?

Almost as if Chippy had read his thoughts, he said, 'You can go all sorts of ways in life. You choose for yourself where you go.'

Denis made a noise which was intended to imply agreement; but did he agree? His choice had been Jean, not Jessie. What happened with Jessie and himself had been accidental, almost. He pursued it now, in his dreams, in his thoughts, as if it was a road he had chosen to travel; but was it?

He was aware, suddenly, of how far he had come in the last three weeks since the train pulled out of Cuddon station leaving his father on the platform. The relationship with Jessie had developed without her being there to in any way influence him. He had created it from the seed sown in the hour or so they had had together the night before he left, and yet it was real. He looked at her and she was there, and when he spoke to her she answered.

Another thought entered his head now. There was the possibility that another seed had been sown that night. It was a possibility which had occurred to him more than once during the voyage, but his sickness and the fact that it was too potentially disastrous to contemplate made him push it away. It was the possibility that Jessie was pregnant.

Again, as if to push the point home, Chippy said, seeming again to read his thoughts, 'They're all bastards, the women you saw back there. Fathered by whites that took their pleasure and then took their hook. Misery, that's what you make when you make life. You make misery.'

CHAPTER TWENTY

Even the introduction of rationing did not alter the tenor of life in Cuddon, for the peacetime diet had been less than the wartime ration for most of the population, and even now there were many who could not afford to use all their coupons. Those who could not would sell them to others better off. The extra money that poured into many of the homes as women went to work on munitions and other occupations did not all go on improving their lot, for as industry re-tooled to produce weapons of war, the production of consumer goods dropped. The shortages of beer which hit many areas of the country were not allowed to occur in the mining villages, as if the government realised what the drop in morale might do to the output of coal.

The pubs were fuller than they had been for years. Even in the immediate pre-war years women were rarely seen in pubs, and then only certain kinds of women. Now they joined the men openly, sipping port and lemon by the gallon.

Jean started at the munitions factory the week after

Denis left to join his ship. She joined the queue of women at the bus stop in Cuddon main street at six every morning, and was back at the same time each night. Ted now rarely saw her during the week, for she was often too exhausted to come out. At weekends they would meet and catch the bus to Caselborn, visiting a pub where they felt safe.

Ted was increasingly impatient of the restriction placed on their relationship by the attitude of her parents, for both were now working and earning money and could have afforded to set up a modest home. He could not understand that her unwillingness to tell them yet was due more to her affection for them than fear of what they might say or do. She would justify her anticipation of their reaction by pointing out to him that both were barely yet seventeen, and even in his impatience he knew that most parents would be regarded as having a legitimate objection to such an early marriage.

'You can see their point of view,' she would say, pleading with him. He would fall silent, and eventually change the subject. It was his way of acknowledging that he could.

In her absence during the week he found himself spending more time with his father. It worried him, now that his mother had died, that the older man seemed to have no friendships other than the casual meetings he had with men of his own age and generation in the pub. Always closer to his father than to his mother, he had, in the months following her death, become increasingly attached to him. It was in a way as if Hoyle had replaced Denis; as if they were mates. He would have liked to have opened out more on the subject of politics, for he respected his father's political martyrdom and was increasingly proud of it. As he read more and became increasingly radical in his young, idealistic way he saw his father more and more as a hero of his times, a victim both of the capitalist system and of the working class failure to unite. He knew him to be a deviationist, for he was rapidly learning the jargon, but found it easy to excuse though hard to understand. He saw it as part of the ageing process, an inevitable falling off over the years, the weariness that follows a lifetime's battle against the forces of reaction. That it might be an intellectual rejection of his earlier beliefs due to his reading and the accumulated wisdom and experience of his years, he would not have accepted even had it occurred to him. In any event, they had continued to turn their backs on any kind of conflict in the conversations between them.

He followed him one night to the pub and found him, as usual, standing alone in the public bar.

'Where's your mates?' he asked, when his father had ordered him a pint.

'Cemetery mostly,' his father said, with only half a smile. 'Given up in disgust and gone afore their hour.'

How was he to tell him that he worried about him in his loneliness, Ted wondered. As close as they had become, it was something they did not communicate directly. It passed between them hidden behind the words, intricately woven. They had never, so far as Ted could remember, seriously discussed a personal matter. He tried now, awkwardly, to put right this failure to communicate.

'You're on your own too much,' he said, lightly as if he made a joke of it.

He sensed rather than saw his father glance sideways at him, as if he recognised the attempt.

'Some people like their own company best,' said Hoyle.

'Do you?'

'I've grown used to it over these last years.'

'I worry about you,' Ted said, looking ahead of him.

It was easier when you didn't look. Again he was aware of his father's glance.

'No need to worry about me, lad,' Hoyle said. 'I'm content enough.' He paused, then said, 'It's good of you to bother, though,' as if he had received an unexpected gift.

They were silent for a moment, then Hoyle said, 'What's up with your sister these days?'

'Jessie?'

'You've noticed nothing?'

'No, but then I've barely seen her since I changed shift.'

'I heard her weeping t'other night.'

'Weeping?'

'In her room, weeping, after she'd gone to bed.'

He would not have gone to her, Ted thought. The same gap existed with Jessie and his father as had existed between his father and himself. Yet he would have lain there, Ted knew, longing to go and comfort her but unable to do so. Why?

It was as if he had spoken aloud, for Hoyle said now, 'I've felt ashamed over the years for the little I've given you. It got so I could barely look at you, leave alone talk, for fear you'd turn your backs on me.'

'Nay,' said Ted. 'Not you.'

'Your mother, you mean?'

Looking for a truth that would not hurt too much, Ted exonerated her in her own words. 'The Square soured her,' he said.

There was a silence, then Hoyle said, 'You're young to be understanding a thing like that.'

It was in Ted's mind to say that it was something she had taught him herself, but it was too private a memory to be put in words. There were things you could communicate, he found, and things you could not.

'You've no idea what it could be?'

'Jessie? No? … No, I've not.'

He remembered the mystery boy friend, but it was not like Jessie to weep for a fantasy, a dream, for all the dreaming she did in her books.

He said, 'I'll talk to her, see if owt's wrong.'

'What about you then?' his father asked, as if he feared the barriers might rise between them again before all the questions were put.

'Nay, I'm reight enough,' Ted replied.

'You and Jean?'

'I get a bit sick of waiting round t'corner so her mum and dad can't see me when she comes out.'

'Chapel at work is that,' said Hoyle.

'Aye, but I don't see why I should suffer it. I don't belong to chapel. Neither would Jean if she'd a choice.'

'You can see their point of view, though, the Colthards.'

'I told Jean I could.'

'I look at it from your point of view, same as they do from hers. You can rush into marriage too soon, pay for it all your life after.'

'You're another against us, are you?'

Ted said it more in hurt than in anger. There were other things than politics, it seemed, that could endanger their relationship.

'I married too soon myself.'

'We want to marry. We're warm with each other.'

'It'd be no good telling you I felt the same about your mam. When you're young you think nobody's felt like you do.'

Again into Ted's head came the often now recurring picture. The old face framed in the golden hair. The ruination of a life. The strident ugliness of his mother's voice echoing around the Square. The awfulness of their life in a house with too many children and not enough to provide. Could there be love in all that? But then there was the other picture, seen through the murk of the years.

'I wouldn't deny you that,' he said to his father.

Hoyle looked at him again and Ted sensed his surprise at this understanding, but again it was beyond him to tell his father who he owed it to.

'It was the Square,' he said, 'not you,' though the man beside him had not asked for absolution, and now rejected it.

'It's been said I brought the Square on meself. When Council dished out houses I got the Square, along with the idle sods that were put there because they wouldn't work. I was known as a rabble rouser in them days.'

'You were right to try and rouse 'em against them that put 'em there.'

'They put theirselves there. There's work-shy buggers in every class.'

'Taking the side of the masters, Dad?'

'You can't fight the masters with them on your back. You put weapons in the hands of the masters when you defend such as them.'

'We're what we're made by them that rules us,' Ted said. It was one of the facts which had rung true to him in his reading and to which he had clung.

'I used to believe that.'

'It's true.'

'I don't believe it any more. I wish I could. It'd all be black and white if I could still believe that.'

'You'd turn your back on all you fought for and the price you paid?'

'Nay,' said Hoyle, vehemently. 'Nay, nay – you mistake me. But I'll not turn me back on the truth, neither.'

They were silent then, a tenseness between them. It was as if each waited for the other. Then Ted said, 'We shall not fall out.'

He turned to his father, smiled, and said again. 'We shall not fall out.' But there was a pain inside him.

'You've an old head on young shoulders, there,' Hoyle said. 'Don't think it's too old to learn, that's all. When there's nowt left to learn it's not Utopia we've come to, we've come to the end of the world.'

Ted watched Jessie closely after that, taking over his father's role as he had said he would. She seemed at first no different to the way she had always been, except that examinations were approaching and she spent even more time with her books, but then that was understandable. Sometimes though, when he was at home, reading or simply dozing by the fire, he would look up at her and see her looking into the far distance with a lost expression on her face as if she had come across some problem in her work that she could not cope with.

'Penny for 'em,' he said once, lightly, hoping to draw her out. She had not seemed to hear him and he had repeated it again, and she had turned her head and looked at him without comprehension as if she had heard the sound but not the words.

'Penny for 'em,' he said, for the third time.

'For what?'

'Your thoughts.'

'Not worth a penny.'

Her smile, he thought, was a bit forced, as if she had conjured it up to disguise her feelings from him.

'I'll give a penny for 'em even so. Twopence, happen.'

'Oh, shut up, I'm busy,' she had said. 'I'm thinking.'

Then she had bent over her work again to show him that it had been that all the time.

Sometimes he would listen in the night, as if he might hear her weeping again as his father had said she had done, but he heard nothing.

***

What eventually drove all thoughts of Jessie's problem from his mind was a watershed in his own life which he had feared but had never really believed would happen.

The year was well into spring by now and with the warmer nights he had taken to meeting Jean at the ruined farmhouse on Saturdays and sometimes on Sunday, too. This was a Sunday evening when he had gone early. She could not come herself until after chapel where she went with her parents. He did some work on the garden, getting rid of the weeds and generally making it tidy after the ravages of winter so that when she came he could say, 'Look, see what I've done.'

She came long before she would usually have come, when in fact she should have been in chapel. He saw her coming down the track on her bike and was glad, though puzzled, that she was early. When she dismounted and leaned her bike in the usual place he saw at once from her face that something was wrong.

'What is it?' he asked.

She did not answer him at once. She came and looked at the work he was doing without speaking.

'What is it?' he asked her again.

She looked at him. It was not her usual expression. It was almost as if she was looking at him for the first time, sizing him up, looking beyond what she saw immediately to that other one who steps out of the flesh for a few moments in life only.

'What do you think it is?' she asked, as if it was a guessing game, but serious. 'You tell me what it is!'

Then he knew, but he did not show that he knew. He pretended ignorance while a confusion of thoughts sorted themselves out in his mind. He played for time.

'How should I know?'

'You should, if anybody does.'

She was cold, almost antagonistic towards him;

contemptuous even. She was also, he sensed, afraid.

'Don't play games,' he said.

'Games!'

The word exploded from her.

'If it's something bad, tell me!'

He resented her coldness. It was as if they were strangers.

'Bad?' she said. Then again, 'Bad?'

He had an instinct to run from her, so much a stranger she seemed, hating him almost.

He said, 'All right then. If you don't want to tell me I'll get meself gone.'

He moved towards his bike. Whether he would actually have mounted it and ridden away he did not know, for she spoke then and told him.

'I'm going to have a baby,' she said.

In later years, in similar situations, the more technical expression was more often used. 'I'm pregnant,' were the catastrophic words, but the reaction was the same. The emptiness in the pit of the stomach, the feel of life at an end instead of beginning. The death wish at the prospect of birth, as if nature at that moment endowed you with the capacity to understand the enormity of having created life.

He stopped when she said it. He turned and looked at her. She met his eyes for a moment then looked down. She waited.

'Why didn't you tell me then?' he said. 'Why couldn't you tell me instead of acting like that?'

'I don't know.'

'Why couldn't you have told me?'

'I don't know.'

'What do you think I am?'

'I'm sorry.'

'Treating me like a bloody stranger.'

'I'm sorry.'

'You should be! You should be by God!' Then he went to her. He stood before her. She did not look up. He touched her hair, then her cheek, gently.

'You should have told me,' he said.

'Yes.'

'It was going to happen, sooner or later.'

'Yes.'

'It's maybe for the best.'

Some of the old feeling came back to him then. The thing he had often felt with Denis. That he was old, and wise, and in charge. That he was master and God help anybody that said he was not. A phrase came to him from his childhood that seemed so far away though he was scarcely more than a child. It was a phrase from a game they had played when he was younger, when they had stood on a wall or a mound on the stacks and dared anyone to push them off, issuing the challenge: 'I'm the cock of the midden.'

The death wish was gone now, though there was a coldness in him at the various agonies which he knew were to come. He sat down on the low garden wall and pulled her down beside him. She sat there, obedient now, willing to be comforted, to let him lead. She put her arm around him and he responded and it seemed to him later, whenever he looked back to that moment, that there were three of them there, three children, comforting one another for the fact of life.

Although it was late when he got home that night, Jessie was still at the table in the living-room, her head bent over her books. She looked up as he entered, pushing her hair out of her eyes.

'Dad's gone to bed,' she said. She looked down, then looked back at him. 'You look tired.'

'I'm all right,' he said. 'I shall get sleep. I'm not on shift till eight.'

He sat by the fireplace and took off his boots. She was right. He was tired. He was as tired as he had ever been. Yet he did not want to sleep. He said to her, because they were both child adults from whom few of the facts of life had been hidden.

'Jean's going to have a baby.'

She looked up. They looked at one another. After a moment, she asked, 'When did you know?'

'Tonight,' he said. 'She told me tonight.'

'Do the Colthards know?'

'I've just come from there.'

'Was it awful?'

It had been awful, but not in a way as awful as he had expected it to be. There had been an outburst of anger from Jean's father while her mother sat weeping in a chair. He had bent his head and listened and had taken it all on himself; absolving her almost as if he had raped her. Colthard had limped around the room in his anger, as Ted had once imitated him at the baths. The memory had come back to him and he had felt ashamed, and some of the genuineness of it must have shown in his face for the man had grown quieter and had eventually moved on to the practicalities. Then at the end of it he had said, suddenly, 'It's a good job you're Doug Hoyle's lad or I'd have whipped you,' as if he did not doubt his physical capacity to do so.

The remark had puzzled Ted, for he had expected his background to be held against him. His father, it seemed, was respected in odd quarters.

'When will you wed?' asked Jessie, not doubting that they would.

'End of the month,' said Ted.

The date had been fixed for him, as had almost everything else. He found himself, in an odd sort of way, liking her father after the initial onslaught which he had listened to more or less in silence.

'What about you?' Ted asked Jessie.

'Me?' She looked at him, sharply. 'What about me?'

'Dad's worried about you.'

'Why?'

'He thinks you're upset about something.'

'About what?'

'I don't know. Are you?'

'I've nothing to be upset about except these exams,' she said, dismissing it, bending her head over the table.

That night, however, as he lay awake, unable to sleep for the turmoil of his own mind, he found himself listening for the sound of weeping.

The happy arrangement whereby the two younger boys had made a new home with their aunt was put in jeopardy the following week. She had a heart attack and was taken to hospital and Ted came home off shift one night to find the old turmoil. Jessie was in the kitchen cooking a meal for them and Hoyle was trying to quieten their excitement at finding themselves back in their old environment. Not, it became apparent, that they preferred it. It was simply a change.

Later, when Jessie had taken them upstairs to bed, Ted and his father discussed the situation.

'Bang in t'middle of her exams,' said Ted.

'First thing that occurred to me,' said his father.

'We shall have to take turns, take the weight off her.'

'I don't know how,' Hoyle said. 'She's like a bloody mule when it comes to doing what she sees as her duty. She was brought up to believe that men sat down when they came back from t'pit, and were served.'

'She's not to spend the rest of her life serving us.'

'You'll be gone afore long, and I can manage well enough. It's them two young buggers upstairs!'

Hoyle had just come back from visiting his sister at the hospital when they talked.

'How was she?' Ted asked.

'She claims she'll be back and ready to take 'em on again in a fortnight or so.'

'What do you think?'

'I've no means of knowing, have I?'

Ted and Jean were to live with her parents. He had not relished the thought, but even if she would come here there was not the room for them. He wanted desperately that Jessie should get away to college, that her life should be changed as his own had been changed, albeit accidentally. He felt guilty at his own happiness, that his life was set on the road he wanted to travel. He wanted desperately that it should be so for her.

CHAPTER TWENTY-ONE

There was no mail in Freetown for any of them. They had gone to Port Harcourt in the Cameroons after leaving Lagos to unload a deck cargo of crated fighter planes. The planes were assembled at Port Harcourt and flown across Africa to take part in the war in the Middle East. They did not go to the Congo this time as Chippy had expected they would. Instead they returned up the coast to Takoradi, a small West African port where dock facilities had been installed, and unloaded the rest of the cargo before proceeding to Freetown.

It was on the voyage from Takoradi to Freetown that Denis saw his first victims of the war. Not that he had been unaware of it on the voyage out. Although the sickness had anaesthetised his capacity for fear, he had found himself at moments very much aware of the possibility of attack from beneath the surface of the sea. He had taken down messages from the Admiralty giving the position of submarines in the area, and at one point on the voyage out the crosses which the First Officer marked on the chart were so closely aligned across their course that it had seemed impossible that the convoy would not be detected.

It was no doubt one of the submarines which had missed the greater prize which had sunk the small coastal steamer, the debris from which they now sailed through. They had heard the distress message on the radio the previous day and had altered course to pick up survivors.

Later, in Freetown, they heard that the steamer which had been sunk had been carrying over two hundred Africans who, with their families, were travelling to work on a building project somewhere up the coast. The debris from the ship had already been scattered over a wide area before they came on the scene, but there were no signs of boats or rafts. As they drew nearer they could see, among the smaller debris, larger floating mounds like the protruding bodies of a school of whales which had come to the surface. The engine room telegraph rang and the speed of the ship decreased as the first of these mounds came towards the ship's bow. All the crew were gathered on the deck. They stood at the rail as the ship steamed slowly into the debris and the first of the mounds came alongside. The sea was flat calm, the surface broken only by the undulations created by the ship's bow, and as it came within the influence of these the mound bobbed gently up and down and, caught in the drag, floated inwards towards the stern so that those who were stood at the rail there were looking down on it.

It was the body of an African woman, grossly distended by the heat of the tropical sun, but distended in this instance in proportion so that it simply seemed that in life she had been quite enormous. She wore a vivid blue dress which had split under the pressure from inside so that at first it looked as if she wore it without the seams sewn. Then, caught in the drag of the propellers, she began to bob quite violently in the water until she vanished from sight at the stern.

The men at the rail were silent. No one spoke as the next mound came into view, and then another, and Denis suddenly realised that they were steaming silently through a grotesque floating graveyard of bodies of men, women and children.

A somewhat larger mound now came towards the side of the ship, which was by now hardly under way. There were two bodies, a man and a woman. They passed under the rail, slowly, the ship barely moving now. Although not distended so much as some of the others, the man's penis had swelled dramatically. It had seemed odd that they should be together when the others were separated, but it was possible now to see why. They were tied together, as if as the ship sank they had been afraid to be parted or as if they believed in some way this would ensure that they stayed together through the moment of dying into some life beyond and not be lost in the darkness of the infinitely uncaring sea.

They passed by now, slowly making their exit, to a silence if anything more profound than that which had accompanied the others. Many of them, perhaps, had wondered whether some insensitive moron among them would relieve his abhorrence of the silence with some ribald on the distended penis; there were those among them who were capable of this. It did not happen, but it was the climax to the event. Up on the bridge the engine room telegraph was rung and the propellers stirred into violent life to carry them from the scene. Turning from the rail now, as they all did almost as one, Denis found that his eyes were filling remorselessly with tears and he looked downwards as if to hide them from the others who with their silence had preserved the dignity of death for people they did not regard with the human dignity they expected themselves in life. Perhaps they wept too, some of them, though not perhaps knowing why.

Denis knew. He knew why he wept. He had seen in the relationship of the man and woman in the water something he immediately recognised though not pertaining to himself or his erstwhile romantic images of the love of men and women. He had seen his mother and father in the moment of their death.

By the time the convoy left Freetown on its way back to Liverpool they had been away for three months. To Denis, seasick and homesick in almost equal proportions, it seemed more like three years. The voyage home would take three weeks. He would have been impatient at this in any case, but by now the original tiny seed of a possibility that had been planted in his mind that Jessie might be pregnant had grown into an enormous and terrifying conviction.

He had gone through the process in his mind. In fact it had come to the point where he went through it now almost daily. In the event he had come to believe that it was impossible for her not to be pregnant. Everything had happened to ensure a pregnancy. Nothing had been done to prevent it. In his ignorance, though more likely in the strength of his feeling at the time, for he was not totally ignorant of the possible consequences, it had simply not occurred to him. Looking back he could not understand why she had made no attempt to prevent him, for pregnancy before marriage in the society in which they lived was almost worse than crime. That she herself had been overwhelmed by the same feelings of desire, curiosity and ultimately uncontrollable enjoyment did not enter his mind. In all the sex talk of his youth, in what was said and what was not said, it was never suggested that women actually enjoyed sex. Sex was for the enjoyment of men. Women endured it.

She would have assumed that marriage would follow inevitably. He was convinced of this. She had permitted it because she assumed he wanted to marry her. Not immediately, perhaps, for they were both little more than sixteen.

He had been desperately hoping that there would be letters at Freetown, and the fact that there were none, which he was assured was not uncommon with short voyages, had been an enormous disappointment. In their absence his imagination created the situations which they would either have confirmed or denied. By now she would be three months pregnant. He knew that women bulged in pregnancy, but not how much or how soon. In any case, he assumed it would by now have reached the stage where it was noticed. In other words, even had she wanted to keep her condition secret pending his return the option would be taken from her. He would return … to what? He tried to imagine the reactions of the various people involved. His father pained, disappointed in him. His mother would see his life in ruins. Her father might possibly attack him, for this had been known to happen in Cuddon. Ted would be the worst. Ted would hate him for it, for he had a deep affection for Jessie.

The possibility that in spite of her having a child he might not marry her never occurred to him. He wanted to marry her. Even the sick, unhappy feeling induced by the disgrace he would have to endure did not obscure the fact. The sensual daydreaming was gone now. In its place his tortured imagination tried to grapple with the problems. Where would they live? How could they face a future in Cuddon where everyone knew, and would know forever?

He hardly ever thought of the child. It was simply not a reality. When he did think of it, it was almost in the abstract. It was the cloud that oppressed him.

'When you make life you make misery,' Chippy had said. He had meant it in a different sense, of course, but it applied. Several times he thought of telling Chippy, when the burden of his secret became almost too much for him, largely because of the burden of his ignorance. There was so much he did not know. Chippy would know, but then he would class him with Andrew for whom he had little regard and more than a little contempt. Andrew had come back to the ship that night in Lagos, boasting of his success with one of the women. The most beautiful of all these there, he had said. If only she hadn't had the touch of the tar brush, he had said, he would have married her. Chippy had been scornful. 'All talk,' he had said. 'You don't boast about something like that. You keep it to yourself.'

They came back to Liverpool three weeks later. In their absence the city had been bombed. 'Worse than London,' one of the dockers said proudly, as if it was some sort of achievement. He and Andrew were given four days leave, starting the following day. Denis was relieved to find that he was expected to stay on the ship for the next voyage. He would have been sorry to have left people he was just beginning to know, especially Chippy. Even Andrew he had come to like in a way, Chippy's contempt having cut him down to life-size, in Denis's mind at least.

They took the overhead railway into Liverpool that night. For the last ten days of the voyage food had been short on the ship due to a failure of one of the refrigerators, and they were looking forward to a good meal. They were disappointed, having forgotten the limitations imposed by rationing, but it was good to be ashore again, though Denis had not been so sick on the homeward journey. Liverpool seemed grey and drab after the warmth and colour of West Africa, but there was about it much of what was best in Britain at that time. It had a purposefulness, an atmosphere of being the core of some highly organised operation, as if someone at last was actually in charge. The tide had not yet turned in the spring of that year, but you could sense that it might; that there was a chance; that all was by no means lost.

After the meal they went to Exchange Station to use the telephones. Andrew to ring his parents, Chippy his wife, and Denis to ring the only number he had which was that of his uncle. It was his uncle who answered. 'Ah, it's you is it?' he said when he heard Denis's voice, with no great surprise, as if he had seen him only the day before. Yes, he would let Denis's parents know, he said. In fact he would go down right away. Apart from this, his voice was somewhat abrupt and matter of fact, as if he obliged from a sense of duty towards Denis's mother rather than from any warmth or regard. It was not what Denis would have expected after the increasingly friendly relations between them since the war, and as he put the telephone down he had a distinct feeling that his worst fears were about to be realised. Jessie was pregnant. He had disgraced the family. The shit, as Andrew would have said, was about to hit the fan.

The following day he staggered to the station with his one large case packed mostly with gifts and caught the train to Cuddon. He had given the time of arrival to his uncle so knew that he would probably be met. Now he wished he hadn't. It would have been better to have gone alone to the house. He spent the journey largely rehearsing his speeches in defence of himself, but in the end decided there was no defence. Honest guilt, he felt, was the only attitude he could take. By the time he reached Cuddon he was totally resigned, to everything except to the situation as it might have been. The return from the war. The hero's welcome. The fatted calf. They were not for him. Sackcloth and ashes were the order of the day, or blood, sweat and tears as Churchill had said in another context. He could not even blame it, as so many people blamed so many things these days, on the war. 'I did it because of the war,' he heard himself saying, and hollow laughter echoed down the corridors of the train.

His mother and father were on the station platform. They were dressed in the clothes they wore only for going out on special occasions. Their faces were turned up to him as the train pulled to a halt, but he could not read them. When he opened the door his father took the case from him and lifted it to the platform. His mother looked at him impassively, her eyes searching his face, but without life, as if she looked for something that would put life there. She had changed, he could see that. She was not as she would normally have been.

His father, who had stood back to give her priority, came forward now as if to embrace him and then, as if at the last moment realising he was no longer a boy, held his hand out and they shook hands stiffly and uncomfortably.

'You'll be hungry,' his mother said, predictably, as if he had just returned from Changi jail.

People on the platform were staring at them. Returning sailors were relatively unusual in Cuddon, which was far from the sea and where most of the population were on some kind of civilian war work.

'We'll get on down home,' his father said, seeming embarrassed, and picked up the case. As he and his mother followed him out of the station and down the road, Denis was aware that from time to time she glanced at him, as if looking for something. But he could not bring himself to look back and meet her eye. It was a strange, silent journey.

They were relaxed in the house. At least, by comparison they were. It was as if one obstacle had been surmounted and the rest, for the time being, could wait.

He took out his gifts and they examined them and expressed their pleasure, genuinely. His mother disappeared into the kitchen to prepare a meal and his father relaxed even more, almost visibly, as if all the tensions he experienced in life were only for her. But that was as it always had been. He went to the cupboard and took out a bottle and looked at Denis.

'You'll have had a drink?' he said, though knowing of course he was under age, as it was even in the home in those days. These were different times, however. Many things were changing, and he was saying so, the bottle in his hand.

Denis nodded. 'Now and then,' he said.

His father smiled, and then turned away to search for glasses, showing that it was a gesture he had not prepared. The smile was like an opiate to Denis. After the tensions of the last few weeks, days, and especially the last few hours, it calmed. 'Nothing,' he thought, 'is going to be so awful as it seemed.' It was all going to be surmountable. He would live through it.

His father poured a measure into the glasses and held one out to him.

'Like liquid gold these days, this stuff. Money won't buy it. You've got to have something else that's in short supply to trade.' He held his own glass up and looked at Denis. 'To them that go down to the sea in ships,' he said, and then, because he was saying that whatever the circumstances he was glad to see him back, and because he meant it, he looked away to take a first sip of the golden liquid. But when he looked back he could not hide the fact that for a moment he had been close to tears, and Denis was reminded of the moment at sea when the steward, Sam, had held him as he almost fell in his sickness, and how for a moment he had thought that his father held him up. 'Nothing,' he thought again, feeling some of the weight lift from him, 'is going to be as bad as it seemed.'

Over the meal they relaxed even more to the point where it seemed that the difference he had sensed in them had been all in his mind. They listened for most of the time, as he told them how it had been, using his blue pencil from time to time to censor things that might upset or offend his mother in the way that all boys do. He enjoyed telling them, relaxing with them in the process, thinking how little pleasure there would have been in it if he had had no one to come back and tell it to. Even his sea sickness, which was the one thing he did not exaggerate in the telling, seemed to compensate in some way for the fact that he had seen no action. Apart from the floating graveyard, that was. When he came to the point of relating this, in the natural sequence of events, it did not come out. It was as if his mind had rejected the reality; as if it had never happened. Then looking at them across the table in the familiar, loved kitchen of his home, he remembered how he had seen their faces looking up at him from the water and was suddenly afraid, but of what he did not know.

Long before they tired of listening he ran out of words. That part of the homecoming at least had been as he had hoped it would be. He had told his story, or as much of it as could be told. Already he felt older in the house, separate from his former being, as if there were two of him there; a younger one who also listened.

That they had something to say to him that they had not yet said he could sense even more strongly now. As his own words ran out, and there were silences, he flinched inwardly each time he thought it might be said, catching a glance from one to the other and reading it as a signal. But it did not come.

He wanted to go now and see Jessie but of course he could not say this. In the end he created a subterfuge. Outside the window of the living-room, dark on all but the lightest of days, the darkness of night had come and his mother had lit the gas, the hiss of the flame licking round the bright mantle as it had done in his moments of homesickness when he had searched for and held each image preciously.

They would not object now he thought if he left them for an hour or two. The excuse was already in his mind. He said, when the moment was right: 'I think I'll go and see aunt and uncle,' glancing at his watch, casually, as if it had just occurred to him that he had a duty to perform. Again they glanced at each other as if they were signalling, and he waited for what they obviously now had to say to be said, but it did not come.

He went for his greatcoat and hat and put them on, trying to disguise the urgency now within him, wanting to be gone before they would be tempted to speak. He had reached the door of the shop on his way to the street before his mother called him.

He hesitated, but knew that he could not pretend he had not heard for the shop bell would ring as he opened the door. He took his hand from the latch and started to return to the living-room. With his hand on the not quite closed door he heard his father say in a low, tense voice, 'Let them tell him then if they want to. Seems we've not been able to bring us selves to it.'

He pulled the door open and went back inside. His mother looked up at him and said, 'Don't be late, will you?'

'I'll not be late,' he said, and went. He went quickly, to get away before they brought themselves to it.

When he turned the corner of the street that led into the Square, it was still as it had been, though why he expected it should have changed in three months he did not know. It was all like that though. He looked at everything now through long years of absence, expecting everything to change at the same rate of change at which he himself had moved on.

A thin sliver of light through the blackout curtains told him that someone was at home. He had floated through the streets rather than walked, as if he was still at sea and in one of his dreams. He knocked. There was the usual pause while the blackout curtain was drawn back and then drawn close again, and then the door opened. In the dim light he could hardly see as she, straight from the light, would be even less able to see him. He said, 'It's me.'

There was a silence and he thought for a moment that she had not heard, and then she said, 'Oh ...' and again, her throat catching on the sound as if she reacted to pain ... 'Oh . . .' she said.

He followed her through the door and stood while she closed it behind them. They were in the small dark square formed by the curtain and the door and inevitably, as she turned, they were touching. It happened then as it had happened before, spontaneously, without any words at first except for the small sound she had made when he spoke to her outside ... 'Oh ...' she said, and again ... 'Oh ...' It was her face he touched first. His hand came out of his dream and touched the reality with the breathtaking awareness, for which life offers no substitute, which comes as it must come rarely when the reality transcends the dream. It burnt into his memory with the indelible permanence with which those moments do from which we never recover.

CHAPTER TWENTY-TWO

They had barely entered the room, or had time properly to look at one another, when Ted came home from the pit. As he came through the blackout curtain, cursing roughly as it tangled with his foot, he caught sight of Denis. For a moment something of the past flickered in his eyes, then he grunted, pulled off his jacket and handed his empty Dudley to Jessie, and sitting on the edge of a chair started to unlace his boots. 'You're back then,' he said, glancing up briefly.

It was the first time that day that Denis had seen the kind of change in people which, in his mind, he had expected. Ted had changed in three months with the rapidity with which people change in the course of a sudden, severe illness. There were shadows under his eyes and his face had thinned down to bone. His manner had always been somewhat abrupt and to the point, but somewhere in his eyes or the twist of his mouth there had been a modifying humour, a hint of something which said, 'I don't really mean it, you know.'

He said now, not looking at Denis, 'I'm off out when

I've changed.'

He was saying that he assumed Denis had come to see him, and that the meeting would have to be short. So he did not know then that Denis had come to see Jessie, or that they had any relationship at all. It was another respite from the tensions which absorbed him and, to some extent, took the edge off his pleasure at seeing her again. To some extent, but not by any means completely. Glancing at her now as she waited to attend to any needs that Ted might have, as she was accustomed to in a house of pitmen, he knew that his feeling for her as she was had a greater tenderness and delight than anything he had experienced in his dreams of her at sea. His eyes were drawn to her again and again in the hours which followed, learning to know her face, as if he would store the reality against the time which would come when he would have only his memory to sustain him.

'Where've you been?' asked Ted, dragging him back to another kind of reality.

'West Africa,' said Denis. 'Lagos – that way on,' as if he was speaking of a not too distant town.

Ted grunted, and glanced at him as if looking for a change in Denis as Denis had seen it in him. For a moment Denis thought he detected a glint of envy in the tired eyes, and then the thought was confirmed.

'It's coal that'll win this bloody war you know,' said Ted in a sudden outburst. 'It's all right for you blokes in your fancy uniforms, having fun with the women, trotting round the bloody world at our expense! There's no glamour in the pit, mate!'

Denis remembered his sickness, the day he first vomited blood and the fear that had accompanied this. 'It's not all beer and skittles at sea,' he said. There was a sharpness in his voice. For the first time he had ever come back at Ted, or challenged his friend's superiority. Out of the corner of his eye he was aware that Jessie had glanced at him sharply. He was encouraged to go on.

'There's not much bloody glamour, either!' he said, using the expletive awkwardly because he rarely swore.

Ted rose from the chair without answering this and picked up his boots.

'I'm off up to change,' he said to Jessie, then went to the foot of the stairs. He paused there, then turned and looked at Denis. There was a touch of the old humour in his eyes and mouth, and with it a cut of the old superiority.

'Learning, are you?' he said, and went on up the stairs.

Jessie waited until they could hear his footsteps on the floor above them. 'I've his dinner to get,' she said then, her voice low so that Denis knew that she still kept her secret. 'We can go out then,' she said. 'Dad's on nights.'

'Is he still seeing Jean, then?'

'Yes, of course,' she said, surprised. 'Didn't you get my letters?'

The letters had been due to arrive an hour after he left the ship to come on leave. To wait for them would have meant catching a later train. He told her this.

'You know nothing about any of it, then, do you?' she said.

'About what?' he asked, his heart in his mouth.

'I'll tell you later. I don't want to talk about it here.'

She went into the scullery. Cupboard doors were opened and shut with unnecessary force as she prepared to get Ted's meal ready. Pots clattered more noisily than they usually did. It was something familiar to him, for it was so with his mother at home when something was on her mind that she had kept to herself. He remembered how his father would glance up at the sound, recognising what it meant, then go back to whatever he was doing, knowing it would either be told eventually, or not told, and that there was nothing to do but sit it out.

Denis sat on the edge of the large shabby sofa that took up too much of the small room, still holding his cap in his hand like a casual visitor, and with his greatcoat still on.

'Aren't you stopping?'

He looked up. She was standing at the scullery door with a loaf in her hand, smiling at him. He loved it, her smile. It came out off the darkness of her life that was in her face when it was still. It illuminated her, transformed her, obliterated the scars of her miserable childhood. He wanted to keep it there for ever, to make it his reason for living. He had never felt with any other person before, so strongly, the need to give. He had not yet learned that you can never completely obliterate the past except in the act of dying.

'You've still got your coat on,' she explained.

'I thought we were going out.'

'I'll be a bit yet,' she said. 'Take it off.'

She said it possessively, still smiling, as if he was hers to be ordered to do this or that. He wanted nothing more. To please her he took it off, though it was cold in the room, glancing at the fire as he did so and at the rag rug where they had lain. Then his eyes met hers and she could read the thought in his mind. She turned back into the scullery, but not before he had seen the smile diminish slightly as if she had sensed a shadow pass over her grave.

He went to the door of the scullery and watched her as she worked. She knew he was there but pretended not to notice him. There was a pan on the gas ring which she stirred from time to time, looking out of the window, or so it would have been if the blackout screen had not been there. But it was as if she looked beyond it, lost in whatever she saw that was in herself, and it was another moment which fixed itself in his memory and from which he would never recover.

He said, with the unconscious banality of words which are ill and too often used because there are no others, 'I love you.' It was already understood between them. There was no necessity to say it, and yet there was no escape.

Then Ted started to come down the stairs and he left her and went back into the room.

In the brief time he had been upstairs Ted had affected the transformation that many pitmen achieve, stepping from one world to another so that it becomes a routine part of their lives whatever degree of exhaustion they feel at the end of a hard day's work. He wore a brown, well pressed suit with wide turn-ups to the trousers. It was a wartime utility suit, but stylish for all that, making the most of little as so many manufacturers learned to do in the war. His shirt was white with the kind of whiteness that used to be achieved by dolly blue without the help of modern washing powders. The tie was excessively colourful as if to react aggressively against the black and white world in which he worked, and his hair was sleekly brilliantined and carefully quiffed at the front. But the shadows were there still under his eyes.

He went to the scullery door, and said, 'I'm ready, love.'

She served him because he was her brother and because of the affection between them, and his acceptance of the fact that she was a drudge in the house when she came home from school was only because it had always been so. No other way of life being known or perhaps being even possible the way things were.

Then he sat at the table, like a king, waiting. It would never have occurred to him, or to her, that perhaps he might help himself.

He looked at Denis, and said, 'How do you like it, then, at sea?'

'All right,' said Denis. It was a fair summing up. A lot

of his enthusiasm had flown out of the window this first trip, but he did not entirely dislike the life.

'See any Jerries?'

'Subs, you mean? I didn't see any. They were there though. We plot their positions on a chart, those the Admiralty know about.'

'Not as rough as they make out then, is it?'

Denis remembered the bodies in the water. 'It's as rough as your job, any day,' he said, challenging Ted for the second time.

'How do you know? You've never done it.'

'You've never done mine.'

The childish exchange, reminiscent of their schooldays which were not so far in the past after all, was interrupted by Jessie coming in with Ted's meal. Because Ted had made him angry now, Denis suddenly resented this.

'We don't get waited on hand and foot, either,' he said, pointedly.

Jessie flushed but pretended not to have heard. Ted digested the statement, thoughtfully.

'You feed yourself then, do you?' he asked, eventually.

'Course not,' Denis said, in the trap.

'You get waited on, then,' said Ted, making it a simple, indisputable fact, not to be argued against.

Jessie went out then, as if she could not bear to hear them arguing. She cared for them both. If they divided then she was divided too, torn between one and the other. Her going left them silent. Ted picked up his knife and fork and ate as if Denis was not there. Denis sat quietly, a storm raging within him. The old battles had been simple and straightforward. He had lost pretty well all of them, but had simply accepted it. It was no longer the case. From now on he would fight, every inch of the way. The battle lines were drawn between them.

***

Ted finished his meal and went, with very little more said between them, though at the door he paused, as if suddenly aware that it was odd for Denis to be staying when, as he assumed, Denis had come to see him.

'You'll be off then?' he asked.

'I asked him if he'd walk me to Clara's,' Jessie said, quickly. 'You know I don't like it in the blackout.'

Ted glanced at them both impassively, then pushed his way through the blackout curtain and the door closed behind him.

They waited a moment, then she said, 'He doesn't mean to go on at you. He's fond of you really.'

'Yes,' said Denis, wanting only to please her, telling her only what she wanted to hear in the way that lovers do when love begins its destructive process, annihilating truth.

Now that Ted was gone he did not dare to approach her, to touch her. The flood gates would open and the inadequate barriers break down. It would all come later, he comforted himself, regretting the delay in spite of the fact that fear had rendered him impotent.

Not that he knew what impotence was; only that something he expected to feel did not seem to be happening. She had said that they would go out. Was that what she wanted? Ted had once said that women often said the opposite to what they really wanted because they liked men to persuade them. Did she want him to suggest that they stayed in the house so that she would know he wanted it to be as it had been before? Did she want reassurance?

'Are we going out?' he asked, testing the water.

'You don't mind, do you?'

'Not if you want to.'

'I don't go out much because of the blackout, and it's dark when I get home from school.'

'We'll go out then,' he said.

She went upstairs for her coat. He waited. He wondered whether she would tell him, or whether he would have to ask her. If he had to ask her, what would he say? He was shy with her still, in spite of the intimacy between them; not really able to believe that she cared for him as she seemed to. When she got to know him better, he wondered, would she be as contemptuous of him as he was of himself? Care for him as little? Have as little respect for him? It always worried him when his mother talked about self-respect as if there was nothing mattered more. If she was right, how sadly lacking he was, for he had little for himself in comparison to others.

What a mess he had made of things, in his ignorance. It did not occur to him that his ignorance in respect of things sexual was as much, if not more, the fault of others as was his lack of any real education. Ted knew about these things. How could there be any excuse for himself if Ted knew? As for Jessie, she was a woman and was required to be ignorant so far as Cuddon was concerned. Sexual education before marriage was tersely summed up in the simple phrase, 'Thou shalt not'.

Wrapped in a masochistic mood of self-contempt he did not know that Jessie had come back into the room until she spoke.

'What's wrong?' she asked, looking at him.

He looked at her with his lying, loving eyes and said, 'Nothing. Nothing's wrong,' he said.

And the cock crew for the second time.

They walked across the pit fields on the pathway they had walked the night they went to the pictures in Caselborn. They had walked there instinctively for it was a safe place to go, though neither had actually said so. It was an open expanse without trees or hedgerows and the older lovers sought the quiet lanes where there were places you could at least hope for privacy if you were so lost in love or lust as not to care about the rough, hard ground or the cold night air. The pit fields were for those who had nothing to hide but their words, the hand on the waist or the odd cold kiss in the darkness which could lead to nothing because there was nowhere convenient to go. The pit fields were safe. They were walked by girls who had no intention of giving anything before marriage, and men who accepted that it would be so. They were walked by girls who wanted to give but did not dare, knowing the consequences, and by men with the same desires and fears. For those who walked the pit fields there was nowhere else to go except the altar and the success or failure of the marriage bed, while under the hedgerows and the stars the lovers lay. The pit fields were safe.

They walked in silence for most of the time at first. Which of them would remember in later years the communication, consummation almost, of hand holding hand? The communication of the rough darkness; voices of picturegoers bouncing back off the stacks as they took the short cut to the bus. Which of them would look backwards mockingly on the unsophistication of their childhood? 'Denis loves Jessie,' carved on the cold night air.

'Which college are you going to in autumn?' he asked.

She named a teacher training college to the west of the county.

'Mixed, is it?' he asked, as casually as he could, not so unsophisticated that he wanted her to know that he had caught the first flickering glance of the green-eyed monster.

Not sufficiently practised yet he did not deceive her. Her voice smiled in the darkness as she said, 'It's a women's college,' and squeezed his hand as if to add,

'Don't worry, I belong to you.'

Yet how could she think of going to college under the circumstances, he thought? Confused images floated through his mind. In one of them he walked up the steps of the college beside her. The principal was there. They flashed the baby. At this point the image froze.

She had told no one yet, not even Ted. He had forgotten for a moment his father and mother. Was it just the relationship they knew about? It would be enough to throw his mother into a state of despair. 'That girl from the Square! The Square of all places!' As if it was another planet. Yet if they had somehow discovered even just a part of the secret, how was it Ted did not know?

He had wanted her to tell him in her own way as he knew she would, must, eventually. But his mind was racing now and there was an empty, sick void inside him. To be so close to happiness as he was then, and yet to be in misery, was more than he could bear. He said, 'What did you mean when you said I knew nothing of it?'

He sensed her glance at him in the darkness. 'Did I?' she asked.

'You know you did. You said I knew nothing about any of it,' he said, quoting her precisely, 'because I haven't got your letters yet.'

They walked a few more steps in silence.

'What did you mean?'

Again she was silent, as if searching for words, then she said, simply, 'It's a baby.'

The night exploded around him. When the echoes had died away he was surprised to find he was still there. Amazingly, too, the empty void inside him had gone, as if the simple fact of knowing the worst had filled it.

'You might help me,' she said now. 'You've guessed, haven't you?'

'Maybe,' he said, not committing himself, throwing it back on her. 'Maybe I have.'

'It's so awful,' she said. 'You missed it all. You were away. I kept expecting you to get my letters and write to me and nothing came.'

'I told you why.'

'I know that now, but I didn't know it then. I thought it was going to happen to me, too.'

'What?'

'The baby, of course.'

'Whose?'

'Theirs, you idiot! Jean and Ted's. You realise it could have happened to us, too, don't you?'

What we sometimes remember as happiness is often just a sense of relief. The intense awareness of life as we walk from the graveside after someone else's funeral; the moment when we discover that the bill is less than we thought.

The pit fields were dancing tonight, or so it seemed to Denis. He had tried to be sober about Jean and Ted and the baby. What did it matter that they weren't married really, he had said, when it was going to happen sooner or later anyway. It was all humbug! Life was humbug! Ted was his friend, he didn't care what anybody said about him; 'It's the war,' he had said once, using the old excuse. 'It's all different since the war,' he said, ignoring the fact that in Cuddon they were hardly aware of the war.

She could not understand his mood and the change in him. She tried to make him understand what it meant, as if he hadn't been through it all in his head before. God, hadn't he! The memory of it only served to feed his euphoria. He took her hand and told her not to worry, that the worst thing she could do for Ted was surround him with gloom. It was bad enough for him, Denis had said, with feeling, without all that. 'It could have happened to us,' she said, several times, not knowing that she was only fuelling the fire.

'You don't care for me, do you?' she said suddenly, out of the darkness. 'You don't really care for me, do you?'

It sobered him, that she should think so. If anything he cared for her more. It was as if they had been shackled together by chains, and the chains had been removed, but they stayed together because it was what they wanted.

'You know I do,' he said.

'What would you have done if it had been us?'

'I'd have married you, of course,' he said, confidently. It had not been marriage he feared, neither the permanence nor the responsibility of marriage. What he had feared most was the stigma, the social embarrassment, what in those days they called the shame. It was a flaw in his character, though he was not really conscious of it as such, or why should he care so deeply what other people thought. Did Ted care? He had borne the other stigma all his life, the one imposed even by his own class, of being 'from the Square', branded for something over which he had no control.

Jessie, too, was branded in the same way, by his mother and people like her. That he might be like his mother himself except in this one instance, in which he was emotionally committed, did not occur to him then. It did not occur to him either that he was branded himself, that in the whole complex class structure in which he lived there were few in the pyramid who escaped.

She had seemed contented with his answer, and then she said, 'We're not old enough to marry.'

'Is Ted getting married?'

'Yes. They're getting married next month.'

'Well then.'

'They're older than us.'

'Not much more than a year. What difference does it make?'

'It makes a difference, that's all.'

'I don't see why.'

She was silent then and he knew it was because she had raised the point for some other reason, and that she didn't believe it either. Then after a time she said, 'Your mother wouldn't let us.'

'That's what you meant before, isn't it?'

'Maybe.'

'Why didn't you say so then?'

Her silence was like a pain in the darkness. It carried the humiliation of the Square, but she didn't want to say that either, though they both knew it to be so.

'I can do what I want,' he said. 'I'm at sea. I'm a man.'

'They'll like that,' she said. 'You turning your back on them because of me.'

'Mum was a Horsborough,' he told her. 'When she married Dad he worked down the pit. She'd have had half Grandad's money when he died if she hadn't done.'

'That's why she'd be against it. She knows what it's like.' She was mulish in her determination to make all the points she could against herself.

'It's not the same,' he said, fighting back. 'We've no money. We're like you.' Then feeling more sure of himself he went on, 'You're a teacher – at least you will be. You went to High School. Look at me. What do I know? I know nothing. Nothing!' he repeated, grinding his face in the mud.

They had gone on like this at intervals until they got back to the house. He had hoped she would ask him in, but she didn't. They stood outside in the Square for a while, for the most part silent. His euphoria had been gone for some time. They all seemed nonsense now, the fears he had had. The fact that it could have been as he feared he discounted. Ted's problems seemed nothing compared to his own. They would marry as they would have done anyway. The shadows under Ted's eyes would disappear and be replaced by other shadows.

Somewhere in one of the houses voices were raised in anger. There was a thud as something thrown inside hit the door, then light spilled into the night as a man came out. He stood at the door and shouted back inside, swearing profusely and indecently, until it slammed in his face. He kicked it once, then again, and then went off round the corner, talking to himself. They heard his clogs as he went, dragging frustration along the pavement.

'You see,' she said, 'that's how it is.'

'We'd go away.'

'I've Dad to think of … the kids.'

'They'll have to do without you when you're at college.'

'That's something else,' she said. 'I might not go. I haven't decided yet. Maybe I'll not go …'

'Why are you telling me all this?' he asked. 'Why?'

'I'm telling you what it's like.'

'I know what it's like.'

'No you don't. You only think you do.'

'I should want to marry you anyway.'

'You'd wait then?'

They were only sixteen. Five years would have seen the end of most of the problems, but she said it as if they might have to wait till late middle age. He could not understand the change in her mood since he had first come to the house. He remembered her voice when he had stood here before and said, 'It's me,' and she had said, 'Oh . . .' and again, 'Oh …'

It was slipping away from him, that moment from

which he would never recover. He wanted to keep it as a healed cripple hangs on to his crutches to remind him of when he was lame. He said, 'I want to come in,' though what he would have said had he been more articulate about his motive was, 'I won't let you destroy yourself,' but maybe she would have said 'No' as she did in any case. It would have been pointless anyway, in the event, for as she said it a door opened down the street and a neighbour shone a torch at them. 'You're back then,' she said. 'Thought you were a long time at school. I'll send the kids in, shall I?'

The torch lingered a moment longer, taking in Denis, and then went out. It would be all round Cuddon tomorrow, he thought, not caring.

It was late when he got back home. He had abandoned all thought of going to his uncle's and had walked back across the pit fields instead, and then on a long winding detour which brought him back into Cuddon at the crossroads. He came down the lane where he had walked the night he saw Tim with Jean Colthard. He could understand now how it had happened. Tim had walked her home that other night when she had joked about being attacked in the blackout. He was a Horsborough. She would have liked that. She would have seen it as a trophy in the game, to acquire a Horsborough, even on a temporary teasing basis. Her brief interest in himself he put down to his Horsborough connection. He had been a potential trophy in the game she enjoyed. The teasing game. It was Ted who had called her a teaser, and it was Ted who had fallen.

It was Tim that Denis could not understand; his interest in Jean. He had associated Tim in his mind with the sophisticated, well-dressed girls who shed their High School gymslips and became women for the weekend, the kind who lived in the houses up where the

Horsboroughs lived. Jean was not sophisticated; worldly in a working class way, but not sophisticated. She was like the women you saw coming out of the Cuddon Arms on a Saturday night, brightly painted, peroxide hair, uncaring of their reputations at a time when women were rarely seen in pubs. They were women who lived for what little fun there was to be had in a Yorkshire mining village in the dark nights of the war. They were good humoured women, many of them unusually attractive in an earthy, physical sense. It was their only currency. They stared the world out boldly, but with a hint of sadness behind their contempt, as if they would have it otherwise given the choice. It was what Denis liked in her, this curious mixture of sadness and bold contempt. But Tim was different. He belonged to another world. He was an intellectual, though it was not a word Denis would have used at that time. The fact that Tim might have been attracted by the very things he had been attracted by himself never occurred to him.

He was no wiser at the end of the walk than he was at the beginning as to the reason for Jessie's sudden change of mood. Everything they had said that evening had passed through his mind again and again, as through a sieve, as he searched for a grain of understanding. She had told him he only thought he knew what her life was like, as if he was wilfully ignorant and as if the gap between them was too wide ever to be bridged. He could not see it. It was something that came to him only in later years, the fact that the gap can only be accurately measured from below, not from above.

His father was alone in the living-room when he got back home. He was listening to the radio, but he switched it off when Denis came in.

'Coal stocks are low. Dalton wants rationing. They're blaming the miners again,' he said.

His father voted Conservative. He was not by any

means the only miner, or ex-miner, in the place who did so, but it set him apart. He drank sometimes at the Conservative Club, but then so did many of the Labour men; the beer was better.

'Years of neglect,' he said. 'Bad owners. Men like Machen that said he'd make the people of Cuddon bleed. And they wonder why miners strike.'

It was a contradiction, or it sounded like a contradiction of his beliefs, but he was simply stating the facts. He was too intelligent a man to do otherwise.

'Your mate Ted's making a name for himself,' he went on. 'Making his voice heard at Union meetings. Studying economics at night school they tell me. Some kind of Communist they tell me. Not the usual kind. One of these groups that split off.'

'Where's Mum?' Denis asked.

'Gone up to bed. Not to sleep though. Reading.' He paused, then added, 'She's not been too well this last week or so. Doctor wanted her in hospital, but she'd not with you coming home.'

'What is it?' asked Denis, fear rising in him.

'Oh, it'll be something or nothing,' his father said, casually to reassure him. 'One of these women's complaints. You'll know about women's complaints when you get married,' he smiled, making a joke of it.

Denis took his coat off and went to the back door to hang it up. When he came back his father was banking the fire up for the night. He said, 'Seems daft when we're supposed to be short of coal. She gets up in the night, sometimes, that's why I keep it going.'

Denis took the bull by the horns. If the woman with the torch talked, and they always did, it would be common knowledge anyway soon in the small community in which they lived. He said, 'I didn't go to see Uncle.'

His father glanced at him briefly, then emptied the last

of the slag from the bucket on to the blanketed fire. He waited for Denis to explain, playing with the poker as he did so, gently touching the coals as if putting them in precise order.

'I've got a girl,' said Denis. 'Ted's sister, Jessie.'

His father looked at him, then back at the fire.

'How long's that been going on?'

'Just before I went away.'

There was a silence. His father prodded the coals, carefully, then said, 'Serious, is it?'

'Yes,' said Denis.

'Bit young to be serious, the pair of you, aren't you?'

'If you're serious,' said Denis, 'you're serious.'

There was a longer silence, and more attention to the coals, before his father said, 'You've heard about young Ted and Jean Colthard from the baths?'

'Yes,' said Denis.

His father put the poker carefully back in its holder and sat down in the opposite chair. He looked at him with his clear, straight eyes.

'It's not that serious, is it?' he asked.

Denis looked at him. He said, simply, 'No,' so firmly that there could be no doubt of it, and it was only as he looked away, embarrassed by the subject rather than the question, that he remembered that it so nearly could have been. Suppose he had had to say yes? How would those clear straight eyes have looked at him then? He had the feeling of having stood on the edge of a precipice without knowing it. It was as if someone had drawn him away, then pointed and said, 'See how far you could have fallen.' The fact of the moment, or as near as he had come to it, was worse than he had imagined it.

He said, 'Mum won't like it, will she?'

'Because of who it is, you mean?'

'Yes. It's a family with a bad name.'

'You worked with him once. You said he was all

right. You told Mum. It was Jessie's mother's fault, you said.'

'I said that, yes.'

'She's dead?'

'Aye, and look what she's left the lass with. Three kids and her father to care for.'

'That's not Jessie's fault.'

'It's not the fault that counts,' his father said, 'it's who picks the bills up at the end.'

'Why should she?'

'She's the kind of lass to duck on it, is she?'

'No.'

'That's your answer, and her credit, then.'

'It's not what Mum'll say.'

His father looked at the fire, buried by what sustained it. After a moment, he said, 'You've years ahead of you yet before you're ready for marriage. If you still feel the same when she's free you'll have nothing to worry about. Your mother'll come round to it.'

'I could be dead then,' said Denis.

He wanted to tell his father about the bodies in the water; about the moments when the anaesthetic of the sea sickness had lifted and let him see fear. He had been less sick on the voyage home. Several times he had stood at the rail at night with other ships silhouetted against the moonlight and seen his death coming towards him through the darkness. He thought for a moment of finding the words with which to explain this to his father, and then he remembered that he himself had been buried alive in the pit when he was fourteen and had barely survived.

'There's something you don't know,' said his father, breaking into his thoughts. 'We weren't sure whether to tell you. Your mother'll want to know whether your uncle did.' He paused briefly and then went on, 'Your cousin Tim's missing. He went out to Burma the week after you left. They had a telegram last week.'

His mother was asleep when he went upstairs. She lay on her back with her head slightly to one side and the book still in her hand. He was glad she was asleep. His father had made him promise not to raise the question of Jessie for the time being. He was in conflict as he looked at her. He loved her as he had always done, but there was resentment too, and he could not understand how she could justify her attitude to Jessie when she herself had given up so much to marry his father. 'She knows what it's like,' Jessie had said, as if in support of her.

He went to his room and lay on the bed without undressing. So Tim was missing. Was he dead? When would they know? All over England it was happening. Women woke in the night and wept. Men too, perhaps. They wept for those who had been told to go, and for those who had gone because they wanted to, like Denis, albeit for badly thought out reasons. Churchill had talked of the darkness over Europe. The end of civilisation as we know it, he had said. There was a chaos in life that Denis had not known in his childhood. Was it that he had only now grown to awareness of it, or was it part of the war? Was it, perhaps, what they were fighting to put an end to?

Tim would have told him, he thought. Tim read and knew about these things. Tim was educated. Even Ted was studying. Economics. It didn't sound like Ted. What possible use was there in studying economics if you lived in the Square? It was a question he could not answer, because when it boiled down to hard fact he would have been at a loss to explain what economics was. He was aware again of his own ignorance, of how much he needed to know to understand any of these things. To understand even Jessie, perhaps, and why the Square shadowed their lives.

He slept. When he awoke he was still in his clothes. He was stiff and cold and afraid, as if in his sleep he had dreamed of death. He lay in the darkness, looking towards the window, like a child waiting for the light.

CHAPTER TWENTY-THREE

When Ted left the house after the argument with Denis he headed for a meeting at the Miners' Welfare. The exchange had depressed him. He knew instinctively that it had been childish to speak as he did, that the responsibility for the sourness that had grown between them was his own. He knew too that it had not been solely directed at Denis, but was part of the general atmosphere in the community when it came to comparing the wartime role of the miners with that of men in the services. In the first two years of the war thousands of men had left the pits to join the armed forces, considering this a better deal. In 1941 some forty per cent of miners were over forty years old, yet worked a longer week than before the war because of the desperate need for coal, yet production fell and strikes increased.

Ted attended most of the union meetings these days. Unless there was some specific grievance of particular interest, they were sparsely attended and he was usually the youngest one there. They were often long and boring, for many of the older men on the platform were obviously fond of the sound of their own voices. Yet he would listen, fascinated, agreeing or disagreeing with the arguments, where he understood them. He could never bring himself to speak from the floor, though often he was tempted to do so. He would rehearse some speech in his head but not deliver it, and after the meeting would chastise himself for not doing so. On the way home he would deliver it to the audience of stars in the night sky.

It was his ambition now to stand on the platform, to be an official. All his reading was directed to this end. It had transcended his ambition to gain a reputation at the coal face, to be a king. Words, and their use in argument, fascinated him. He could use them to work up a passion within him which both surprised and excited him. He could not understand how men could stand on the platform and drone on endlessly and boringly about issues which seemed to him simple and clear cut.

They were there again when he entered the hall at the Miners' Welfare on this night, the same old faces.

'The lad's here, we can start now,' one of them joked as he entered. He flushed but was pleased that his visits had been noticed.

The meeting was about pithead baths. Funds had been allocated to each pit in alphabetical order and now it was the turn of Cuddon. Yet a ballot had to be taken at each pit to see if the men wanted pithead baths. If a pit voted against it went to the bottom of the list and might not get another chance for years. Yet some pits had so voted, and the men on the platform obviously feared this might happen at Cuddon, for both the union committee and the management wanted to do away with the old practice whereby the men washed at home; the big zinc bath in front of the fire, the labour of filling and emptying it, the often repeated injunction of the wife to 'sit still or you'll stir the muck up'.

At the back of the determination of many of the men to keep things as they were, Ted knew, was the old belief that bathing every day weakened the back and softened the limbs. Even in large families, where bathing could go on for the better part of a night, the hostility to pithead baths could exist.

Ted desperately wanted the baths to come for soon he would be married and the job of preparing his bath would be Jean's or he would not be regarded as master in his own home. While initially they were to live with her parents he knew there would be no peace until they had a home of their own and the chances of getting one with a bath were as remote as to be almost non-existent. It would be one more arrow to her bow, the labour of dealing with his pit muck. Moreover, he wanted himself to return home clean as men in other jobs did.

Since the men on the platform wanted the baths, and no voice was raised from the floor where, in any case, only Ted and half a dozen others sat, the only practical decision made that night was to choose a date for the ballot. A few other minor matters on the agenda were dealt with and the meeting came to an unusually early close.

It was a clear, fine night when he came out on to the street. In earlier times he would have gone to the pub or the club, but with marriage looming he was desperately trying to save. He started to walk back home but his unspoken speech of the night was still ringing in his head and eventually he turned off the road and made his way to where the stacks started to slope and began to climb.

It saddened him that the building of pithead baths should be in doubt when the funds were available. That the men might make a conscious decision against them. Initially a believer in the theory that bathing weakened the back, he had been to a lecture the union arranged when a doctor lectured the men on the desirability rather than otherwise of regular bathing, and had accepted this and abandoned his old belief. Why did not sufficient of his mates do the same, so that the baths would not be in jeopardy? Was it fear; superstition? There were many superstitions in the pit based on all too real fears, especially among the older men. Their lives were riddled with fear, superstition, distrust of authority and most of these were, in their own terms, soundly based, rooted in some deeply felt experience.

He warmed as he climbed and the night air flavoured with the smell of the stacks filled his lungs. Below him a crack of light showed through an inadequate blackout, and around him, against the lighter colour of the sky, he began to see the shape of the headstocks of other pits, most of which he recognised.

He stood on the spoil which represented the labour of generations of pitmen, spoil brought from the bowels of the earth since before the Industrial Revolution. He looked down on Cuddon. He had never been as demeaningly conscious of living in the Square as Jessie had, but he was equally conscious of it in a different way. He would not run from it as he would have had her go. He knew there would be pain in its destruction even for him. Whatever else it was it had been their home. Already in his vision of the future it was doomed, and he saw in his mind a picture composed from the memory of other buildings he had seen demolished. He saw the broken wall still covered with the faded, fusty wallpaper in the room where his mother had died, and where she had said to him, 'The Square soured me.'

He looked down on it now, conscious of the spoliation of life that the stacks represented, as they also represented the wealth of the country he had been born in. He could see no alternative than to be committed to the destruction of the Square. To go on as they were was unthinkable; to run from it an act of shame.

He was not ashamed. He was proud, even, of his inheritance, for without it the excitement that generated his ambition to destroy would not be there. It was all the dross in his life, but it was all the colour too, and the hope. Words gathered in his mind as they did at the meetings, forming an articulate expression of what he would never acknowledge as dreams, but which he saw as future realities. He saw himself on the platform with an audience before him. All the faces he knew were there: his father, his wasted life too late rewarded with a crumb of employment; Jean with her hatred of the pit and Cuddon conflicting with her feeling for him which had trapped her forever, perhaps, with their forthcoming marriage; Jessie, feeling herself permanently belittled, marked for life, trapped by the death of her mother if the boys had to stay at home. Then, too, there was that other woman that he saw in his mind more and more these days, the woman his mother might have been, the face blurred but smiling, framed in gold in the gallery of his life.

He said aloud, 'Not wasted,' and again, 'Not wasted,' as to reassure them of hope. Tears pricked at his eyes, but he pushed them away. Tears belonged to the past, not the future.

CHAPTER TWENTY-FOUR

Memories of the days when he had shared a bedroom with his brother Stan had begun to fade from Denis's mind since he had left home to go to sea. The illness which had destroyed Stan's mind was as little understood still, it seemed, as when it had happened. Whenever Denis did think of his brother it was not Stan's real face he saw, but the face on the photograph on the living-room mantelpiece. A face frozen in a time now gone.

They went to see Stan the next day. His parents were going anyway, and Denis had promised his mother that he would visit his brother when he came back from the voyage. They took the bus to Leeds in the morning. Denis sat next to his mother. His father suggested that he did, knowing that she was proud of him in his uniform though she pretended that nothing was different. She didn't niggle at him now as she used to do. 'Unfasten your coat … straighten your tie … push your hair out of your eyes …' All the mother things. Even for her, it seemed, he had to some extent grown up.

They spent an hour in Leeds, waiting for the bus that would take them to the mental home where Stan was incarcerated. Leeds was drab and grey as most cities were in wartime. It was hard to say why. The buildings were the same, though lacking paint. The trams still rattled through the streets and most of the shops were open. Perhaps it was the people, thought Denis. He watched their faces as they passed by. Few dawdled; most of them seemed to be going somewhere; but their faces were tired, expressionless for the most part, as if they had shut out life, pulling the curtains on it until the morning. In years to come they would say, 'How we laughed! What a spirit we had!' Aching nostalgically for those grey, mirthless, spiritless days.

The home was a nineteenth-century institution. Twenty years later in the brave new post-war world that never, never had it so good it was still a nineteenth-century institution, with trimmings. They sat on folding wooden chairs in a dark green corridor, waiting for Stan to be brought to them. Once his mother's hand touched his own by the side of the chair, and she got hold of it and squeezed at it as if she waited in dread, knowing the futility of the visit, and wanting to reassure herself that at least he was still there.

Then he came, Stan, looking because he had been told that someone was here to see him, but seeing no one he knew. His mother stood and took his arm and pretended, as she pretended throughout, that he knew who they were and why they had come. It was a year since Denis had seen him. It was one of the obligatory visits, for in those days he was told that he should come, not asked whether he wanted to. For some reason, then, he had been able to close his mind to it. It was something to be gone through. You sat there and waited until it was over.

Stan had changed. Denis observed him, caught at the

eyes whenever they flickered over him, looking for recognition. He called him Stan, and talked to him as he had talked to him when they had slept in the room together when Stan was, as they sometimes put it, himself. That was five years ago. No one knew, it seemed, though some might have pretended to, what it was or why it had happened. He had got worse, and after he came to the home, much worse. Now there was nothing. They sat, Denis, his mother and father, on the hard wooden chairs in the dark green corridor talking to someone who wasn't there.

It was the middle of the afternoon when they came out. They walked back through the grounds to the road where they would wait for the bus into Leeds. There was a soft dampness in the air that deadened the sound of the traffic so that their footsteps on the gravel seemed to fall almost into silence. When they reached the gateway from which the iron gates had been removed in answer to the government's plea for scrap metal, it started to rain.

'Even the weather's against us,' said Denis's mother.

She made no other complaint.

He went that night to see his aunt and uncle. Since they had been away seeing Stan there had been no one to tell his mother that he had not been the previous night. Neither had there been any opportunity for gossiping customers to pass on the news about Jessie and Denis which must surely have spread to some extent since the previous night. In any case, he felt, Tim would have wanted him to go. He remembered his uncle's abruptness on the telephone which he had interpreted as a coolness towards himself, and knew now what it was. He would stay for as little time as he decently could and then he would go to the Square and see Jessie.

***

They were sitting closely round a very small fire when he arrived. He wondered if the coal shortage had hit them, too, but doubted it. There were always miners willing to sell a percentage of the only perks of the job, their home coals. Most likely, he thought, his Uncle Maurice had seized on the war as an excuse, as others did, to save money. He had always been known as being a bit on the tight side, unlikely to miss the opportunity to use the cloak of patriotism to reduce his outgoings.

Doris was at home, as well as his aunt and uncle. She was about to be conscripted, his father had told him with a certain amount of satisfaction. She was faced with a choice of work in a factory (the thought warmed the cockles of Denis's heart), or service in the WAAF or ATS. It was a sore point, his father had warned him, trying to disguise his satisfaction. His Conservative philosophy obviously did not extend to support of people like the Horsboroughs.

Looking at them, as they sat there, Denis could in no logical way associate them with Tim. His aunt came from a very similar, prosperous middle class home. She had simply exchanged one comfortable home for another. She had not, as Denis's mother had, abandoned it all for what Denis could only suppose was a love that he did not recognise in his parents except in the odd moments when the mask of their privacy dropped. The kind of books that Tim read, the music he listened to, his entire view of life would be alien to her. And yet she loved him, because she had given birth to him, and if he had been killed the whole of the rest of her life would be diminished by this. It was not love as Denis recognised love these days, but he knew of no other word for it. How many kinds of love were there, he wondered.

Part of his uncle, too, would die if Tim was dead. Denis knew this instinctively from the little knowledge he had of them and their relationship, as alien as that between the mother and the son.

He could tolerate his uncle and aunt, even at moments feel some slim affection for them, but he had no feeling at all for Doris who encapsulated all that he most disliked about his wealthy relatives. When, in later years, he listened to talk of the class system it was always Doris who entered his mind and coloured his reactions. At parties he would see one then another, ticking them off. The world seemed to be full of Doris and her kind. In his Revolutionary period, soon to come and as soon to depart, it was always Doris's face that appeared in the sights of the machine gun he was about to fire. It was a very long time before he was able to disassociate his personal dislike of Doris from his political thinking, and sometimes he would wonder if he ever had.

She was not unattractive. He had never heard of any men in her life, but he supposed there must be some. Watching her as she looked into the fire as his uncle told him about Tim, he found himself associating her, grotesquely, with Ted. Ted would know what to do with Doris, Denis thought with sadistic glee. Ted, in fact, was what Doris needed, he thought; Ted's arrogance, his confidence, the way in which he weighed people up and found them wanting. It never occurred to him then that in a way it would not have been an attraction of opposites, but of like to like. That what he disliked in Doris he had always tended to admire in Ted.

His Uncle Maurice had insisted on Denis reading Tim's last letter, as if it was some sort of Last Testament. It was odd and stilted and not like Tim, as if he had found it hard to fill the pages to take it to a decent length. Then, towards the end, he came to a passage that made him pause and read it again.

'Give young Denis my love if you see him when he comes home again,' Tim wrote. 'I hope he reads the books I lent, though maybe he won't. They're all things that started me thinking the way I do happen to think. I know you don't like the way I think, but it's me. Maybe he'll react against them and think like you do, then you'll be pleased. In a way he's the reason why I think as I do. None of us has done anything to deserve to have more than his part of the family have, especially me, and I'm not belittling your hard work Dad, or even Grandad's, though I never had much time for him.'

Then he read on and came to the end and passed it back to his uncle.

'I thought you might like to read it,' his uncle said, smiling at him for the first time that evening. 'Especially the bit about you.'

'Oh Tim and his daft ideas,' said Doris.

Her mother glanced at her sharply as if she spoke ill of the precious dead; as if the final telegram had already arrived.

'A lot of intelligent people share his ideas,' said her father. 'People who are helping to win this war.'

Denis's estimation of his uncle leapt up like warmed mercury. 'We shall want something better than we've had in the last twenty years if we win it,' Horsborough went on. 'I know who he means when he talks about the hard-faced men. Your grandfather always overdid it. Probably why I was soft with you.'

'Not soft enough to use your friends to help me get out of this conscription.'

'What makes you think I could?'

'Les Bannerman managed it for Helen.'

'He mixes in different circles to the ones I mix in then. In any case,' he said, 'why shouldn't you do your bit like everybody else, like most decent people anyway?'

'Three bloody cheers!' thought Denis, holding back hard on a grin. It went of its own volition as he thought, suddenly, of Jessie doing her bit in another war. Ready to give up college and look after her father and children not all that much younger than herself. Risking the feeling she had made it plain she had for him, with no spoils of victory to look forward to, nothing to gain. He remembered her bitterness in their last words together the night before. Was it because she felt that it would all come to nothing, that she would lose him anyway? He got to his feet and picked up his hat.

'I've got to go and see some friends,' he said.

He saw the surprise on their faces. He had been there for less than half-an-hour. It would have disappointed his mother, he knew, but already his feet were taking him of their own accord in a direction she would not have approved of either.

'Would those be your friends in the Square?' asked his aunt. So that was why she had been cold with him.

'We have a cleaner from the Square. She said she saw you there last night.'

'She talks too much,' said Horsborough sharply. 'Probably talks about us, too. You should get rid of her.'

'You've got to scrape the barrel these days,' his aunt said. 'Take what you can get. I never thought we'd have to have anybody from the Square in this house.'

He had an excuse ready in case Ted was there. He was coming to collect the books that Tim had lent to Jessie's father. The kids were at home, so he used it anyway, telling it to the boy who came to the door.

He stood like a stranger inside the room, holding his cap. It had been easier when Ted was there. The older boy was twelve and the other a year younger. They had the hard, knowing eyes that so many of the boys in the Square had, nothing being hidden from them by parents who had long ago given up trying. But they were not, like their parents, defeated; they still had the optimism of their youth. They were not like Jessie, he thought, and wondered why she was different, by what almost impossible circumstances she had survived to win the only scholarship to the High School in a year, and then to lose the optimism by which they survived.

She was ironing when he entered, her face flushed by the heat of the steam that rose from the clothes. Two local girls were there too. He knew, instinctively that she did not want them to know that there was anything between Denis and herself. They would, he guessed, make her unhappy with the teasing cruelty that children are capable of. Her eyes signalled her gratitude for the excuse, and she sent one of the boys upstairs to get the books. The girls looked at Denis and whispered and giggled and he found himself flushing with a mixture of irritation and despair. She spoke the girls' names, sharply admonishing them and, to his surprise, they obeyed. It was strange to hear her wielding such authority, standing there with the iron in her hand, knowing too much too soon about where the path to the altar can lead to.

This was what their life would have been like perhaps if she had had a child and they had been obliged to marry, young as they were. He knew enough by now to see briefly beyond the joy (and there was no other word) of being with her to the harder reality beyond, but the alternative, of leaving her now even if only until tomorrow, seemed infinitely worse. He had again the feeling he had had so strongly the night before of something slipping away from him. She felt it too but seemed resigned to it as if some bitter experience had taught her, less than a step from childhood, that there was no return.

What would she do, he wondered. Would she come to the door with him? He was sick with the frustration of wanting to see her alone.

Then Jean came in. She came as always as a flash of colour in the room, and as if she had seen Denis only yesterday. She seemed untouched by her troubles, uncaring as to who knew, as if it had never happened.

'Whcrc is he?' she asked Jessie, after greeting Denis.

'Rowe Lane Club.'

'I'm supposed to follow him up there, am I?'

'He didn't say.'

'He wouldn't, would he?' said Jean, as if it was no more than she had expected. 'Anyway, he knows where to find me. Not that he likes coming to our house. Mam and Dad, sitting there saying nothing. Just looking at him.'

She laughed, as if it was all a huge joke. 'Doesn't make sense, does it? They think he's the worst thing that ever walked on two legs, but they'd have a dicky fit if they thought he wasn't going to marry me.'

The boy came down with the books, and gave them to Jessie. She held them out to Denis and he took them from her.

Jean stood. She said, 'Oh, well – short visit!' She looked at Denis and said, 'You can walk me back.'

He looked at Jessie. She wanted him to stay, and yet she didn't. Their eyes met briefly. She looked away resigned.

They picked their way through the rubble of the Square in the darkness. Once Jean stumbled and fell against him and he held her briefly to stop her falling. Absorbed as he was in another and in the mental torment of love he was aware in the moment of physical contact of her sexuality. She wore it as she chose the colours she wore, like a bright flame. She laughed, as if aware of what he had felt.

'That was nice,' she said, 'Shall we do it again?' Even her pregnancy and commitment to marriage, it seemed, did not repress her.

'Where've you been?' she asked.

'Africa,' he said, casually.

'Oh Africa,' she said, unimpressed, as if it was somewhere the other side of Cuddon. 'If you ever go to the States,' she said, 'I take size nines in nylons. Seamless'll do.'

He wondered what Ted would say if he turned up at the door one day with a packet of size nines.

'When do you go back?' she asked.

'Day after tomorrow.'

'You'll be away for the duration, then, more or less. It'll be the last of Cuddon for you. You'll not come back when it's over.'

'Who says I won't?'

'I do. You're not the type. There's more to you than Cuddon. Live inside yourself, don't you? The quiet kind.'

'What's wrong with Cuddon?' he said, remembering his homesickness, when there was nowhere on earth he wanted more to be.

'I wouldn't know where to start.'

'You'll be going yourself then, will you?'

'Me?' she said. 'Me? Fat chance!' For the first time she sounded less than tolerant of her situation. 'Come back any time you like,' she said, 'me and Ted'll be here. Ted'd not leave if they pulled it down. He'd dig himself a cave in the stacks and shack out there!'

'Ted's all right,' he said, loyally, taking it as some sort of overall criticism of Ted.

'He's more than all right. He's better than you know. The only thing wrong with Ted is Cuddon. Must be the sulphur in his blood.'

They turned out of the narrow streets of terraced cottages into Cuddon main street where at least there were lamps, though dimmed and shaded for the blackout.

'You go that way, I go this.'

'I'll walk up with you,' he said. 'I've nothing else to do.'

She accepted his offer with silence. They turned to the left towards the station. The street was deserted. They walked from one dim pool of light to the next and for the first time she was silent so that when she eventually spoke again what she said sounded like a contradiction.

'I like talking to you,' she said, as if they had been engaged in some deep intellectual conversation. 'Ted never talks to me about things that matter. He spends all his spare time reading books but he never talks to me about what he reads.'

'Reading?'

'Twice a week to the library up at the Welfare.'

It didn't sound like Ted, but neither did economics.

'Haven't you got a girl yet?' she asked him, later, as they stood at the end of the road which led to the baths. There was the teasing note again in her voice.

'Maybe,' he said, wanting suddenly to tell her about it but not daring. Jessie might not want her to know. Or Ted for that matter. To make it clear that he wasn't all that far behind Ted in other respects, either, he said, 'I'm reading a lot too. I read on watch in the wireless room. Stuff that Tim lent me.'

'Tim?'

He had forgotten almost about the night he had seen them together. Something in her voice reminded him now.

'How is he?' she asked. The casual note that covered, or attempted to cover, something of importance was in the way she asked. He could tell. It was something he practised himself.

'He's missing,' he said. 'Didn't you know?'

He thought for a moment that she had not heard him. Then in the darkness beside him she said, 'Oh …' and

then again 'Oh ...' It was so much as Jessie had said it
the night before that it caught incongruously on his ear
for a brief second as a note of joy. He did not know then
how closely akin are the sounds of joy and pain. He said,
though why he did not know, 'I know about you and
Tim.'

'Know?' she said. 'Know what?' as if she had either
not heard or not understood.

'I saw you,' he said, 'one night on the lane. Before I
went off to sea.'

There was a silence again before she spoke. When she
did her voice was quite different, as if she had made the
sort of adjustment in the darkness that a mimic makes on
stage when he turns his back on the audience for a
second before turning round to face them as someone
else.

'Oh, it was nothing,' she said ... 'Wouldn't have
worked out if it had been ... Men don't want you for
your brains anyway, even if you've got any ... They
don't even want you for yourself, whatever that is ...
Surprised you, did it? Me? Him? ... Well not me,
perhaps, but him – I'll bet that surprised you? ...'

'In a way.'

'Only in a way? My God, it'd have surprised his
mother, wouldn't it?' She said, with the kind of class
masochism that he recognised in Jessie, using the light-
hearted jargon the aircrews had created to cover despair:
'No future in it, is there?' And then, using the knife she
had used to wound herself she turned it, unknowingly,
on him:

'I'm only a few streets removed from the Square, me,
aren't I?'

When he had got back to the ship he seemed to have
been away much longer than the four days. Already he
felt to have more than one foot in this world of grey,

rust-streaked ships, the dark flood of the river and the seemingly chaotic activity of the docks, the endless movement.

He left his case on deck at the top of the gangway and climbed the ladders to the wireless room to tell the first sparks he was back. Andrew was in there with the headphones on, the muted blast of trumpets rattling the ear pieces. Denis tapped him on the head to make his presence known, then took the headphones off.

'Where's the First?' he asked.

'On leave. I've only been back an hour. How were the judies back home then?'

'Bang on,' said Denis, as was expected of him. You didn't hang your soul out to dry in this kind of atmosphere. He had seen Jessie once for half-an-hour the previous night by dint of waiting for the bus on which she came from school. He felt strange in his uniform as she came towards him in hers, looking so much younger than she looked in the shabby clothes she wore at home. When she got home she would change and put on her years, carefully saving this other temporary world, keeping it clean for appearances. He had worn the uniform because he had wanted to be different. He had forgotten why. To compete with Ted? To impress Jean? To lift him towards some image he had of himself that put him apart? Whatever the reasons they were smouldering in the ashes now; now that he only wanted to belong.

Belong where? To Cuddon, with Ted and Jessie alienated from his own pathetic inheritance there by the Square? To this new world into which he was moving, where if you weren't a man you nevertheless behaved like one because you were in a man's world?

He left Andrew listening to the radio and went on deck. Army gunners were checking the Oerlikons and the twenty-five pounder gun on the stern. Civilians were inspecting the de-gaussing gear, an immense amount of wire which wound its way round and round the ship to render magnetic mines ineffective. What a lot of trouble war was, he thought. The danger, the grief, the destruction; you expected that. But the sheer effort devoted to this one single purpose he found as stupefying as the contemplation of infinity.

The First Officer trotted past him on the way to the bridge and grinned at him in passing. 'Hadda good leave?' he asked, not waiting for the reply.

In the cabin which he shared with Andrew he unfastened his case and opened his locker to put his things away. He had left a good deal behind him to make room for all the presents he had taken home, including the books which Tim had lent him. He remembered what Tim had said in the letter about the books. Some of them he had read, or had attempted to read. One or two had made him think about things he had not really thought about before, but nothing had engulfed him. There had been no blinding light. He picked one up now which he had barely looked at, even though he felt he must make the effort because Tim had made the effort for him. It had always been the last in the queue, as it were, for it was an anthology of poetry. He opened it now at random and looked at the first two lines of a poem:

'Go and catch a falling star,
Get with child a mandrake root ...'

What did it mean? He knew that there was a world which was beyond his present understanding. He had not yet fallen into the trap of believing that because he could not himself see a meaning there was none. The music he had heard in the corrugated iron bungalow in Lagos had extended his willingness to listen to other music, and somewhere inside him there was a growing chorus of sound which had wound itself into his dreams and his fantasies.

'Go and catch a falling star,
Get with child a mandrake root ...'

There was, perhaps, a kind of music there too. For a long time now he had sensed that he was approaching some sort of crossroads, some place where he would have to pause and decide in which direction to travel. He was aware of deeper divisions among people he knew than the physical divisions which separated the Square from Cuddon Hill, or the economic factors which created them. Jessie was of the Square, and yet not of the Square nor of Cuddon Hill. Tim was of Cuddon Hill, and yet not of Cuddon Hill nor of the Square. About his aunt and Doris, and probably his uncle, too, there was a poverty of the senses which he had always in the past associated with material poverty, with life in the meaner streets of Cuddon. But it was not so.

Had he a choice, or was it all an accident, something over which he had no control? The music had been an accident, he felt, a question of him being in the right place at the right time. He resented the possibility that it was all beyond his capacity to influence, that he could not reach out and experience of his own volition, as educationally poverty stricken as he sensed himself to be, the deeper experiences that he sensed brushing past on the fringe of his life.

He turned another page and read on.

CHAPTER TWENTY-FIVE

The wedding of Ted and Jean took place at the Registry Office in Caselborn. There was much debate about it beforehand, due to Jean's condition. In the normal course of events Jean's mother would have insisted on a white wedding in church, with all the trimmings, but in these circumstances she vacillated between her life's dream, her beliefs, and the thought of the eyes focused on the site of the bulge to be as the bride walked down the aisle on the arm of her resigned father. Ted knew Jean's mother would never be resigned; would never forgive him; would go to her grave damning him if she lived to be a hundred. She was not the type to play merry hell, tear him apart in one awful session and then make the best of it as Jean's father had done. He would catch her watching him sometimes, her expression still incredulous, unbelieving, as if no exercise of the imagination would ever truly convince her that it had really happened.

Jessie woke him early on the morning of the wedding. When she had left the room he lay for a moment looking up at the ceiling where snow had blown under the tiles one winter and left a rippled pattern of damp on the distempered plaster. It was a pattern that was etched in his mind, his first visual impression of each day according to the quality of light that came through the morning window. More memorably it belonged to the last moments between wakefulness and sleep, when the light from the coke ovens would flare up and reveal it and make it a focus for his thoughts.

The two boys beside him had stirred but gone back to sleep. It was the last time he would lie with them in that inadequate bed. When night came again he would be in bed with Jean, and all the nights after. The permanence of it entered his mind for the first time, blending with the excitement of the thought, bringing another dimension to his life. But they would not be alone for long. The child would be born. He would be a father.

Some of the incomprehension he had seen in the eyes of Jean's mother stirred in his mind then. How had it come to be? That he should be a father? He turned his head and looked at the sleeping faces of his brothers beside him. It was almost as if he looked at them for the first time; asked himself where had they come from and where were they going. He had no illusions that his mother and father had planned their entry into the world, any more than that of Jessie or himself. They were accidents. They were the misfortunes that followed the reaching for the night sun in the dark existence of the Square. Yet beyond the Square, in the wider world he had never seen but which he had read about, in houses like that in which the Horsboroughs lived, in other towns and in other lands, this same thing came to be. As he thought of it, it appalled him that such terror and misery, such potential for joy and for the deep, caring love he had found himself capable of experiencing with Jean should have such accidental beginnings. How innocent his brothers looked in sleep; yet he knew them to be knowing in sexual matters, obscene almost in their talk of girls when they thought him to be asleep and deaf. Such another face as theirs would enter the world because of him, and they in their turn would perpetuate themselves. He thought of the moments of grief in his life when he had wished not to be, not to exist, and the enormity of casual creation rose like a giant wave of slag as if it would obliterate the morning. A great darkness entered his mind so that he almost gasped as if the wave was already engulfing him, bringing him to sudden wakefulness.

He got out of bed, dressed quickly and went down the stairs.

'Decided to go through with it have you?' his father grinned from the table where he was eating breakfast. 'We thought you'd happen decided to stop upstairs.'

Not a word of condemnation had passed his lips when Ted had told him that he had to marry Jean. It was almost as if he had expected it.

'You could have done worse,' was all he had said.

He looked jovial now, almost. Ted thought, 'He's pleased. He's glad for me.'

Jessie, too, was smiling, though she had wept a little the previous night when she had reminded him that it was his last night in that house. Then as he comforted her she had said, 'If I was a man I could get married, too.'

'What do you mean, if you were a man?' he had said. 'What do you think I'm getting wed to – a bloody horse?'

'It's men that decide.'

'Decide what?'

'Oh, I don't know,' she had said, her mind obviously now in a tangle, 'it's just better for men, that's all.'

Then he had sensed that she was belittling herself

again, but blaming her sex this time rather than the Square, and he had become impatient with her.

'You should give yourself credit for what you are, not what you've got landed with,' he had said, almost angrily.

'What am I?'

'You count. You've more brains than me, for a start.'

'I'm no better than average at school.'

'You must be. You won a scholarship. Best part of that lot are paid for.'

'They're bred to it.'

'To what?'

'To use their brains.'

Then his anger would have spilled over, but he could not fight her. He loved her too much. Oh, how he loved her, he thought, looking at her now in the morning of his marriage. His father, too. It glowed in the darkness of their lives, this love he felt for them. It was different to his feeling for Jean. It was compounded from the trials and tribulations of their life together over the years; the shared deprivation; the coming together for warmth. It was only partly flesh and blood. He was aware of it as something important created in the passage of time. He would go away but it would never leave him.

He said, 'Do I get fed before I get wed?'

'We've got a poet in the family,' she said.

'Poetry's for women.'

'Denis reads poetry,' she said, adding quickly, 'so he said that night he was here.'

'Always thought he was a bit of a cissie, Denis,' said Ted, joking.

She flushed then, but joked back at him, 'I'll tell him what you think of him.'

'Nay, he's all right is Denis,' said Ted, an acknowledgement which, from him, was an accolade. 'He can't help his relatives.'

'What relatives?'

'His mother for a start.'

'What's wrong with his mother?'

'She didn't like us being mates, his mother.'

'Because we live in the Square?'

Ted sought around for some other reason that would apply to himself alone, but his father who had been listening chipped in now.

'She was brought up so like a lot of others,' he said. 'It's grained in her like the Square's grained in us.'

'More shame on her,' said Ted.

'It's how people are,' said his father. 'Human nature, that's what it is.'

'Time human nature got changed then!'

'Going to change human nature are you?' his father asked, smiling, and behind the smile was the old, tired acceptance of things.

'I'll get me honeymoon over first,' said Ted, pulling back from the argument with an effort, making a joke of it.

They went on the bus to Caselborn, Ted, his father, Jessie, the two boys and a mate from the pit who was to be best man. Ted would have asked Denis, but Denis had returned from leave and would be at sea now. As the bus dragged out of Cuddon Ted thought he would have liked Denis to have been there at his wedding to Jean. Denis had 'liked' Jean. It would have been another victory, another assertion of the old superiority. Even though at that moment a picture of Denis's mother came into his head it did not occur to Ted that his battle was really with her. That deeply rooted within him was the very thing which angered him in Jessie; the humiliation of being from the Square. He looked around the bus. Two Cuddon women were in the seat across from him. They were talking in low voices, and he knew instinctively that he was the subject of the conversation and that the talk was not complimentary to him. He remembered a picture he had seen in one of the books he borrowed from the library. A Jew was being driven through one of the streets of a city in Germany before the war. Round his neck hung a placard with 'Jude' boldly written on it, and he was obviously being taunted by storm troopers and passers-by. Yet in his expression there was dignity, as if by some enormous effort of the will he removed himself from the present and contemplated better times. Ted felt instinctively that the woman across from him would have been one of the taunters, joining with the mass for reasons she would not be articulate about. He tried to assume the expression of dignity he remembered on the face of the Jew in the picture, but then he caught her eye and, unable to resist the temptation, winked at her. She flushed and turned away, an outraged expression in her eyes, and he made a mental note to succumb to similar temptations in the future in the same way.

They were outnumbered at the Registry Office, many of Jean's relatives having turned up, most of them, Ted thought, for reasons of curiosity rather than affection. He could feel himself being examined, weighed up and probably found wanting. For a moment the old temptation to thrust his hands in his pockets and turn his back rose up in him, but as it did so he became aware of Jean and caught her eye. She was trying to smile at someone who was talking to her, but he could see it was an effort. He could guess that before she left home that morning her mother would have made an hysterical scene; her final protest. She would not make it in public, being bred to keep up appearances, and indeed he saw her smiling now as if it was the happiest of occasions for her. Yet he knew that she would be haunted for the rest of her life by that tiny presence in the womb of her daughter on this day. For a moment he felt a twinge of regret, remorse, responsibility; a confused mixture of these. 'She was brought up like a lot of others,' his father had said of Denis's mother. 'It's grained in her like the Square's grained in us.' Ted pushed it away from him, the brief remorse. He would live with her civilly for as long as they needed to for Jean's sake, but he could do no more. He could not bend to the mother; could not accept the view of himself her attitude expressed. He would be himself as he was or he would be nothing.

He was always confused about the rest of that day in Caselborn. After the ceremony they had retired to a room above a caterers in the town where a simple reception was provided by Jean's parents. What he did remember was how he had been able to pick out the guests who were from her mother's side of the family, from those who were related to her father, for they were a family rather like Denis's. Jean's mother had 'come from money'. Nothing like the affluence of the Horsboroughs, but infinitely above the simple artisan background that Colthard himself came from. You could see it to some extent in their clothes, but mostly in their attitude. Their very presence, Ted thought, they probably regarded as a condescension, a charitable act. Few of them talked to him, whereas a number of Colthard's people made the effort to bridge the embarrassment of what all of them, no doubt, regarded as a forced marriage.

Ted had not contemplated the possibility of a honeymoon, for as much as he had tried to save, a weekend in Blackpool would have been almost beyond his means. Jean's mother had insisted, however, and was to pay, and again he had accepted for Jean's sake. He would have preferred Blackpool himself, for this was where most of the people he knew went, or had done before the war. He had heard, however, that nowadays it was inundated with RAF types and had no desire to be permanently reminded of his civilian status, so that when it was announced that they were to go to some relatives of the Colthards who had a small boarding house in the Lake District he agreed without argument, though he knew neither where the Lake District was nor what it was like.

His father and Jessie came to the station with Jean's mother and father. His father and Colthard conversed warmly and amicably as they walked there and Ted could tell, from snatches of the conversation, that they were talking about their time in the pit together when they were both boys. The mother endured this talk of the pit with remote disapproval. Perhaps it was from her that Jean had got her own deep dislike of the pit, thought Ted, yet it did not worry him. Jean was free of the narrow morality that motivated most of her mother's life. The rest, he felt, he could cope with.

In the compartment with Jean, looking down on the four waiting faces on the platform, he longed for the train to pull out. His eyes caught at Jessie's and he saw that they were moist, but only because, he knew, she was happy for him. He had got what he wanted and she knew it, he thought, and perhaps she saw in this some hope for herself, though it was little enough she would ask. What did she want? He realised he did not truly know. What had happened in the relationship with the boy she had said she 'liked'? He did not know who it was, or whether it was someone she had felt for without declaring herself, for she had obviously wanted to keep it to herself and he had respected her privacy. Yet he wished now that he had talked to her more, had broken through the wall of reserve she built around herself to protect what she felt was her inadequacy and the ugly scars of her background as if, almost, she suffered them as a physical deformity.

She was no more like their dead mother than Jean was like the woman who stood beside Colthard on the platform now. Yet what did he know of his mother in the totality of her life? Only his father knew to what extent she was the victim of the same environment which might now deform Jessie, the one Ted himself both gloried in and wanted to destroy. More and more now he saw his mother as a victim, and as he so saw her the later image of the strident, unlovable woman he had known was replaced by that other image which he saw as the woman his father had married. She was what the Square had made her, not what she had made of herself. He could not see the contradiction of his refusal to see Jean's mother in the same light, to see only the people he cared for as victims. He could not see the limitation of his compassion as a flaw in himself.

A hiss of steam came from the engine.

'Don't do anything I wouldn't do,' said Colthard, conventionally, but earning himself a quick glance of annoyance from his wife.

His father looked at him and smiled but said nothing, and Jessie's smile was moistly fixed as if she dare not let go of it.

'We'll see you in a week,' said Jean, beside him. Then as a tear ran down her mother's cheek she said, desperately, 'Cheer up, Mum!'

The train started to drag out with merciless slowness. Expressions were fixed and held as the distance grew. The solitary tear on Jean's mother's face became a river, that now began to fade from view. The figures grew smaller as the train picked up speed, then it rounded a curve and they were gone.

Ted pulled on the strap that slid up the window, then turned and looked at Jean. 'We're on the way,' he said, as if the revolution had at long last come.

CHAPTER TWENTY-SIX

It was six months after Ted's wedding that Denis came on leave for the second time. The ship had made its usual run but had then been diverted to Karachi, returning via Durban and the West African ports. In spite of the length of the voyage there was again no mail, but they put it down to the diversion. Then again, with so many ships being sunk, mail often ended up on the ocean bed. There was nothing they could do but endure the silence; no one to complain to. It was just the war.

He read many books now in the long hours on and off watch. The ship had a reasonable library, provided by various organisations on shore. Many of the books were book club editions of popular works, but there were unusual titles too; works on history, science, psychology and political theory. He read anything and everything, voraciously, skipping whatever he could not understand, then moving on to the next one. Finding his vocabulary limited for some of the books he read, he had bought a dictionary when in port and used it regularly, gradually adding to his store of words. He had developed a taste for sophisticated novels, though why he did not know for they described a world he did not know in terms which he could barely understand. London was the background for many of them, and from the pages of the books a portrait of the city to which he had never been began to emerge. He had already decided that when the war was over he would go there. He saw himself walking in streets whose names he had read which seemed, in the books, to be perpetually fog bound. What he would do when the war was over he did not know, except that he knew now that he would not stay at sea. It never occurred to him that the war might be lost; that the peace which followed the end might be dominated by the enemy so that the totalitarian compulsion to do what you were told rather than what you chose, a situation which you were obliged to accept in a war, might be the norm for the rest of his life. In Ted's world such a situation could exist, but then he did not believe in the possibility of Ted's world either.

He wrote to Jessie whenever there was a possibility that mail could be posted. His feelings for her were no less than they had been, but his long absence from home made it all somewhat abstract. His letters were brief, sometimes almost abrupt, for he could never write in anticipation of the post and the decreasing likelihood of him ever getting a reply made him doubt whether she would ever get them. Moreover he knew that they were read and censored and this inhibited him, so that often he found himself unable to describe his true feelings or to continue the arguments they had had on his last leave.

They docked in Glasgow eventually after two days lying at anchor in the Clyde. The following day he caught the train to Cuddon and leave. The trains were as dirty and crowded as he remembered them, the same dimmed light falling on the same tired faces. There was no hope of victory in the faces, no hope for a brave new world to come. Most of the people in his compartment were much older than himself. He looked at them from time to time as they slept or stared blankly into the darkness beyond the reflections in the carriage window. Were they too tired, too immensely weary, he wondered, to care any more? Would peace, when it came, come too late?

He knew what it was to be tired, but not to be old and tired, though he could imagine how it might be. He had seen it in Cuddon on the faces of the older men coming off shift, carrying the darkness of the pit with them still into the more merciful darkness of sleep. The war had saved him from that. It had not saved Ted, but then Ted did not want to be saved. It was part of the difference between them.

It was raining when he got off the train at Cuddon station, and a wind had sprung up. The gas lamps in the subway that by-passed the level crossing flickered proudly as if they were conscious of the fact that they were the only public lights left undimmed. When the war ended they would lose this special status. All over England the lights of wartime would flicker out as people became once again nothing more than themselves. He came up the steps from the subway and started down the main street towards home. They would never know that world outside, he thought, those that had stayed in Cuddon. They would live in the place they were born in, close to the womb of life, for the most part undreaming.

The street was empty, for it was late, but as he came towards the road that led to the baths a figure came from the other side and a face looked palely towards him, unrecognisable in the dark. For a moment whoever it was seemed to hesitate, as if to wait for him, then suddenly carried on down the road away from him.

***

Although the house was in darkness, Ted did not mount the stairs too quietly. It was not too late for Jean's mother to be still awake. If she went to sleep before he got in, her first remark to Jean the next day was always, 'And what time this morning did he get in?' It was barely eleven now, giving her little cause for complaint, though she would undoubtedly use what little there was.

He had been to the club, following a union meeting. He was never sure which she objected to most, the union or the club. She had asked Jean once why he attended all the union meetings.

'He's going to be an M.P.,' Jean had said, rashly.

Her mother had looked at him speculatively ever since, and her attitude had definitely changed, though very slightly. It was her insurance against the possibility that he might succeed, that she might have a Member of Parliament for a son-in-law. She would like that, he thought. He could imagine her attitude then, and the thought strengthened what had become his driving ambition. The Square, which had been the seed of that ambition, was less in his thoughts these days. Pay and working conditions in the pit increasingly occupied his mind, and he was becoming known to the men on the platform as the spokesman from the floor for the younger end, the lads. He had spoken several times to one of the union men who was also on the Council and was the chairman of the housing committee. He did not wish to use his contact to jump the queue for a council house, but he was desperate now to leave the Colthards, and was increasingly sorely tempted.

It worried him sometimes, especially when he went back home where his father, Jessie and the boys were living, that his political motivations were widening, taking him away from them. One of his mates had joined the Communist Party and he had himself begun to toy with the idea. When they talked it was not about the local issues that were the subject of union meetings, but about a concept, which he had not yet fully grasped of a completely new society. It was as if the Square became a symbol rather than a reality, yet he needed it still. Sometimes he would go to see them simply because he knew that when he came away his anger would be renewed, his ambition revitalised. It never occurred to him to wonder what he would do for sustenance if it went.

He entered the bedroom he shared with Jean quietly and undressed and climbed into bed. He had thought her asleep, so still and silent she was, then she said, 'What time is it?'

'Eleven.'

'That's all right then.'

'All right with her, you mean?'

'I have it to put up with as well as you.'

He knew the battles she had with her mother, taking his side. 'I know you do,' he said, reaching out to touch her.

She took his hand and held it against her belly, swollen with his child.

'Say hello to your son.'

'Hello, son,' he said. 'Your old man's back from the boozer.'

'He'll not stay in Cuddon when he grows up.'

'Who says he'll not?'

'I do. I shall drive him off with a stick if he turns out a donkey like you.'

'There's worse places than Cuddon.'

'Name one.'

'Whole world's in a bloody mess,' he said.

She was silent for a moment, then she said, 'I felt like going up to our place today.'

She always called it that when she spoke of it; 'our place.'

He remembered their times in the room upstairs in the ruined farmhouse. He remembered the time she had come back to him.

'I told Dad about it,' she said after a moment, hesitantly as if she feared he might be angry. They had never told anyone else.

'I thought we weren't going to tell anybody,' he said, chidingly but without anger.

'He knows it. He knows who it belongs to. He thinks it could be bought.'

'He's dreaming,' said Ted. 'Where would we get the money?'

'He thinks he could get round Mum's brother to lend it. A mortgage, he said.'

She twisted Colthard round her little finger. It came from being an only child, Ted thought.

'He's dreaming. It's a dream.'

'We could try.'

He said, after a moment, 'I don't want to.'

'I don't understand you.'

He didn't understand himself. He only knew that somewhere inside him foundations were shaking.

She said again, 'I don't understand you.'

'It's a dream,' he said, turning his back.

His parents had been in bed when Denis had arrived home. His father had come down and let him in, and then had insisted on waking his mother, saying she would not forgive him otherwise. There had been a tearful reunion. Now, in the following morning, her eyes followed him everywhere.

'You're growing up,' she said, after studying him over breakfast.

'Of course he's growing up,' his father said.

'He's growing up too fast.'

The shop bell rang then.

'We should have closed.'

'We can't shut up shop on a Saturday,' his father said. 'I'll go if you like.'

'I'll go,' she said, reluctantly, and went.

'What's trade like?' Denis asked his father.

'Better than before the war. The money's there. Government can't do enough for pitmen now they want coal. Lads haven't got used to it yet. When they get given what union's asked they get to thinking they can't have asked for enough. Then there's women and girls on munitions. There's council houses with more than ten pound a week coming in. Trouble is, we can't get enough to sell. There's a shortage of anything you can name.'

'No news of Tim?'

'He's dead,' his father said after the briefest pause. 'We'd have told you last night except we wanted you to get a night's sleep behind you.'

He looked down at his plate, as if the details were written on it. 'That's all they know. It's happen all they ever will know. We didn't write you. Thought we'd save it till you got back.'

Brief flashes of Tim alive came into Denis's head, like a flip through a photograph album.

'Your mother took it badly.'

Tim had been the only member of that part of the family that had really cared about them, thought Denis. With his Uncle Maurice it was simply the odd spasm of conscience, and the women cared nothing at all for them really. He remembered how they had used his mother in the past simply to care for the house while they were away, and how when they bought things from the shop they always expected to pay trade price. He remembered how he had found her weeping, alone in the drawing-room in which she had been a child, cut off from her past because she had married out of her class. He thought of Doris who had passed him in the street, disowning him. Anger rose up in him. He felt belittled by his relationship to them, rather than the other way round. Yet his mother had in a sense adopted their attitude in respect of Ted, because he was from the Square, and would have done so with Jessie no doubt. Because he loved her his anger was confused now. He could not understand how she could do to others what had been done to her. He looked up and found his father's eyes on him. There was understanding in them, as if he could read his thoughts.

He said, 'There's going to be a lot of changes after this war.'

'Everyone says that,' said Denis, as if he wanted to believe it but found belief difficult. Would Doris change; or his aunt? Would Ted change in his hostility to all of them? Hands in pockets, back turned? Would his mother warm towards Jessie, accept her as the child of the attitudes which had soured her own life? Was it only necessary, to bring about all these and all the other changes in the hearts of people, to win the war and bring it to an end? Was that what they were fighting for?

'They mean changes for the better, most of 'em when they say it.'

'Don't you?' Denis asked him, surprised.

'There'll be some for the better,' his father said, 'but most for the worst I reckon. If we win it we shall all be expecting prizes. We shall expect too much. It was like that after the last lot. A land fit for heroes they promised us, and look what we got.'

'I shall leave Cuddon,' Denis said, taking advantage of his mother's absence.

'I should want you to,' his father said. 'Well, half of me would. I thought you might marry young when you told me about young Jessie Hoyle. Given it up, have you?'

'I don't know,' said Denis.

'Her aunt died. She's given up her chance for college. She's looking after the home.'

'I didn't know.'

'Doesn't she write you?'

'No,' said Denis. 'Not any more.'

'Stay free as long as you can,' his father said. 'You could be chained to Cuddon for life.'

They were standing on either side of the living-room when Ted entered the house. Jessie with her apron around her, caught in the middle of house work. Denis was by the fire, looking down at it and away from her almost as if he did not know she was there. The boys were tearing around upstairs, their feet thumping the floorboards.

'Back again then,' said Ted to Denis, genuinely pleased to see him. Then he went to the foot of the stairs. 'Cut that racket,' he shouted at the top of his voice, and there was silence above.

'You shouldn't let 'em take advantage of you,' he said to Jessie.

'They're just lads.'

'Nowt worse than lads, unless it's men,' Ted grinned, looking at Denis for confirmation. 'I'm living at the Colthards' now, you know.'

'Jessie just told me.'

'Till we get something else.'

Jessie picked up a broom and started to sweep the floor as if, now Ted was here, she was excused conversation.

'Where's Dad?' Ted asked her.

'Gone down the allotment to see to his birds.'

'I'll go down there then.' He looked at Denis. 'Coming?'

Denis looked at Jessie, but she did not look up.

'I'll come,' he said.

She looked up then.

'Might see you again some time,' Denis said.

Upstairs the uproar broke out again. Ted went to the bottom of the stairs and shouted as he had done before and again there was silence.

'Lads!' he said.

They went out.

Denis left Ted and his father at the allotment and walked across the pit fields in the direction of the Horsboroughs'. He would not go there though. He was done with the Horsboroughs now Tim was dead.

His brief conversation with Jessie had hurt.

'Didn't you get my letters?' he had asked her.

'Yes, I got them.'

'Why didn't you write?'

'There wasn't any point.'

He had thought that they were back to the same old argument, but then she had said, 'I'm going with a lad from the Square,' and had looked away from him.

'Who is it?' he had asked, as if it mattered.

'Jack Farrer from number nine.'

He knew Jack Farrer, remembered him from school. Two years older than himself and with the same jaunty, aggressive quality that was part of Ted. Yet the quality that made Ted different, his moodiness and unpredictability, he did not have. Without it he was like most of the Cuddon men, totally male, totally dominant in their treatment of women, essentially worldly, chained to a materialistic pattern because of their role as breadwinners in a hard society. There was none of the inner conflict in Farrer, he thought, that he had always sensed in Ted.

Let her have him then, he thought now, walking blindly with nowhere to go. In his mind he abused her.

Let her have him. Let her grow old before her time and live in the Square forever, forever belittling herself and destroying herself in the process in spite of her dreams of other worlds; the worlds she read about, but would not reach out for. For he knew that if she could have reached out for him with hope she would have. It was as if she had heard his own attempts at persuasion as the voice of an enemy and had acted to silence him. As if in the long dark tunnel of a war she could see no possibility of an end; no light.

His bitterness extended to Ted now. He had given up the fight no less than Jessie had, Denis thought; had let the darkness of Cuddon close round him. His father's words echoed in his mind. Ted was chained to Cuddon for life now, and Jean with him. Of the four of them, Denis would be the only one to escape. Yet he, too, had so nearly been caught in the same predicament, wanting it almost.

Was it all an accident, then? He remembered Miss Maddy, and the time of her death in the ticket office at the Baths where he had found her. Childless, unmarried, no chains of that kind had bound Miss Maddy to Cuddon, yet when she died Denis was not the only one who had wept for her. It had been as if in her passing she had taken a part of the place with her, so much a part of the scene she had been, giving herself, creating a warmth about her which he was remembering now, though she was gone into a greater darkness than Cuddon.

His steps faltered as his thoughts became confused. Images dark and light flashed through his mind. He looked at the sky as if in the light he might still see the stars shining above the pit fields where he walked. They were there though he could not see them. When night came they would shine. Whenever he looked up, from wherever he was, on a clear dark night he would see them. Yet, for him, they belonged to the pit fields more than to that other world outside. He sensed already that perhaps it would always be so; that there were other chains than those that bound the other three physically to Cuddon; that even the act of going would bind him.

20252569R00215

Printed in Great Britain
by Amazon